NEMESIS

Also by Lindsey Davis

The Course of Honour
Rebels and Traitors

NEMESIS

LINDSEY DAVIS

MINOTAUR BOOKS ✹ NEW YORK

NEMESIS. Copyright © 2010 by Lindsey Davis. All rights reserved. Printed in the United States of America. For information, address St. Martin's Press, 175 Fifth Avenue, New York, N.Y. 10010.

www.minotaurbooks.com

Library of Congress Cataloging-in-Publication Data

Davis, Lindsey.
    Nemesis / Lindsey Davis.—1st U.S. ed.
        p. cm.
    ISBN 978-0-312-59542-5
    1. Falco, Marcus Didius (Fictitious character)—Fiction.   2. Private investigators—Rome—Fiction.   3. Murder—Investigation—Fiction.   4. Rome—History—Vespasian, 69–79—Fiction.   I. Title.
    PR6054.A8925N46 2010
    823'.914—dc22

                                                                                2010021847

First published in Great Britain by Century, a division of Random House

First U.S. Edition: September 2010

10 9 8 7 6 5 4 3 2 1

PRINCIPAL CHARACTERS

Marcus Didius Falco	a man of mixed fortunes and seeker after truth
Helena Justina	his true love, sought and won
Falco's family	low grade, but not as bad as they seem:
Junilla Tacita	formidable wife to the deplorable Geminus
Maia Favonia	Falco's sister, the best of the bunch
Flavia Albia	heart-broken and ready to break heads
Katutis	Falco's secretary, a disappointed man
Helena's family	high class, but not as good as they look:
Aulus Camillus Aelianus	keeping a low profile
Quintus Camillus Justinus	keeping his career on target, thanks to:
Claudia Rufina	his wife and financial backer
Lentullus	an accident waiting to happen

Falco's associates in Rome

Lucius Petronius Longus	an upright vigiles enquirer (low pay)
Lucius Petronius Rectus	his brother, feeling off colour
Nero	their ox, another one gone missing
Tiberius Fusculus	Petro's second in command
Sergius	their whip man (always encouraging)
Clusius	a devious rival auctioneer (low motives)

Gaius	a dubious apprentice (high hopes)
Gornia	a tight-lipped porter (no comment)
Septimus Parvo	a family lawyer (*absolutely* no comment)
Thalia	a contortionist with a problem to wriggle out of
Philadelphion and Davos	her lovers, keeping well off the scene
Minas of Karystos	a lawyer, on the up
Hosidia Meline	a bride (on the make?)

Also in Rome

Tiberius Claudius Laeta	a smooth bureaucrat with high aspirations
Momus	a rough-edged auditor with low habits
Tiberius Claudius Anacrites	the Chief Spy, a high-flyer of low worth
The Melitans	his agents (dodgy connections)
Perella	an assassin who wants a new job (her boss's)
Heracleides	party-planner to the stars
Nymphidias	his thieving chef
Scorpus	a singer, spying on spies (an idiot)
Alis	a fortune-teller who blames Mum (a wise woman)
Arrius Persicus	a philanderer, oversexed and over-budget
A courier	newly wed and newly dead
Volusius	Mum's boy, a numerate victim

In Latium

Januaria	a waitress at Satricum, an all-rounder
Livia Primilla & Julius Modestus	complainants in high dudgeon
Sextus Silanus	their nephew in Lanuvium, in low spirits
Macer	their loyal overseer, gone missing
Syrus	their runaway slave, fatally roughed up
A butcher in Lanuvium	a very careless creditor
The horrible Claudii	neighbours from Hades:
Aristocles and Casta	cold-natured, hot-tempered parents (deceased)
Claudius Nobilis	so notorious, he has 'gone to see his granny'
Pius and Virtus	the twins, 'working away from home'
Probus	'upholding the family name'
Felix	'lost'
Plotia and Byrta	downtrodden wives
Demetria	runaway wife of Claudius Nobilis (low esteem)
Costus	her new boyfriend (asking for trouble)
Vexus	her father (anticipating the worst)
Thamyris	employer of Nobilis and Costus (over-confident)
Silvius	an officer of the Urban Cohorts, undercover

Plus full supporting cast
Jason the python, dogs, missing persons, slaves (non-persons),
personal beauticians, impersonal magistrates

And featuring
The Praetorian Guards   bastards!

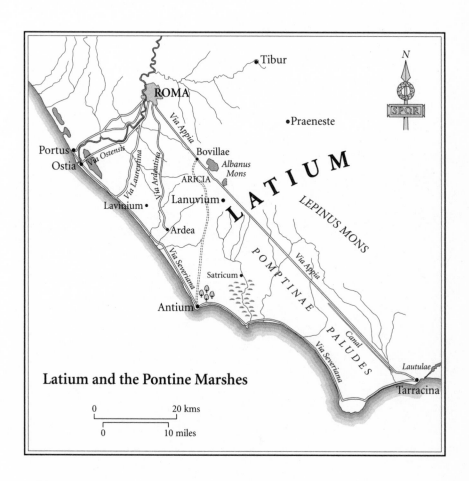

Latium and the Pontine Marshes

ROME AND LATIUM: SUMMER, AD 77

I

I find it surprising more people are not killed over dinner at home. In my work we reckon that murder is most likely to happen among close acquaintances. Someone will finally snap after years of being wound up to blind rage by the very folk who best know how to drive them to distraction. For once it will be just too much to watch someone else eating the last sesame pancake—which, of course, was snatched with a triumphant laugh that was intended to rankle. So a victim expires with honey still dribbling down their chin—though it happens less often than you might expect.

Why are more kitchen cleavers not sunk between the fat shoulders of appalling uncles who get the slaves pregnant? Or that sneaky sister who shamelessly grabs the most desirable bedroom, with its glimpse of a corner of the Temple of Divine Claudius and almost no cracks in the walls? Or the crude son who farts uncontrollably, however many times he is told . . .

Even if people do not stab or strangle their own, you would expect more to rush out into the streets and vent their frustration upon the first person they meet. Perhaps they do. Perhaps even the random killing of strangers, which the vigiles call 'a motiveless crime', sometimes has an understandable domestic cause.

It could so easily have happened to us.

I grew up in a large family, crammed into a couple of small, sour rooms. All around our apartment were other teeming groups, too noisy, too obstreperous and all packed together far too close. Perhaps the thing that saved us from tragedy was that my father left home— his only escape from a situation he had come to find hideous, and an event which at least saved us from the burden of more children. Later my brother took himself off to the army; eventually I saw the sense of it and did the same. My sisters moved out to harass the feckless men they bullied into marriage. My mother, having brought up seven, was left alone but continued to have a strong influence on all of us. Even my father, once he returned to Rome, viewed Ma with wary respect.

As she continually reminded us, mothers can never retire. So, when my wife went into labour with our third child, in came Ma to boss everyone about, even though she was becoming frail and had eyesight problems. Helena's own mama rushed to our house too, the noble Julia Justa rolling up her sleeves to interfere in her genteel way. We had employed a perfectly decent midwife.

At first the mothers battled for dominance. In the end, when they were both badly needed, all that stopped.

My new son died on the day he was born. At once, we felt we were living in a tragedy that was unique to us. I suppose that is how it always seems.

The birth had been easy, a short labour like our second daughter's. Favonia had taken a week to seize upon existence but then she thrived. I thought the same would happen. But when this baby emerged, he was already fading. He never responded to us; he slipped away within hours.

The midwife said a mother should hold a dead baby; afterwards she and Julia Justa had to wrestle to make Helena give up the body again. Helena went into deep shock. Women cleaned up, as they do. Helena Justina stayed in the bedroom, refusing comfort, ignoring food, declining to see her daughters, even distant with me. My sister Maia said this day would be black in Helena's calendar for the rest of her life; Maia knew what it was to lose a child. At first I could not believe Helena would ever come out of it. It seemed to me, we might never even reach that point where grief only overtook her on anniversaries. She stayed frozen at the moment when she was told her boy was dead.

All action fell to me. It was not a legal necessity, but I named him: Marcus Didius Justinianus. In my place many fathers would not have bothered. His birth would not be registered; he had no civic identity. Perhaps I was wrong. I just had to decide what to do. His mother had survived, but for the moment I was alone trying to hold the family together, trying to choose what formalities were appropriate. It all became even more difficult after I learned what else had happened on that day.

The tiny swaddled bundle had been placed in a room we rarely used. What was I to do next? A newborn should receive no funeral rites; he was too small for full cremation. Adult burials must be held outside the city; families who can afford it build a mausoleum beside a highroad for their embalmed bodies or cremation urns. That had never been for us; ashes of the plebeian Didii are kept in a cupboard for a time, and then mysteriously lost.

My mother revealed that she had always taken her stillborns to the Campagna farm where she grew up, but I could not leave my distraught family. Helena's father, the senator, offered me a niche in the tumbledown columbarium of the Camilli on the Via Appia, saying sadly, 'It will be a very small urn!' I thought about it, but was too proud. We live in a patriarchal society; he was my son. I don't give two figs for formal rules, but disposal was my responsibility.

Some people inter newborn babies under a slab in a new building; none was available and I jibbed at making our child into a votive offering. I don't annoy the gods; I don't encourage them either. We lived in an old town house at the foot of the Aventine, with a back exit, but almost no ground. If I dug a tiny grave among the sage and rosemary, there was a horrendous possibility children at play or cooks digging holes to bury fish bones might one day turn up little Marcus' ribs accidentally.

I climbed up to our roof terrace and sat alone with the problem.

The answer came to me just before stiffness set in. I would take my sad bundle out to my father's house. We ourselves had once lived there, up on the Janiculan Hill across the Tiber; in fact, I was the idiot who first bought the inconvenient place. I had since worked a swap with my father but it still seemed like home. Although Pa was a reprobate, his villa offered the baby a resting place where, when Helena was ready for it, we could put up a memorial stone.

I wondered briefly why my father had not yet come with condolences. Normally when people wanted time alone, he was a first-footer. He could smell tragedy like newly cooked bread. He was bound to let himself in with that house key he would never give back to me, then irritate us with his insensitivity. The thought of Pa issuing platitudes to shake Helena out of her sadness was dire. He would probably try to get me drunk. Wine was bound to feature in my recovery one day, but I wanted to choose how, when and where the medicine was applied. The dose would be poured by my best friend Petronius Longus. The only reason I had not sought him out so far, was delicacy because he too had lost young children. Besides, I had things to do first.

My mother was staying at our house. She would continue to do so, as long as she believed she was needed. Perhaps that would be longer than we really wanted, but Ma would do what she thought best.

Helena wanted no part in the funeral. She turned away, weeping, when I told her what I planned to do. I hoped she approved. I hoped she knew that dealing with this was the only way I could try to help her. Albia, our teenaged foster daughter, intended to accompany me but in the end even she was too upset. Ma might have made the pilgrimage but I gratefully left her to look after little Julia and Favonia. I would not ask her to see Pa, from whom she had been bitterly estranged for thirty years. If I *had* asked, she might have forced herself to come and support me, but I had enough to endure without that worry.

So I went alone. And I was alone, therefore, when the subdued slaves at my father's house told me the next piece of bad news. On the same day that I lost my son, I lost my father too.

2

As I turned off the informal roadway into Pa's rough carriage drive, nothing appeared amiss. No smoke came from the new bath house. There was no one in sight; the gardeners had clearly decided that late afternoon was their time to down tools. The gardens, designed by Helena when we lived here, were looking in good fettle. Since Pa was an auctioneer, the statuary was exquisite. I thought Pa must be down in Rome, at his warehouse or his office in the Saepta Julia; otherwise on a warm summer evening I would expect to hear a low buzz and chinking wine paraphernalia as he entertained associates or neighbours, sprawling on the benches that permanently stood out beneath the old pine trees.

I had come in a closed litter. The dead baby lay in a basket on the opposite seat. I left it there temporarily. The bearers dropped me by the short flight of steps in the porch. I banged my fist on the big double doors to announce my presence and went straight indoors.

A peculiar scene met me. All the household slaves and freedmen stood assembled in the atrium as if they had been waiting for me.

I was startled. I was even more startled by the size of the sombre crowd filling the hallway. Tray-toters, pillow-plumpers, earwax-extractors, dust-dampers. I had never realised how many staff Pa kept. My father was missing from the scene. My heart started pounding unevenly.

I was wearing a black tunic instead of my usual hues. Still lost in the horror of the baby's death, I must have looked grim. The slaves seemed prepared for it, and oddly relieved to see me. 'Marcus Didius—you heard!'

'I heard nothing.'

Throats were cleared. 'Our dear master passed away.'

I was taken aback by that crazy phrase 'dear master'. Most people knew Pa as 'that bastard, Favonius' or even 'Geminus—may he rot in Hades with a bald crow perpetually eating his liver'. The bird would be pecking sooner than expected, apparently.

The whole bunch were deferring to me with new-found humility. If they felt awkward doing it, that was nothing to how I felt. They stood trying to hide the anxieties that characterise slaves of a newly dead citizen while they wait to know what will be done with them.

It could hardly be my problem, so I gave them no help. My father and I had been on bad terms after he left Ma; our reconciliation in recent years was patchy. He had no rights over me and I took no responsibility for him. Somebody else must be designated to deal with his effects. Somebody else would keep or sell the slaves.

I would have to tell the family he was gone. That would cause all sorts of bad feelings.

This was turning into a bad year.

Officially, it was the year of the consuls Vespasianus Augustus and Titus Caesar (Vespasian, our elderly, curmudgeonly, much-admired Emperor, in his eighth consulship, and his lively elder son and heir, notching up his sixth). Later, 'suffect' consuls took over, which was a way of sharing the workload and the honours. The suffects that year were Domitian Caesar (the much-less-liked younger son) and an unknown senator called Gnaeus Julius Agricola—a non-notable; some years afterwards he became governor of Britannia. Say no more. He was too insignificant for a civilised province, so the Senate finessed him by pretending that Britain was a challenge where they wanted a man they could trust . . .

I ignore the civic calendar. Still, there are years you remember.

Duty began weighing on me. Death wreaks havoc on survivors' lifestyles. For years I had been forced to play at being the family head, since my father reneged and my only brother was dead. Pa ran away with his redhead when I was about seven—an even thirty years ago. My mother never spoke to him again and most of us were loyal to Ma. Even after he returned sheepishly to Rome, calling himself Geminus as a half-hearted disguise, Pa kept apart from the family for years. More recently he did impose himself when it suited him. He was a snob about my connections to a senatorial family, so I had to see most of him. Recently my sister Maia took over his accounts at the auction house, one of my nephews was learning the business, and another sister ran a bar he owned.

Once the twittering slaves made their announcement, I foresaw big changes.

'Who is going to tell me what happened?'

First spokesman was a wine-pourer, not quite as handsome as he thought, who wanted to get himself noticed: 'Marcus Didius, your beloved father was found dead early this morning.'

He had been dead all day and I did not know. I had been struggling with the baby's birth and death and all the while this had been happening too.

'Was it natural?'

'What else could it be, sir?' I could think of a few answers.

Nema, Pa's personal bodyslave, who was known to me, stepped up to give me details. Yesterday, my father came home from work at the Saepta Julia at a normal time, had dinner and retired to bed, early for him. Nema had heard him moving about this morning, apparently at his ablutions, then came a sudden loud thump. Nema ran in and Pa was dead on the floor.

Since I was known to spend my working life questioning such statements, Nema and the others looked worried. I suspected they had discussed how to convince me the story was accurate. They said a slave with some medical knowledge had diagnosed a heart attack.

'We did not send for a doctor. You know Geminus. He would loathe the cost, when it was obvious that nothing could be done . . .'

I knew. Pa could be stupidly generous, but like most men who accrued a lot of money he was more often stingy. Anyway, the diagnosis was reasonable. His lifestyle was tough; he had been looking tired; we were all not long returned from a physically demanding trip to Egypt.

Even so, any doubts would bring the slaves under suspicion. Legally, their position was dangerous. If their master's passing was seen as unnatural, they could all be put to death. They were scared—particularly scared of me. I am an informer. I fix credit checks and character references. I deliver subpoenas, act for disappointed beneficiaries, defend accused parties in civil actions. In the course of this work I frequently run across corpses, not all of them persons who have died quietly of old age at home. So I tend to look for problems. Jealousy, greed and lust have a bad habit of causing people to end up on a bier prematurely. Clients may hire me to investigate the suspicious death of a lover or a business partner.

Sometimes it turns out that my client actually killed the deceased and hired me as a cover, which at least is neat.

'Shall I fetch the will?' asked Quirinius, whose main job had been to detain creditors with sweet drinks and pastries on a patio, while Pa scarpered by a back exit.

'Save it for the heir.'

'Back in an instant!'

Dear gods.

Me? My father's heir? On the other hand, who else was there? What friend or close relation, other than me, could Pa have lumbered? He knew half of Rome, but who counted with him enough for this? Had he died intestate, it would have become my role in any case. I had always imagined he *would* die intestate, come to that.

Misgiving gave way to dread. It seemed Pa was going to make me responsible for unravelling the complex rats' nest of his business affairs. I would have to become familiar with his dubious private life. A named heir does not automatically inherit the estate (though he is entitled to at least a quarter); his duty is to become an extension of the dead man, honouring his gods, coughing up for his charities, preserving property, paying debts (a frequent reason to back out of being an executor, believe me). He makes arrangements for specified bequests and tactfully fends off people who have been disinherited. He shares out the booty as instructed.

I would have to do it all. This was typical of my father. I don't know why I felt so unprepared.

The will was apparently hard to find. That wasn't suspicious; Pa hated documentation. He liked to keep everything vague. If he had to have written evidence, he tried to lose the scroll among a lot of mess.

The slaves kept staring. I cleared my throat and gazed at the mosaic floor. When I was bored with counting tesserae, I had to look at them.

They were a mixed bunch. Various nationalities and jobs. Some had worked for Pa for decades, others I failed to recognise. It was unlikely he came by any of them in the usual way. Not for my father a trip to the slave market when he needed a specific worker, with genteel haggling then a routine purchase. In his world, many business debts were settled by payment in kind. Some executors find antique vases of great value, which have been payments in lieu of fees. But since my father dealt in antique vases anyway, he accepted other commodities. He had acquired a curiously colourful *familia* in this way. Sometimes it worked out well; he had a wonderful panpipe-player, though he himself had a tin ear. But most of the staff looked unimpressive. Bankrupts' cast-offs. Two kitchen staff were blind; that could be entertaining. A gardener had only one arm. I spotted a few vacant expressions, not to mention the usual rheumy eyes, raw wounds and sinister rashes.

While we went on waiting, they plucked up courage to petition me. Very few of these frightened household members were already freedmen; Pa had made lavish promises, but never got around to issuing formal deeds of manumission. That was typical; he managed to screw decent service out of his staff, but preferred to keep them reliant on him. I quickly learned that many of these anxious souls had families, even though slaves are not allowed to marry. They pressed me to grant their freedom, plus the same for various wives and children. Pa did own some of these, so their fates could be untangled and regularised, if I was willing. But others belonged to neighbours, so that was a mess. Other owners would not appreciate me trying to fix up fairytale solutions for *their* handmaids and bootboys.

Another worry for the slaves was where they would all end up. They realised that the villa might have to be sold shortly. They might be heading for the slave-market and a very uncertain future.

While we hung around in embarrassment, surprisingly one of the women asked, 'Would you like to see him now?'

I nearly said *must I?* but that would have been an impiety.

Don't be like that, my boy! Is it too much to show respect to your poor old father? . . .

A freedman was guarding the room. A curtain of scent wafted at me from the doorway, cassia and myrrh, traditional funeral incenses, the costly ones. Who authorised that? I hesitated on the threshold then went in.

I had viewed plenty of corpses. That was work. This was duty. I preferred the other kind.

No need to wonder about identity. On a rather fine couch in this dim room off a peaceful corridor, lay my deceased parent: Marcus Didius Favonius, also known as Geminus, descendant of a long line of dubious Aventine plebeians and honoured among the dealers, tricksters and shysters of the Saepta Julia. He had been washed and anointed, dressed in an embroidered tunic and a toga; given a wreath; his eyes had been closed by respectful hands and a ridiculous flower garland positioned round his neck. His haematite seal ring, his other gold ring with the head of an emperor, and the key to his bankbox at the Saepta lay in a small bronze dish, emphasising that the trappings of his life were no longer needed. Lying on his back, laid out so neatly on two mattresses, that garrulous sociable soul, now permanently silent, seemed thinner but essentially the same as when I saw him last week at our house. Unkempt grey curls warned how my own would be in a decade's time. A lifetime of enjoying meals and doing business over cups of wine showed in his solid belly. Still, he had been a short, wide-bodied man who was used to moving heavy furniture and marble artefacts. His hairy arms and legs were strongly muscled. Down in Rome he often walked, even though he could afford a litter.

This motionless corpse was not my father. Gone were the characteristics that made him: the bright, devious eyes; the raucous, complicated jokes; the endless lust for barmaids; the aptitude for making money out of nothing; those flares of generosity that always led to pleading for reciprocal favours and affection. Gone for ever was what my mother called his cracking grin. No one could more surely clinch a deal. No one enjoyed making a sale so deeply. I had hated having him in my life—but now suddenly could not envisage life without him.

I backed out of the room, feeling queasy.

In the entrance hall Quirinius, flustered, told me, 'I thought I knew where his will was kept, but I've searched high and low and I can't find it.'

'Gone missing?' As a professional habit, I made it sound ominous; not that I cared.

He was reprieved. To my surprise, we were being joined by new arrivals; people had come from the city for the funeral. Bemused, I learned that messengers had been sent earlier today to the family and my father's business colleagues. My litter must have crossed with them.

Word must have flown around Rome. Father had belonged to an auctioneers' burial club; mainly he went for the wine. Although he had not paid his subscription for the last six months, the other members seemed to bear no grudges (well, that was Pa). Undertakers had been marshalled. A calm dignitary was in charge.

Gornia, the elderly assistant from the antiques warehouse, was one of the first comers. 'I brought up an altar we had kicking about, young Marcus. Rather nice Etruscan piece, with a winged figure . . .' A benefit of the profession. They could always lay hands on an altar. They had access to most things, and I was just thinking Gornia might help me pick out an urn for the ashes, when one of the funeral club people produced an alabaster item which apparently matched my father's instructions. (What instructions?) The man handed it to me discreetly, brushing aside my murmur about payment. I had the feeling I had blundered into a closed world where everything would be made easy for me today. The debts would come later. Probably not small. I, of course, would be expected to pay them, but I was too sensible to upset myself thinking of that before I had to.

A remarkable crowd gathered. Men I had never seen before claimed to be decades-old colleagues. Squeezing out tears that could almost be genuine, strangers gripped my hand like familiar old uncles and told me what an unexpected tragedy this was. They promised me assistance with unspecified needs. One or two actually winked heavily. I had no idea what they meant.

Family arrived too. With sombre gowns and veiled heads, my sisters—Allia, Galla, Junia—pushed through to the front, dragging with them my nightmare brothers-in-law and Mico, Victorina's widower. I viewed this as deep hypocrisy. Even Petronius Longus appeared, bringing my youngest sister Maia, who at least had some right to be here because she had worked with Pa. It was Maia who thrust a set of tablets at me.

'You'll need the will.'

'So I am shocked to hear. He kept it at the office?' I was just making conversation. I shoved the thing through my belt.

'This was his latest version!' Maia scoffed. 'Some urgent change had to be made last week so he brought it down to the Saepta. He did love fiddling with it.'

'Know what it says?'

'The misery wouldn't say.'

'Haven't you looked?'

'Don't be shocking—it's sealed with seven seals!'

No time to be amazed by Maia's restraint (if that was true), another marvel happened. A small figure, veiled in blackest black, jumped nimbly off a hired donkey (cheaper than a carrying chair), with the manner of one who expected reverence. She received it. At once the crowd gave way for her, and apparently without surprise at her presence. If the day had seemed unreal before, it became madness now. I didn't need to peek beneath the veil. My mother was taking back her rights.

Luckily no one could see her expression. I knew she would not throw herself inconsolably on the bier, or rend her hair. She would send Pa to the Underworld with a cackle, delighted that he had gone first. She was here to make certain the renegade actually left for the Styx. The smug words I heard through that veil all day were, 'I never like to gloat!'

I saluted Ma gravely and made sure a couple of my sisters led her by the hands, with instructions to ensure that she always had a good view of proceedings and that she didn't pinch any silver trays or old Greek vases from the house. I knew how a son ought to handle his widowed mother. I had advised enough clients on this point.

A procession lined up, like some reptile slowly awakening in the sun. In a daze, I found myself propelled to the front of a long funeral train. We made our way a short distance to an area of the garden that Pa must have already chosen as his resting place. He had planned everything, I gathered. I was fascinated to find he had this morbid streak. His corpse was carried on a bier, on its double mattress, with an ivory headrest. I was one of the eight bearers, with Petronius and the other brothers-in-law—Verontius, the crooked road contractor; Mico the worst plasterer in Rome; Lollius, the constantly unfaithful boatman; Gaius Baebius, the most boring customs clerk in that far from rollicking profession. Numbers were made up by Gornia and a fellow called Clusius, some leading light in auctioneering, probably the one who hoped to scoop up most of my father's business in the next few weeks. There were torches, as is traditional even in daytime. There were horn-players and flautists. Curiously, they all could play. To my relief, there were no hired mourners wailing and, thank Pluto, no mime artists pretending to be Pa.

The undertakers must have brought equipment and, unnoticed, had already constructed a pyre. It was three levels high. Funereal odours soon covered the hillside: not just more myrrh and cassia, but frankincense and cinnamon. No one in Rome would be able to buy banquet garlands today; we had all the flowers. High on the Janiculan, a breeze helped the flames get going after I plunged in the first torch. We stood around, as you have to for hours, waiting for the corpse to be consumed, while people with no sense reminisced about Pa. The kinder ones simply watched in silence. Much later I was to drown the ashes with wine—just a mediocre vintage; in respect for Pa, I reserved his best for drinking. Though I was still not certain how much of the organisation was my responsibility, I invited everyone to a feast in nine days' time, after the set period of formal mourning. That encouraged them to leave. It was a good step back down to Rome and they had gathered I was not offering overnight accommodation.

They knew I had special troubles. They had all seen how, just before the undertakers opened my father's eyes on the bier so he could see his way on to Charon's ferry, I had clambered up and laid upon his breast the body of my one-day-old son.

So on the sun-drenched slopes of the Janiculan Hill, one long, strange July evening, we paid our respects to Marcus Didius Favonius. Neither he nor tiny Marcus Didius Justinianus would have to face the dark alone. Wherever they were going, they set off there together, with my tiny son clasped for eternity in the strong arms of his grandfather.

3

I shed some tears. People expect it. Sometimes at the funeral of a reprobate it seems easier than when you are honouring a man who really deserved grief.

Before they left, the jostling started. Relatives, business associates, friends, so-called friends and even strangers all made subtle or blatant attempts to find out whether they would receive a legacy. My mother stayed aloof from this. She and Pa had never declared themselves divorced, so she was convinced she had rights. She was waiting for my sisters to take her back to Rome, but they were queuing to come up and speak to me, showing affection that unsettled me. I could not remember the last time Allia, Galla or Junia had felt the need to kiss my cheek. One by one their feckless husbands each clasped my hand in strong, silent communion. Only Gaius Baebius came right out with a concern: 'What's going to happen about Flora's, Marcus?' He meant the Aventine bar that my sister Junia managed for our father.

'Just give me a few days, Gaius—'

'Well, I suppose Junia can go on running the place as usual.'

'That would be helpful.' I ground my teeth. 'I hope it's not a chore. Apollonius is a perfectly good waiter. Or if Junia really can't face it, why doesn't she just close up the shutters, until we know what's what?'

'Oh, Junia won't give way to her grief!'

Junia stood in uncharacteristic silence, forced by the situation to have her husband speak for her: he like a true Roman patriarch and she like an inconsolable bereaved daughter. Yes, the lies and deceit had started.

I caught Maia's eye and wondered again whether she had sneaked a look at the will. I could have unsealed the tablets. It is traditional to read a will in public straight after the funeral.

Stuff that for a game of soldiers. I wanted to inspect and evaluate this dodgy document when I was safely by myself. It remained in my belt. Every time I bent a few inches, the chunky tablets stuck in my ribs, reminding me. Every time someone fished for information, I played at being too overcome with sorrow to think about it.

'Cut that out!' muttered Petronius Longus, while *he* acted out supporting me. 'Some of us know you would have gone to live as a pork-chop trader in Halicarnassus if you could have escaped being your father's son.'

'No point. He'd only have turned up,' I answered gloomily. 'Offering me a cheap price for bones—and expecting me to leave the marrow in as a favour.'

Petro and Maia stayed until last, helping to shepherd out the rest, then giving orders to the slaves. 'Keep the house running as normal. Keep it clean and secure.'

'You will have instructions later this week about the funeral feast, then you will be told where you will each be working afterwards . . .'

I watched them, moving now like a long-established couple, although they had only lived together formally for one or two years. They had met after Maia was married and a mother, a status she respected with more diligence than her late husband deserved. Each now had children from first marriages, all of whom were currently outside in the portico, quietly occupying themselves. Throughout the day Petronilla, Cloelia, Marius, Rhea and Ancus had behaved in magical contrast to the brats my other sisters dragged along. They would have shown up my own pair, had I brought them. My daughters were cute but unmanageable. Helena said they got it from me.

Petronius, tall and hefty, was not in formal funeral clothes, but had simply thrown an extra-dark cloak over the battered brown gear he usually wore. I guessed that back in Rome he was due at the vigiles' patrol house for a night shift. I thanked him for coming all the more; he just shrugged. 'We've got a really puzzling case, Falco. I'd welcome your advice—'

My sister laid a hand on his arm. 'Lucius, not now.' Maia, with her dark curls and characteristic quick movements, looked odd and unfamiliar in black; she usually flitted about in very bright colours. Her face was pale, but she was businesslike.

I would have hugged her, but now the house had emptied, Maia broke away and threw herself onto a couch. 'Did you see this coming, sis?'

'Not really, though Pa had complained of feeling off-colour. Your Egypt trip knocked it out of him.'

'Not my idea. I had banned him. I knew he'd be a menace, and he was.'

'Oh I realise. Look,' Maia said, 'I won't annoy you with details, but I went quickly through the diary with Gornia. We will carry on with all the booked auctions but won't take any new orders. You'll have a lot of sorting out, whatever happens to the business.'

'Oh Jupiter! Sorting out—what a nightmare . . . Why me?' I finally managed to voice it out loud.

Petronius looked surprised. 'You are the son. He thought a lot of you.'

'No, he thought Marcus was a self-righteous prig,' my sister disagreed in a casual tone. She threw insults as if she had hardly noticed doing it, though her barbs were generally apt and always intentional. 'Still, Marcus always does a good job. And apart from behaving like a bastard at every opportunity, Father was a traditionalist.'

'Maybe all fathers are bastards,' I commented. I like to be fair. 'He knew what I thought of him. I told him often enough.'

'Well, he knew you were honest!' said Maia, laughing a little. She had faith in me. I had never felt certain just how she regarded Pa. We were the two youngest in our family, long-time allies against the others; she was my favourite and held me in great affection. She had worked with my father because he had paid her, at a time when she had been desperate financially. Newly widowed then—it was about three years ago—she appreciated being in a family business during that hard period. She needed the security. Pa, to do him justice, offered it. He railed against having a woman interfering yet he let her do much as she wanted as his office manager. He recognised how good she was at organisation. He also liked having one of his own privy to his secrets, rather than a hired hand or a slave. That was why he let Junia run Flora's Caupona too, even though her attitude upset half the customers. And that, I suppose, was why he landed me with his will.

I pulled it out. I held the tied and sealed tablets nervously between both hands, making no attempt to pull the strings undone. 'So tell me about this, Maia.' Maia just sniffed. 'He rewrote it last week? Why was that?'

'One of his whims. He sent for the lawyer straight after that drama-dealer, Thalia, came to see him at the Saepta.'

'*Thalia?*' That was unexpected.

'You know the creature, I believe? She wears the shortest skirts in the Empire.'

'And frolics suggestively with wild beasts.'

'Who is this? Should I know her?' Sitting on the end of Maia's couch, his long legs crossed and his hands behind his head, Petronius showed himself keen for gossip. Maia kicked him, and he massaged the bare soles of her tired feet for her; neither really seemed aware they were doing it.

I shrugged. 'Have Helena and I not mentioned her? She's a circus and theatre manager. Runs actors and musicians—does rather well. Her speciality is exotic animal acts. I do mean exotic! Her indecent dance with a python would make your eyes water.'

A gleam came into Petro's eyes. 'I'd like to see that! But Marcus, my boy, I thought you gave up your fancy girlfriends!'

'Oh I have; honest, legate! No, no; she's a family friend. Thalia's a good sort, though I hate her pesky snake, Jason. I could have done without her travelling to Alexandria with my damned father. She came to buy lions. Pa cadged a free ride on her ship. I believe that was the first time they met, and I can't imagine they would have any business together back in Rome.'

'Oh, they were close!' Maia snorted. 'They rushed into a closet with the door closed and there was some ghastly giggling. I did *not* take in a galley tray of almond fancies.' She looked prudish. 'When they emerged, Thalia seemed extremely happy with the outcome and our father positively glowed—the revolting way he did when some busty fifteen-year-old barmaid gave him a free drink.'

Petronius winced. I just looked rueful. 'Thalia's a woman of the world, Maia, with her own money; she can't have been scrounging. What she likes from men, insofar as she likes them for anything, is purely physical . . . What did Geminus say?'

'Nothing. I could see he was bursting to make *some* grand pro-nouncement,' Maia replied, 'but the Thalia woman glared at him and for once he held his tongue. Immediately she left, the lawyer was booked, however. Next day Geminus went into a huddle with *him*. He couldn't resist letting on he was playing with his will. Since he was dying to tell me the details, I refused to show any curiosity.'

Like Maia, I hated to be manipulated into feeling any interest. I was exhausted. I decided I would have dinner here, sleep at the villa, then rise early to go home to Helena. I tossed the will on to a low table. 'It will keep.'

'My bet is, that will be a whole year's work and twice as much trouble,' Petronius warned.

'Well, I'll give it proper attention tomorrow. The timing must be a coincidence, Maia. I can't imagine Thalia's visit was connected.'

Then Maia exclaimed, 'Oh, Marcus. You can be such an innocent!'

After Maia and Petronius left, the slaves found me something to eat and somewhere to sleep. I had to stop them putting me in my father's room. Assuming his legal identity was bad enough. I drew the line at his bed.

Food revived me. Pa always ate well. The excellent panpipe-player whootled gently for me too. I was ready to be irritated, but it was quite relaxing. He seemed surprised when I congratulated him on his arpeggios. It looked as if he was hanging around in case I required other services—not that my father would have stood for that. I dismissed the musician without rancour. Who knows what kind of debauched household he originally came from?

Then, of course, I did what you or anyone else would have done: I opened up the tablets.

4

My life changed for ever at that moment.

My father's will was quite short and surprisingly simple. There were no outrageous clauses. It was a routine family testament.

'I, Marcus Didius Favonius, have made a will and command my sons to be my heirs.'

So it was legally proper, but well out of date. Despite all the talk of revisions, this had been written long before he died—twenty years ago, to be precise. It was soon after my father returned to Rome from Capua, where he had originally fled with his girlfriend when he left home, and when he set up again as an auctioneer here, trading under the new name of Geminus. Flora, the girlfriend, never had children. At that time 'my sons' meant my brother and me. Festus later died in Judaea. Clearly Pa, who had been close to him, had never been able to face writing him out.

The customary seven witnesses had signed. They ought to be present again when the will was opened, but to Hades with that. Some names were vaguely familiar, business contacts, men of my father's age. I knew that at least two had died in the intervening period. A couple came to the funeral.

As was customary, the tablet named some people who might have had a claim but specifically disinherited them as main heirs: Pa chose to dispense with the equal treatment that the law would have given his four surviving daughters if, say, he had died intestate. I could see why he had never made my sisters aware this would happen. Their reaction would be vicious. The bastard must have imagined with enjoyment my discomfiture when I had to pass on the news.

He left no instructions about making any slaves free. They too would be disappointed, though executors can be flexible. They were bound to know that, so they would continue canvassing me. I would take my time over making decisions.

Next came a list of specific annuities to be paid out: quite a high figure to Mother, which surprised and pleased me. There were smaller sums for my sisters, so they had not been ignored completely. It was usually assumed married daughters had received their share of the family loot in their dowries. (*What dowries?* I could hear them all shriek.) Nothing had been done for Marina who, well after the will was made, became my brother's lover and mother of a child who was presumed to be fathered by Festus. An enormous sum was earmarked for Flora, Pa's mistress of two decades, though since she had died that no longer counted. I would keep quiet about it; there was no point upsetting Ma. After that, the rest went to the specified heirs: 'my sons'. So with Festus dead, everything else my father had owned would come to me.

I was seriously shocked. It was completely unexpected. Unless I uncovered enormous debts—and I reckoned Pa was too canny for that—then he had bequeathed me a substantial amount.

I tried to stay calm, but I was human. I began to reckon up mentally. My father had never owned much land—not land in the traditional Roman sense of rolling fields that could be ploughed and grazed and tended by battalions of rural workers, not land that counted formally towards social status. But this was a grand house in a splendid location, and he had owned another, even bigger villa on the coast below Ostia. I only discovered his place at Ostia last year, so there might be further properties he kept secret. The two I knew about were well staffed—and house-trained slaves were valuable in themselves. Above all, these houses were furnished expensively—crammed to the rafters with wonderful goods. I knew Pa kept instant-access funds in a chest bolted into the wall at the Saepta Julia and he had more money with a Forum banker; his cash flow rose and fell with the ups and downs of self-employment, much as my own did. However, throughout his life, his real investments followed his real interest: art and antiques.

I looked around. This was merely a bedroom for casual visitors. It was lightly furnished, compared with the areas Pa used himself. Even so, the bed I was lolling on had intricate bronze fittings, a well-upholstered mattress supported on decent webbing, a striking wool coverlet and tasselled pillows. There was a heavy folding stool in the room, like a magistrate's. An old Eastern carpet hung on one wall on a runner that had gilded finials. On a shelf—which was grey-veined marble, with polished onyx ends—stood a row of ancient south Italian vases that would sell for a figure big enough to feed a family for a year.

This was one unimportant room. Multiply it by all the other rooms in at least two large houses, plus whatever stock was crammed into various warehouses and the treasures currently on display at Pa's office in the Saepta . . . I began to feel light-headed.

Complete upheaval faced me. Nothing in my life could ever be as I had expected: neither my life, nor the lives of my wife and my children. If this will was genuine, and it was the latest version, and if my brother Festus really had died in the desert (which was undeniable, because I had spoken to people who saw it happen), then I would be able to live without anxiety for the rest of my days. I could give my daughters dowries lavish enough to secure them consuls, if they wanted idiots as husbands. I could stop being an informer. I need never work again. I could waste my life being a benefactor of out-of-the-way temples and playing at patron to dim-witted poets.

My father had not just made me his legal representative. He had left me a great fortune.

5

The morning after the funeral I returned home at first light.

After only a few hours' sleep I felt drained. My house still lay quiet. I crawled on to a couch in a spare room, unwilling to disturb Helena. It was still barely a day since her labour and loss. But by then she had been told about my father, so was on the alert. Just as she always heard my return from late-night surveillances, Helena roused herself and found me. I felt her drop a coverlet over me, then she slid under it too. She was still distraught over the baby, but now the greater need was to comfort me. Our love held strong. Extra trouble brought us back close. For a time we lay side by side, holding hands. Too soon, the dog snuffled in and found us, then we began the slow slide back to normality.

When I told Helena she had married better than she thought and might be about to acquire a stupendous dress allowance, she sighed. 'He never mentioned his intentions, but I always suspected it. When you raged at him, I think Geminus enjoyed secretly knowing that one day he would give you all this. Because you are a realist you would accept his generosity . . . He loved you, Marcus. He was very proud of you.'

'It's too much.'

'Nonsense.'

'I can say no to it.'

'Legally.'

'I might.'

'You won't. Just say yes, then give it away if you feel that way later.'

'It will ruin my life.'

'Your life is in your own hands, just as it always was. You won't change,' Helena said. 'You need to work. It is what you enjoy: grappling with puzzles that no one else will undertake and righting society's wrongs. Don't become a man of leisure; you'll go mad—and you'll drive the rest of us crazy.'

I pretended to think she just wanted reasons to pack me out of the house every morning as before. But she knew that I accepted she was right.

During the nine days of mourning, Helena and I told everyone that 'in the style of the divine Emperor Augustus and his unparalleled wife Livia', we would not be seen in public. Platitudes always work. Nobody considered that we regarded Augustus and Livia as two-faced, double-dealing, power-mad manipulators.

After the nine days, we could both just about face people again. Helena Justina was beside me at the feast, when I returned to the Janiculan.

I knew what the funeral feast would be like. I thought the day would hold no surprises. Even more hangers-on managed to bring themselves up the hill than had struggled there for the cremation. Free food, free drink, and the chance to hear or pass on gossip, brought fools out in flocks. Relatives we had forgotten were ours somehow turned up. Mother's brothers, Fabius and Junius, who were rarely seen together because they feuded so tenaciously, both came all the way from the Campagna; at least they brought root vegetables as presents, unlike the other shiftless guests. If they had ulterior motives they were too dumb to say. I thought Fabius and Junius were simply acknowledging the end of an era that only they and Ma now remembered.

I had primed my more reliable nephews—restless Gaius, over-weight Cornelius, sensible Marius—to pass among the throng, muttering that there were far more debts than anticipated and that I might refuse to be the heir . . . It held off some of the graspers from overt begging.

Together Helena and I went through the motions of hosting the banquet. Stuffing merrily, people were no trouble. As the long meal drew to a close, I watched the tall and stately Helena Justina pass among the guests with my secretary, Katutis, at her shoulder. He was new. I had acquired a trained Egyptian scribe at just the right moment. He was thrilled to have deaths in the family; it provided more work than I found for him normally. While Helena prised out people's names, Katutis busily wrote them all down in level Greek script in case I needed to know later. I was nervous that some of Pa's dubious business arrangements might jump up and bite. Helena had also pointed out several women who looked like off-duty barmaids, flaunting their best outfits and seemingly unaware that mourning women should leave off their jewellery. These blowsy, bulging dames might just be good-hearted old friends of my social papa; perhaps they adored him as a lovable rogue who left good tips by his empty wine-cup. Or they could have deeper motives. Helena was collecting their data along with details of all those old men who felt no need to explain who they were, as they called me Young Marcus and tapped their bulbous red noses as if we shared enormous secrets.

As we went about our duties, Helena murmured, 'I have said we are hoping for a mention in the *Daily Gazette* society column: *Seen at a banquet in his elegant Janiculan villa to celebrate the life of much-admired man-about-the-Forum, Marcus Didius Favonius, were the following persons of note* . . . Now watch the would-be persons of note rush up to help Katutis spell their names right.'

'I don't want Pa in the news.'

'No, darling. Why alert the tax authorities?' Helena's voice was thin, but she was regaining her sense of humour. Inheritance tax is five percent, paid into the Treasury's military fund. The army was going to like me a lot.

I had used my mourning period for the traditional purpose of starting to inventory the legacy. For most people nine days is enough to cover this formality; I had barely tickled the edge.

Supposedly incommunicado, I had worked like a bath-house stoker among Pa's many possessions. I set aside the least desirable items to sell to pay the tax. I also established with Gornia that we would auction some stuff that would either fail to sell, or sell for a disappointing amount; this would show picky officials that my inventory valuations were blamelessly modest. A citizen is obliged to pay his taxes, but may adopt any legal measures to minimise the damage. I knew all about that. I had been Vespasian's Census fixer. I investigated every variation of fiscal fraud and tax-dodging—and I now planned to use my experience. Pa would expect it.

I had had an interesting chat with a treasury official about whether, if I sold goods at auction, I must pay the one per cent auction tax on top of the five per cent for inheritance; you can guess his answer.

'Thalia is here; have you seen her, Marcus?'

'I glimpsed her.' She was lurking at the far end of a table, looking more wrapped up and respectable than usual. 'Nice of her to hang back and not bother us.' In fact her demure behaviour had set up anxiety.

'I shall have a word!' Helena declared, making me oddly apprehensive.

As she paraded through the guests, Helena identified the surviving witnesses to Father's will: four of those shaky old fellows who had grasped my hand interminably. I made sure they each had a drink poured from the special amphora of Falernian, which probably shortened their lives by several months; it flowed like rich olive oil and was dangerously potent. Their presence allowed me to read out the will formally. I pretended the contents came as news to me; nobody was fooled. A restrained silence fell. My sisters heard their fates without making a public scene, but assumed foreboding expressions. Ma was too heavily veiled for anyone to see her reaction. She had seemed quiet all day, as if losing the old devil at last had knocked all the spirit out of her.

Soon afterwards, people began to leave. Helena told me it was because I was viewed as tight-fisted. 'Everybody is whispering that things would have been very different—they mean, more money for them—if Festus had survived.'

That suited me. But many just went because the food and drink were running out. There had been plenty. Some of it was going home in people's pockets. Anyone who brought their own napkin made sure they took it away laden.

'I swear there were some "grieving friends" who came with little baskets specially,' I complained to Maia. Then I noticed her basket.

'Marcus, darling, I'm family. Any leftover egg-and-anchovy tart is mine!' She backed down slightly. 'You don't want waste, do you?'

Helena had identified my father's lawyer. Once we were freed from saying farewells in the portico, she brought him to me indoors.

He was surprisingly young, twenty-five or so. He introduced himself as Septimus Parvo. His accent was decent, though not screamingly aristocratic; it sounded as if he had learned how to speak from an elocution teacher, after a plebeian upbringing. His dress was neat, his manner polite. He told me he avoided cut-throat court cases at the Basilica Julia, instead working as a backstreet family lawyer.

'I'll keep your name handy then. I'm an informer myself. We may be able to do business.' The veiled surprise in Parvo's expression reminded me that most people expected I would now retire. It was still too early for me to be certain, though I thought Helena was probably right; work would always claim me. 'You're far too young to have prepared my father's will, Parvo—assuming the date is right?'

'No, my own late father did that. We have worked for many years with Didius Geminus—we always called him that. Or do you prefer to say Favonius, Falco?'

'To be frank, I just called him an incorrigible swine.'

The young man kept his expression neutral. He managed to avoid glancing around the salon we were in: the walls were drab because Pa never paid out for fresco decorators, but the room was adorned with a fabulous collection of furniture. Given how much I had just inherited, Parvo may have been wondering at my attitude.

Helena rejoined us. She led in Thalia. It was the first time I had ever seen the circus entertainer looking nervous. Normally she was as brazen as she was statuesque, even when not wrapped in her python.

'This is Thalia, Parvo. Have you met?'

She was a tall, striking woman, with muscled thighs like wharfside baulks, which were impossible to ignore through a fringed cloak that barely covered her toned body, minute skirt and tightly laced circus boots. Faced with this vision, Parvo inclined his head twitchily, as if he could tell Thalia ate men like him as pre-lunch snacks. 'No— but I heard a lot about you, Thalia.' Always a wily operator, Thalia made no reply to that thumping phrase. 'We are about to discuss the will,' Parvo murmured, acknowledging that Thalia should be part of the conversation, though not immediately saying why.

The women seated themselves in comfortable half-round chairs, filling in time by arranging cushions. Thalia folded the cloak so it just covered her legs, in a curiously modest gesture. I glanced at Helena, then waited. She had given me a 'don't say anything impetuous' look, the put-down that strong-minded wives inherit from their mothers. You know, the look you should always pay attention to, though the mischievous Fates somehow make you foolishly ignore it.

Parvo must be a piecework lawyer, not paid by the hour. He moved things along: 'Falco, when we spoke just now, did I detect a query?'

'Only that I was surprised by the will's date. I understand Pa made frequent revisions—and didn't that include one last week?'

'Yes, I brought that for you,' Parvo replied calmly. 'It is a codicil. Your father did indeed frequently make changes, but he always left the will itself alone.'

'Your fee for a codicil is much cheaper than your fee for a new will?' I guessed drily.

Parvo smiled his acknowledgement of what Pa called value for money and others might stigmatise as meanness. 'Apart from that, a codicil is often a more flexible way of giving instructions.'

I braced myself. 'So what usefully flexible orders has the old beggar left?'

Without comment, Parvo passed me a scroll, the ink so fresh and black it almost still smelt sooty. I read it. I raised my eyebrows and passed it to Helena, who read it too. We both looked at the lawyer.

'Marcus Didius Falco, your father hereby makes a solemn request of you called a *fideicommissum*. That is a good faith undertaking.' Filthy misnomer. Good faith did not come into this. 'It affects any child of Marcus Didius Geminus, otherwise Favonius, which is born to him after the date of this codicil—including a child born posthumously. You are charged with treating any child that you know your father intended to acknowledge as your sister or brother, according to the terms of the will.' Parvo knew what instruction he was handing me. A new female child must be given the same as my sisters' annuities. A *male* child would halve my inheritance. 'I shall leave you with that, Falco. Should you have any queries, anything at all, I gave your wife my address. Delighted to meet you, Helena Justina—and you too, Thalia.'

Being an experienced family lawyer, he fired the arrow then at once made off.

Helena and I turned to our old friend Thalia. Helena balanced her chin on her clasped hands, in silence. It was left to me: 'Do I gather, Thalia, that you are pregnant?'

She eyed me ruefully. 'Properly caught out, Falco.'

Thalia looked well-preserved. Across an arena she could pass for a lithe girl, but near to, I put her at approaching forty. Gracious Roman manners barred me from suggesting she was too old for this. Maybe she had thought so herself, while freely indulging in love play. That sexual promiscuity of an athletic kind had occurred was in no doubt. Thalia referred to her appetite for pleasure as consistently as she denounced as pitiful the brave men she bedded.

'Would this have been on your Egyptian trip?'

'I wondered why I was feeling so queasy all the time in Alexandria.'

'Geminus believed he was responsible?'

'Oh, he didn't need persuading. The sweet duck was ecstatic,' boasted Thalia. 'It must have happened on the boat when we were going out to Egypt. We had a few cuddles to keep out the sea breezes.'

'I'm rather surprised by the results!'

Thalia grinned. She was recovering her confidence. 'I can't say I'm happy to be a mother at my age—but when I told him the news, your dear father was just thrilled. He was so proud to find out his ballista was still firing missiles.'

I believed that. Pa—vain, foolish and ridiculous—would eagerly take the blame.

'You told my father you were expecting, he accepted it was his responsibility, and if he hadn't died, he would have acknowledged the baby?'

'That's right, Falco,' said Thalia meekly.

'What does Davos say?'

'Nothing to do with him.' Davos was Thalia's long-lost love, in theory. Helena and I had witnessed them being reunited out in Syria. It had seemed like a heart-warming development—for about three months. As far as I knew, he was now leading a summer theatre tour in southern Italy. No chance of pinning this baby on Davos. *'The Girl from Andros'* and her pal *'The Girl from Perinthos'* would give him foolproof alibis.

'And have you mentioned it to Philadelphion?'

'Why would I do that?'

Thalia gave me a hard defiant stare. She was sticking to her story, even though she realised I thought it much more likely her child had been procreated by a womanising zoo keeper we knew in Alexandria. He was firmly married—and what's more had a tenacious official mistress. None of that had stopped him unofficially discussing the price of lion cubs with his old crony Thalia in the humid privacy of her travel tent.

'You're right.' I managed not to appear angry. 'Philadelphion had enough baby animals to hand-rear.'

I rarely pray to the gods but on this occasion it did seem permissible to offer up a plea to Juno Lucina, light-bearer to pregnant women, that Thalia was not expecting male twins or triplets to reduce my heritage even further. Suddenly I knew how that old mythical king felt about the interlopers Romulus and Remus. I saw why he put those threatening twins straight into the Tiber in a basket; if I did it, I would make sure there were no nearby female wolves available for suckling.

'So Marcus, my dear,' Thalia wheedled. 'It's lucky we know each other so well—now that I'm going to be giving you a little sister or brother! And do I gather the precious babe is to receive a bit of money from your lovely father?'

'Get it born first!' I answered her, perhaps too cruelly.

6

You hypocrite—I saw your face!' Helena accused me. She smoothed her skirts, rattling her bracelets in annoyance. 'Marcus Didius Falco—' That was a subtle clue. Helena used formality like a fisherman's trident. I was well speared. 'Can it be that you have become a miser, over a fortune you never expected—and it's only nine days since you heard about it?'

'Human nature. The dark side of greed.' I forced a grin cautiously. 'What I really hate is this pregnancy of Thalia's being passed off as our problem. Pa was riddled with vanity and befuddled by drink if he couldn't see she was conning him. Being fleeced by a friend is loathsome.'

Helena shook her head. 'What if she's right? No child can ever truly know its father, nor any father know his child. Unless there is some way of testing the blood in our veins, we are all left with the word of our mothers—and most of us are none the worse for it.'

'The world is full of wicked mothers who have no idea who their children belong to. Roll on the day some scientific investigator finds out how to prove paternity. Maybe that silver-haired fox Philadelphion will do it.'

'Given that Philadelphion may be the real parent, that would be a nice irony. But uncertainty has advantages,' Helena maintained. 'Besides, you can't blame Thalia asking Geminus for help—'

'She's a highly successful entrepreneur. What help can she need?'

'She can't dance with the python during a pregnancy!'

'I would not put it past her. Modesty isn't in her repertoire.' Even Thalia's normal acrobatics were gross. 'If she's out of action for a while, her troupe will go on working. She'll have funds.'

'But Marcus, she wanted to plan for the baby's future. She didn't know your father would die,' Helena insisted. 'No one expected it.'

'I agree, she can't have intended settling down with him—she's far too independent.' I shuddered at the thought of Thalia as a stepmother. 'Still, she got him to promise something. He obviously told her he would change his will. And she was happy for him to do so!'

'As you said—she is a very good businesswoman.'

Growling, I went off to the Saepta Julia, where I was burying my anger in the monumental task of exploring my father's affairs.

It was the day that crawler Cluvius turned up. He was nagging to know whether I intended carrying on Pa's business, or could Cluvius and his auctioneer cronies siphon off work that would have been ours? 'People approach the Guild for advice. We assume you don't want to be bothered, Marcus Didius . . .'

On the spot, I decided. 'Business as usual!' I snapped crushingly. 'I'll be lending a hand myself.' I had spare capacity. Informing was quiet in summer. People are too hot to worry about professional fortune-hunters marrying their daughters. Of course they *should* worry—because long steamy July and August nights are when those bold girls are most likely to let lovers in at the window . . .

'Feel free to ask any of us for advice then,' Cluvius offered peevishly.

That clinched it. From that moment I became a joint auctioneer-informer. I would manumit one or two of the better slaves from Pa's ménage then train them up as freedmen assistants, a few in the auction house, a couple on my client casework. There could be a handy crossover. The auction helpers could scout for people in the kind of difficulty I solved as an informer. And it was traditional for both trades to operate out of the Saepta Julia.

Strange how you can worry for years over your career, and do nothing about it—then alter it instantly without a qualm. This was like falling in love all over again. Certainty thumped down on me. There was no going back.

'Yes, Cluvius; I'm moving back into my old office. That will help me keep an eye on the competition!' I may have looked naïve but if Cluvius knew that the 'office' I referred to was where I had once worked with the Chief Spy picking off Census defaulters, he might see me as a more serious rival. Anacrites and I had done well. Even Vespasian, a byword for stinginess, had felt moved to reward us with social elevation. I had skills; I had contacts too. I rubbed my gold ring thoughtfully, but Cluvius still didn't get it.

He was leaving. Thank you, gods!

He dropped one more innocent-sounding question from the doorway to catch me off-guard. I hadn't seen that feeble trick since Nero appointed his racehorse a consul: 'I suppose nothing came of that amphitheatre contract? Tricky, pinning down the Treasury; I dare say it fell through . . .'

I knew nothing about this. I tapped my nose, implying some delicate and secret deal. As soon as Cluvius wandered off, I bounded into the back of the warehouse and briskly tackled Gornia.

The porter groaned. 'Oh, he must be on about the statues.'

Not news I wanted. The last time Pa and I were involved in statuary—our one and only operation together—we caught a bad cold. I could hardly bear to remember. Pa claimed he'd learned his lesson. Maybe I had too. Or maybe he at least could never resist a challenge . . . 'If that leech Cluvius is curious, do I sniff nice profits?'

'Oh just let Cluvius wet himself.' Gornia, a spindly old cove with about sixty years of working for Pa behind him, was as exciting as that porridge our forebears called a national dish. I mean, before they discovered the better joys of oysters and expensive turbot. 'You don't want to worry about him, Marcus Didius.'

I wondered if I could trust Gornia. His attitude was an aspect of the business I had not yet resolved. Even though he had stuck by Pa, he might not be so loyal to me.

'Statues? Amphitheatre? Gornia, would that be the great lump of unfinished masonry our beloved Emperor is dumping on the south side of the Forum? Where Nero's giant lake was? Where they need so much travertine cladding, they had to open a new marble quarry?'

'That's the beauty. Soon to be covered with statues,' said Gornia, looking nonchalant. 'They need thousands of the buggers, I believe.'

'*Thousands?*'

'Well, there will be three tiers of eighty arches, at least two tiers with some statuary in each arch.' He seemed well informed on the building plans.

'So "thousands" actually means a hundred and sixty? Two hundred and forty if they do the top tier?'

'Big fellows! Plus the odd hero driving a quadriga, with a full rack of fiery steeds, to shove up over entrances.'

I slumped on a stone seat. Foreboding dropped on me like a smelly old blanket, but I leaned back with a nonchalant air. 'Whisper to me what my cherished papa had to do with it?'

'Well . . . you know him!'

'Yes, I am afraid so.'

'He tried anything.'

'Tell me the worst.'

'The old fool lined up to supply a few old stone toffs for the exterior.'

I had already learned that Gornia avoided discussing problems. He had handled Pa by keeping out of awkward chats. When he did comment it was wry, dry and plastered as floridly as a banker's dining room with dangerous understatement. 'How many stone toffs,' I asked gently, 'is "a few"?'

'Not sure I know.'

'I bet. Does my sister have figures?'

'Oh, he didn't want to involve Maia.'

'Why not? Dodgy contract?' With Pa, no contract at all was more usual. I had another thought. 'Was this transaction off the books?'

'Our books?'

'No, the Treasury books. Don't say this is a corrupt deal?'

Gornia looked disapproving. 'He always said you were a prig, Marcus Didius!'

'I don't mess with the government; that's why I'm still alive. Was Pa behind with the order or something?' I remembered that his Rome warehouse had been significantly short of statues when I surveyed the stock.

'He sent samples. We'd scraped the moss off the second-hand ones. The officials were happy.'

'So what's the problem?'

Gornia looked shifty. 'Who mentioned a problem?'

'You did, Gornia, by not coming clean. What's up? Are we over-due on deliveries, or are we done?'

'It's our call. They pay by the piece, as and when. They're just happy to get enough suitable figures. Anyone who can meet the specifica-tions is in. The spec,' Gornia added quickly, 'is simple; there's a height rule, that's all.'

'That will be for visual uniformity.' I sounded like an interior de-signer. 'I bet it's surprisingly difficult to find ready-mades to fit the arches . . . We have stock?'

'The old man collected a marble or two at the place on the coast, I believe.'

'Be more specific?'

'Oh . . . maybe a hundred,' said Gornia.

'*A hundred?*' My voice was faint. 'That's bulk-buying by a maniac.'

'You did ask. Don't worry about it, I told you.'

'I am relaxed.' I was anxious. 'So, Gornia—excuse me, but why don't we just hand this huge batch over, and collect our fees? I don't want to be stuck with a glut of forgotten heroes and disgraced gener-als.' Everyone who might buy such junk had gone to their summer villas at Neapolis. There, many would be gazing at horrible statues my father had sold them on previous occasions, and thinking *never again.*

'It will work out,' Gornia assured me. 'Geminus said to hold off a bit . . .' He looked embarrassed. 'We ought to pay for them.'

Now I saw it. This was neither unexpected nor insurmountable: 'Daylight! No ready funds?'

Odd, that. There were plenty of funds, as I knew well. In fact I was looking for outgoings, to set against the inheritance tax.

'We had the collateral. We just couldn't pass it to the vendors. I went. I went down there with the cash myself. Geminus always sent me, because I look so ordinary,' Gornia told me endearingly. 'Nobody ever robs me on the road. But I couldn't find them.'

'His suppliers?'

'They vanished.' Gornia looked relieved to squeeze it out. 'Bit of a novelty, isn't it?'

My father had been in many scrapes. Sometimes debt featured, but he covered it eventually. His cash flow only faltered temporarily. He was good at what he did.

It was rare for anyone in Rome, and never Geminus, to try to pay a creditor but to fail. I was used to the other system: those with claims came forward at a run. Their invoices were immaculate. They brought their own strongboxes to take away their cash. I coughed up. They were happy. End of story.

I decided I had better look at these statues myself. Then I would seek out the suppliers. I was an informer; I should be able to track them down.

I knew many good reasons why people who *owe* money vanish. But when people who are *owed* payment disappear, it tends to be because either they have grown old and confused—or they have quietly died. If Livia Primilla and Julius Modestus (those were their names) had passed away, fellow feeling made me want to help whatever poor heir needed to collect in this debt.

I just wanted to be a good citizen. But this was when the situation gently began tipping from straightforward into the kind of dark enquiry I was used to.

7

Modestus and Primilla lived at Antium, nearly thirty miles away. I dreaded announcing to Helena that I was going on a trip. The baby's death still gnawed. It was the wrong time to leave home. However, some god was on my side. Some deity with time on their hands in Olympus decided Falco needed help.

I entered my house with a cautious step. After working the key gently, I let the door swing to with care, glad no one was acting as door porter. I had the classic bearing of a guilty bastard slinking in and hoping to avoid notice. It was the ninth hour, evening, the period when busy men return, freshly bathed and ready for a good dinner. In houses all through Rome such men were about to have ructions with tired wives, layabout sons or indecent daughters.

Drawing upon six hundred years of a Roman's right to behave crassly, I flexed my shoulders. This house was where Pa had lived for twenty years but quite unlike the Janiculan spread. Crammed against the Aventine cliff on the Tiber's bank, our town house lacked the depth to allow a classic atrium with an open roof and vistas across peristyle gardens. Here, we lived vertically. I felt easy with that because I had grown up in the tall apartment blocks where the poor fester. We lived mainly upstairs because sometimes the river flooded in. Plain rooms off the corridors on the ground floor were non-domestic and silent at this hour. I walked across the empty entrance hall and went up.

Albia, my foster daughter, rushed down towards me. She was trying not to trip over the hem of a blue gown she thought particularly suited her. Her dark hair looked more fancifully arranged than usual, though with a lopsided tilt as if she had pinned it hastily herself. She burst out excitedly, 'Aulus has come home to Rome!'

Well, that could be good. Or not. He was a promising fellow. Still, she was too happy about his arrival. Something would have to be done. Helena was not up to it; this would be my problem.

Aulus Camillus Aelianus was Helena's brother, the elder of two. Though neither was a disaster, as pillars of the community this pair wobbled. Aulus once loathed me because I was an informer, but later saw sense. He was maturing; I liked to think he benefited from my patronage. Like his brother Quintus, he worked with me sometimes, when I felt strong enough for in-depth training of the hare-brained. Lately Aulus had been away studying law, first in Athens then Alexandria. This could either make him more useful to me, or give him a separate new career.

I was aware Albia and he had struck up a friendship. As a father who expected the worst, it made me glad Aulus was spending time abroad, since he was a senator's son and Albia was a foundling from Britain with a bleak history; they had no scope for romance, and anything else was unthinkable. On our recent family travels to Greece and to Egypt I had noticed Helena try to keep them apart, with limited success. Albia saw no problem. Aulus was something of a loner, and taking his time getting suitably married, so he liked having Albia to giggle with. He must know it could never go further. They were chums. It would pass. It had to.

'Aulus is *here*?'

'Come and see him!' Eyes bright, my innocent fosterling rushed ahead of me into the salon where we received visitors.

I detected a strained atmosphere at once.

Helena was sitting in a basket chair, her feet very neatly together on a footstool. She looked pale and weary. Our small daughters, Julia and Favonia, were lolling against her knees. Those scamps had been subdued since we lost the baby. Even at four and two, they had a good sense of trouble. Now Father was home but for once they did not hurl themselves upon me, shrieking. Their dark eyes came to me, with the open curiosity of children who recognised a crisis; my intelligent tots were watching closely what would happen now.

'*Aulus!*' Albia had cried out with joy too readily. He grinned, but it was sheepish. He was a poor actor. Albia's chum had come home looking indefinably hunted.

Albia tensed. She was very bright. I moved alongside and took her hand, like any fond father in company. But Albia was not like other people's daughters. She had come from the rowdy streets of Londinium, a harsh, remote city. Her Roman sophistication was a cloak she soon hurled off, immediately anyone upset her.

Seated on a couch, Aulus was a couple of years short of thirty, with a flop of dark hair, athletically built. Right beside him—when there were various other seats available, some more comfortable—perched a silent young woman. If there was trouble in the room, she was it. I kept tight hold of Albia.

Of foreign appearance, the young woman wore layers of expensive drapery in dark silk-shot linen. Her gold necklaces and ear-rings were rather formal for an unannounced visit to friends. Aulus must have brought her from Athens, but if she was Greek, she was not bearing gifts.

'Marcus!' Family gatherings were Helena Justina's strong point; she could direct bad-tempered relatives like a theatre producer getting an uncoordinated chorus into line. 'And Albia, my dear—here's a surprise.' Over our children's heads, her dark eyes sent me complicated messages. Without appearing to hurry, she began unhappily: 'Aulus has come back to Italy to settle down. He thinks he has learned enough; he wants to use his knowledge.' That, and his talent for upsetting everyone, I reckoned.

'So who's your new friend?' I asked him bluntly.

He cleared his throat. 'This is Hosidia.' He looked hopelessly at Albia.

'Hello, Hosidia.' I don't discriminate. I use the same brisk tone for tipsy barmaids showing their bosoms, hard-hearted females who have knifed their mothers, and Athenian dames who are looking down their nose as if they think I am the slave who cleans the silver. This Hosidia appeared to be costing up our metalware—the comport with the honey-glazed nutty titbits and the small but exquisite drinks tray. (Thanks to my father's perfect taste, our best service was small, but second to none.) If she had been under investigation, I would have put her on the suspects list. I really did not like the way she was assessing my pierce-patterned wine strainer.

'Marcus Didius Falco,' Aulus introduced me formally. He sounded unsure how Hosidia would react. I thought he could not know her well; nowhere near well enough, if I had judged this situation right.

Helena wanted Aulus to come clean, but as he held back she said politely, 'Hosidia is the daughter of my brother's tutor, Marcus. You remember the famous professor, Minas of Karystos, don't you?'

Jupiter help us! I raised an eyebrow, which Hosidia could take as admiration of her papa's intellect if she chose. In front of his daughter, I refrained from saying, 'That disgusting boozer, never in the classroom, trying to kill his students with his terrible all-night parties?'

Minas of Karystos was a decent court prosecutor when he could stand up straight, though that was rare. I knew Decimus Camillus, my father-in-law, was appalled by the shameless fees Minas charged. Perhaps this explained the son's recall. Camillus senior had decided to staunch the haemorrhage of cash. He can't have banked on the tutor's daughter.

Helena was looking overwrought. 'Marcus, would you believe my little brother has gone and got married?'

'No!' Call me a cynic, but I believed it all too sourly.

Aulus would have been an easy mark. He thought himself astute, but that just put him in more danger.

I saw it all. Albia, however, was taken aback. After one wild glance, she wrenched her hand free from mine and tore from the room.

Nobody commented on Albia running out. I thought Aulus jumped, but he stayed put.

Helena continued bleakly, 'The wedding happened in a rush, because of Aulus coming home. Minas is delighted—'

Minas must have set it up. However big a rissole Minas of godforsaken Karystos was in Athens, the glory of Greece had passed away. Rome was the only place for any ambitious professional. Marrying off his sombre daughter to a Roman senator's son must have been in the mind of the unscrupulous law teacher from the moment he grabbed his new pupil, fresh off the boat, and promised to make him a master of jurisprudence.

Demonstrating to the newlyweds how a good husband arrives home, whatever shocks await, I crossed the room sedately, then bent and kissed my dear wife's cheek. In the style of a good Roman marriage, she was the companion who shared my closest secrets, so to demonstrate our private affection to Aulus and his bride, I murmured a love greeting in Helena's neat ear. I managed not to nibble her lobe, though I considered it, which may have shown in my face.

'Seems Albia may want to leave town,' I then muttered. 'I could vanish to Pa's *villa maritima* for a few days. Call it executor business. Shall I take her away for some breathing space?'

Helena kissed me back formally like a matron who knows the father of the family is up to no good. 'Let's talk later, darling.'

In the style of a good Roman marriage, I took that as settled.

8

Toward nightfall, to escape the tantrums that were rattling shutters in my house, I went out to see Petronius Longus. He was on duty with the vigiles, at the Fourth Cohort's secondary patrol house. It was a calm, masculine environment where only the grunts of criminals being brutally thrashed ever disturbed the tranquillity. July and August were always quiet. Members of the public used fewer oil lamps and cooking fires, so they set fewer of their tenements on fire. For the vigiles, nights became tedious. Patrols could be stood down. While they waited for emergencies, the firefighters liked to sit in their exercise yard telling one another moral fables. Well, that was one way to describe it. They were ex-slaves, a rough lot.

Petronius sat apart in a small office, wrestling with his latest unsolved case. Drink was barred on these premises, but he gave me a slurp from the beaker he had under the table. He hid it again in case the tribune dropped in, then we swapped gossip.

'Helena is hopping mad at her brother, and our girlie is distraught.'

'Albia's how old? Seventeen?—Thundering Jove, was it that long ago you and I were in Britain during the Rebellion?' That was when she must have lost her parents. 'Did Aelianus touch her?' We were fathers. We were paranoid with good reason. We had been lads in the army together, then dirty bastards about town. We knew what happens.

'Albia is bound to deny it.' I had not asked her. Why invite tears? Indeed, why give your daughter a reason to hurl abuse at you? 'He's been away a lot, which is one good thing,' I went on gloomily. 'We ran into him a couple of times when we were travelling, but as far as I know, they just wrote to each other.'

'Oh *letters*!' scoffed Petro darkly. He did not have my literary leanings. 'Soulmates, eh? Falco my friend, you are in deep donkey shit.' He handed me his beaker again, though it was a joyless panacea. 'What's his new wife like? A looker?'

'A spender.'

'And a Greek prosecutor's daughter?'

'Guilty until proven innocent. We met her father in Athens. As a boozer he makes Bacchus look restrained.'

'Jupiter and Mars!' Petronius Longus viewed all lawyers as pests. Lawyers so easily demolished the criminal cases he put together; he ignored the fact that this feat was achievable because the vigiles' definition of 'proof' was simply a man whose face they did not like who walked down a street where they happened to be. 'How are the senator and his wife taking this?'

I laughed drily. 'Considering all three of their children have now, without permission, taken a spouse who is either foreign or plebeian, Helena says Decimus and Julia are calm. They have to be careful showing opinions, because not only is the Hellenic bride living in their house with the captured Aulus, but her go-getting, influence-seeking, hard-drinking Athenian father came to Rome too. Of course he would do. A niche among the ruling class, with access to a wine cellar? His sole purpose in fixing up the marriage.'

'The bastard!'

I shared Petro's curse, then put my troubles aside and let him tell me his. He was stumped on a peculiar case: a family who went to their mausoleum to hold a funeral discovered that someone had broken in and dumped an unknown body. Foul play among the tombs was commonplace. Some people would have just chucked out the corpse for the crows, but this family was sensible enough to notice disturbing elements. It was the body of a well-kept man of mature age, not the usual young rape or mugging victim, and he was laid out in an odd ritual position.

'Violence. Someone really enjoyed it.' Petronius was very experienced. He knew when death had been caused by an unexpected drunken fury and when it had a perverted smell.

'You think there will be other victims?'

'Dreading it, Falco.' He dealt with atrocity all the time, but never became inured to humans' absence of humanity.

I told him if anyone could solve this case it was him, and I meant it. Then I went home to be ready for an early start next morning on the trip to my father's villa.

'Is this the future?' Petronius joked. 'You swan off to your extravagant holiday home—while I get stuck here with a sordid serial killer?'

I grinned and told him to get used to it. He ought to know I wouldn't change.

Albia and I went down to the sea on the Via Laurentina. All the best people have villas north of where that road hits the coast, turning towards Ostia. My father had his place a little to the south. He said he liked the privacy. There were reasons. They were mostly commercial, relevant to his dedicated avoidance of paying import tax.

Pa had left me a litter and bearers but I had forgotten I owned it. Automatically, I hired a donkey cart, which gave me an excuse to concentrate on driving. Albia sat bolt upright beside me. Throughout her childhood she had been a scavenger for both food and affection; she still had stick-thin arms and, when she was unhappy, a gaunt look. No fancy ringlets today; she had let her hair dangle loose, though Helena had run with a bone comb and tidied her up for the trip. Even though there was bright sun beating on the highway, the girl hunched in a shawl, making herself suffer.

We rode twenty miles in silence then Albia could no longer keep it up. She was bursting to accuse me of cruelty. 'Why do I have to be dragged along with you? Am I forced to work in your business, like some horrible slave?'

'No, I have a posse of grateful slaves and freedmen for that now. They may be Paphlagonian poltroons but unlike you, Flavia Albia, they are meek.'

'I hope they all cheat you.'

I was the villain. Nothing new. 'Bound to. So cheer up, will you?'

We drove on for a while.

'I'd like to rip his head off.' Aelianus deserved all he got, but I owed it to the senator and Julia Justa to preserve his well-barbered bonce. So I merely said Helena and I hated to see Albia so unhappy; we had thought she might appreciate a chance to avoid Aulus. 'Yes,' agreed Albia thoughtfully. '*Then* I'll rip his head off—when he thinks he's got away with it.'

Helena Justina had taken in our British waif because she was so spirited, so torn with grief and loneliness, and had been so unjustly served by fate. Found as a baby in the ruins of Londinium, no one knew or would ever know whether Albia was a Briton or some half-and-half little bun, a dead trader's offspring born to a local woman, maybe. She could even be fully Roman, though it was unlikely. When we offered to adopt her, we had wormed a certificate of citizenship out of the British governor, who owed me favours. We now gave Albia education, sustenance, security and friendship, though not much more was feasible. In the snobbery of Rome, she would have a hard fight. I was middle-class now, with the Emperor's approval, but since I had plebeian origins, even my own daughters would need more than elocution lessons if they were to be accepted. I lived with a senator's daughter but that was Helena's choice. It was legal, but eccentric.

'I hope Aulus did not make you any promises.' I broached the subject tentatively, still not brave enough to say I hoped he had not slept with her.

'Of course he wouldn't; I'm a barbarian!' Albia snapped furiously. Her voice then dropped. 'I was just stupid.'

'Well, it must seem impossible at the moment, but one day you will get over him.'

'I *never* will!' Albia retorted. Her loves and hates were equally intense. I had a dark feeling she was right; she never would recover. After knocking about with street life in Londinium, Albia knew how to stay safe at that level, but she had trusted Aelianus. He was one of the family, *her* family now. She had dropped her guard.

'Maybe it's a good thing we are going to Antium, or I might rip his head off myself.'

'You never would,' sneered Albia bitterly.

'Since he is actually married, there is not much I can do about the situation, and you know that.'

'If he wasn't married would you do anything?'

I gave her no answer. Aulus was overdue for marriage. I thought his choice was a disaster, but I would have seriously opposed any offer for Albia—for both their sakes.

'You talk about righting injustice, but you never do it,' she grumbled.

'*Conciliation*—there's a fine Latin word . . . I hope you never have to see me stick a sword in someone's ribs.' It had been known. But I believed retribution should fit the degree of the crime. 'Aelianus has been thoughtless and disloyal. Young men are like that. Young women can be just as bad—or worse.'

'Oh I don't expect anyone to stand up for me!' Albia was back on the verge of tears now. My heart ached for her. 'You are both men. He is your friend, your relative, your assistant. You will stick by him—'

'He was your friend too.' I was nervous that Aulus might have the crazy idea they could carry on as friends. He was that kind of innocent. 'I'd say, value your past—but move on and forget him. Do it for yourself.'

Poor Albia was far from being ready to move on. She turned away but I heard her weeping all the rest of our journey to the villa.

9

Silence.

Pa's shoreline villa can never have rung with a summer social life, because he was rarely in residence; the one time I was here before, I had gathered activity was infrequent. Having an absentee owner was typical for a seaside villa. For security, he left more than a skeleton staff, though they lived in a separate wing from the main house. They stayed on the alert because he would turn up at any time—it depended what incoming ships from Spain or the East had agreed to quietly offload artworks at sea to save him paying duty. He and Gornia then took a boat out into the shipping lanes. It was not a process I intended to repeat. Mind you, I would keep the boat.

I reminded the slaves who I was and explained the situation. They made themselves look downcast over my father's death, though did not feel called upon to shed real tears. This was much as I felt myself, so I did not complain.

Naturally they assumed Albia was some fluffball I wanted to seduce behind my wife's back. That is what slaves always think. It's the male behaviour most see from their masters. Wearied by driving, my reaction was short-tempered.

I felt old. Once, finding myself with custody of a delightful young girl, I would have been tempted. I could still remember those happy days, but ambivalence was a vice I had lost. I was married. Albia was family. I viewed her as a grumpy teenager I had to keep safe despite her yen for rebellion, while she saw me as hideous, elderly and past it, just like any father.

Disappointed of scandal, the slaves—who seemed good-natured enough once they got used to a situation—made us a barbecue on the beach. Grilled fish, freshly caught from the sea and smoke-cooked in a drizzle of olive oil, can mend most griefs. Albia tried to continue the feud. But she smiled slightly when I pointed out that she was enjoying not enjoying anything. At least she ate. Being forlorn had not affected her appetite.

Next day I surveyed the property. It was even bigger and more luxurious than I remembered, and packed with treasures. Albia followed me around with her mouth agape, muttering, 'This is *yours?*'

'It's mine. Or only half of it, if Thalia's sprog pops out with male genitalia.'

'You could castrate him.' Albia's harsh new mood produced intriguing legal questions.

This villa, protected from sun and storms by pine trees, was where Pa had kept his favourite collection, items he really liked and enjoyed. I liked them too. I would have to come back soon for a long visit; there was so much stuff to catalogue. I needed to bring Helena, to show her the glorious location, the rampant antiques and furnishings. Maybe this would become our permanent summer retreat. If she hated the place, which I thought unlikely, there was so much to sell I would have to time our auctions carefully, so as not to flood the market.

'Are you planning to liberate any faithful slaves in your dear father's name, Marcus Didius?' The usual question.

As ever, I responded with a noncommittal sigh. I could free a percentage in Pa's name. I would do it if I could. I wanted to evaluate them first. What happened to them would have nothing to do with how well each had served my father during his life; it depended on how much manumission tax I would have to pay if I freed them or what price they would fetch in the slave market. Any with specialist training or pretty faces were in greater danger of being either kept as slaves or sold. Already I was thinking like a tycoon. If they had a high market value, I was less inclined to give them their release.

The monumental statues for the amphitheatre contract were lined up in rows in the woods. Close to, they were a ragbag: anonymous men of note in triumphal poses, batoned and breastplated; some were weathered about the face and drapery as if they had already adorned public places. I wondered if they had been stolen from their plinths; however, some had their plinths with them.

One batch appeared new. They had been carved to the same model, but with different arms or helmets. I was not surprised. Jobbing sculptors regularly provide a basic figure in an old-fashioned toga, then let you commission a true-life head of your grandaddy at a cut-price rate. So why not cloned dignitaries for an amphitheatre?

I counted them. One hundred and eleven. Jupiter! Pa had cornered the market. Trust him. The Flavian amphitheatre would be virtually: *statues courtesy of Geminus*. No wonder that creep Cluvius wanted me to step aside and let him muscle in.

I gave instructions that the statues were to be brought up to Rome using whatever haulage system Geminus had put in place. 'And I want to see a hundred and eleven arrive. A hundred and twelve will prove to me that you are really conscientious.' My humour was lost on the steward. Foolish; if he failed to notice my jokes, he could end up at the slave market.

'I could stay here to supervise,' volunteered Albia.

'No thanks.' I was not giving her a chance to bolt. 'Lass, if you want to run away, check logistics with me first. For a workable escape you need a plan, a budget, detailed road maps, a stout stick, proper footwear and a good hat.'

'You are no fun, Marcus Didius.' Albia openly acknowledged that I read her well. 'I want to go back to Britannia.'

'No.'

'Helena's Aunt Aelia would let me stay with them—'

'I said no, Albia.'

On to the next stage of our trip.

We could take the coast road down to Antium, a straight run but a poor track, all dreary dunes and sandflies, or we could go by sea. For that we would have to go up to Ostia, almost ten miles in the wrong direction, then the misery of a major trading port, followed by horrible seasickness for me. I opted to continue by cart, south down the Via Severiana, maybe fifteen miles. It only took a day, though it was a long hot one. We then stayed at a mediocre inn. It looked over a sea packed with delicious wildlife, yet the dish of the day was week-old eggs. Even my omelette was tough.

Next morning we tried to find the statue-sellers. Gornia was right. Their house was locked up, with nobody there. Not even a watchman answered our knocking. Albia tried to climb in from a balcony but the place was well shuttered.

I made standard enquiries. Primilla and Modestus had kept to themselves, as prosperous middle-rankers often do. They had a substantial home on the seashore, no obvious financial worries, no ugly rumours about why they did a flit. None of the neighbours had seen them for months or knew where they had gone. True, the neighbours shied away from my questions, though this was a town where imperial celebrities had long clustered; people were discreet.

Antium was once the capital of the Volsci, who tussled with Rome over a long period in the remote past. Once it became ours, the city lay far enough from Rome for men of means, wanting to avoid riots and creditors, to favour it as a retreat. Palatial villas lined the shore. Cicero owned a grand place. The disgustingly rich Maecenas had a house. The old imperial family, the Julio-Claudians, had a particular liking for this spot. It was at Antium that Augustus received formal acclaim as Father of his Country. Caligula and Nero were born here; Nero founded a veterans' colony and created a new harbour.

The new Flavians were bound to arrive on this part of the coast soon. Land agents must be keeping lists of suitable homes for up-and-coming Caesars whose pocket money came from the spoils of war.

This was a superb location for commercial dealers. The town had a slightly dusty, off-season look but it could easily perk up. By reputation the fine foreshore villas were beautified with exclusive original art and expensive modern reproductions. Most of the enormous houses were still lived in, and by people with funds for house and garden makeovers. It was astonishing that a pair of reputable art dealers would leave a place with such potential.

A Temple of Fortune was the big public monument. I applied there for information. Since Gornia's fruitless visit, a certain Sextus Silanus, a nephew of Primilla's, had left a message that enquirers should consult him. I had to pay the priests extortionately to be told; it would have been friendlier if the nephew had just chalked up a note on his uncle's locked front door.

The bad news was, Silanus lived at Lanuvium. To get there we had to take an unnamed road through famously unhealthy country on the northern edge of the Pontine plain. The Pontine Marshes have a fearsome reputation. Still, they should have dried out in summer and Lanuvium was on a spur of the Via Appia, which led straight back to Rome.

10

Lanuvium was an extremely ancient hilltop city in Latium, on the
Alban Hills, lying just south of the Via Appia. The town was
dominated by a clutch of temples, especially the richly endowed
Temple of Juno Sospes, to which belonged much of the land between
here and the coast. We knew, from passing through it, that the soil
was unusually fertile, though the area was very thinly populated. For
most of the route we saw no one but a few pasty-looking slaves. The
state of the road suggested vehicles were unusual and the labourers
stared at us as if they never saw travellers. Well, they stared until
Albia glared at them. Then they turned away nervously.

'There are many rivers draining the hills; they carry down rich
alluvium silt.' I was taking on Helena's role, had she been with us. Just
because Albia had a broken heart, she need not be ignorant. 'So the
Pontine plain has some of the best land in Italy for grazing animals
and growing crops, but you won't see many people. The water table is
very high and the sand dunes on the coast trap the floods, so for
much of the year, especially south of here, it is a pestilential place.
Clouds of biting insects make the marshes almost uninhabitable—
keep yourself well covered up; they carry horrible diseases.' We were

north of the real swamps, which suited me. Attempts had been made to drain them. The attempts all failed.

The high citadel at Lanuvium must be healthier. From its acropolis there were gracious views over the plain to the faraway ocean. Like most places with vistas, this had been heavily colonised by the villa-owning fraternity. To cater for their property maintenance needs, small artisan businesses thrived. Silanus was a terracotta specialist.

A row of freckled children sat on the kerb outside his premises. When our cart drew up, they all swarmed aboard. I tried to strike a bargain that they would look after the outfit, by which I meant they were not to kick the donkey or remove the wheels. I hoped they were too small to shift the money chest. Feigning acute shyness, none of them spoke. When I went into the workshop, Albia stationed herself at the doorway, observing the nippers sternly. In her present mood, she was scary; that would work.

The children must have inherited their freckles from their mother. She never appeared; I soon gathered she was dead—probably exhausted and deceased in childbirth, judging by the perilous number of offspring she had left behind.

Silanus was a stocky, pockmarked fellow with the faint tetchiness craftsmen have, caused by the anxieties of sole trading. As a gesture to personality, he wore a bracelet on his upper left arm that was pretending to be gold. His tunic was dull and ragged, but he was in work clothes so that told me nothing. The stock in his shop was good: well-made, fancy Greek-style acroteria for roof finials, a few gargoyles, routine racks of tiles and wall flues, plus the usual decorative wares for the home, plant tubs and balcony trays. It was all handsome. I would have bought from him.

He gave the impression he wanted to be friendly, but was biting it back. I softened him up, mainly by telling him how much cash I had brought for his uncle and aunt. He was stuck in an awkward situation. His relatives had mysteriously vanished. They had no children. As the only nephew, he felt obliged to take charge, though he did not even know if Primilla and Modestus were alive. Unlike me, he felt he had no legal position as an heir, so was not free to negotiate.

I sympathised. 'So what happened? I work in this line; maybe I can give you advice.' Silanus was not the type to trust informers, or even to know what we did. 'Silanus, whatever has gone on? I saw their house at Antium; it's quite deserted. Your uncle and aunt must have had staff, but they too have dematerialised. Have you brought the slaves here?'

Appreciating his practical difficulties must have won his trust. Silanus sighed. 'They ran away. I haven't started a fugitive-hunt. Let them go, if they can make a life.' This man was neither greedy nor vindictive. A decent sort. Not something I often came across. I tried not to find it suspicious.

He seemed upset about his missing aunt and uncle, troubled by the situation, completely dispirited. 'I was told that my uncle left first, then my aunt went to look for him. She had the sense to order one of their slaves to come and tell me, if she too vanished.'

'So where did Primilla and Modestus go?'

'You don't want to know, Falco.'

I was agog. 'Try me.'

'They went to see the Claudii.' Silanus spoke as if I ought to know what that meant. When I merely raised my eyebrows, he went back to the start of the story. 'Uncle and Auntie owned property, farmland. Made their money that way, originally, but you know how it is. Nobody stays on the plain, because they soon get sick. Anyone sick soon passes away. Only slaves can be persuaded to stay there for husbandry. People who can afford to move do so. They come up to the hills or go over to the coast. So about twenty years ago Modestus became an art dealer in Antium—though they always kept their land.'

'My father did business with them, as I told you; Geminus knew them for a long time . . . So whatever happened?'

'A boundary dispute flared up. I knew about it—squabbles have been grumbling on for years. Some of their neighbours are notoriously difficult to deal with. A few months ago cattle strayed on to Uncle's land and did a lot of damage. Modestus likes to assert his rights—he went to have it out. He never came back. Aunt Primilla is a spunky woman herself; she set off to find him. She too has never been seen since.'

'These neighbours are the Claudii you mentioned? . . . So have you reported it? Called in the authorities?'

'I did my best. It was a long time before I heard anything. Once I knew my folks had gone missing, I had to get someone to look after my business before I could go over to Antium. I managed to interest the local magistrate. A posse went to investigate. They found nothing. The Claudii all denied ever seeing my relatives. So nothing can be done.'

'That sounds feeble!'

'Ah well . . . it's the badlands, Falco. Strangers don't go there.'

'What—upset the web-footed marsh sprites and they drown you?' I was amazed. 'Troublemaking is a homely Pontine tradition and everyone has to put up with it?'

As I raved, Silanus looked boot-faced. 'The fact is, Falco, I know perfectly well what happened. My aunt and uncle upset the wrong people and have paid for it. Nobody can find any trace of them. No one locally saw anything. There is no evidence. So I'm not going to tackle the Claudii and be made to disappear myself, am I? So yes, that is how bullies get away with it—but no, I will not leave my children orphans.'

I asked if he wanted to hire me to investigate. He said no. Partly, that was a relief. I was reluctant to do country work. Especially in the Pontine Marshes. That's suicide.

This would not have done for me, yet I did understand why Sextus Silanus was letting the mystery rest. He was practical. How many times had I advised clients to take such a sensible route (and how many had ignored me)?

Regarding the money Pa owed, we agreed that I would hand it over and call the account closed. Silanus would bank the cash at the Temple of Juno Sospes, until enough time passed for him to feel he could have it himself. Realistically, that would be soon. One glance at all the children he was bringing up said it. And I did not blame him.

He came out to collect the money. Shooing his freckled infants off the cart, he confirmed he was a single-handed parent; he had six under fourteen.

I bought a load of his fine terracotta wares. It would pay a few food bills for him, and anyway I liked the stuff. Albia helped me choose.

As Silanus waved us off, he asked, with a desperation I could almost forgive, 'Your daughter seems a very nice young lady—Does she have a husband, Falco?'

'Get lost!' Albia and I roared in unison.

Bad timing, Silanus.

I I

This strange disappearance of two respectable art dealers continued to haunt me. Driving allows you time to muse. Still, I had concerns of my own. If Silanus wanted to abandon hope, it was depressing, but his own affair. I went on my way, relieved of the cash and freed up to sell the statues. The curious episode was over.

Or was it? I should have known better.

The Via Appia is a legendary highway built four hundred years ago by Appius Claudius. It runs down across the Pontine Marshes, straight as a javelin for fifty miles between Rome and Tarracina. That entails causeways where it crosses swamps, but the northern part is wide, well-paved and, if your donkey can summon the energy, pleasantly fast. I had hired a decent working beast; she didn't bite or lie down in the gutter, though nor did she exert herself. We trickled sedately down a sliproad and hit the famous highway just before it climbed the Alban Hills, passing Lakes Nemi and Albanus.

Giving a friendly lecture to Albia (who barely responded) I had to admit that Appius, a great builder who also constructed the first

Roman aqueduct, was better than average, for a patrician. As a free-born city boy, I found some of his policies questionable—allowing the sons of manumitted slaves to enter the Senate and extending the vote to rural folk who owned no land. Still, Appius Claudius also published the law, stopping the priests from keeping it as their private mystery. That made him a patron of informers.

We went north for ten miles. With only another two or three to go, we reached the tombs among the stone pines that line the approach to Rome's Twelfth District. On a bright and baking afternoon this sometimes lonesome vicinity made for good travelling. We hit shade. I was cheerful; I could detect the smell of home and the donkey could sniff her stable. Albia just snuffled miserably but soon I could hand her over to Helena.

Then we ran into the vigiles. Since the Twelfth is looked after by the Fourth Cohort, these were a section of Petro's men.

Outside the city boundary, discipline evaporated. Some, inevitably, were lying under pine trees for a nap. However, others applied themselves fairly well. They told me they were on the case Petronius had told me about: the corpse dumped in a mausoleum. One ritual laying-out was not enough for Petro. Armed with crowbars and a love of violence, his troops were bashing open mausoleums and peering inside for other bodies that ought not to be there. In the crumbly roadside necropolis, many tombs were so ancient nobody knew who built them. They were easy to search, once the vigiles scraped the sleeping vagrants off their worn old entrance steps. Others, even the oldest, were still used by families; thanks to good diet and our nation's virility, some Roman clans had long pedigrees.

One cranky owner must have stipulated he had to be present; I saw Tiberius Fusculus, Petro's trusty, hiding his impatience while the blighted toff fumbled interminably with a padlock. I pulled up the cart and when Fusculus was free again, he strolled over. He was overweight, hot and red-faced. Albia gave him a drink of water. 'Take it all. Who cares?' She dispensed her generosity with airy fatalism, as if she herself did not care if she died of thirst.

Avoiding Albia's aggression like a wise man, Fusculus told me that no more corpses had been found. 'Well, plenty—' Fusculus joked, '—but none we link to the case.'

'Will Petronius pull you off it soon?'

'Not yet, Falco. Obstinate beggar is convinced we have turned up a ritual killer.'

'Then Petronius Longus must sit it out until the next new moon, or there's a "rho" in the month, or the red tunic comes home from the laundry—whatever weird trigger tells this killer it's time for him to shed more gore.'

'Normally,' Fusculus agreed, 'the boss would be happy to lie low. Especially in summer when he likes to get home early to your revered sister and have a nap on their nice sun terrace.'

I was amused. Petro had his eccentric side; he never liked anybody knowing his habits and he had not even told his men that he was living with Maia. They all knew of course. 'What's different?' I asked.

'Sealed lips. State secret.'

'Very grown-up! And are you going to share it?'

'Absolutely bloody not, Falco. This is so utterly *sub rosa*, one word to you and I'd be spit-roasted with a bunch of oregano pushed up my bum.'

Tired of boys' talk, Albia interrupted. 'I suppose, Tiberius Fusculus, that means Uncle Lucius has not told *you* his thinking on this?'

He gazed at her almost as speculatively as Silanus had before he asked if she was married. 'Bright girlie. No, *Uncle Lucius*—tight bastard—has not revealed his mighty thoughts.'

I grinned. 'I'll have to ask him myself then.'

'You do that, Falco.' Fusculus reapplied himself to searching tombs. I clucked up the donkey. As the cart jerked and moved off, Fusculus called after us without rancour, 'The big clue is—we found luggage!'

Interesting.

It was *so* interesting I was dying to ask Petronius about it. First, I returned the cart to the hire stables, took Albia home, and gave a good show of being safely back with my family. After about half an hour

I nipped out to see Petro. Helena spotted me going. I winked and promised to share any gossip as soon as I came back. She sighed, but did not intervene.

Petronius, amazingly, was trying on his toga. This rare sight made me chortle—until I found out why. It was dusk, so the sweltering streets had cooled a fraction; not enough for loading pounds of heavy white wool on your shoulders, though. No option, it seemed: Petro had to stand in for his tribune, Rubella. The Fourth Cohort's senior officer had been summoned to a high-status conference on the Palatine.

Petronius would normally have been taken along too, in order to whisper corrections whenever Rubella got information wrong— mishandling facts was any lazy tribune's prerogative. As it was July, Rubella was away. Since he had not bothered to inform the Prefect of Vigiles he had snatched a vacation, if Petro wanted, he could land Rubella in mule dung. However, he would be a fool to do so.

'Falco, you know what I think of Rubella—'

I assured him I thought the same. Marcus Rubella was an over-promoted, super-ambitious, unreliable, self-seeking squit. However, I thought he was the best the cohort would get. 'Fill me in, Petro.'

'On *Rubella?*'

'On the case, idiot.'

'We found a hidden pack that must have belonged to that murder victim. Maybe he noticed he was being followed, so he tucked away his stuff just before he was grabbed.'

'What's the palace connection?'

'He was carrying a draft petition to the Emperor.'

'About?'

Petronius winced. 'Ghastly moans. Complaining about local crime. *This public disgrace has been allowed to fester far too long; the authorities in our region simply will not address the issue . . . The Emperor should take the initiative and refuse to tolerate nuisances caused by criminals who boast they have special protection . . .* Nobody will ever listen, of course. Still, I shoved it onwards to the top—gave the poor bastard his last chance of an audience. Least I could do, I thought.'

'You know who he is?'

'I said it's a draft, you noodle! Nobody signs their name on a private rough.'

'Silly me! So it was no help?'

'I'd have kept it, if it had been useful. Obviously I had to mention to the scroll-beetles that the writer was discovered ripped open from crotch to gullet, with his hands removed.'

The details were new. I pulled a face. 'Pluto! That would have made your report attract notice.'

'Seems so. What came over me? Now some schnoozle wants a brief.'

'Minding his back,' I said. 'You'll handle it. You know your stuff. And you've been there before.' Petronius had attended at the Palace with me. We once had a policy discussion with the Emperor and a full phalanx of flunkies. Vespasian took our measure. Even so, we ticed a money-making commission out of him that time. 'Who sent the summons?'

'Some grunt called Laeta.'

I pulled up short. 'Claudius Laeta? I'll come with you.'

'Keep out of it. I don't need a nursemaid, Falco.'

'Laeta is trouble. Appearing amenable is his speciality. Then he'll extract your balls and twist them up in an old knitted sock, swing it round his head and knock you down with your own magic machinery.'

'For a spare-time poet, your imagery stinks,' opined my old friend dourly. But he must have been nervous about the meeting, because he let me tag along.

Unlike him, I did not go togate. Laeta was head of the main secretariat. The man had sent me on so many dubious missions, he would receive no respect from me. The only good thing about Laeta was his constantly trying to double-cross Anacrites, the Chief Spy. I watched from the sidelines and tried to play them off against each other.

Petronius and I ambled gently from the patrol house. I was enjoying my return. I threw back my head and breathed in the last heat of a warm city day. I heard the low buzz of voices from families and groups of friends, eating, chatting, gathering to enjoy those quiet hours of the day before they resumed their usual habits of fornicating with each other's wives and cheating each other at business or dice. Strings of shrieking garland-girls were going home; nobody would buy dinner flowers now. Sounds of flutes and a drummer vied with the clatter of crockery from an alley, obviously the back door to several bars. Wafts of frying food, swum in oil and enlivened with thyme and rosemary, floated just above street level.

I had missed Rome. Petronius pointed out with a grin that I had only been away three days, during which I should have been happy, since at Pa's villa I had all those expensive new possessions to count. Always generous, Petro bore no grudge for my good fortune. Like me, perhaps he did not yet take it seriously.

On descending the Aventine, to cross to the Palatine we had a choice of passing around the Circus Maximus at the starting-gate end or hoofing down past the apse. The racetrack was absolutely in our way. Even if Petro could have used influence to get inside and cut straight across, there was no point because then we would have had the Palatine's vertical face ahead of us. Since we both grew up on the Aventine, we were used to this inconvenience. Sometimes we detoured one way, sometimes the other. Either by-pass was long and frustrating. As it was his meeting tonight, I let him choose; he opted for the starting-gates, then wending gently through the Forum Boarium. It stank of raw blood and butchery but gave us a clear run at the Palatine via regular approaches. Petronius was not in a mood to slide through a back door and get lost in the pernicious maze of corridors.

He presented himself to the Praetorian Guard, managing not to be rude to those braggarts. If I stood on my rights with the Guards when they threatened to push us around, Petronius would shrug and dump me. I followed my friend's lead meekly.

Neither of us had any idea at that moment, but we were beginning an adventure that would be as difficult and dangerous as any we had ever attempted. And its connection with the Palatine overlords would be much more than simple bureaucracy.

12

The tall vaulted corridors of the old Palace had their usual evening hush. This was the time I liked to come here. The crowds of jabbering petitioners had given up and gone home, leaving residual odours of garlic sausage and sweat. People were about, but the daytime tension relaxed. The night shift was efficient, but unexcitable. They put anything important or awkward on hold for the day shift.

Slaves padded past us, setting out oil lamps. Under our frugal Emperor, there was never quite enough light. The slaves had mastered the art of implying they had too much work to break off and tell us whether the office we were looking for was down the right- or left-hand corridor, let alone to admit whether the imperial family was in residence or had all gone away to some summer villa . . .

Systems here had stayed the same since Tiberius organised this part of the Palatine. The imperial livery had changed and there was less open fornication; little else altered. Emperors came and went while bureaucracy continued, as rampant as mould. Vespasian and Titus lived in Nero's repulsively opulent Golden House on the other side of the Forum, while élite secretariats kept their old offices in this historic complex. The bigger the name, the grander the office. Laeta had a suite. Its doorknobs were gilded and a quiet slave constantly mopped the marble floor outside. She was probably there to eavesdrop on pre-admission visitors.

'This place always reeks of suspicion,' Petro mumbled, keeping an eye on the mopper. Once she looked up and automatically he smiled at her. Like any healthy Roman male, he kept in practice as a flirt.

I agreed. 'To say they all plot is like saying slugs eat lettuce.'

Laeta worked late. As a bureaucrat he genuinely believed his vital work required more than an ordinary business day, even from an expert like him. He kept us waiting. That was to make us impressed that he should find time for us. Petronius and I slouched on corridor benches below a high, elegant ceiling and remarked loudly that being so disorganised at his rank was pathetic. We made sure the usher heard. Enlivening the life of underlings is a ploy worth spending time on.

Maia and Helena said we had never grown up. We could be mature—though kicking our heels in boredom brought out the worst in us.

Finally Petronius was called in and I followed. When he saw me on his marble threshold, Laeta looked irritated. He was a middle-aged, middle ranker with an astute gaze. He was bursting to ask what I was doing there; he wondered whether somebody had failed to brief him on a policy issue—or, worse, had he been briefed but had forgotten it? He felt obliged to nod a greeting, but some unease showed.

We shimmied across the doormat—a pleasing integral mosaic—and began our next role-play. It involved extravagant respect from Petronius, while I stared as if flattering a senior official had never occurred to me. Petro declared he was honoured to meet such an important man of whom (he said) he had heard much, all of it impressive. Laeta fended off a blush. Everyone must suck up to him, but he was unsure how to take it from us. Well, I said he was astute.

Tiberius Claudius Laeta was a rising comet, experienced but still with a decade or two of conniving in him. His forenames indicated he had been a slave in the imperial house, freed under a previous emperor; from his age it would be Claudius. The imperial household had produced many senior bureaucrats, including my bugbear Anacrites, who had wormed his way up to be Chief Spy very quickly and, to me, quite unaccountably; he was the kind of light garbage that floats. Anacrites was younger than Laeta and had been freed by Nero— hardly a recommendation, to have that eye-rolling maniac think well of you.

'You submitted a man's petition, Watch Captain.' Prepared for the meeting, he waved it at us.

'Found in a murder victim's baggage,' Petro confirmed. 'I assessed it as the dead man's last words. Delivery seemed the decent thing.'

'Yes, you explained—' Laeta laid down the tablet abruptly, hoping to cut off bloody descriptions of the corpse. I made a grab to see what was written. Laeta was too refined to snatch the tablet back but watched jealously, like a man seeing his lover depart on an international journey.

The complaint was as Petro had described. The handwriting was decent, the language civil service Greek. If the author was not a professional scribe, he had certainly had general clerical training. One aspect surprised me: a tone of familiarity. 'Had this man written in before?'

'One of our regulars.' Laeta sounded weary.

'Classic aggrieved citizen?'

'Let's say, *detailed*!' Free Roman citizens have the right to petition the Emperor. That did not mean Vespasian personally read every scroll. He thought he did. So did those who made petition-writing their hobby. In truth, officials like Laeta censored out the batty ramblings of obsessives, at the same time as they were checking for unhinged threats against the Emperor's person and simple-minded do-gooders offering religious advice.

'Bit of a menace then?' Petronius asked, more mildly than me.

Laeta was too professional to insult a member of the public. His duty required him to be fair, to defend the high principle of equal access to the Emperor. 'On the one side—' elbows on the table, he turned back his left hand as if holding up a market weight, '—he has the right to campaign. And on the other—' he balanced the hypothetical weight with his other hand, '—resources are limited, so we just cannot investigate every perceived problem.'

Perceived said a lot. No wonder Laeta looked relaxed. He *perceived* he could ignore such stuff.

'Did this fellow always make the same complaint?' I asked.

'Usually. He worried over law-and-order issues. He was agitated about a large tribe of petty criminals who should, in his opinion, be exterminated. The fact is,' Laeta informed us smoothly, 'all over the Empire, groups exist who arouse their neighbours' prejudice, perhaps because they seem feckless or a little different. They live rough, they rebuff approaches from the community. People suspect them of stealing, of luring away women, insulting priests, depressing property values and having lewd habits. Drink and putting curses on cattle are a constant theme of complaints.'

'Living next door to deadbeats can be a real problem,' Petronius corrected him. He had no truck with social misfits. He didn't believe curse tablets could make cows barren, but he did reckon that when people bestirred themselves to complain formally, the thefts and assaults they protested about were probably real. To him, Laeta's bland remarks were official excuses for inaction.

To be angry about neighbours' bad behaviour would seem a crazy waste of time where we grew up. On the Aventine, there were too many persons of lewd habits to write petitions about it. Everyone drank, to take away the pain of existence. Nobody wore themselves out trying to have ethical standards. Even joining the army when we were eighteen was such a nod to the establishment it had made Petro and me objects of raucous derision.

'Of course we take all such reports seriously,' Laeta assured us. Tell that to the man who wrote in, I thought.

'You rush to rootle out the villains?' I teased him. 'Their horrid shacks are upended by military-style machines, their filthy possessions tossed away, and the pilfering layabouts are made to take regular jobs in nasty occupations?'

Laeta scowled. 'We ask the district magistrate to make enquiries.'

'And if your correspondent writes again—*when* he does, since he refuses to give up—you just send another soft request to the same magistrate who let everyone down the first time?'

'Dispersed responsibility, Falco.' Laeta let my jibes trickle off like river water from a cormorant.

'Well, it's hardly corrupt, but I'd define it as inept and complacent.'

'Always yourself!' smiled Laeta. 'I do admire that, Falco . . . Sometimes these complaints die down,' he said to Petronius, as if addressing the reasonable man in our pairing. 'So much better if a situation is dealt with peacefully, and at the local level. Nevertheless, should there be a flare-up that the local authorities cannot handle, it will be tackled—tackled aggressively.'

'This involves more than bad neighbours,' Petronius assessed. He was glum. 'Now a man has died. Tortured, killed, and his body deposited in a blasphemous way. He appears to have been coming to Rome to appeal to the Emperor personally. That, to me, places a moral duty on Rome to look into what happened—and to pursue the victim's complaints.'

'Quite.' Laeta, too, became more subdued. He clasped his hands on the surface of his shining marble table. Mention of moral duties always casts a blight on bureaucrats. He admitted, in a frank way that from him was an apology, 'It now appears the man's petitions were justified.'

We had reached the crux of the meeting. Claudius Laeta half rose from his throne-like chair, so he could wriggle out of his toga. In palace code, this told us whatever was said next must be in confidence. Petronius Longus eagerly shrugged off his own formal robe. He and I moved closer to Laeta. We three were alone in the enormous room, but all of us dropped our voices.

'What are we dealing with?' The expert now, Petronius was terse, calm and impressive.

'The misfit family are called the Claudii. Mean anything?'

I had heard the name only recently so I pricked up my ears, though Petronius shook his head, asking, 'Are they in Rome?'

'They may set their sights on moving to the city,' Laeta answered. 'So far we are spared.'

'Did your writer name names?'

'Often. He mainly railed against a brutish wastrel called Claudius Nobilis.'

'Anybody talked to him?'

'I believe he is frequently the subject of enquiries. However . . .' Petronius glanced my way as we waited. 'It is a little delicate.'

'Why?' I asked bluntly.

'These people are freedmen,' Laeta said. 'Not just anybody's freedmen—they originally came from the imperial family.'

Petronius chewed it over for a moment then clarified: 'The current Emperor's family name is Flavius. So not Vespasian's *familia*?'

'Yes and no.' Laeta's backside must be purpose-made for fence-sitting.

I saw the problem all right. 'All the imperial possessions passed over when Vespasian took the throne. Not just official buildings and mansions, but all the Julio-Claudians' vast portfolio of palaces, villas and farms—together with, presumably, their battalions of slaves. Claudian freedmen might transfer their respect to the Flavians—if they thought there was anything in it for them. As there generally is, with imperial connections.'

'The Flavians in turn must have been happy to accumulate powers of patronage—or not, in this case!' joked Petro.

Claudius Laeta had a chilly demeanour as we scoffed. 'Most freedmen of the old imperial house transferred their allegiance to the new.'

'And that's why you are here!' I told him, with a wicked smile.

He cut me off. 'We acknowledge an inherited problem. Someone tried to dump it in the past—unsuccessfully. Slaves *should* be freed as a reward for good service—' Just what my father's band all kept reminding me. 'It is clear this clan were disposed of because they were perennial pests.' Laeta sniffed. Slaves and ex-slaves are riddled with snobbery. 'None ever held a useful position or trained in a specialism. When they were freed, none took decent work or tried to set up businesses. Their imperial past makes them arrogant; it is thought—both by themselves and others—to give them protection from the law.'

'Wrong of course?' I asked.

'They exploit the belief, and people are afraid of them.'

Petronius and I shared another glance. 'So it will look bad,' he suggested, 'if moves are made against them on your orders, Laeta—but you find no evidence and can make no charges stick?'

'Indeed.'

'So what's the plan? I assume you asked me here because there is one?'

Laeta powered into a summary: 'Local initiatives have failed. Time and time again, in fact. I want to send expert examiners from Rome. Look at it with fresh eyes. We need a sophisticated approach, backed up by energetic action.'

The usual plan, apparently. The one that usually fails.

'You want them evicted?' A shift behind his eyes told me—and Laeta, if Laeta was observant—Petronius Longus thought this was asking for trouble.

'Only,' Laeta insisted, 'if the accusations are true. If these people are causing a very serious nuisance.'

'Murder would be defined as "very serious"?'

'Yes, murder would justify intervention from Rome. More than one murder certainly.'

'What action has been taken so far?'

'Your dead man was reported missing, by relatives I understand. Regional forces did visit the Claudii, since they were implicated . . .'

'And the regionals buggered it!' Petronius was frank, but Laeta looked unfazed. Well, he started life as a slave. He had heard crudity in many languages. As an official in Rome, he shared Petro's sneer at the regions too.

'Perhaps they were under-experienced . . . They found nothing. It means any new investigation has to be conducted with extra sensitivity. It would be a bad day if imperial freedmen—which the Claudii are, and that must never be forgotten—came to accuse the Emperor of harassment.'

I asked, 'Have they lawyered up?'

'Not yet.' Laeta clearly assumed they would. Social menaces are well versed in finding legal teams to defend them, and an imperial connection was attractive; it guaranteed the brief would attract notice.

'Can they afford it?'

'There are always lawyers, Petronius, who find it a challenge to take on the government.'

'*Pro bono?* That really would be a glory of democracy,' I scoffed.

'It would be a pile-bursting pain in the arse!' Laeta's turn to be crude.

'So you want the vigiles involved?' Petronius Longus was torn between his yearning to pursue an intriguing case and his distaste for taking orders.

Laeta flexed his fingers. He summed up the position in a careful intellectual way: 'The Praetorians would look heavy-handed. The army is never used against Roman citizens in Italy. Yes, it seems right to use the vigiles. And since you have prior knowledge, Petronius Longus, you should lead the mission.'

'Going out of Rome?'

'Going to Latium.'

'My tribune will need a docket.'

'Your tribune will be comforted with all the honeyed instructions he requires.'

'This is Marcus Rubella,' Petronius warned, on the verge of smiling.

'Ah, the wondrous Rubella!' Laeta had met him. 'Then I shall use my most impressive seal when I write to him.'

'Better bump up his budget,' I advised. 'To help him calm down.'

Laeta tinkled with laughter. 'Oh Falco, there are limits!'

Foreseeing a long summer away from his family, Petronius became grumpy. He could not refuse when the Palace commanded. If this had been his own idea, he would have been gagging for it; orders from a scroll-beetle were much less welcome. He tapped the dead man's tablet with a heavy index finger. 'So does the petition-writer have a name, Laeta?' Claudius Laeta made a show of ruffling through other documents to check.

I leaned towards him and offered helpfully, 'He is called Julius Modestus—am I right?' When Laeta confirmed it, I was not surprised.

13

Petronius shot me a dark look. He thought I had known all along. In fact, I had only just decided for sure the coincidences added up.

To Laeta I breezed, 'Lucius Petronius and I are already on this. We have been working together; I am just back from reconnaissance.' Now it was Laeta's turn to look annoyed with me; he thought I was angling for payment. He was right too. 'If you are sending in head-quarters assessors it makes sense to include me. I'll do it for my usual rates.'

'You're too expensive, Falco.'

'You can't afford to peel manpower off the Fourth Cohort. Petronius and I have history as a team; he can't tackle this alone—and if Vespasian wants to distance himself from these freedmen, he knows I'm his man.'

To my surprise, Laeta reluctantly nodded. Probably he thought if this went wrong, he now had someone else to blame.

'It's more than neighbourhood annoyance,' said Petronius, impatient with our negotiations. 'The tomb death was not a singleton, an accident of tempers flaring; Modestus had been stalked, all the way to Rome. He was mutilated—the killer returned to the body for more of that after death.'

I saw Laeta moisten dry lips. 'I need to demonstrate we are dealing with more than one random murder.' He was still worrying over the bureaucracy.

'Modestus' wife is also missing, most certainly dead too. Not even a body,' said Petro. 'The killer may have kept her corpse for—'

'I see!' Laeta must be squeamish.

'Treats in the larder,' explained Petro relentlessly. Laeta closed his eyes. Petro scowled sombrely, mentally dwelling on the circumstances.

'Other murders are likely, going back over many years, Laeta,' I weighed in. 'Petronius reckons this killer will strike again, until he is captured and stopped.'

'Ah, one of those!' Laeta pretended to be a crime expert. 'No one has ever suggested the Claudii are *that* bad.'

'When such murderers are exposed, people are always surprised,' I pointed out. '*He kept to himself, but he never seemed violent. None of us had any idea*—that's how repeat killers get away with it. Only with hindsight does it all seem bloody obvious.'

I was supposed to have the reputation for mischief, but it was Petro who asked, 'You came up through the imperial household yourself, Laeta. Did you ever encounter these backwoodsmen? Were you slaves together?'

Claudius Laeta battled a shudder. 'No; absolutely not. Though it's a small world. I am sure you could find palace staff who have met them in the past . . . But during their time in the imperial *familia,* these were merely low-grade rural slaves. It is said they worked originally at a villa beloved of the Emperor Augustus at Antium. Nero tore it down—how typical of the man—and rebuilt on a scale that he fancied was more glamorous. Probably at that time the Claudii were deemed superfluous. You know, there is a difference between rough country slaves, labouring anonymously in the fields as shepherds, mowers, tillers or harvesters, and those of us who are fortunate enough to be trained for duties close to emperors.'

'Understood!' Petronius could be a bastard. 'So, they were batch field workers . . .' He kept pushing. 'Your paths never crossed?'

'No.' Laeta remained polite but cold. 'You could ask Momus,' he added offhandedly to me. He managed to imply I had no scruples in my choice of personal contacts.

Momus started life as a gruesome slave-overseer. Since he lacked both intellect and morals, he had been assigned to a palace audit section; according to him, his job description was to audit the spies. Interpreting that as an order to cut staff numbers, Momus strove to make Anacrites fall down a very deep well or float off a high parapet. I got on well with Momus. Laeta, who was more fastidious, regarded him as a major disease—but possibly useful.

'He is foul—though he knows the slave rostas. I intend to have a chat!' I assured Laeta happily. Now Laeta was wondering if Momus knew any secrets about *him* and would Momus tell *me*? 'Careful intelligence will be needed on this case, Laeta. I suppose it's a coup for you, grabbing the job from Anacrites?'

'So sad for him.' Claudius Laeta beamed, a disconcerting sight. 'I hear the Emperor has posted dear Anacrites on a mission to Istria—insultingly straightforward and boringly diplomatic. Here, he could have been gaining praise by saving the Emperor from association with the menace of the Claudii—Anacrites will be *livid*!'

Laeta was smiling. Petronius Longus and I were smiling too. The job stank. But we were all united in a bond of happiness that we had a chance to snatch credit away from the Chief Spy.

Before we left, Laeta found it in himself to say to me, a little awkwardly, 'I was so sorry to hear about your father and your child, Falco.'

He had left it too late in the conversation. It failed to come over as genuine. I brushed his condolences aside.

14

As we left, Petronius and I took a detour past the smelly hutch Momus normally occupied; there was no sign of him. I did not make enquiries. Momus was grisly; I preferred not to know about his leisure time. His room must have been shabby to start with, but he had let it grow squalid; in a palace full of slaves with buckets and sponges he had no need to endure this. Even Petronius, who saw the world's worst in his work for the vigiles, raised an eyebrow at the rancid accommodation.

On the opposite side of a long corridor lay Anacrites' office. Now we knew he was away, I opened the door and invited Petro inside. They had met a couple of times and Petro had a personal interest. Anacrites, who made a habit of hanging around my family, at one time took a shine to Maia. Maia saw through him; sensing he was dangerous, she backed out of whatever relationship they had. His response was to send men who trashed her home, terrifying Maia and her four young children. Even now, Anacrites could not see how that vicious action only proved she was right to drop him.

I would pay him back. He thought he had got away with it. He still hung around my mother as if she had adopted him, and he greeted me like an old, affectionate colleague. He would learn.

The good result had been Maia taking up with Petro soon afterwards. He knew her story. He, too, had not forgotten. Like me, he was determined to deal with Anacrites one day, one day at the right moment.

The spy's room was cramped but at least clean. It had an almost medical smell; I had always noticed that, though never pinpointed the source. One of his staff must have endemic veruccas, or enduring the spy day in and day out had given someone migraines.

We strolled over and squinted sideways at the stuff on his table, deliberately shifting pens and styluses in subtle ways, to worry him when he came back. Everything had been laid out pedantically; he was bound to notice changes.

There were no confidential tablets; Anacrites was tenaciously secretive. Petronius looked with longing at some secured cupboards, but we were not in a mood to force locks. Usually, however late it was, our bugbear had a dandruffy clerk or one of his dreadful agents moping in here with him. As soon as he was sent abroad, they must have all rushed off. The room was strangely still and quiet. The strife and duplicity that emanated from it had been placed on hold.

We stared around, then Petronius shook his head slightly, bemused. I wriggled my shoulders as if to slough off the very air the spy had breathed. We left without a word.

By the time we emerged from the rambling old buildings, the night had taken a shift onwards. Still simmering with remains of the day's heat, Rome had become its darker self. Families and workers were back in their homes. The streets now carried streams of delivery carts, each alley ringing with the trundle of battered wooden wheels and the bloody-minded curses of crude drivers. Stray dogs ran for their lives from heavy-duty wagons that were so laden they could neither swerve nor stop in a hurry. Even the burglars and muggers who emerged at dusk kept their sandalled feet well back from the kerb.

We sensed their presence, as they skulked through streets where they had conveniently blown out any lamps. None of them bothered us. We looked too capable.

I saw Petronius savour the warm air, trying to tell whether various wafts of smoke from baths and cookshops meant fire duty for the vigiles. He was in full professional mode, alert for any kind of trouble.

He and I made a few quick plans as we strolled, via the winding lane at the foot of the Capitol, back to our own haunts. He then returned to the patrol house, up on the Aventine. I watched him go, with that familiar fast, loping stride. Quietly I continued along the Marble Embankment to my house.

15

'Marcus, darling, you should be ashamed! Why ever didn't you tell us about the funeral?'

Let's call Marina my sister-in-law, though it had always been a title of convenience. She and my legionary brother, Festus, had never lived together, though the ditsy dumpling claimed they would have done, but for his tactlessness in getting himself killed. She still made out our scamp would have settled down on his return—a concept he guffawed at, as I more accurately recollected. Suggestions of marriage always made Festus need a very large veal pie and so much drink to wash it down he would fall unconscious on the caupona counter.

Still, he had loved children. Once Marina had a baby we all agreed to accept as fathered by Festus, she needed somebody to sponge off. The Didius family pitied her plight. We understood want. We admired efficient begging too. Little Marcia was a dear child (possibly a factor that should make us think she was not ours), so we subsidised Marina for her daughter's sake. I say 'we'. The others always left the fine details to me. By details, I mean actually handing out cash.

Inevitably my father's death had brought Marina, dragging Marcia, to pay respects (her words). She had her large beautiful eyes on the legacy.

'Marcia will be no trouble. I brought her a lunch pack. I'll pick her up when I've run a few errands . . .'

Marina was a fabulous specimen, though common. She turned heads so frequently she had no idea it was possible for a woman to walk past a scaffold, a wine bar, a fish stall or a cohort of soldiers without whistles and loud invitations to share grimy fellows' flagons. It looked as if the food she had so unnecessarily brought for her daughter was part of a workman's sardine ration, in fact. Women loathed her. Helena, and even young Albia, greeted her arrival with embittered sighs. While they hoped she would leave quickly, I prayed she had not worked out how much money to ask me for. She had, of course.

'You never even invited Marcia to your party at Saturnalia. Everyone ignores us nowadays. Whoever thought Festus would be so quickly forgotten? Marcia hadn't seen her gramps for ages and now she'll never have the chance again—' (Wails from Marina's well-primed daughter.) 'Geminus was *so* fond of her; it's *such* a tragedy! And I blame you, Marcus.'

Since the child was listening, I refrained from spelling out that Geminus lost count of his grandchildren, and that my niece could have been brought to see Pa at the Saepta any day. Suitably prompted, he would have reminisced about Festus and handed out hot pancakes. Given his eye for a promising woman, Marina would probably have walked away with some piece of jewellery. The fact was, she had been too busy leading her life of play and pleasure—until she heard that Pa was gone and how much he had left behind.

Marina dumped Marcia on us 'to play with her little cousins'. Marcia was a fast-growing skinny-rib of ten, so she and my much younger girls had nothing in common, but Marcia spent hours diligently tying hair ribbons and my daughters were willing little dolls.

Primed by her mother, Marcia set about charming me in her own style. 'Uncle Marcus, just give us the money.'

'What money?'

'A big bag of cash to make us feel less sad that Grandpa died.'

'How does that work?'

'Mother is happy, so I'm happy—and you will be happy too. You don't want us littering up your smart hall every morning.'

'Is that going to happen?'

'Yes, *Marcus darling*—' Marcia did a priceless imitation of her effusive mama. 'Until you give in, I shall be dumped here to work on you.'

I said I was packing for a business trip to Latium.

My niece turned withering great brown eyes on me. What she lacked in her mother's extraordinary beauty—and she was on course to inherit most of that—she made up in character. If the character was dubious, it only proved a Didius really had spawned her. A handful at three, at ten she was now ferociously bright and spirited.

Marcia suggested that, if I was busy, I should simply give her the password for my Forum bankbox, then she would withdraw a sum she thought suitable. Nothokleptes, my banker, would probably be so surprised he would hand over everything.

I said Marcia must be joking, then we both collapsed in giggles.

Two days later it was Marcia, a dedicated gossip-winkler, who told me that Petro's brother was at Maia's house.

'Petronius must have sent for him. Auntie Maia is put out.'

'Nobody knew Lucius even had a brother!' Helena exclaimed. We were at lunch, tucking into our own goat's cheese, olives and flatbread, plus more sardines; Marina's scaffolder must be really keen on her, though he had a tedious diet.

'Lucius has a brother.' I wiped my oily chin on a napkin. 'Rectus. He lives in the country; Petro despises that.'

'His brother is always off-colour,' Marcia informed us. Information stuck to her like mud on a wall. 'He has marsh fever. First it nearly killed him, now it keeps coming back. But Lucius Petronius has turned down the official guide you were offered by the man at the Palace and asked his brother instead. He trusts him. Anyway, he's brought Nero.'

'*Spot!*' Helena and I corrected her briskly. Nero was an ox, of dubiously rakish character. Petronius, his poorly brother and some hick cousins jointly owned him. Calling the beast by the name of an emperor who had been damned-to-the-memory could be defined as an offence. I was once arrested for it in Herculaneum—though the real reason was that Spot tried to rape a donkey. A snooty Herculaneum citizen, its owner, failed to see the funny side.

'If this is the same ox, he's a sex maniac. I'm not driving him!'

'Why do you need a guide?' Helena interrupted, swift to pick up any detail I was trying to hide. She homed in on the fact that when I first discussed Laeta's mission, I implied Petro and I were just retracing my journey to Antium. She fixed me with accusing eyes. I acted casual. It never works.

'They need a guide,' Marcia piped up before I could stop her, 'to show them the way in the Pontine Marshes. That's where they have to find the murderers, if those men go into hiding and think nobody will ever dare to go after them there since it is so horribly unhealthy.'

'Thank you, Marcia,' I replied coolly. She gave me her clever-little-girlie smile. I would have biffed her, but refused to be dragged down to her level.

Helena Justina, my companion in work and my soulmate in life, was now inspecting me as if I was one of the more repulsive insects from the fetid swamps under discussion. 'O father of my children—' She adjusted an ear-ring, an expressive punctuation. 'Would that be the Pontine Marshes which have such a reputation for disease and death?'

I wiped my chin again as if I had missed a smear the first time. I placed the napkin on the serving table, neatly alongside my food-bowl; I straightened my spoon, rearranged my chewed olive stones in a more aesthetic pattern, then could no longer stall. 'We may not have to go there.'

'But if you do, Falco?' Helena generally called me 'Falco' when I had let her down unspeakably—and had been so careless that she found out.

I had done my research. I spent the past couple of days in libraries— not what people generally expect of informers, but unless there is a good reason to hang around barmaids and Forum lags, I like to use reputable sources. The scrolls depressed me. 'The good thing,' I chirruped, 'is that we are going in summer, when much of low-lying, scenic Old Latium dries out.'

Unfortunately, Helena was well read too. 'Marcus, the modern theory is that drying out the land seasonally has only provided better summer breeding-grounds for flies!'

'Olympus, is that what they say?' I was genuinely glum.

A row of silver bangles jingled together on Helena's left arm. 'The flies are hideous. Even in the forests, clouds of them rise up at every step. The Pontine Marshes are so dangerous nobody will live there. What's that proverb—*You grow rich in a year, but you die in six months?*'

Sometimes I liked having a partner who supplied me with background. At other moments I understood the men who married girls who had no time for arguments as they devoted themselves to athletes and actors. 'I won't be staying a year—not even six months.'

'Six hours will be too long if the wrong fly bites you.'

'Either we can pin the killings on our man, or we come straight home. In any case,' I countered feebly, 'as Marcia said, Petronius Longus is in charge of the logistics. He is bringing the best possible guardian—his own brother.'

My niece Marcia gave us a sniff that reminded me of my mother at her most disparaging. 'Everyone thinks Petronius Rectus has gone off like a pint of bad prawns.'

Much later, that evening when the house was quiet, Helena Justina and I discussed my journey properly in my small private study. I sat in an old basket chair I kept there purposely, so she could lean her elbows on the arms while she told me what a swine I was. At other times, the dog jumped up on it. Tonight, Helena pinched my reading couch, so I was reduced to the chair and the dog jumped on my lap.

Helena had thrown off her shoes and her jewellery, pulled out the ornamental pins from her fine hair and was massaging her head with those long fingers as if the pull of a chignon had made her scalp hurt. But I was the real headache.

'Listen, fruit. The old rules apply. If you ask me not to, I won't go.'

Helena thought about that, for about two heartbeats, which was longer than usual in fact. 'The rule is we travel together, Marcus.'

Now I was stuck, as she intended. If I said it would be irresponsible and unfair to our children for both parents to risk death in the marshes, it just emphasised how stupid it was even for one of us to go.

Helena did not wait for me to bluster. 'I can't come. Julia and Favonia need me here for reassurance.' They had played up a lot after we lost the baby. They probably needed me here too. Typically, Helena did not waste breath pointing that out.

'I am sorry a big case has come up so soon. Well, maybe I'm sorry it has come up at all.'

'Marcus, I know you will always need to work.'

'I could become a full-time antique dealer, a permanent auctioneer. Do you want me to do that?'

Helena made an impatient gesture, left-handed; lamplight hit silver in a ring I once gave her. We had not addressed the issue of my future, but now we dealt with it. 'I think you will be good at it,' Helena told me, 'but you would hate to do it permanently. You enjoy being an informer—it was one of the first things that struck me about you. And you're very good. So be honest. You and Lucius Petronius have been offered a mystery and as usual you can't resist.'

'My connection with Modestus caused it. Apparently a new career won't save me from mysteries!'

'So your argument is, you owe something to Modestus? Not profits. I know what the statues brought in.'

'You checked!'

'I check a lot of things,' Helena said, to worry me. I grinned happily. I kept few secrets from her. She was too likely to expose me.

When the statues went forward to the amphitheatre project, their modest price was the best Geminus could negotiate. Vespasian never wasted cash. 'Pa always decried sudden swish rewards,' I said. 'He reckoned it's the regular accumulation of small sums that matters, not a hiccup that may thrill you for a moment yet never come again.'

Helena smiled. She had been oddly fond of my father, as he always was of her. 'He was right—though I believe he had his thrills too. What pleased your father could be a beautiful artefact—' Often in the form of a willing woman, though I refrained from interrupting with that comment. 'But to him, any business finesse was delectable. You inherited it, Marcus. You get the same boost from your work. So you want the satisfaction of explaining what happened to this man and his wife, especially when nobody else can solve it. Then, since no one else will take them on, you and Lucius see these Claudii as your challenge.'

Helena understood—but explaining was not the point. 'You don't want me to go.'

'That's not it, Marcus. *I want you to come back!*'

Helena took in a breath, not despair, more exasperation. It was no more than if I had gone out in my newest tunic when the streets were muddy. She would let me go to the marshes once I promised to take care. Promises were not worth making in this situation, though for her I stretched the point.

Next morning, Helena and Maia visited apothecaries. A large basket of herbal ointments to keep away flies would be going on the mission with us. If we were sensible men we would use them.

If Petro and I were not sensible, our women would find out. So we thanked them politely for caring and agreed to take precautions against dying. 'You are taking swords, aren't you? What's the difference?'

I loved Helena Justina. I wanted to survive with her for many years. But did she think Hercules slathered himself with brimstone and pennyroyal when he departed for his twelve labours?

Actually it was worse. Petronius and I had been supplied with bunches of nettles to hang all around the ox cart, then numerous soapstone boxes of a concoction in which not only pennyroyal but wormwood, rue, sage, tansy, myrtle and spearmint were mingled in an olive oil base. Some individual ingredients were attractively aromatic, but the combination smelt foul.

'I'll use this stuff, if you will,' I told Petro.

He said, anything would be worth it to save us being bitten. For bites, he showed me, our determined women had sent another box. Their sandalwood and lavender bite-salve would scent us like a pair of Pamphyllian dancing masters. We were hard men, but that really terrified us.

16

We detoured to call on Sextus Silanus. We had to pass on the tragic news of his uncle's death. Petronius would explain the circumstances. My role would be to watch this conversation unobserved, judging the nephew's reaction. He had benefited financially from the death. Some investigators would pin the murder straight on him. When motive gives you a quick way to clear up a case, who needs facts?

Silanus came to the shop door, saw our cavalcade, recognised me, and expected the worst. Petronius Longus always looked as if he had a grim purpose. His bearing and sombre face gave away the reason for our visit. The numbers in our group also indicated that Modestus and his fate were at last of official concern.

We had the ox cart, containing some of us and our baggage. On dilapidated mules were a couple of Petro's men, all he could safely scrounge from duty: Auctus looked too fragile to fight fires but he had been in the cohort for years and everyone accepted him; he was riding Basiliscus, a skeletal beast with a bent ear and bad breath. Ampliatus had an eye missing and rode a brindled, knock-kneed mule called Corex who kept running away. Although the vigiles are ex-slaves, most were not quite so off-putting; these were the only two men who would volunteer for our destination.

Petronius had left Fusculus behind in charge, though we wished we could have had that steady fellow with us. Somebody had to do Marcus Rubella's vital job; at least, that would be Rubella's view.

In charge of the cart, Petro's brother had a similar relaxed driving style, holding the reins in one hand loosely and letting the ox make his own pace. Otherwise there was little resemblance between them. Maybe there had been a frisky lupin-seller in the neighbourhood just before Rectus was born, though I did not risk the joke. Rectus was older, shorter, of squashy shape and slumped posture, an unsociable fellow who seemed hard to like. They had had very little to do with one another for years. I was sure Petro once told me his brother was a bit of a fixer and mixer, though he gave no sign of it. Perhaps age or the marsh fever had slowed him down. When anyone asked Rectus about the fever (which we did frequently, because we were all petrified), he just grunted; if pushed further, he let out a sardonic laugh and turned away. I decided not to discuss him with Petronius. Let him volunteer a comment if he wanted to.

Completing our party was a brother of Helena's, Justinus. I worked with him in Rome and had also taken him on missions in rough country. I knew he would be reliable. Helena had begged me not to expose him to danger, but he was no longer a lad; it was his choice. He was keen to escape the bad atmosphere at home, caused by his brother's new wife and pushy father-in-law. On this trip Justinus had brought his barmy batman, Lentullus. The dopiest, clumsiest ex-legionary in the Empire, Lentullus was devoted to Quintus in a wide-eyed way. He limped badly on one leg and would probably try to tame the Pontine flies as pets.

I planned that if we ran into hostility from local dignitaries, resentful of imperial interference, then Camillus Justinus, as a senator's son with the smart travel clothes and uppercrust accent, could be shoved forward to charm them.

We first tackled officialdom at Lanuvium. I was right; we were given the brush-off. If there's one thing I hate about travel outside Rome it is small-town magistrates who think they count for something. The petty toffs who ran Lanuvium had so little sense of proportion they called their town council the Senate and their magistrate a Dictator. That was the title used in ancient times for a leader with unrestricted powers who was called upon to rescue the nation in an emergency. On mention of the Claudii, the Lanuvium Dictator rapidly assumed other emergency powers: declaring that this problem was outside his jurisdiction. He kindly suggested we try Antium instead.

He had cow dung on his boots and I wasn't certain he could read—yet he managed to dismiss Laeta's request for civic aid as briskly as if he was swatting wasps on a saucer of relish.

'I'm getting a feel for this,' Petronius remarked in annoyance as we left.

'You mean,' suggested Justinus, 'it feels like stepping in a slurry pit?'

'And helplessly falling over!'

We spent the next half-hour despondently embroidering this with such details as falling in the manure while wearing your best cloak and with a girl you fancied watching . . .

Our detour to Lanuvium was partly a waste of time, but we did see Silanus. Petronius had asked him a few questions that confirmed the body found in the tomb was his uncle: a man in his sixties, nearly bald, thin build; usually wearing a lapis signet ring, which had not been found. I saw Petro thinking that the killer might have kept it as a trophy and that if we ever caught up with him, the ring might be good evidence. Her nephew said Livia Primilla was about fifteen years younger; in good health, blue eyes, greying hair, kept herself nicely, wore good clothes and jewellery. Unfortunately, even though they dealt in statues and must know the artistic community, the couple had never commissioned portraits of themselves.

Silanus gave us directions to his uncle and aunt's farm. It was near Satricum, adjacent to land farmed by the Claudius freedmen: 'If you can call what the Claudii do *farming*.'

They did own cattle: Silanus said his uncle had a long history of bad relations with them but the most recent ugly incidents began when the Claudii let a rampaging bunch of young bullocks break down a fence. Modestus had an overseer who went to demand compensation for the damage, but was badly beaten up.

Silanus confirmed that Modestus had a hobby of writing angry letters. He had complained directly to the obnoxious Claudii. He also badgered the town council in Antium; those wits'-end worthies may have lost patience with his demands. After he and Primilla disappeared and Silanus appealed for help, the magistrate had to investigate, but his men may not have put much effort into it.

'Some of the Claudii are just loafers; they go into town and act up—minor thefts from homes and businesses, insults, writing their names on walls, guzzling wine then causing a disturbance after dark . . . You know.'

'Everyday life, where we come from,' Petronius said, though he made it clear he was sympathetic.

We were indoors at the time; Silanus went to look outside to check what his children were doing. Lentullus, a big child himself, was talking to them; he had them feeding grass to the ox. 'One or two Claudii have more violent reputations. People don't like anything to do with them.'

'Particular names?' asked Petro.

Silanus shook his head. 'When Modestus was railing, I had my own troubles. It always sounded like exaggeration. Anyway, there never seemed much I could do . . .'

'A man called Nobilis has been mentioned.'

'Means nothing to me.' Silanus fell silent. Now he blamed himself for not taking more interest previously.

I said quietly, 'You were right the other day. Why make yourself another victim? Your conscience is clear. Leave it to the professionals.'

I had watched Petronius silently weighing up the nephew as a harassed family man of basic honesty. Turning a piece of terracotta in his big hands, Petro asked, 'A slave brought you the news of your aunt's disappearance—can I speak to him?'

'Syrus. I don't have him,' said Silanus. 'There was a man I owed money to. I handed over the slave to pay off the debt.'

He had paid the butcher. That's how it is. Syrus may have loyally carried out instructions from Primilla that had brought him on a day's journey, and the result of his information would make Silanus and his children financially secure. But unlucky Syrus was a slave. His reward for diligence was to be exchanged for half a year's supply of skillet offal.

Our conversation seemed to have finished. But as Silanus saw us off outside, he brought out awkwardly, 'I have to ask—are you expecting to find Aunt Primilla?'

I let Petronius answer. 'We shall do all we can. You understand that we already suspect what happened. Whether any trace of her remains is a question I can't answer yet. I'm sorry.'

Silanus accepted it. But he had one more worry. We had told him how Modestus died. 'Will she have suffered . . . the same kind of injuries?'

Petronius Longus grasped his shoulders. 'Don't think about it. She won't be suffering now. My advice is, try to live as normally as possible until we report back. Whatever happened to Livia Primilla is long over.'

He would not give fake reassurance, nor could he offer comfort.

We had brought what remained of the late Julius Modestus with us from Rome. In such circumstances, the vigiles used a tame undertaker to cremate the body before it was returned to the family. All Silanus received was a plain urn with the ashes.

Petronius implied the cremation had been carried out when they thought the dead man might never be identified. But I saw the nephew's face. He recognised concern for him: preventing any chance that he or his children might see the decayed, beaten, mutilated and tortured corpse.

17

The butcher in Lanuvium was typical. He was built like an unhealthy boxer, with a cleaver through his belt. A row of meat joints hung along the front of his shop, just where his horrible nitty head would bang into them all day. He had blood on his tunic. It looked and smelt as if it was weeks old so if you ate his meat you would keel over. But if we all avoided the produce of off-putting butchers, we would be stuck with a diet of lettuce leaves and the Empire would be overrun by beefy barbarians.

He no longer possessed the slave Syrus. We groaned, thinking this was the start of an interminable chain of petty debt pay-offs. In Rome it would have been. The butcher would have sweetened a brothel-keeper who then passed on the goods to buy a sack of hay . . .

Sophisticated barter had yet to arrive in Lanuvium. They were simply careless. 'Syrus? I only had him two days. He ran away.'

'Not much of a debt cancellation!' Petronius grinned. 'If I were you, I'd take the old "sleep-with-my-sister" settlement next time.' City wit really goes down well in country districts. The butcher gave him a glare that made me squeamish. Still lost in his joke, Petro appeared to ignore the frosty looks but went on in formal vigiles mode: 'Have you reported your slave as a fugitive, sir?' The 'sir' was satirical, if you knew Petro.

'What's the point?'

'He may turn up.'

'That good-for-nothing is long gone.'

'Well, we do like to have runaways listed properly; apart from being useful if we catch them involved in a felony, it helps deter the next one from trying it if he knows he'll be on a list for the bounty-hunters . . . Where do you think this Syrus is headed? Would he go back home to Antium?'

The butcher was full of bluster and certainty. 'Oh he's chased off where they all go—straight up to the Via Appia, hop on the back of a winecart, and disappear in Rome. They think the streets are paved with gold. Maybe they are. I think I'll go myself one day!'

Petronius Longus remained undaunted. 'Better give me his description and I'll have a docket sent on your behalf in case he's rounded up. You may get him back, sir. The Rome vigiles are adept at spotting country runaways . . .' He implied that agricultural incomers stood out in our sophisticated city. It wasn't true. A loser in flight from a farm looked little different from one on the loose from a town house—well, once the townee had rolled up his smart uniform and shoved it under a bush. 'Let me take down a few details. Height?'

'Middling.'

'Weight?'

'Middling.'

'Distinguishing marks?'

'None visible.' The butcher leered. 'I hadn't got around to inspecting his rude bits!'

'Trained for any fancy duties?'

'General runabout.'

'I suppose,' Petronius deduced, 'he was wearing a rough-sewn, homespun tunic and worn country shoes? Well, thank you for your keen observation, sir. That gives us some very useful points to go on.'

Petro was a po-faced, placid humorist. The butcher could not decide whether he was being mocked or praised.

18

We could have stayed the night in Lanuvium but we all agreed that somewhere else—anywhere else—might suit us better. I remembered there was a hamlet about halfway down to Antium; it would put us well on our way tomorrow, so we headed off there. It was a very ancient settlement, a place that made us feel we had strayed into Old Latium back when it was New. They claimed to have ninety inhabitants; they must have been counting in their goats. I kept expecting to run into the old hero Aeneas, tramping across this low-lying bog that the gods had sent him to colonise, still wearing the loincloth in which he escaped from Troy.

There was a cluster of poor houses, gathered together for company because it was near a crossroads; about a mile further on, a bridge crossed a river. There, a rutted track led off the narrow road. Rectus said the track wandered south, passing close to Satricum, so we could have nipped down there immediately, but we still planned to try in Antium to learn about the official efforts to find Modestus and Primilla. We only expected disdain from another magistrate. But why abandon a well-tried system just because it doesn't work?

A man and his wife conjured up basic meals for travellers. If there were places to stay, we preferred not to investigate. We ate, drank, told stories, then camped out. Next day, the man had gone to check his fig tree, but his wife made us a simple breakfast. Then we pressed on.

At Antium our qualms proved groundless. The magistrate was not going to be the least bit unhelpful; we were not even able to meet the man. His house was locked up and he was away.

'So . . .' Petronius Longus mused thoughtfully. 'If you live in a scenic old town on the coast, when summer comes you still have to go off on holiday?'

'That lummock with the fig tree nipped down here and warned him you were coming,' gloated his brother. This was pretty well the first opinion he had volunteered on anything. The rest of us gazed at Petronius Rectus and carefully kept quiet, as we belatedly assessed him as a crackpot fantasist.

We asked around. That was a lark. Half the people refused to speak to us, the rest said they knew nothing.

After these fruitless forays, we did move on to Satricum. It was another very ancient township, on low-lying ground, right at the edge of the Pontine Marshes. Around this remote crossroads, cultures had clashed for aeons. The warlike Volscians had fought over the archaic place; they probably still lived here. Not only did it feel as if we might bump into a bunch of slant-eyed, smiling Etruscan ancestors, there was an end-of-civilisation atmosphere, brought about by the little town's proximity to the dreaded wetlands.

A tightly built settlement was going about its business. Up on a hill stood a temple to Mater Matuta: the mother of the morning, Eos, Aurora—the rosy-fingered harbinger who unlocks the gates of heaven so the sun can roll out each day. We climbed the acropolis like good tourists and saw the ancient goddess, chiselled in pitted stone, enthroned and mourning her son Memnon, killed at Troy by Achilles, whose corpse lay across her lap.

She was a goddess of provender as well, and a game girl who had been cursed by the jealous Venus into a habit of taking many lovers (the kind of curse most young girls fervently pray for). The Mater Matuta at Satricum looked a bit weathered for lovers, but had done her job with opening the gates for Helios today. The sky was clear blue and the sun shone brilliantly.

'That's the Pontine deception,' Petronius Rectus informed us gloomily. 'Gorgeous weather, vegetation blooming—death behind every bush.' As a travel companion, the man was a laugh a minute.

We went back to our lodging house, in need of a drink.

It had taken us a while to find an inn that could accommodate seven of us. Satricum might be a crossroads, but most people who came this way must be heading somewhere else. It had little to attract visitors. The main feature was the old temple; that was hardly a unique shrine. Mater Matuta once flourished all across mainland Italy. She had a temple in Rome, right beside the Cattle Market Forum and so close to my house the memory made me homesick.

Perhaps a mother mourning her dead son was a sight I was not yet ready for. Heaviness fell upon me. I lost myself in my own thoughts.

Most of us were spinning out the evening in the inn courtyard. Auctus and Ampliatus, the two vigiles, were outside on a bench at the roadside. Although they were ex-slaves, we were equals on this trip and the rest of us genuinely wanted to include them; they stubbornly remained aloof. Meanwhile, as Justinus was a senator's son it was his birthright to chat up the girl who had served us. He was, however, unsure whether Lentullus, who had only recently joined his household, would report to his wife Claudia anything he got up to. Petro and I had our wives under control, or so we convinced ourselves; even though flirting with bar staff went against our noble natures, we did the necessary with the waitress, just as we had done for the past twenty years.

We were picking her brains. What did you think I meant, legate?

Because it was the largest roadhouse in the area—the only acceptable inn, it seemed—this had to be where the posse that came to look for Modestus and Primilla also took a breather. At first the waitress was reluctant to say much. The riders from Antium counted as local to her; we were foreign. Under the curious eye of his older brother, Petronius set about persuading her how much he hated gossip and admired a discreet waitress, but how much more he liked a civic-minded young woman who poured wine so nicely while she revealed all. (All she *knew*, legate; don't go off pop.) It took him about ten minutes before she had sat down with us and was gabbling information just as fast as he could ask the questions. Rectus, Justinus and Lentullus were impressed. I had seen Petro reach this point in half the time, but in those days he was young and in army uniform.

Her name was Januaria. She looked fifteen, was probably twenty, and would be killed by hard work before another decade passed. She had stabled our ox, cooked our dinner, explained the wine list (that took no effort), pulled heavy benches closer to the table, filled jugs from a cask and served us, including several detours to the two vigiles outside. None of us had asked, but it was understood that if we wanted, she would go to bed with us as well; all seven, if necessary, on whatever rotation basis we suggested. It would probably cost no more than a soft-boiled egg.

Januaria obligingly told us a posse turned up here about two months ago. A town magistrate who was hoping to go home as soon as possible arrived on horseback, in charge of volunteers who were hoping at least for a fight. After a hearty lunch, they toddled off into the marshes to tackle the Claudii. Following ingrained tradition, those scurrilous runts all swore blind they never saw Modestus or Primilla after the broken fence incident. They provided alibis for one another, in the usual way of large families.

'Then there wasn't much more to be done. Suspicion fell mainly on Probus and Nobilis.'

'Nobilis and Probus? *Noble* and *Honourable*?' I could hardly believe the irony of these names.

The simple girl didn't see my point. 'Those two are the best known—and most feared. They hang around together a lot. But Probus now has his own business—he buys and sells harness; second-hand mostly.' That probably meant stolen, though she did not suggest it. 'Nobilis has been working for Thamyris, a grain supplier in Antium, though Probus swore blind to the militia that his brother had gone away. So he couldn't have done anything, could he?'

'Away where?' asked Petronius. 'Campania? Rome? Overseas?'

'No, somewhere real foreign.' The girl knew nothing of other regions of Italy, let alone the overseas provinces. Our glorious Empire meant little to her. She had never even been to Antium, which was only seven miles away.

'When did he leave?'

'We haven't seen him in Satricum for months, but that's not unusual. The Claudii come and go.'

'Do you think he fled because he knew people would be looking for him?'

'He's never been scared before.'

I shoved Petronius along his bench and muscled in. It took effort. He was bigger than me and resisting like a recalcitrant old hog. 'So, excellent young lady with the beautiful eyes—' Januaria giggled as if no man had ever chatted her up before. Clearly few from Rome stayed here. 'What do you know about these rascals, the Claudii? Are there many of them?'

'Plenty. They live a bit rough, except some of the girls, who got away and married and have families.'

'I'm Falco, by the way.' I gave her my best smile, the version with dimples, which has been called seductive.

Sadly Januaria lost her chance with me. There was a landlord keeping an eye on her in case she snatched five minutes to herself. We never found out whether he was her husband or father, or even her owner if she was a slave. Around here, arrangements were freestyle. All three situations might apply simultaneously. In Rome we have a wide range of social entertainments on offer; in country dumps they tend to be stuck with witchcraft and incest.

The man was a waddling, inquisitive slob in a meal-sack apron. When he put in an appearance, the girl slid to her feet and made off indoors. She knew he had come out to stop her gossiping. Maybe he beat her if she slacked. In the country, people who may be kindness itself to their valuable animals treat staff management as harshly as an arena blood sport.

We never found out his name. We never wanted to be that friendly.

He just liked to do all the talking himself. They had a system. This wastrel chatted to customers; Januaria did everything else.

'Oh yes, fine sirs! I can tell you all about the Claudii!'

He said he remembered them arriving here. He was a child then. They had been manumitted in the time of the Emperor Gaius, which would be forty years ago. Freed from the rural farms of Antonia, the Emperor Claudius' mother, they arrived near Satricum and took possession of some soggy fields they claimed had been given to them. No imperial land agent had ever come to question it, though that could be because the sodden fields in question were rubbish. The Claudii hit the district like a plague of rats. Since then, anything portable had to be locked up, which the landlord said included all women younger than great-grandmothers.

The father was called Aristocles. He was a cold, odd man who certainly beat his children; people reckoned he knocked his wife about too, though some said that in fact he was frightened of her. Others maintained both parents acted together as a terrible team; the mother once hit a three-year-old so hard he lost an ear. This matriarch, a woman known as Casta, had borne about twenty offspring, in whom she showed little interest, although they all strangely revered her. The children were feral and generally disliked. The boys became renowned for wild tempers. They had bad relations with their girlfriends, when they were able to find any. Their sisters, who knew no other kind of man, tended to ruin any hope of a new life by choosing work-shy, thieving wife-beaters who resembled their own kin. The whole family were regularly suspected of burglary and arson, though it took a brave person to accuse them. Criticism of one was viewed as an attack on them all. It would bring the whole tribe into town, out for retaliation.

'Isn't it rumoured they have imperial protection?' I asked.

'Oh they do. Everybody knows about it.'

'How does that work?'

'We just all know. The Claudii have powers in Rome looking after them. That's why nobody official tries to clear them out. That's why most of us steer clear of them.'

'Did they give the posse from Antium any trouble?' Petronius asked.

'Oh no, laddie. Resistance would have proved they were up to no good, wouldn't it? That's their trickery. When troops go down there to their camp, they act meek as lambs. They make out that all complaints against them are dreamed up out of local spite. They pretend to be helpful. They throw open their doors to let their places be searched.'

'But no evidence is found?'

'They are very clever.'

Petronius leaned his chin on his hands. He was thinking about bullies who fester in society, accepted as a hazard of life, while they terrorise communities for years. He had to deal with situations like this in Rome. There were foul alleyways that nobody went down. Even the vigiles would only venture there in groups and they whistled loudly first, to let it be known they were coming. They would not want to surprise anyone. They gave the specially violent ones good time to get away.

The landlord decided he had said enough, though he gave us directions for tomorrow. Rectus, our intended guide, looked down his nose; the information was of the 'take the first turn out of town then just keep going straight' variety. This always leads you to sharp bends and forks in the road with no signboard. 'You can't miss it,' said the innkeeper, complaisantly. Our hearts sank.

We turned in early. My dinner lay heavy in my guts and even after it deigned to go down I had an ache in the pit of my stomach. I cannot have been the only one. We all knew we were about to visit one of the most dangerous areas on earth.

19

First thing next morning, Petronius and I handed round the insecticide ointments Helena and Maia had made us bring. Amidst a lot of joshing about the reek, and how scared of our women Petro and I must be, surprising amounts were applied to exposed skin. Petronius Rectus called us a bunch of fragile florets, but even the two vigiles dipped into the pots and daubed their foreheads.

None of us bothered much with breakfast, except Rectus. Since he had already had a dose of marsh fever, nothing worried him. We were tense, but he was placid. Immediately he had stuffed himself, he harnessed up Nero the ox, then without a word, threw his pack on the cart and set off. Luckily the rest of us were ready to go. You couldn't call the man surly; he just never bothered to communicate. His distaste for talk was religious. Being in his brother's company seemed to make Petro equally gloomy. I didn't try to chivvy him out of it; I was gloomy myself.

There were towns on the coast, west of us; there were stopping points along the Via Appia, to the east. Between them, once we put Satricum behind us, the way ahead was a vast empty quarter. We had a sense that the sea was somewhere over on our right hand, less than ten miles away though we never caught a glimpse. When Appius

Claudius struck his great road south from Rome, he only added to the problems of this low-lying interior, his hefty causeways interfering with the water table. There were tracks, down which the ox could just haul his cart, though in narrow parts we had to dismount and manhandle the vehicle. These tracks all had the look of overgrown, deserted byways that would take you miles into nowhere then peter out without warning.

Everywhere had a wild beauty. The sun burned bright, its effects tempered by coastal breezes. Seabirds and marsh birds cried incessantly. Clouds of butterflies roamed fitfully, seeking out aromatic mints and oregano. Crickets jumped ahead of us. As we expected, there was a mass of insect life. Black bugs and tiny midge-like flies swarmed in clouds everywhere we stopped for a breather, along with worrying bright red things that looked as if they had already dined on blood. I reckoned there must be snakes too.

We were crossing great tracts of scrubland. We did see small fields, planted with grain or fast-growing crops to take advantage of the short summer period when the land at least partly dried out. Everything that grew, grew with astonishing vigour; the soil was both well watered and enriched with silt from all the rivers and tributaries that poured off the Lepini mountains. We never saw anyone tending the fields.

Where there had been grazing to keep down the foliage, the ground was covered with maquis—small, very tough bushes, some of which were broad-leaved, though more were of the vicious, prickly kind. If you stepped too far off the track, you were likely to find yourself sinking suddenly up to the ankle in swamp water. Its suck would be ominous. Once you managed to pull out your foot safely, your heart would be pattering.

Where there had been no attempt at agriculture, larger vegetation had grown. There were wild olives and figs, which could have been reassuring as domesticated trees, though left to nature they had become enormous rampaging monsters, forming impenetrable thickets. Rectus broke his silence to say happily that the forests would be even thicker, the further across the marsh we went.

Sometimes in the distance we glimpsed cattle, generally where the levels remained flooded. They probably belonged to someone, but were not visibly herded. We did not risk approaching them. Trampling the edges of dark saltponds and stagnant pools where fallen vegetation putrefied, these beasts in their lonely location gave me a grim shiver. Once in Germania, I had had an encounter with a wild aurochs; I glanced at Camillus Justinus and knew he too was remembering our narrow escape from that huge bovine throwback.

Supposedly, the threat here was human. The Pontine Marshes had a sinister reputation as a place where brigands and highwaymen holed up. They must be brigands who could endure being bitten, stung, afflicted with foot-rot and driven crazy by isolation. We were gathering an idea of what to expect if we ever found the people we had come to interview.

We knew that the Claudii deliberately lived far enough from habitation to make visits inconvenient. We were fit men, equipped for this, but by afternoon we felt exhausted. We were despondent too, thinking we might never track down our quarries. Rectus assured us we were not lost. That depended how much faith we put in him.

'I wish I was one of those herons and could just flap up and fly out of here. I bet this is a place where you could wander in endless circles!' chattered Lentullus when we paused for rest. He must be twenty-five now, but he wittered like a mindless child. Justinus and I had known him since he was an army recruit with a fervent imagination and a knack for getting into trouble. We reminded him that we got him safely back to civilisation last time; he looked unconvinced.

'Stay on the track,' Justinus warned his bright-eyed batman. 'If you get stuck in a deep sinkhole I'm not pulling you out, in case it brings a boggle-eyed sprite swirling to the surface.' Now who was using too much imagination?

We all had the creeps. Long periods of silence descended on us. The invigorating effect of fresh air turned into sun-glaze and skin-burn. Eyes were dry. We started to itch, but when we slapped at imagined insects, they were never there.

Something about wild places brings misery to the surface. I began to be afflicted by griefs and guilts I thought I had left behind in Rome. Now that I had mastered the endless tasks involved in Pa's estate, my brain found space to heal itself—which it did as spitefully as possible, by way of reliving moments of misery. Over and over, I went through again that long day of Helena's labour and how we lost our baby son; over and over, I daydreamed that I was back at my father's villa, while his gaggle of slaves informed me he had gone.

Avoiding the others, I lolled in the cart, thinking about life and death. Death, mostly.

When it was too late to get back to Satricum the same day and while we all tried to avoid raising the unwelcome subject of having to camp out for the night on this sodden ground, we came upon something.

We had been travelling an intermittently raised track through shoulder-high brushwood. Occasional clearings widened out in a ragged fashion. Somebody must use this route. In one part they had actually laid wicker hurdles where the track had sunk, though the hurdles had then been half submerged too. Quite suddenly we broached a bigger space. A tilting heap of trash grew out of the ground amongst a fungoid clutter that was definitely human in origin. It looked abandoned. It looked like the windblown rubbish that piles against bushes in forests. Not so, though. Someone had carefully collected this detritus, over a long period. There was a lopsided shack at the heart of the mess which appeared to be roofed and lived in.

'This is it, boys!' declared Rectus, as if he had knowingly led us to it.

'Ooh, I don't like it!' crooned Lentullus, like someone listening to a ghost story around a winter fire.

We stood and looked. Nero the ox lowered his head and nuzzled around in clumps of reedy grass. His tail flicked manically, as he was tormented by flies. We were too tired and dispirited to advance on the hovel immediately. If a will-o'-the-wisp had wafted out in a swirl of mist and cried *'Boo!'* we would have turned tail obediently.

One end of the building had a squashed look and slumped low, as if it was in the process of being swallowed by the swamp. This was a lean-to with nothing to lean against. At times over various decades, attempts had been made to patch up rotten parts. Items of hardware that may have been stolen from other people's porticoes or looted from stationary vehicles on market day were attached like trophies: a Medusa-faced tile end, a metal knocker solidified with its own verdigris, half of a baker's giant stone flour grinder. Around the shack were piles of old building materials, large-scale food containers that dribbled rancid waste, cartwheels, broken pieces of armour and incomplete fishing equipment. There was a table groaning under masses of machinery parts—rusty bits off pulleys, cranes and ploughs—ugly metalwork the purpose of which had been long forgotten and which would never be identified and reused. It all looked shabby. Most totters would have rejected it.

Parked between what must have been the door and a window that had been boarded-up was a row of heavy-duty spears and javelins. They were cruder than army issue, gross objects made for intimidation. No one in Rome could have such a vile armoury displayed against his house; decent folk just had a lantern they forgot to light most evenings and a tile saying *cave canem* to act as a cheap watchdog. Weapons were illegal in the city. In the country, anything was permissible. Out here in the wild, the hunting excuse let any small-time character who wanted to look big decorate his home with this all too obvious panoply. It didn't mean he was able to use it properly, though even an amateur who wielded one of those wicked beasts would be capable of inflicting harm.

Petronius Longus reached into the ox cart and quietly buckled on his sword.

I would have followed suit, but just then a man appeared in the tumbledown abode. Above three snaggled wooden entrance steps, with rotten treads, it had a two-part stable door. Without warning, he looked out through the top. Perhaps he had heard us coming. Obviously he had seen us now.

Petronius and I at once strode forward to speak to him. Wild barking announced that a vile-tempered dog was behind the lower section of the door, desperate to attack us. The man wore a filthy sleeveless tunic, a week-old beard and a scowl. No chance of a civilised traveller–host relationship here: he wasn't going to ask us in for pastries in a mock-marble peristyle. When Petro said we had come from Rome—a pedigree that must have been obvious—without a word, the rude householder swung back the lower door so that a powerful, ragged mastiff came bounding down the steps in a slather of rabid froth and sheer blind rage.

Justinus and Lentullus rushed forward. As always in a crisis, Lentullus knew no fear; he acted before he thought, then he fainted with terror afterwards. That was how he had nearly lost his leg. Now he grabbed the ferocious, snarling dog with both hands around its neck as it leapt at us. He hung on, intent on saving his beloved master. The man from the shack loped after the dog and lunged for it feebly; more by luck than judgement, he looped a chain around its heavy neck and clapped on a padlock. 'Good boy, Fangs! He's just being friendly,' he mumbled, in the manner of all lacklustre owners. He had no understanding of his dog's capabilities and strength, no hope of controlling it. He would be lucky if he wasn't found one day, savaged to death by his own animal.

We stepped away. The berserk Fangs was now straining to drag his chain free of the big tree to which its other end was fixed. He so much wanted to kill us, he seemed likely to strangle himself. We would have no qualms about letting him. Thwarted, he started hurling himself at the tree.

'Sorry, I forgot he was there. We don't see many people and he gets excitable. Quiet, boy!'

There was no way the dog could be silenced, until the owner lobbed half an old amphora at him. It missed. The weighty crock could well have cracked the canine skull. Fangs seemed to know about this wine-jar trick. Immediately he piped down and slunk to the base of the tree where he just sat, bored and whining.

We all stood in the clearing and went through introductory formalities.

'I am Probus, one of the Claudii,' said the man from the shack. 'I expect you have heard of us.' He folded his arms and stared, not openly hostile yet proud of their notoriety.

'One of the brothers?' asked Petronius, not denying we had been told about these people.

'That I am.'

'Are you the family spokesman?'

'Can be.'

'Do any of the rest live around here?'

'Several.'

'Give me some names?' Petro appeared quite patient, though I thought he wanted to kick this swamp slug in the throat. In Rome he would have had the bastard up against a wall; the problem here was lack of walls. Nobody wanted to go near the tree where Fangs was chained. Pushing a suspect hard up against the shack would most likely cause the whole wreck to keel over.

'Names?' Probus gave Petro a slow look, then wiped his nose on where his sleeve would be if he had sleeves. His arm was hairy enough, and muscular. He slouched like a wimp, but I bet he fought dirty. 'Names, eh?' He was medium height, well built in a slovenly way, with his belt drooping to groin level and a small paunch hanging over it. 'Everyone around here knows who we are.'

'I come from Rome,' Petronius told him again in a mild tone. 'SPQR. I'd like to hear some details.'

'I'm very busy,' Probus boasted. 'No time to draw a family tree.'

'And there are a lot of you, I gather.' Petronius still sounded friendly. I was waiting for him to explode. A cloud of midges began to swirl in front of my face and I biffed at them in irritation. 'Did I hear of twenty siblings?'

'Justus was the eldest—' Probus counted on his filthy fingers. He had on a silly face, playing clever bastards. I felt my attitude harden.

This could be the swine who had tortured a man for remonstrating about a trespass, beat him, cut off his extremities and left him to moulder. The gods only knew what had been done afterwards to the missing wife. That probably happened close to here.

'Go on,' Petro encouraged him, far too politely.

'Justus dropped dead last year—according to you lot, he probably died of a bad conscience. Then two girls, me, Felix—Felix, the happy and fortunate—and a clever little sod too; well we lost him early, naturally . . . another sister, the twins Virtus and Pius, and Era, then triplets who all died at birth, Providentia, Nobilis—he's the one you people usually blame, every time an apple falls from a tree and the owner squeals, *Those Claudii stole it!*—'

I had had enough. Probus continued his long list, but his sly, teasing attitude was more than I could take. Every name made me angrier. 'Let's stop messing about!' Petronius snatched at my arm but I shook him off. 'Probus, you know why we have come. A body was found; it was not pretty. Stop lying and admit that Modestus and his wife came here to complain.'

I strode forward. The thug stepped back in mock alarm. 'Oh they came!' he delighted in telling me. His black teeth showed in a gleeful grin. 'And they're not here now—however many of you cocky Romans barge about looking for them!'

That was all he said, because I socked him. I hit him low and hard, then as he doubled up, I struck again. If I had been alone with him, I would have carried on for half an hour. I felt so much aggression, I startled myself.

'*Falco!*'

Petro and one of the others dragged me off. 'Don't make me wish I hadn't let you come,' muttered Lucius Petronius, eye to eye with me and speaking low.

I wrenched free and stumbled away from him. Then I left him to deal with it. I walked off stiffly into the forest by myself.

20

I strode through the woods in a straight line. No point getting lost. When I came upon a path, I poked a stick in the ground, upright, to show me where to turn on my way back. I had no plan. I was not following the precept that sometimes on a bogged-down investigation, striking out blind can lead you to a clue. I was just overwrought.

I had calmed down by the time I came across more marsh-dwellers.

I walked into a similar campsite, just as poor as the last, just as untidy, just as unedifying. It had scenic advantages, however. It looked out on fields, for one thing. They were not bad fields either, my country background told me that, though their boundary fences were in a bad state.

Three horrible hutments, arranged in a rough triangle, formed a kind of shabby hamlet, not one to feature in a tourists' guidebook. What distinguished these from Probus' lair was that each had a couple of beaten-up chairs outside for admiring the view or making it easier to shout abuse at the sky. Each had a washing line. No man who cultivates a reputation as a dangerous long-term pest pegs out his smalls. So a couple of the Claudius women were in view, one slowly hanging up limp garments, another seated in a dispirited pose on the steps of what was probably her home. Her cowed demeanour suggested she was not allowed to use the chairs. On a nearby patch of ground, some tousled children were kicking a bucket about; I counted four though from the racket there could be others.

The girl with the laundry had the thin body of a child of fourteen and the face of someone two or three decades older. Pain lurked in her eyes. It would stay there. She had seen things she would never forget but she was never going to share them. Her drab dress was short, shapeless, frayed, a grey piece of rag that looked older than she was. Nonetheless, she wore a string of crude stone beads and even a bangle that could pass for gold for a pawnbroker who was ninety and short-sighted. Some man who wanted to signify she had a lot to be grateful for had given her those. She should have thrown them back and got free of him.

Surprisingly, the women did not take offence that I had stepped out of the undergrowth. It did not mean they would be helpful.

'The name's Falco. I'm looking for Nobilis.' No surprise at that, it seemed. 'I think I took a wrong turn. You're . . . ?'

'Plotia,' said the one with laundry. 'You want Nobilis?' She nodded to the centre shack. I had the impression it was empty. 'Gone away.'

'Beach holiday at Baiae?'

'Gone to visit his grandma.'

'Is that a joke? I hear he's a tough nut.' Plotia just stared.

I walked closer. After the incident with Fangs, I looked around, in case there were other guard-dogs. Reading my thoughts, Plotia said, 'We never have animals.' Her gaze flickered; she stated sombrely, 'Well not for long.'

I swallowed. Petronius once told me that pathological murderers tend to start their killing sprees while they are children. Find a man who takes prostitutes off the streets as a personal vocation, and he'll probably have a set of neat jars with his childhood collection of dissected rats. I had suggested all boys are curious about dead animals. Petro said most just pick them out of the gutter; we don't trap them on purpose and deconstruct them. Most of us don't eviscerate our own pets.

'What is your connection to the Claudii?' I asked the women.

'I'm married to Virtus.' It was still Plotia answering. 'Byrta belongs to Pius.' *Belongs to* was a term that would have delighted our ancestors; my Helena would disdain it. [Note to scribe: delete that 'my'. I don't want my balls pickled.]

Before I could ask, Plotia added, 'Both not here. Pius and Virtus work up in Rome.'

That was news. Petronius would be sure it was not good news.

'I'm from Rome.' I played friendly. 'What do your men do there?'

Plotia just shrugged. A Roman wife may be her husband's closest confidante in theory, but not around here. I guessed marriage was a one-sided contract among the Claudii. Wives had to take foul language, thrashing and forced sex, if I was any judge. Then they bore endless children, who were battered and buggered too. They would all learn to keep their heads down, to judge carefully from bad moods what it was safe to say or do, and never to ask questions. They were bound to have been ordered not to talk to strangers.

Many a slave knew that existence. Maybe it was how the Claudius men had learned to impose themselves on weaker souls.

'Nobilis have a wife?' I asked.

'She left.' At the mention of escape, Plotia looked jealous. Even Byrta perked up. From her perch she was listening to everything. 'He never recovered.'

'I bet there was all Hades of a row.' Plotia laughed briefly. 'Still, she got away from him?' Neither woman reacted to the way I phrased it. 'Where did she go?'

'No idea.' That meant not allowed to tell. 'Nobilis knows. Antium, I think. She set up with someone else, so Nobilis stopped that—'

'Really! How?'

'The usual way!' Plotia said scornfully. 'The girl took refuge with her father afterwards, I heard.'

'What's her father's name—and *her* name?'

Plotia and Byrta glanced at each other. This information must be on the banned list. Nonetheless Plotia told me the father was a baker called Vexus. The wife was Demetria.

'Does Nobilis now accept her going?'

'Yes—if "accept" means constantly saying he'll get the girl one day.' I sighed. 'When did they split?'

'Three years ago.' And it still rankled with the husband? Demetria must be a brave soul to break free of that control. Or was she so badly crushed that *anything* was better than life with Nobilis?

'If that's his house, can I have a look round?'

'He won't like it,' Plotia said flatly. Strangely, she then made no objection. It might be part of the Claudian plan to appear helpful whenever they were directly confronted. I took my chance and went to the door. It was unlocked—almost a jeering invitation to search. Even at that point, entering the house Nobilis lived in sent a shiver down my spine.

I wondered if the posse from Antium had searched here. It must have done them no more good than it did me. The freedman's house was crammed with stuff with an obsessive neatness. The collection of rubbish looked as if Nobilis had lined it up in rows, just waiting to upset enquirers by failing to provide clues.

Plotia came to the door behind me. She was gazing around as if she too had never stepped inside before. 'He keeps everything. He's got stuff that goes back decades.'

That was true, but if Nobilis killed Modestus, he had not kept the statue-seller's lapis lazuli signet ring. There were no locks of hair from victims, no lovingly cared for boxes of different girls' underwear. I found no old calendars with scored marks to signify killing days. No bloodstained weapons. No ropes with cut ends that could be matched to ligatures around dead men's necks.

I had been an informer long enough to expect disappointment.

I searched until I had had enough, then I came back outside.

'Find anything?' called Plotia, now squatting alongside her sister-in-law, with the early evening sun on her face.

'No. Does Nobilis have anywhere else he hangs out? Some special annexe, where he plays boys' games alone?'

Both women merely gave me odd looks.

This place was a shack to me, but maybe it had a subsidiary hovel, some even more secret hideaway where Nobilis committed his worst deeds. If so, either he kept it from his relatives or they were playing dumb. 'Just one last thing—did either of you see the quarrel with a neighbour called Modestus?' Both Plotia and Byrta shook their heads, rather too quickly. 'You know who I mean?' I insisted. 'He disappeared after a bust-up here, then his wife came to look for him and now she's missing too.' When the women continued to blank me, I said in a sombre voice, 'Modestus is dead. Murdered—on a journey to petition the Emperor. This isn't going away, so you may as well tell me. You still deny seeing the argument?'

'Probus and Nobilis talked to the old man.' For the first time Byrta found her voice. She had a common country accent and her attitude was the wrong side of aggressive. 'It did get heated—Modestus was an idiot, and pushy with it. Our lads never did anything to him. He just went away.'

'You sure of that?' I don't know why I bothered asking. I included Plotia in the question; she was keeping quiet now. She looked away and I knew she was not going to help me. 'Nobilis and Probus were the ones Modestus argued with?'

'They never touched him,' repeated the pale, thin woman as if this was a religious chant and if she said a word wrong, some sacrifice would be invalidated.

'That right? I'll be off then.'

'We'll tell the boys you came!' Plotia mocked my wasted effort.

'Don't do that, please. If there's talking to do, I'd rather do it my-self.'

Then, Plotia and I shared a brief glance. It was possible I had made a connection with at least one of these drear, isolated women—some bond that might help our investigation later.

More likely, she was just thinking I was an idiot.

21

I met my companions as I walked back through the woods.

'Next time you want to play good officer/bad officer,' Petro rebuked me mildly, 'let's agree it in advance, shall we? You know I hate always being the nice fellow. When is it my turn to put the boot in?'

I asked if his being sweet to Probus had achieved anything; he growled, 'Guess!'

'I wish I'd hit him harder, then.'

'Yes, if it helped whatever's eating you!' He knew what that was. Petronius was a loyal, affectionate family man. He knew I had grief I had not yet dealt with, and I was guilty about leaving home.

He smacked me on the shoulder, then we walked side by side. The others watched us warily, letting Petro play nurse. I outlined what the women had told me, not that it moved us forward.

The others had been carrying out sweeps, searching the woods in wide circles, looking for bodies. We went back along the path, passing the three hutments. Justinus stayed there to search the two women's homes with Auctus, one of the vigiles. The rest of us moved forward.

Looking for a good spot to camp because there was no chance we could return to Satricum that night, we were heading for what seemed to be more open country. Justinus and Auctus caught us up, having also had a fruitless search at the shacks. We kept moving along the boundary fence, distancing ourselves from where the Claudii lived. We found a place where the fence had been broken down and rebuilt; a notice had been erected on the far side, warning off trespassers in the name of Julius Modestus. Despite its fierce semi-legal language, only a short way further on we came upon another boundary breach. A group of wild-looking cattle which probably belonged to the Claudii stood on the Modestus land, eyeing us inquisitively.

No one said anything, but we kept going, rather than pitch camp too close to the big-horned beef.

We had a tent, but the ground was too wet and spongy for pegs to grip so we just hung an awning off the side of Nero's cart. As dusk drew in, I fetched out the ointment Helena had provided. This time there was no grumbling. As insects bothered us incessantly, we all dipped our fingers in the pot and slathered it on. Everyone tugged down their tunic cuffs and tightened their neck-scarves.

We lit a fire, which may have kept off some of the wildlife, though there was still plenty. We ate a nearly silent supper, not even discussing our plans for tomorrow, because we had none. Any chance of sleep was finished off by hundreds of croaking frogs. Then cattle turned up too, splashing, huffing and coughing, sounding enormous as they do in the dark. The vigiles jumped up from time to time, to shoo beasts away. Groaning, we tossed and turned all night, between bouts of miserable scratching.

At first light, people made a move stiffly. Basic ablutions were tackled. Lentullus, a shy soul, went off by himself. Soon a frightened shout alerted us: the Claudius cattle had found him in mid-pee. Although he was country-born, he was no match for these mad-eyed, jittery bullocks and heifers, who were galloping around trying to herd him against the fence. His bad leg had stopped him escaping fast enough.

'Typical Lentullus!' muttered Justinus, as we all set off to rescue him. It took a while. We had to drive the cattle to the far side of the boundary fence, then we clambered over it and left them safely out of reach. Behind us, they lowed hoarsely in frustration.

When we made it back to camp, we found a disaster. Straight away we saw that our ox was missing.

'Was he loose?'

'He was not!' Rectus was quick to clear himself of blame. 'I had him hitched to the cart.'

The cart was still there, along with some of our kit, though it was strewn around. The vigiles' two mules, who were almost uncatchable, stood under a tree looking on.

'How could strangers get Nero to go with them?'

'A bucket of feed would have him trotting off without a murmur.'

We searched around, following deep, water-filled hoofprints, but the trail lost itself in the maquis. Now we were stuck: miles from anywhere in a dangerous marsh that was inhabited by criminals of every type, knowing somebody must have been watching us—and they had stolen our ox.

22

We did keep searching as long as it was feasible. Several more days passed, but we lost heart now we were walking and carrying all our kit. We still had our mules, though once we lost Nero, Corex and Basiliscus had odd looks in their eyes as if they wished they had bolted; Corex had never been a group player anyway. We had to abandon the cart, another expensive loss for the Petronius brothers. Our task came to seem pointless. Nothing that bore any relation to a crime scene turned up. Looking for corpses in that sodden, scratchy, empty area was hopeless. The marshes were endless, horrible, ominous. Without a definite lead, we could wear ourselves out until the flies and disease finished us, yet achieve nothing. Depressed beyond bearing, we took a vote and agreed to give up. We had done our best. We had done more than anybody else had ever bothered to do.

The trip back took a long time and the first stage, heading back to Satricum, made us more sore-hearted than anything. When, still humping our packs, we passed the shack where Claudius Probus lived, he sniggered openly. He blamed the ox theft on the bandits who were supposed to have colonised the marshes. Curiously, we never saw any sign of such bandits. My guess was that the Claudii had seen off all the competition in these parts years ago. Most bandits are cowards, who avoid serious confrontation.

When we reached the good road and collapsed at the Satricum inn, the landlord expressed great surprise to see us. However, he was eager to hire us extra mounts, and very conveniently had some donkeys available; the two vigiles went with him to inspect them. Petronius sat set-faced, glaring as if he now thought the landlord was responsible for our loss of Nero.

Helena's brother Justinus went indoors to talk to the waitress, Januaria; neither Petro nor I had the heart. He returned looking thoughtful. 'She was talking about foreigners—that's anyone they don't count as local, I suppose. Some foreigners who take a road through the marshes don't come back; well, not this way.'

'That is because they have had their transport stolen!' Petro snarled.

Quintus and I exchanged glances. If the girl had made him think what she said was significant, I trusted him.

Petronius continued to resist. 'You head south, because you're going south. When you get there, that's where you want to be. So you stay there. In the south.'

'Logical,' I cracked. 'For simpletons!' I was feeling tetchy myself.

He carried on ranting. 'It follows that miserable inn-folk to the north don't see you again. They won't see *me* again either, once I get back to Rome.' Petro took a swig of wine from his beaker, spat, slammed down the cup in high disgust, then strode out, shouting to us all to move. He had had enough of the countryside. He was going home.

Petronius Longus and Petronius Rectus drove us all mad, maundering on at one another about the value of their stolen ox and abandoned cart. At least that ended when Rectus took his leave at the Via Appia. He returned to his farm in the Lepini hills. 'He was my bloody ox as well!' shouted Lucius Petronius after his departing brother.

I knew why he was so livid. The theft showed him up. He expected another ear-bashing from the cousins who owned part-shares in Nero. They were bound to suggest that an officer of the Roman vigiles ought to be able to hang on to his draught animal, especially when stuck in the middle of wetlands that were famous for criminal activities. 'My barmy brother was in charge of him—I should have known what was coming!'

I was welcomed home quietly. Helena had a sniff at me to ensure I had been using the anti-insect ointment. Ever the thoughtful husband, I had made sure I rubbed in some more just before I turned my door key. Helena herself was still subdued. Once we would have rushed straight into bed together, but with the baby's death so recent that would not happen.

I prowled around, checking the house. Things seemed well under control. Helena ran a good household and she had grown up in a senator's house, full of staff. Slaves from Pa's house were being tried out here a few at a time. I had never been able to buy good ones because I found the process so uncomfortable, but these seemed to know what was expected of them.

'Just tell me which you want to keep,' I told her, discussing slaves in order to avoid more painful subjects. Tired as I was, I raised a laugh. 'I can't believe I said that!'

'All you need to decide,' Helena answered drily, 'is whether you intend to continue your old frugal life, or should I now plan domestic extravagance and show-off socialising? We need more style. I changed from pottery beakers on the breakfast table—Gaius found some flagrant gilded goblets at the warehouse that I think will pass as morning water cups, though they won't do when we are entertaining consuls and international trade moguls.'

'Oh I leave all that to you, fruit. Don't skimp; just commission new from the most fashionable designer.'

Helena continued the joke. 'I'm so glad you said that. I've found a man who does the most *marvellous* art glass. I think it is important, Marcus, that our girls grow up knowing the finer things in life—even if they promptly break it . . .'

We tired of playing games. I flopped on a couch and Helena knelt to help pull my boots off. She was simply dressed for home in a long white tunic, with plaited hair just wound in a circle and secured with one long bone pin. My real wealth lay in the love in her eyes. I knew that.

Albia was still moping; she had stopped throwing perfume bottles at the wall, though she had taken to disappearing out of the house for long periods. Perhaps she went walking by the river, wafting along like a water sprite wronged by some heartless god. When she did come home, Helena suspected she was writing screeds of tragic poetry. 'I blame myself, Marcus; I gave her the education. Is this to be the Empire's heritage: putting barbarians at a social disadvantage—yet equipping them to complain?'

'Any further visits from Aelianus to inflame things?'

'No; he's busy. Father decided that now both Aulus and Quintus are married, it is make or break time to put them up for the Senate.' That was all I needed: electioneering. Helena grimaced too. 'I mentioned that it would be inconvenient for you, just when you are tied up with the legacy and need them to assist in your casework. But Papa is giving them one last chance to become respectable—he hopes to inveigle Minas of Karystos into a financial contribution.'

I scoffed. 'We know Minas better than that, I think!'

'Yes, he is as much use to Aulus as an in-law as he was as a professor. I suppose it has struck you,' Helena murmured warily, 'that *you* are now in line to be badgered for money, Marcus.'

'What? Everyone always supposed I wanted your father to pay *my* debts. Can the senator now be hoping to sponge off me?'

'I believe he may try to talk to you,' Helena admitted, smiling.

Thank you, Geminus. Now I was a plebeian-born, middle-class upstart who had to play banker to his aristocratic relatives. 'Will it cause a family crisis if I say get lost?'

'Not from me,' said Helena. 'Neither of my ridiculous brothers is fit to govern a beanfield, let alone the Empire.'

'Then they will sail into the Senate. Perhaps I *should* make an investment, then demand political favours from them? If a bunch of ex-slaves living on frogspawn can have friends in high circles, why not me?'

'You don't need favours from anybody, Marcus.'

I kept my head down for a few days. Life ran its usual furrow in the Aventine, though his tribune was back, so Petronius Longus had too much work at the station house. Invigorated by the sea air of Positanum, Rubella started sniping because Petro kept nipping off to the Forum Boarium, the riverside cattle market, to scrutinise any animals that came in. 'Just in case Nero turns up.'

'Nero's long gone,' I snapped, for which I received a mouthful of bad language. Fine. I told the high-handed Petronius that I had plenty to do at the Saepta Julia. So I immersed myself in my own business. We were not estranged, just having one of those tussles that keep a good friendship fresh.

Without my restraining presence, Petronius Longus chalked up a 'missing' poster in the Forum. It gave Nero's identifying features: answered to Spot, left-hander when yoked in a pair, dun coloured, four legs, tail, left-eye squint. Petro even drew a mug-shot. His depiction of Nero's perpetual line of dribble was particularly sensitive, in my opinion. I saw two granary clerks almost wetting themselves as they guffawed over the artwork, but they took it more seriously when they saw what size reward my stubborn friend was offering.

He was presented with a lot of mangy animals by rustlers who had just 'found' oxen wandering, but never his own.

The day I saw the poster, I was at the Forum to meet my banker, that morose ledger-fixer, Nothokleptes. His fingers could fiddle an abacus like no other's. He wanted to hire me a larger bankbox (for which there would be a larger fee) while I needed to explain that my sudden acquisition of large sums was not due to illegal money-lending scams or fraud on twittering old widows. Nothokleptes was quickly convinced I was legit; with a fine grasp of Roman nomenclature, he stopped referring to me as 'Falco, you shameless bankrupt' and now schmoosed, 'Marcus Didius, my dear respected client'. He claimed he had always known I would come good, though I had no recollection of this astrological forecast in the long dark days when I was begging for credit.

I still had to get used to my new position. I admit I was surprised when Nothokleptes seated me at a little bronze-legged table and sent out a lad to buy me a custard pastry. It was soggy, with not enough nutmeg topping, but I saw that my financial fortunes must have officially turned around. Thanks again, Pa!

Mellowed by egg custard, though with mild indigestion, I climbed up the Aventine to visit my mother. She was out, putting the world to rights. So I called at the house nearby where Petro and Maia now lived. She said he was sleeping. Then she backed me into a daybed on their sun terrace and forced a dish of salted almonds on me. I was beginning to see why men of wealth were also men of girth.

'Lucius has come home from Latium in a foul mood, and it can't just be losing that ridiculous ox. I blame you, Marcus!' Maia tolerated me more than my other sisters did, but she followed the trend. Petro's first wife, Arria Silvia, always thought I was a bad influence. That was even though, according to me, our worst adventures had always been his idea.

'I never did anything!' Why did a discussion with relatives always make me sound like a truculent five-year-old?

'I suppose that's what the low-lifes in the marshes all said too! Lucius keeps mum, but I can tell you got nowhere. You'll have to buck up,' Maia instructed me. She was a decent sort, when not being abrupt, hasty-tempered, condemnatory and unreasonable. That was her good side; her wild side was frightening. 'Get this case moving, will you?'

'It's his case.'

'He's your responsibility.'

'No—he's thirty-six years old and a salaried officer. Besides, he wasn't even my responsibility when we were young soldiers drinking our way across Britain while the tribes rampaged around us.'

'I can't live with him this grouchy,' Maia insisted. 'You're supposed to be the investigator, so stop loafing and get sleuthing.'

I promised I would, but sloped off home. Helena was slightly more sympathetic—if only because she felt her role was to appear always more rational than my female relatives. Putting their noses out of joint with her blameless serenity was, according to Helena, in the noble tradition of Cornelia, the mother of the Gracchi, every wise matron's heroine.

'You are not going to send me out pavement-bashing with a flea in my ear, I hope, darling?'

'Of course not.' Helena paused. 'Though I am *very* surprised, Marcus, that you have made *no* attempt to find those Claudii who work in Rome, or learn where Claudius Nobilis went off to!'

I knew when I was beaten. I crawled out of the house like a slug with a spade put halfway through him.

I had no intention of being bossed. Pa, who knew just how to live a worthwhile masculine life, had bequeathed me one thing of greater worth than its book-value: I now possessed his bolt-hole. As nonchalantly as possible, I took myself to the Saepta Julia.

Now I was so prosperous, I even had two bolt-holes. I was still paying rent on a cubbyhole Anacrites and I once hired, back when we were working on tax matters. I had affection for the place that had acquired me middle rank. I was using it now for the legacy paperwork, so it was stuffed with scrolls and piteous pleas for the inheritance tax clerks to give me time to pay. I didn't need more time, but today Nothokleptes had impressed upon me the need to delay bills so he could invest the capital in short-term sure prospects. 'The more you have, the more you can make, young Falco. You realise that, surely?' I certainly realised the more I had, the more my banker could cream off for himself. 'Only the destitute pay up prompt, for fear they won't have any money later.'

I had told Nothokleptes I would have to get used to this principle— but that I was a fast learner.

I sat in the cubbyhole, thinking, until boredom took over. Then I sauntered along the Saepta's upper gallery, enjoying the vibrant life going on at this level and below, just as Pa used to do. I could see why he loved this place. There was never a dull moment, as fat jewellers and paranoid goldsmiths swaggered around trying to bamboozle would-be customers, while pickpockets tailed the customers and guards wondered absently whether to tackle the pickpockets. There were constant cries from food-sellers who wandered the building with gigantic trays or weighed down by garlands of drink flagons. Wafts of grilled meat and suet patties vied with the reek of garlic and the stench of pomade. Every now and then some man of note—or a nobody who thought he was one—pressed through the throng with a train of arrogant slaves in livery, trailing sweaty secretaries and put-upon fan-danglers. Disdainful locals refused to be pushed around, resulting in loud altercations.

I enjoyed watching the gallery rage, then stepped over a vagrant and entered the office. My nephew Gaius, Galla's second eldest, was loafing there. He looked me over. 'You don't want to waste your time here, Uncle Marcus. Why not give me a couple of thousand a week and I'll run the place for you?'

He was at an indefinable point in his late teens, old enough to be useful, not old enough to trust. He looked like a tattooed barbarian, though with infected sores where the woad should be. He was a sweetie underneath; we sometimes used him for babysitting.

'Thanks for the kind offer, Gaius. I don't need help. We just put chipped old pots on show by the door and idiots rush in to pay huge sums for them.'

Gaius dropped into a stone throne, his favourite lounger, where he spread himself like a potentate. He was drinking Pa's flagon of Campagnan red, supposedly kept for celebrating big auction gains or for numbing the pain of losses. He waved me to a cheery cup that advised me to drink now for I would die tomorrow; as I poured a tot, Gaius warned me in serious tone, 'You want to take a lot of water with that, Uncle Marcus. It's probably too strong for you.'

'Yours is neat?'

'But I am used to it,' smiled Gaius. His brass-necked cheek came straight from my louche brother Festus, from Pa, and a long line of previous Didii. I made no attempt to remonstrate. Like Lucius Petronius, I was thirty-six and had learned when there was no point arguing.

We talked, with surprising sense from Gaius, about an auction held in my absence. 'Things are looking up again, no question. People stayed away to begin with, thinking nothing would be the same without Grandpa, but customers are trickling back.'

'They are learning you're up to it. One or two may even have heard good things about me.'

'Don't bank on that, Uncle Marcus! Yet again, we failed to shift that two-handed urn with the centaurs battling, but that's been around for over a year; the artwork's crap and people are bored with the subject. I'm going to organise fake bidders next time. See if we can force some interest.'

'Geminus didn't really want to sell that pot,' I said. 'It hung on so long, he grew fond of it.'

Young Gaius shook his head like a Greek sage. 'There's no scope for sentiment in this business!' Then, to my surprise, he asked shyly whether Helena and I were getting over the baby, and complimented me on my handling of Pa's funeral and memorial dinner.

Business over, I called in a passing peddler, bought Gaius a flatbread stuffed with chickpeas, and left him to it.

I sauntered back towards the centre of town, passing the Theatre of Balbus and the Porticus of Octavia as if I had no clear idea where I was going. I had made up my mind, however. I turned away from the river, then climbed up to the Palatine via the Clivus Victoriae. I gained entrance by telling the guards I needed to see Claudius Laeta. But I was going to see Momus.

23

'Falco! You cack-handed, two-timing, pompous backstairs bastard—seems a century since I laid eyes on your ugly bum-crack!' Momus represented the refined element of the Palatine.

He was sprawling on a bench like a big blob of sea anemone, one that had let itself go. Even his headlice were low-grade. He had a paper of nuts lying next to him, but was too lethargic to dip in and munch. 'Torpor' would have been his cognomen, had he been refined enough to want his entitlement to three names.

Thinking about imperial freedmen, as I was for the case, I asked him what family name he used. Momus gave me a wide shrug, astonished anybody asked that question. He was so informal he had never bothered to work out his nomen.

'Who was on the throne when you got your cap of liberty?'

'Some useless pervert.'

'Sounds like Nero.'

'Probably the Divine Claudius.' Momus made 'Divine' sound like an obscenity, which in the case of that old duffer Claudius it traditionally was.

I leaned on a wall, as far away from his body odour as I could get without retreating into the corridor. There was nowhere to sit. Most people who came to see Momus were slaves he was brutalising. He didn't offer them a stool for beatings and buggery. He might be as low as a palace officer could get, but he was one level up from them so he took the traditional seat of power while they cringed in whatever desperate position he chose for them and waited for their punishment.

'So were you a contemporary of an obnoxious bunch of imperial freedmen called the Claudii? Most live in the Pontine Marshes, though I'm told they have connections with Rome.'

Momus took a long time rubbing his bleary eyes, then surprisingly he said no.

I said quietly, 'I thought you were famous for knowing the entire *familia*?'

He pulled a face. He was not intending to help me. That was unusual. Normally our loathing of Anacrites and our distrust of Laeta made us allies.

'Somebody knows them,' I said. '*Somebody* is rumoured to protect them.'

'Not me, Falco.'

'No, I never saw you as the patron type!' Even just talking to Momus always made me feel I had let down my own moral standards. I may be an informer but I do have some.

Momus laughed, but no ice was broken in his reception of my joke.

'Half the towns in Latium are shit-scared of treading on their nasty toes,' I told him. 'And you claim you don't know them? Leaving me no choice, old crony, but to suppose you must be shit-scared of this *somebody* who watches over them.'

Momus did not move a muscle.

I blew out my cheeks slowly, as if impressed by the scale of the problem. That was easy. I was genuinely marvelling. Momus liked to be outspoken. His silence was not part of his routine sea-anemone lolling. If he had had tentacles, he would have stopped waving them as soon as I mentioned the Claudii. Momus was taking a lot of trouble to show no reaction, but his grime-engrained skin acquired extra sheen. I could have wiped his greasy, sweating face and then oiled a wheel-axle with the rag.

Eventually he growled, 'Don't mess with this, Falco. You're too young and sweet.'

He was being ironic, but the warning had a note of real concern. I thanked him for the advice and took myself to see Laeta.

I knew he would be there. In the first place, he enjoyed pretending his burden of work was terrible—and in the second, he really was the most important scroll-bug in the imperial bureaux. At this time in the summer, the betting was that all three of his masters, Vespasian and both his sons, were taking their ease at some family villa, perhaps out in the Sabine hills where they originated. When that happened, Claudius Laeta was left at the Palatine to run the Empire smoothly. Few people ever noticed that power was temporarily in his hands.

As an informal gesture to the fact that it was after business hours, Laeta had a singer intoning an epode. The musician was heavily emphasising the iambic trimeters and dimeters in a long, slow, lugubrious piece that used the style aficionados call affected archaism. It was music you could never dance to, nor would it lull you to sleep, raise your spirits or encourage a fine-featured woman to sleep with you. Laeta had one finger placed against his brow to indicate subconscious delight. I wondered why men who listen to such torture always think themselves so superior.

The Dorian dirge subsided. Laeta had made an almost imperceptible gesture, so the singer left. Going voluntarily saved him having me drag him outside and bind him by his tasselled wristbands to a fast-moving cart.

'I'm glad you dropped by, Falco.' Always a bad start.

Laeta then told me that Anacrites was back from whatever mission the Emperor had let him loose to ruin. Instead of waiting for more orders, the Chief Spy had taken it upon himself to follow up the Modestus case. 'I have informed Marcus Rubella he can drop the investigation,' said Laeta, barely looking up from his deskful of documents.

'That stinks!'

'It's a done deal, Falco.'

'You think Anacrites is fit for this?' I demanded.

'Of course not.' At this point, Laeta did look up and meet my eyes. His were clear, cynical and unlikely to be swayed by protests. 'Think yourself lucky, Falco. Tell your vigiles friend too. This case may go very mouldy before it's over. If the spy thinks he wants the job, that's typical of his misjudgement—but let him go ahead and bungle it. We can all watch Anacrites get nasty black squid ink down one of those barley-coloured tunics he insists on wearing.'

Laeta always wore white. Classic. Expensive and aristocratic. By implication incorruptible—though I had always assumed he was very corrupt indeed.

I dropped my voice. 'What's going on, Laeta?'

He laid down his pen and leaned his chin on his hands. 'Nothing, Falco.'

I folded my arms. 'I can spot official lying. You can tell me the truth. I have the Emperor's confidence. I thought you and I worked from the same order sheet.'

'I am sure we do.' Claudius Laeta gave me the look some bureaucrats use. It made no denial of a cover-up and seemed to assume I knew everything he did. I felt I could see distaste for whatever game Anacrites was playing.

'I thought this was a confidential enquiry. How did Anacrites even find out about it?'

'Your crony Petronius put in a claim for a replacement ox and cart. An auditor strolled up the corridor and mentioned it to the spy.'

'Oh no! I wonder what that was worth? I do see the Treasury will quibble—but the adjudicators are perfectly capable of turning down expenses without bringing in Anacrites. It's nothing to do with him.'

Laeta for once allowed himself to be rude about another official:

'You know how he works. He spends most of his time spying on his colleagues rather than enemies of the state.'

'Shall I challenge him on this?' I asked.

'I advise against.'

'Why?'

Laeta's eyes were keen and oddly sympathetic. 'Take a steer from a friend. Anacrites is always dangerous. If he really feels he wants this work, stand back.'

'That's not my style.'

Laeta leaned back with the palms of his hands on the edge of his table. 'I know it's not, Falco. That's why I am taking the trouble, out of respect for your qualities, to say, just let this one go.'

I thanked him for his concern, though I did not understand it. Then I left his office wondering what exactly the Chief Spy could find fascinating in a bunch of belligerent marshfrogs killing a neighbour in a feud about a boundary fence.

My style was, as Laeta may have realised, to march straight up the corridor to Anacrites' office, intending to ask him.

Once again he was absent.

Two of his men were there this time, eating folded flatbreads. I had seen them before. I reckoned they were brothers, and for no logical reason I had placed them as Melitans. Anacrites had had these idiots watching my house last December. I was looking after a state prisoner temporarily and, in his own tiresome style, he tried muscling in. Just like this, really. If he thought I was being noticed by the Palace, he could never leave me alone.

The legmen had taken over his room as if this was their base, where they were allowed to eat their supper before they were sent out on their next assignment. One was actually sitting in the seat Anacrites normally used. Even spies have to eat. That included the unfortunates Anacrites employed. Any over-familiarity was his problem.

When I looked in, the pair straightened up slightly; they rearranged their foreign-looking features so they seemed helpful, though neither bothered to ask what I wanted. They made vague attempts to hide their vegetable turnovers until they saw I didn't give a damn.

'He's out?'

They nodded. One raised his bread two inches as an affirmative. I didn't ask where he had gone, so they did not need to tell me. They knew who I was. I wondered whether they guessed why I wanted to talk to Anacrites.

He was obsessively secretive, too close to make a good commander. His men probably had no idea what he was up to. That was the problem with him: half the time he didn't know what he was doing himself.

24

For some reason, when I left the Palace, the night seemed full of threats and unhappiness. Rome had its seamy side. I seemed more aware of it tonight. I noticed caterwauling and unhappy cries, both near and distant; there seemed to be a bad smell everywhere, as if while I was in the Palace some major disaster with the drains had occurred. Darkness insinuated lower areas, creating pools of menace where there ought to be streets. Monuments that stood amidst a few lights looked cold and forbidding instead of familiar.

Back at my house, however, there was peace. The children were in bed, perhaps even asleep. Albia was in her room, plotting against Aelianus. The lamplight was mellow, there was food and drink on a side table, a sleepy Nux thumped her tail at my appearance then went straight back to snoring in her happy doggy dreams.

I sat sideways on a reading-couch with a cup of wine in one fist, not even drinking yet. Helena curled up beside me. She was sweet-scented from the baths and now wearing an old, comfortable red gown, no jewellery, with her hair loose. She put a light rug over her bare feet for comfort, wriggling her toes. I looked for signs that her grief for the baby was diminishing; she allowed my scrutiny, though with pinched lips as though she would flare up if I asked the wrong question. But then she took my hand; she was judging my progress back to normality just as I assessed hers. I too concealed my feelings, as I rubbed my thumb over the silver ring on her third finger.

Once we both relaxed, I told her about being pushed to and fro at the Palace. Sharing news was our habit, always had been. I passed on what Laeta and Momus had said, while Helena at first listened. When I ran out of details and sipped my wine slowly, she spoke up.

'Anacrites has commandeered the job because he is jealous, perennially jealous of you—and of your friendship with Petronius. He thinks you have a better life than him. He is afraid you may jostle him aside and gain favours from the Emperor. He wants what you have.'

'I don't see it.' I put down the winecup; Helena reached over and sipped thoughtfully, before replacing the cup. I half smiled but kept talking. 'Sweetheart, he has status; from what I hear, he has money too. Jupiter knows how he got there, but he's top man in intelligence. Even that time he took out of action with his head wound never seemed to affect his position. He has a secure career, salaried and pensioned, very close to Vespasian and Titus—whereas I'm a luckless freelance.'

'He envies your freedom,' Helena disagreed. 'It may be why he tries to sabotage your cases. He realises your talent, hates how you can choose to accept or refuse work. Most of all, Marcus, he longs for you to be his friend. He *loved* working with you on the Census—' He drove me mad on it. 'But he's like an angry young brother, jumping up and down to get your attention.' She had two younger brothers. 'He has done this before to you and Petro. So, treat him like a tiresome brother; just ignore it.'

I went with the simile. 'I don't want the nasty little menace to have a fit and smash my toys!'

'Well, keep your toys on a high shelf, Marcus.'

It was late. We were tired, not exhausted but not yet ready to go up to bed. In a family household, this was a rare moment of quiet. We stayed hand in hand, savouring the situation, re-establishing our strong partnership after a period of upset and absence. Helena caressed my cheek with her free hand; I bent and gently kissed her wrist. We were a man and his wife, at home in private, enjoying one another's presence. Nothing really intimate was occurring—or not yet—but the last thing we wanted was an interruption. So that was when the bastard came, of course.

I mean, Anacrites.

I was dimly aware of noises downstairs—not urgent, no cause for us to involve ourselves. Then a slave I did not remember owning knocked and came in. This was what it meant to be wealthy: total strangers were living in my house, knew who I was, addressed me humbly as their master.

'Sir, will you receive a visitor?'

The visitor must have had a suspicion what my answer would be. He followed the lad and rudely pushed in after him. 'I do apologise for calling so late—I just heard about your father, Marcus. I came immediately!'

Helena murmured, 'Thank you,' to the young slave, so he would know we saw it was not his fault. He slipped away. She and I remained in position just long enough to let anyone less crass than the spy see he was intruding. He had probably come from the office; he even looked around as if hoping for a titbit tray. Failing a guest went against our idea of hospitality, but like stoics we refused to offer him refreshments.

I stood up, sighing openly. A mistake, because it allowed Anacrites to bound right up, grasping my hands in his. I wanted to snatch back my paws, apply them round his beautifully barbered neck and strangle him; but we were standing on an attractive rag rug, and I was reluctant to defile it with his corpse.

'Ah, Marcus, I am *so* sorry for your loss!' He let go of me and turned to Helena who had stayed on the couch out of his reach. 'How is this poor fellow doing?' His voice was doleful with sympathy.

Helena sighed glumly. 'He is managing. The money helps.'

Anacrites took a second to catch on. 'You two! You joke about absolutely everything.'

'Graveyard humour,' I assured him, resuming my place beside Helena. 'A grimace in the teeth of Fate, to hide our desolation. Though as my smart wife says—Geminus left me a stupefying legacy.' I bet Anacrites had made sure he knew that before he came. 'Apart from the inconvenience of probate, rummaging through his coffers does assuage the grief.'

Anacrites took a seat opposite, though we had not invited him to do so. He leaned forwards, elbows on his knees. He was still addressing me with the unbearable earnestness people ladle like sweet sauce over the bereaved. 'I am afraid I never really knew your father.'

'He kept out of the way of people like you.' This was not always true. Once, Pa had thought Anacrites was sniffing too closely around my mother like a gigolo—an idea so unbelievable we had all believed it at the time. My outraged father, taking it personally, rushed to the Palace and took a swipe at the spy. I was there and witnessed the crazy fist-swinging. Anacrites seemed to have forgotten. Perhaps the bad head wound a few years ago excused selective memory loss. It did not, however, excuse anything else he did.

'And how is your dear mother?' He had been Ma's lodger for a time. Though she was so shrewd in many things, she thought he was wonderful. He in turn spoke of her with veneration. He knew it made me sick.

'Junilla Tacita bears her loss with fortitude,' Helena interposed gravely. Anacrites looked at her, grateful to encounter a normal platitude. 'She only gloats in the afternoon; she says in the mornings she's too busy around the house to taunt his ghost.'

I smiled gently at the spy's discomfiture.

He wore an umber-coloured tunic, his idea of sophisticated camouflage. His skin looked strangely plump and smooth; he must have come from the baths. With that oiled hair and a straight bearing, he could be called personable; well, by a woman of the night, with time on her hands and bills to pay. I doubted that any decent woman ever looked at him, not that I had seen him seeking female company since Maia dumped him. I was convinced he had no friends.

He was a strange mixture of competence and ineptitude. Undoubtedly intelligent, he was an able public speaker; I had heard him spout excuses like any clerk covering up his failures. There was no need for him to endure a tiny office and low-grade agents; his was a high public position, attached to the Praetorians; he could have conjured up a decent budget if he had applied himself.

His next foray was to say to Helena, 'I hear your brother is back from Athens—and married! Wasn't that unexpected?'

This was typical. Laeta had said Anacrites only returned to Rome three days ago, yet he had already discovered private facts about my family and me. He pressed too close. If I complained it would sound paranoid, yet I knew Helena saw why I loathed him.

'Who told you that?' She sat up abruptly.

'Oh it's my job to know everything,' Anacrites boasted, giving her a significant smile.

'Surely you should only watch the Emperor's enemies?' Helena retaliated.

'Helena Justina, you were pregnant!' Anacrites exclaimed, wide-eyed, as if it had only just struck him. 'Has the happy event occurred?'

'Our baby died.' I bet the bastard knew that too.

'Oh my dears! Again, I am *so* sorry . . . Was it a boy?'

Helena bridled visibly. 'What does that matter? Any healthy child would have pleased us; any lost child is our tragedy.'

'Such a waste—'

'Don't upset yourself over our private troubles,' Helena said coldly. He had pushed her too far. 'I suppose,' she jibed, 'a man in your position does not know what it is to have family? You must always have looked intelligent. When some unknown slave girl bore you, were you taken up as soon as that was spotted, to be regimented in a soulless stylus-school?'

Anacrites relied on pretending we were all best friends; otherwise, I fancied there might have been real venom in his expression. 'As you say, they could spot potential. I was indeed favoured with government training from a young age,' he replied in a quiet voice. Helena refused to show shame. 'I knew my alphabet at three, Helena—both in Latin and Greek.'

Though she did not remark on it, Helena had already taught our

Julia both alphabets, plus how to write her name in ruled lines. Perhaps she relaxed slightly, however. For one thing, Helena always enjoyed sparring. 'And what else did they teach you?'

'Self-reliance and perseverance.'

'Is that enough for the work you do now?'

'It goes a long way.'

'Do you have a conscience, Anacrites?'

'Does Falco?' he countered.

'Oh yes,' replied Helena Justina sternly. 'He leaves home with it daily, along with his boots and his notebook. That is why,' she said, fixing him with a steady gaze, 'Marcus was so interested in working on the Julius Modestus case.'

'Modestus?' Anacrites' bafflement seemed genuine.

'Compulsory letter-writer,' I put in. 'Dealer from Antium. Found stone dead in a tomb—hands cut off and hideous rites committed— after a squabble with some marsh-waders known as the Claudii.'

I thought Anacrites twitched. 'Oh you were involved with that?' It was disingenuous; he knew it, and looked shifty. 'I pulled back the case from Laeta. He should never have been involved. In fact, I'm glad I've seen you tonight, Falco. I need a handover review. Shall we say mid-morning tomorrow at my office? Bring your vigiles friend.'

So not only was he pinching our case from Petro and me, the un-mitigated bastard wanted to pick our brains to help him solve it.

'Petronius Longus works the night shift,' I said curtly. 'He needs his mornings for sleep. You can have us at the start of the evening, Anacrites, or go begging.'

That would give us two time to liaise first.

'As you wish,' responded the spy; he managed to make out I was surly and unreasonable, while he was all sweetness and toleration.

I was burning with frustration, but just then the door of the room crashed open and in flew Albia. 'I heard there was a visitor. Oh!' She must have been hoping for Aelianus.

'This is Tiberius Claudius Anacrites, the Emperor's chief of intel-ligence,' Helena told her, using over-formality to rile him. 'You met him at Saturnalia.'

'Oh yes.' A friend of her parents: Albia lost interest.

'Why Falco,' the spy then exclaimed. 'Your foster-daughter is growing into a fine young lady!' This was the kind of indefinable threat he had taken to throwing at me. If I ever caught him so much as saying good morning to Albia unsupervised, I would truss him with poultry string and pay to have him cooked in a baker's oven. By the slow-roast method.

'Flavia Albia has led a sheltered life and is extremely shy.' Helena always supported the girl, though sometimes gently teased her. 'But she will be a delicate ornament to womanhood any day now.'

'Well,' Anacrites answered silkily, 'you must bring Flavia Albia with you—oh how silly; I didn't mention this—we have so much catching up to do! I absolutely insist you come to my house for dinner. The formal invitation will be here the minute I can make arrangements.'

I did not bother to decline. But King Mithridates of Pontus had the right idea: the only way I would eat at the spy's house was if I had first spent three months taking antidotes against all known poisons.

'I thought I might lash out on a Trojan hog,' Anacrites confided in Albia, as if they had been close friends for years. He was a man with poor social skills trying to sound big in front of a young girl he thought would be easily impressed; she of course stared at him as if he was crazy. Then she flounced off, slamming the door behind her so hard the pantiles on our roof must be in danger.

As soon as Anacrites had gone, Albia reappeared. 'What is a Trojan hog?'

Helena was dousing lamps as we made our way to bed. 'Exhibit cookery. Only a show-off would serve it. On the principle of the Trojan horse, it carries a secret cargo. A whole pig is cooked then slashed open suddenly at table, so the contents spew out everywhere; the guests think they are being bombarded with raw entrails. The innards are usually sausages.'

Albia considered. 'Sounds brilliant. We had better go to that!'

I groaned.

25

Petronius and I walked into the Palace next evening side by side. We were silent, our tread measured, both outwardly impassive. Anacrites had played this trick on us before. It didn't work then—trust him to repeat the same manoeuvre.

As we neared his office, one of the pair I called the Melitan Brothers came out. When the man drew level, we made space for him to pass us. Afterwards we both stopped, pivoted on our boot heels and stared after him. He managed to keep looking ahead all the way to the end of the corridor, but could not help glancing back from the corner. Petro and I just stood there, watching him. He nipped away out of sight, ducking his head anxiously.

We strode into Anacrites' room without knocking. As Petronius opened the door, he said loudly, 'Standards are slacker than ever. He looks too foreign to be scuttling about like a rat, so near the Emperor—if I had a Palatine remit, I'd make him prove citizenship—or he'd find himself in a neck-collar.'

'Who's your runt?' I demanded of Anacrites. He had been lounging in his usual pose, with his boots—a rather fine pair of russet calfskins—on his desk. He swung rapidly upright, knocking over an inkwell, while his clerk sniggered.

'One of my men—' Petronius guffawed at that, while I winced, miming pity. Anacrites mopped ink, thoroughly flustered. 'Thank you, Phileros!' That was a hint for the clerk, a puffy, overweight Delian slave, to make himself scarce so the spy could talk to us confidentially.

I pretended to think it was an order to fetch refreshments. 'Mine's an almond tart, Petronius likes raisin cakes. No cinnamon.'

Petro smacked his chops. 'I'm ready for that! I'll just have mulsum with it, not warmed too much, double honey. Falco takes wine and water, served in two beakers if they run to it.'

'Hold the spice.' I steered Phileros on his way as if the rest of us needed to get on. The clerk left, and Petronius made a point of closing the door.

It was a small room, and now there were three of us filling it. Petro and I took over. He was a large character, with substantial thighs and shoulders; Anacrites began to feel cramped. If he looked directly at one of us, the other went out of eyeshot, probably making rude hand gestures. I seized the clerk's stool, shoving all his work aside, none too gently.

Then we sat still, with our hands clasped, like ten-year-old girls waiting for a story. 'You first!' ordered Petronius.

Anacrites was beaten. He abandoned any attempt to follow his own agenda. We were all supposed to be colleagues; he could not force us to play straight with him.

'I have read the scrolls—' he started. Petro and I glanced at each other, grimacing as if only a maniac ever read the case papers, let alone relied on them. 'Now I need you to sum up your findings.'

'*Findings!*' said Petronius to me. 'That's a sophisticated new concept.'

Anacrites was almost pleading with us to settle down.

Abruptly, we became fully professional. We had agreed in advance we would give him no excuse to say we had been uncooperative. I briskly set out that I had encountered Modestus' disappearance through his business deal with my father. I did not mention his nephew, Silanus. Why should I? He was neither a victim nor a suspect.

Petro described the discovery of the corpse and its identification from the letter Modestus was carrying. He spoke in a crisp voice, using vigiles vocabulary. He gave an account of our visit to the Claudii; how we had interviewed Probus; searched the area; found nothing.

'What were you planning next?' asked Anacrites.

'Since the next move is all yours, what do you think?' snapped Petro tetchily.

Anacrites ignored the question. 'Do you have any other leads?'

Petronius shrugged. 'No. We have to sit back and wait until another corpse turns up.'

Anacrites applied a sombre expression, which we dutifully mirrored.

'Look, you can leave this all to me now. I can handle it.' Time would show if that was right. He closed the meeting. 'I hope you two stalwarts don't feel I took your case away.' We refused to look sore.

'Oh, I have plenty to do chasing tunic-thieves at the baths,' sneered Petronius.

'Well, this isn't quite on that level . . .'

'Isn't it?'

Anacrites then brought in the ploy he'd tried on me last night: he mentioned his plans for a dinner party, inviting Petronius too. 'I had such a wonderful time when Falco and Helena entertained me at Saturnalia—' Saturnalia may be a time for patching up feuds, but believe me, I was pushed into that hideous arrangement. 'Such a glorious family atmosphere . . . Have you eaten with them at their house, Lucius Petronius?' Of course he had! He was my best friend, living with my best sister. 'I feel it's time I issued some invitations in return . . .'

Previously noncommittal, Petronius Longus straightened up. He looked the spy directly in his weird eyes, which were almost two-toned, one shifty grey, one browner—and neither to be trusted. He stood up, placed both fists on the spy's table and leaned across, full of menace. 'I live with Maia Favonia,' my pal declared heavily. 'I know what you did to her. So no thanks!'

He strode out.

'Oh dear! I was hoping to smooth over any unpleasantness, Falco!' Anacrites was ghastly when he whined.

'Not possible,' I told him with a sneer, then I followed Petro from the room.

Outside, Phileros was hanging about nervously with such an enormous tray of confectionery his stretched arms could hardly hold it. Petronius cared about the poor, since he so often had cause to arrest them. He had ascertained it was all paid for out of the spy's petty cash, not the shabby clerk's own pocket. So we swept up as many cakes as we could carry, and took them away with us.

We gave them to a tramp, of course. Even if they were not dosed with aconite, to eat anything provided by Anacrites would have choked us.

There was no chance we would allow Anacrites to have our case. Earlier in the day Petronius and I had agreed on the same system as the last time he tried muscling in. We would proceed as normal. We would simply keep out of the spy's view. Once we solved the case, we would report to Laeta.

According to Petro, he had Rubella's support. I did not press for details.

Although we had implied to Anacrites we had reached a dead end, we had plenty of ideas. Petronius had issued an all-cohorts notice to look out for the runaway slave called Syrus, the one who had worked for Modestus and Primilla then was passed on to the butcher by their nephew. Petro's men visited the other cohorts to inspect any slaves they had found roaming. There was another alert too: for the missing woman, Livia Primilla, or more likely her body.

It was too risky to have official warrants for Nobilis or any other Claudii; Anacrites was liable to hear about it. Nonetheless, efforts were being made to trace the couple who were supposed to work in

Rome, using word of mouth among the vigiles. There was also a port watch for Nobilis, arranged through the Customs service and the vigiles out-station at Ostia. Meanwhile Petronius was having his clerk go through the official records of undesirables, looking for members of the family listed in Rome. If the two called Pius and Virtus had become astrologers or joined a weird religious cult, that could turn them up.

Rubella would not permit Petronius to leave Rome again, so I was going back to Antium: I would be looking for the estranged wife of Claudius Nobilis, hoping to hear about life on the inside with the Pontine freedmen.

First, came an assignment close to home. When I returned, Helena met me at the door.

'Marcus, you have to do something and it must be now, while Petronius is at the station house. Your sister sent a message; she sounds upset—'

'What's up?'

'Maia needs to see you. She doesn't want Lucius told, because he will be too angry. Maia had an unwelcome visitor. Anacrites went to see her.'

Never mind Lucius Petronius. I was damned angry myself.

26

My sister Maia Favonia had more locks on her door than most people. She had never recovered from coming home one day a couple of years ago to find everything in her home destroyed and a child's doll nailed up where the knocker had been. Anacrites left no calling card. But he had been haunting her neighbourhood after she split from him; she knew who had given her the warning.

I had moved her out the same night. I took her away with us on a trip to Britain and by the time she came back, she and Petronius Longus were lovers; her children, a bright bunch, had democratically elected that friendly vagabond as their stepfather. Maia took a new apartment, closer to Ma's building. Petro moved in. The children preened. Everything settled down. Even so, Maia installed a tumbler lock and a set of large bolts, and she never opened the door after dark unless she knew who was outside. She had been fearless, happy and sociable. Terror left its marks. Maia would never get over what the spy had done.

Petronius and I had sworn an oath together. One day we would exact retribution.

They lived, as most city people did, in a modest apartment. One floor up, a communal well in the courtyard, a small set of rooms to arrange as they liked. Petro, who was handy with a hammer, had fixed the place up in shipshape style. Maia had always had her own casual glamour and, given her work for Pa at the Saepta, she furnished it with dash. Our mother's house centred on its kitchen and a table where onions were always being chopped; Helena and I liked to relax in private in a room where we read together. Any house where Maia lived had a balcony as its heart. There she kept a trough of plants that could survive breezes and offhand treatment, plus battered lounging chairs with mounds of well-squashed cushions, between which was the bronze tripod where she served a constant supply of nuts and raisin cake.

I wondered if Anacrites had been allowed into that insiders' sanctum this time. He knew how things worked. The damage to Maia's previous much-loved sun terrace, when he trashed her place, had been particularly vile.

Helena had come with me tonight. Maia greeted her with a sniff. 'Oh he's brought a woman to worm out all the secrets, has he? You think I'll be softened up by girls' chat?'

Helena gave an easy-going laugh. 'I'll sit with the children.' We had glimpsed them, doing schoolwork in subdued silence: Maia's four, who ranged from six to thirteen, plus Petronilla, Petro's girl, who lived here most of the time now because her mother had a new boyfriend. Petronilla had condemned Silvia's latest conquest as 'a lump of mouldy dough'. She was eleven and already scathing. So far, Petro was still her hero, though he expected daddy's little girl to begin disparaging him any day now.

A shadow darkened Maia's face. 'Yes,' she said urgently. 'Yes, Helena. Do that.' So the children knew Anacrites had been here, and they needed comfort.

I was shepherded to the balcony. Maia closed the folding doors behind us. We sat together, in our usual positions.

'Right. You had a visitation. Tell me.'

Now we were private, I could see how badly Maia was shaken. 'I don't know what he wanted. Why now, Marcus?'

'What did he *say* he wanted?'

'Explaining is not his style, brother.'

I lay back and breathed slowly. Around us were the noises of a domestic district at nightfall. Here on the Aventine, there was always a sense of being high above the city and slightly aside of the centre. Occasional sounds of traffic and trumpets came from a very great distance. Closer to, owls hooted from the gilded roof trees of very old temples. There were all the normal wafts of grilled fish and panfried garlic, the rumpus of angry women berating tipsy men, the weary wails of sick or unhappy children. But this was our hill, the hill where Maia and I grew up. It was a place of augury, foliage gods and slaves' liberation. It was where Cacus the hideous caveman once lived and where the poets' association traipsed about singing silly odes. For us the flavours were subtly distinct from every other Rome region.

'Better start at the beginning,' I told Maia in a quiet voice.

'He came this morning.'

'If I am to evaluate what this bastard is really up to,' I said quietly, 'then start *right* at the beginning.'

Maia was silent. I gazed across at her. Normally you think of your sister as she was at eighteen. Tonight, by the flicker of a pottery lamp, every year was etched on her. I was thirty-six; Maia was two years younger. She had survived a wearisome marriage, births, the death of one daughter, a cruel widowhood and ensuing financial hardship, then a couple of crazy dalliances. There were at least a couple; I was her brother, what would I know? Her worst mistake was when she let Anacrites home in on her.

'You never really told us: was it serious?'

'Not for me.' For once Maia was so unnerved she opened up. 'I met him, you know, after he was hurt and you took him to Mother's to recuperate.' Maia was the kind of daughter who was always popping into Ma's house to share a cabbage—keeping an eye on the old tyrant. 'After Famia died, Anacrites turned up one day. He treated me respectfully—that was a change after Famia using me as a boot scraper for all those years . . .'

'You liked him?'

'Why not? He was well dressed, well spoken, well set up in an official position—'

'Did he tell you about his work?'

'He told me what it was. He never discussed details . . . I was ready,' Maia admitted. 'Ready for a fling.'

I could not resist my next question. Be honest, legate, you would have begged to know too: 'Good lover?' Maia merely stared at me. I cleared my throat and played responsible. 'You made it clear all along that you wanted nothing permanent?'

'At first it could have gone anywhere.' I controlled a shudder. 'But I soon felt he was pressing too close. There was something about him,' Maia mused. 'Something just not right.'

'He's a creep. You felt it.'

'I suppose so.'

'Instinct.'

'I certainly see him as a creep now.'

'I don't understand. I *never* understood why you had anything to do with him, Maia.'

'I told you. He comes over well when he wants. The man had had a terrible head injury, so I thought any oddness was because of the damage.'

'Well, I like to be fair—only I knew Anacrites long before he had his skull bashed in by some bent Spanish oil producers. He was sinister from the start. I've always thought,' I told Maia, 'the head wound only made his character more visible. He's a snake. Untrustworthy, obnoxious, poisonous.'

Maia said nothing. I did not insist. I never wanted to push her into admitting she had been fooled.

'We had nothing in common,' she said in a depressed voice. 'As soon as I told him there was no future, I felt so relieved it was over—' So true. Women are not sentimentalists. I remembered how she had immediately begun flirting with Petronius, who happened to be available.

'Anacrites would not believe that we were finished—then he turned vindictive. You know the rest, Marcus. Don't make me go over it.'

'No, no,' I reassured her. He had hung about, morosely stalking her, until the fateful day he had her home destroyed. I could see my sister growing tense as she tried to avoid those memories. 'Just tell me, what happened today, Maia?'

'For some reason, I opened the door—I don't know why. He hadn't knocked. There he was—standing in the passage, right outside. I was completely shocked. How long had he been out there? He got inside before I caught my breath.'

'Then what?'

'He kept pretending everything was normal. It was just a social call.'

'Was he unpleasant?'

'No. Marcus, I hadn't seen him, not to talk to, since I gave him his marching orders.'

'Were you scared?'

'I was worried Lucius would come home. There would have been a horrendous row. Anyway, I pretended he was there, asleep indoors, so I shooed the spy away. You know Anacrites—I thought he probably realised I was lying.'

'So what did he say?'

'That was the funny thing.' Maia frowned. 'He tried small talk—not that he knows how to do it. His conversation is zero. That was one reason I couldn't continue with him. After Famia, I needed a man who would respond if *I* talked to *him*.'

I laughed. 'Oh, you get banter from Lucius Petronius?'

'He has his hidden side; don't all of you!' scoffed Maia. 'I was about to mention the *incident,* when Anacrites actually brought the subject up himself. Apologised. According to him it was "an administrative mistake". Then he pleaded his injury, said he couldn't remember properly. He tried to make me sorry for him by telling me how tired he had been, how he had to cover that up so he didn't lose his job, how he had lost years of his life through being bludgeoned . . . Anyway— and this is what I wanted to tell you, Marcus—Anacrites seemed mainly interested in that case he's taken off you,' said Maia. 'The warty melon kept trying to extract from me just what you and Lucius have found out.'

'And you said . . . ?'

'I had nothing to tell him. You know Lucius.'

Petronius never believed in discussing his work with his women-folk. Anacrites should have approached Helena instead—she knew everything; not that she would break my confidence. He was too scared of her to attempt it, of course.

Anacrites had upset my sister for nothing. He had angered me too—and if Petro heard about this, he would be livid.

Maia and I agreed that Petronius had better not be told.

27

With Petronius stuck in Rome, grounded by his tribune, I made another trip to the coast.

This time Helena came with me. I took her to see Pa's maritime villa. I brought Nux as well, since my household was completely ruled by the dog. Luckily tearing through the pinewoods and racing along the beach suited her just fine. Nux was prepared to allow us to keep this wonderful place.

Helena also approved, so we spent several days discussing how to arrange things to suit us, turning the house into a seaside family home rather than a businessman's retreat. While we were working, some of the slaves reported a man hanging around in the woods. He was a stranger to them, but from their description, I wondered if it was one of Anacrites' agents.

We knew a woman who lived with the priestesses at a temple in Ardea. Driving off with a deal of commotion, Helena went to visit her. I stayed at the villa; I made myself visible shifting furniture and artwork to outbuildings, then spent time loafing on a daybed on the shore while the dog brought driftwood to me. The mysterious sightings stopped. I hoped the agent had gone back to Rome to report that I was at the coast for domestic reasons.

It would be typical of Anacrites to waste time and resources. He should have been pursuing the Claudii. Instead he was obsessed with Petro and me. He knew us well; he knew we would try to pip him on the case. But that cut both ways. We understood him too.

On Helena's return we went down to Antium. We were enjoying our break from the children, and we did love to be out and about on enquiries. She was right: I must never stop doing this work—and when it was feasible I must always let her join in.

Helena was charmed by Antium, with its shabby, outdated grandeur. As always happens, there was nothing we wanted to see at the theatre, though old posters told us annoyingly that the week before Davos, our old contact who was Thalia's lover, had presented a play here. I would really have liked the chance for a chat with Davos!

Exploring more successfully than I had had time to do with Albia, Helena and I managed to find decent local baths then a cluster of fish restaurants. We lingered over a fine meal, eaten out of doors with grand sea views from the lofty precipice where Antium stood. This was always an hour when we liked to come together, to relax, review the day and reassert our partnership. With just the two of us tonight, it was like old times—that elusive condition married people should seek more often.

As we savoured the last of our wine, I took her hand and said, 'Everything will be all right.'

'The case, Marcus?'

'No, not that.'

Helena knew what I meant.

We enjoyed the evening a little longer, then I went to pay the bill and ask the restaurant-keeper where he bought his bread. His baker was not Vexus, Demetria's father; still, the man gave me suggestions where to start looking next day.

I went on my own, leaving Helena to take Nux around the forum.

It took me some tramping of narrow streets. Vexus worked at the edge of the city, with one small oven and not even his own grind-stone. It was a rough, depressed quarter with dusty streets where half-starved dogs lay on doorsteps like corpses. There were better shops, with a better clientele, in the smarter areas. This man, a short, thick-set ugly-faced fellow, baked heavy dark ryebread for the poor. He looked as if he had been miserable for the past thirty years. I began to understand how his daughter, growing up here without a future, might have settled for one of the Claudii. Even so, there seemed nothing basically wrong with the home she came from. Unless she had only one eye in the middle of her forehead yet failed to attract men with her novelty value, there was no reason for Claudius Nobilis to assume she was so desperate he could treat her badly.

I bought a bread roll to start the conversation; it never works. As soon as I said what I wanted, Vexus turned unhelpful. He had not overflowed with customer care to start with. I introduced myself and I might have been trying to sell him a silver-boxed ten-scroll set of Greek encyclopaedias. Used ones.

'Get lost.'

'I want to help your daughter.'

'Leave my daughter alone. She's not here and she's had enough trouble.'

'Can I see her?'

'No.'

'I don't blame you—but my enquiry won't harm her. Maybe I can get the Claudii off her back.'

'I'd like to see that!' Vexus implied I wasn't up to it.

'Will you at least tell me about Nobilis?'

'Mind your own business.'

'I'd like to—but those wastrels on the marsh have become the Emperor's business. I'm stuck with investigating. So let me guess: your girl married Nobilis when she was too young to know what she was doing—against your advice, no doubt? It went sour. He beat her.' I wondered if the father was violent too. He looked strong, but controlled. Still, men from boot-menders up to the consulship have been known to conceal their domestic brutality. 'Did they have any children?'

'No, thank Jove!'

'So Demetria decided to leave, but Nobilis would not let her go. She came home; he hated it. She found someone else, and he put a stop to that . . . Right?'

'Nothing to say.'

'Is she still with her new man?'

'No.'

'Nobilis put the scares on?'

'Half killed him.'

'In front of her?'

'That was the point, Falco!'

'So the new man caved in?'

'He got rid of her,' agreed her father bitterly.

A ghastly thought struck me. 'Don't say she went back to Nobilis?'

Vexus pressed his lips together in a thin line. 'Thankfully, I put a stop to that.'

'But she was so frightened, doing what Nobilis said became a possibility?'

'No,' said the baker, with heavy emphasis. 'She was so frightened it was *never* a possibility.'

That was all he would tell me. I left details for Demetria to contact me, if she would. No chance. I heard the tablet with my name on it thump into a trash bucket before I got back outside to the street.

I asked about Demetria around the neighbourhood. I met nothing but hostility. The atmosphere felt dangerous. I left before a riot could start.

28

I had another lead to follow: Petronius and I had been told by the waitress at Satricum that Claudius Nobilis worked for a corn dealer called Thamyris. He lived outside town. I took Nux and Helena and drove out to his place, a scattered set of barns and workshops off the coast road that went south.

Thamyris was a wide, squat, shabby typical countryman, in his sixties, wearing the usual rough tunic and a battered hat which he kept on even though when we arrived it was the lunch break. He and his men were gathered on benches, a peaceful group. They had mastered the art of making their working day revolve around the time they took off. Some were eating, some whittling. There was easy-going chat. Nux jumped from our cart and went to sit with them. She guessed correctly they would pet her and feed her titbits.

Nobody showed any curiosity about us. If we had wanted to buy grain we would have had to wait. The men stayed where they were and carried on enjoying their break; Thamyris stayed put and talked to us. Helena was allowed to sit on one of the benches, which a lad willingly swept of straw first, using the back of a fairly clean hand.

I explained what I wanted. Thamyris replied slowly and thoughtfully, as if he had answered these questions before. I asked him; he said he was always being consulted these days about Claudius Nobilis. For years the man had worked in this labour gang unremarked, but now the local authorities had a definite eye on him. It might have been awkward, had he not already taken himself off somewhere.

'Do you know where he's gone?'

'He said something about the family. Knowing what they are like, I kept my nose out of that.'

'So who else has been asking about him?'

'Men from Antium. A man from Rome.'

'I'm supposed to be the man from Rome—who was the other bastard?'

'Someone like you!' The grain dealer enjoyed the joke. I pressed him for details and came to the conclusion he had been visited by one of Anacrites' runners.

While I brooded on that, Helena changed the subject pleasantly: 'What was your impression of Nobilis when he worked for you?'

Thamyris summed up like an employer who noticed things: 'He did the work, though he didn't push himself.'

'Did he fit in? Was he one of the lads?' I asked.

'Yes and no. He never said much. If we were all sitting around like this, he would be with us. If we went out for a drink together in the evening, he would tag along. But he always tended to move off a little distance from the group.'

'Did he strike you as at all odd?' Helena then wondered.

'He had his obsessions. He liked talking about weapons. He collected spears and knives—nasty big ones. He seemed a bit too interested, if you understand me.'

I nodded. 'Trouble?'

'He never gave me any.'

'But he came with a reputation?'

'That I don't deny. People said he had been accused of thieving as a child, and I did hear that years ago a woman said he had raped her.' Thamyris seemed unconcerned. On the scale of country crime, rape tended to rank with shouting boo at chickens.

'So why do you think he left?' asked Helena. 'We heard he was "going to see his grandmother", whatever that means. What's the mystery?'

'A classic excuse.' Thamyris gave a laugh. It was the irritating kind that suggests someone knows a lot more than you do and intends to take a very long while revealing it. 'When people want time off.'

Helena asked, 'So what was up with him? Was he upset? Did he have a quarrel?'

'Better ask Costus.' Hearing his name, a corn cockle on another bench looked over. 'Nobilis!' called his boss in explanation.

'Oh him!' The younger man exclaimed dismissively; then he just went back to whittling.

I raised my eyebrows. Thamyris dropped his voice. 'Had a fling.' I showed that I still didn't get it. 'Costus.' The voice lowered even further. '*With Demetria!*'

I left Helena to draw out anything else she could from the dealer, and strolled across to Costus. He was a handsome chunk, who looked none too bright—in fact, if he had moved in on the wife of the violent Nobilis, he couldn't be. 'You're brave!'

'Stupid,' he conceded.

'I'm looking for your war wounds.' I could see no recent bruises, though his nose and one ear had a squashed look. Without a word, he pulled up the lower edge of his tunic to reveal a ferocious, fairly new knife scar running from below his hip to his belly-button. It was healed, but he must have been laid up and in some danger for a long time. I whistled through my teeth. '*Very* brave—and no wonder you seem subdued.' The Claudius women had told me it was three years since Demetria had left Nobilis. She must have already known Costus, through his working with her husband; were they lovers before, or was it only after she left that this young man had provided a consoling shoulder? 'Did Nobilis stop working here because his wife left him for you?'

Costus shook his head. 'She just left him. Then he went to pieces. He couldn't accept it.'

'You took her over afterwards?' A couple of his workmates were now watching us quietly. 'Do you know where she is now?'

'Nope.'

I bet he did.

Costus lied to me, and his comrades impassively watched him do it. They were all in the cover-up. But I had seen that his lunch consisted of a variety of items, which had been folded up for him in a very clean napkin. The package was not bought from a food-seller. Unless Costus was living with his doting old mother, he had other female company. He was a duffer, in my view, but a woman might find him good-looking.

I thumped him on the back in a rueful gesture. Just as I had with the baker, I wrote my name and other details on the back of an old bill from my pocket, which I placed on the wooden table. 'Better be off. We're heading back to Rome tonight. Probably stop over at Satricum to admire the scenery . . .'

Helena and I thanked everyone for their helpfulness, then we left. We took the road that went across the marshes, stopping at the inn for a night in Satricum as I had mentioned.

We hired a room, and took our time settling in. Easier said than done; the rooms here might be tolerable to men on tough missions where each needed to show the others he was hard. As a husband and wife we would need to hug together very tightly, to keep the bed-bugs out. We stuck it in the room as long as possible then went to find a meal.

I hid a smile when Helena told Januaria, 'I hear you made friends with Camillus Justinus!'

'He's a bit of all right!' agreed the waitress admiringly.

'My brother.'

Januaria was taken aback, but briefly. 'Is he married?'

'Oh yes. He has two little boys.'

The girl sniggered. 'I bet his wife curses him!'

How true.

We ate, then sat behind empty bowls regretting it. Night fell. We had almost given up when the gods smiled. Nux growled a warning in the back of her throat. Costus with the straight nose and biceps from the corn-supplies place sidled up out of nowhere. After shy negotiations, promises of confidentiality, and a small inducement in coinage, he wriggled back into the darkness, then reappeared, leading by the hand a woman we knew would be Demetria.

The baker's daughter was bolder than I expected. That probably meant her relationship with Nobilis had been tempestuous. Sometimes it works that way. Demetria had an ugly air of defiance, probably not caused by her past history. She came with it from the egg; her truculence was a symptom of social ineptitude. Had she ever gone to school, which I doubted, she would have been the awkward one on the back bench.

She was in her twenties, plain-faced with a snub nose, loose, flyaway hair and a faint sour smell as if somebody spilled milk on her several days ago. She wore a drab brown dress with one sleeve rolled and one to the cuff. It wasn't a fashion statement. She was too lazy to notice it. Her girdle was a rope that would have doubled as a bullock halter. She wore no jewellery. I guessed she had never worked, so had no money herself, and the men she chose were never generous.

It was all a waste of time, of course. Demetria admitted she still lived with Costus, pretty well in hiding. He had dragged her along tonight to see us hoping there would be money in it. She might have had enough spirit to run away from Nobilis, but on the whole Demetria's instincts were to do as she was told.

She would not talk about her marriage to Nobilis. She did not accuse him of violence against her, nor of battering her lover. Whatever pressures to keep quiet had been embedded in her by Claudius Nobilis, they were still firmly in place.

She had no idea what Nobilis got up to nowadays or where he had gone off to; she had no contact with the family—though when I said I had spoken to the other two women, she asked after Plotia and Byrta. She swore she knew nothing about what happened with Modestus and Primilla and since she hadn't lived with Nobilis then, it seemed reasonable. When I asked if she had ever had reason to suspect visitors were vanishing at the compound, she denied it.

'So why did you come to find me?' I demanded in exasperation.

That was when she came straight out and said Costus wanted her to beg for money. I could hardly complain. As Helena sniggered afterwards, offering facts for a cash reward was what I did as an informer.

I replied that when *I* made the offer, facts did exist.

There was one outcome. I asked Costus if he had been there when the man from Rome that Thamyris mentioned had turned up. According to Costus, it was a couple of days before. The description he gave of peculiar eyes, greased hair and smooth-talking sounded suspiciously familiar; it could almost be Anacrites himself.

'Did you hear what was said?'

'He took Thamyris out of earshot.'

'So you've no idea what he wanted?'

'Oh yes!' Costus seemed surprised anyone should think his employer would keep a city man's secret. 'He ordered the boss that if anyone came asking about Nobilis or the other Claudii, he was to say nothing.'

'Did he reinforce that order?'

Costus laughed bitterly. 'One or two suggestions. Just in case we forgot. Like—he'd close down the business, crucify Thamyris, sell his wife into a brothel, send us as slaves to the galleys and cut off our goolies first. Do you think he can do it?'

'Oh yes. It's the regular tactic used by the Praetorian Guards.'

29

On the journey home, Helena and I discussed the situation. Costus' story confirmed all the rumours about the Claudii having protection. Whoever was looking after their interests must be powerful, if they used the intelligence network to do their dirty work. Anacrites had not dared threaten Petro and me; even he was not that stupid. But he had no scruples about intimidating members of the public. He assumed we would never find out. For us, this signalled ulterior motives. He would know that if we once became intrigued, we would latch on to him like rat-dogs.

He had slipped up. I for one would not rest now until I uncovered his real interest—and Petronius was the same. I was all set to tear into the spy's office and threaten him with the same punishments he offered Thamyris—especially the part about castration. Maia must have the old veterinarian tools her dead husband used when he looked after the Greens' chariot horses; she would happily loan me his equine nut-crusher.

Helena urged me to play clever. 'Don't alert him, Marcus. Let's carry on as normal, pretend his agent wasn't spotted. I suggest when we get home, we see if he has invited us to dinner as he threatened. If he has, we should go along to his house, and sniff the air before you tackle him outright.'

'I would rather sniff a heifer's bum, after a week's diarrhoea.'

'Your rhetoric is so refined! . . . Listen to your wife's good advice.' Helena shook her finger warningly: 'Find out just whose fixer Anacrites is. Who wants him to protect these marsh-men's interests?'

'You are right, as ever.' It was time to address the point. 'It must all be to do with these Claudii having an imperial background,' I told Helena. 'I sensed that Laeta and Momus know what's going on. Some old influence has carried over . . . I don't believe it's the Emperor.' Vespasian had a few close cronies; his cabinet of private advisers were men like Helena's own father who had known him for years, long before he counted. He had never been regarded as someone who protected favourites.

'Nor Titus,' Helena decided. She and Titus viewed each other with admiration—more admiration than I liked. Still that just meant Titus Caesar was a fine judge of womanhood. Like his father, he was basically straight.

Helena was still ticking off candidates: 'Domitian's more questionable.' I had a feud with Domitian. He didn't scare me, but if he was in on this it was best to know. 'Of the great and powerful at the Palace,' Helena concluded, 'there would only be Claudius Laeta. He would not have invited you and Petro to investigate Modestus, if his interests lay in a cover-up.'

'Give the man credit—he knows we're too good!' I grinned at her.

'Laeta does not take stupid risks,' she corrected me coolly. Helena had a wonderful sense of humour, though little tolerance for silly beggars' backchat. 'He doesn't play with knives for a cheap thrill. He sees his role as protecting the administration, so the Empire can run smoothly.'

'So what do you think?'

'It could be some consul or ex-consul who has never crossed our path.'

'Most of them!' We kept out of general politics.

'I can ask my father. Not that he tends to know strong-arm thugs.

His friends in the Curia are benign. Men who read Plato over their lunch, philanthropists who think a commission should look into health issues among the urban poor.'

I said the Claudii were a health threat in Latium.

Helena was still considering the argument. While I ducked out if there were too many alternatives, she liked to be thorough, with no feeble 'decide that later' topics; she worked through every point. She would say I was a typical man; I thought her a highly unusual woman.

'We ought to consider, Marcus, not just who this person of influence is, but *why* he supports the freedmen. It's been a long while since mighty men in Rome aligned themselves with criminal gangs.'

'People like Clodius and his terrorists? He provided himself with brutal enforcers; everyone was scared of them and together with his very patrician name, it gave him enormous power . . . Nothing like that happens in the city now.'

'It cannot be about anything the Claudii offer to their protector,' Helena said. 'He may be ambitious, but he must be able to manage his career without their help. So why does he bother? What hold do they have over him?'

She was right and I agreed: 'What's he scared of? A bunch of second-rate ex-slaves, living out in a marsh, miles from civilisation, selling scrap and beating up their wives? I can't see how they have any influence with anyone who carries serious weight in Rome. And he must have weight. It takes a real someone to make Anacrites jump.'

'Could it be simpler?' Helena suggested. 'Could they be under the protection of Anacrites himself?'

We both laughed and agreed that was totally unlikely.

Back in Rome, it emerged that the visitor who had threatened Thamyris could not have been Anacrites. The man who went to Antium must have been an agent. Petronius confirmed that the spy had been in Rome. The vigiles had seen him.

Things had moved on. While Helena and I were away, the Seventh Cohort had been called out to the necropolis on the Via Triumphalis.

This burial ground was across the river, north of the city, unlike where Modestus was discovered. Passers-by had alerted a caretaker to what looked like a shallow grave, dug without permission close to the road. In it was a fresh, mutilated corpse.

30

Julia and Favonia had been playing quietly on the floor with their pottery animals. As soon as we walked in, they remembered they had been abandoned by us, their callous parents. They jumped up, grew red in the face and ran away screaming loudly, real tears streaming down their faces. It was a classic scam.

Helena Justina gave me a quizzical look. 'Maybe two is enough?'

'Agreed!'

Albia, too, refused to welcome our return but stalked off like an offended dog. That gave Nux the same idea, even though she had been on the trip with us.

The message from Petronius about the new murder was irresistible. I changed my tunic and boots, then washed my face. I thought about a comb-through but settled for the windswept look. Being back in Rome had fired me up enough; being neat would be too much excitement. Sometimes I needed to remember when I lived in Fountain Court and was a rough rascal.

At mid-morning I set out from home, with a knife down my boot and just enough money in my purse to cover emergencies. My mind was clear and my step spry. However, I had the faint edgy feeling of a man who needs to reimpose himself on his customary surroundings. Adultery and cart-crashes could have occurred without me knowing it. I might have missed the crucial capture of that balcony thief from the Street of the Armilustrium. Old Lupus could have gone on his long-promised cruise of the Mediterranean—for all I knew, taking that pudgy waitress from the Venus Scallop, instead of his miserable wife, the one with pigtails who was always cadging off Brutus from the fish stall. Once I reached Maia's, she would fill me in on these essentials, but first my way took me to the Fourth Cohort's station house.

Petronius had finished the night shift and gone home. Fusculus was there and gave me the story.

'Same modus as before?'

'Apparently. Body found at the necropolis—though not in a tomb this time. There's a difference from the Appia and Latina sites, where you find patrician surnames and bloody big mausoleums. The Via Triumphalis is a big burial ground with a mixed clientele, slaves to middle rank. Its burials are mixed, everything from old skeletons popping out of shallow graves to grey stone urns with nice pointy lids or half a broken amphora lying on its side to hold the deceased's ashes.'

'About our level!' I said, grinning.

'Not as fancy as that inscription your papa fixed up for himself, Falco! No *This is my memorial which may never be sold, with a frontage of a thousand feet*; no pretty Etruscan funeral altar, with dear little wings on it.'

I was not yet ready for jokes. I could satirise losing Pa, but thinking about my tiny son demanded respect. 'Fusculus—that's a large cemetery with a litter of confusing graves. Why did this corpse attract attention?'

'You know some crazy killers want to yell out, *Look at me; I've done what I wanted and you can't catch me!* Petronius reckons the dead man was placed near the road specially, so someone would notice.'

'Did you see the body?'

'That was indeed my privilege.'

'Modestus was middle-aged. Someone similar?'

'No, this one's young. Slight build—easy to overcome.'

'How was he set out?'

'Obviously ritual. Face down, arms outstretched sideways like a crucified slave. Well, when I say full length, Falco, that is excluding both his hands which, having been hacked off, were placed very neatly either side of his head. Same groundplan as Modestus. And like Modestus, when the Seventh rolled him over, they found him sawn open from his gullet to his privates.'

'Any other mutilation?'

'That was enough!'

'As vindictive as the Modestus killing?'

Fusculus gave that thought. 'Maybe not. He had been thumped, but probably during initial attempts to subdue him.'

'Then apart from the fact he lost his hopes in life, you could say he did not suffer?'

'So nicely put! His clothes were there. Shoes, neckerchief—and bright new wedding ring still on his severed hand. Mind, I don't think anyone would try selling what was left of his tunic in the flea market—not after he was slit open.'

'Ring left behind—so theft not a motive?'

'No money on him, so maybe. His donkey's missing, but anyone could have pinched that from the roadside if the killer left it.'

'And do we know who he is?'

'We do, in fact!' Fusculus left me waiting. It was the end of the night and he soon lost interest in teasing. '. . . A carter reported his courier missing. Young fellow. Just got married, so the bride started jumping as soon as he failed to report for his dinner. Her very first attempt at seafood patties—now he'll never know how terrible they were . . . He'd been sent out with a parcel—the Seventh haven't found the parcel, but it was in his donkey pannier. That caring citizen, his master, reported him gone because he thought the lad had simply scarpered with the goods.'

'So this parcel-boy was heading out of Rome, not coming into town? And not on the Pontine Marshes side?'

'No. So the Seventh *were* assuming it's the same killer, because of the method, but those on high say different.'

'Not the Claudii? That's the Anacrites verdict?' I was angry. 'Tiberius, my lad—this points us in the other direction much too obviously!'

'Funny thing,' murmured Fusculus. 'That's what Petronius Longus decided.' He pretended to look impressed that we two could so swiftly come up with the same suggestion. 'Mind you, he always likes to be a wild man over theories. If seven people say a cabbage-seller did it, the mighty Longus will arrest the baker. He'll be right too. Clever bastard.'

Going on my way, when I reached the door I whipped back with a sudden last question. This was a trick to reserve for suspects, really, but Tiberius Fusculus was one person in the vigiles who appreciated stagecraft. 'Have you discounted a copycat?'

'Ah, Falco, there's always that delight to cause confusion!'

Petro had been going to bed when I arrived, but he stayed up to gossip. We went out to the balcony. He closed the folding door. That was how he did things. Through the slats I could see Maia waggling her fingers at us and sticking out her tongue. Ma would have listened secretly. Helena would have dragged the door straight open again and brought a stool for herself.

He gave me further details. The Seventh Cohort, all halfwits in Petro's opinion, had been first on the scene. The Via Triumphalis, which runs out of the city on the north-east side, was the Seventh's beat; they had jurisdiction over the Ninth and Fourteenth districts, including any burial ground just outside the boundary. They consulted the Fourth Cohort. They knew Petronius had the Modestus case, though they had been unaware of the Anacrites complication. The Fourth's tribune wanted to be a Praetorian Guard and spies were a Praetorian subdivision, so as it had a bearing on his own position Rubella stuck by the rules. He notified Anacrites of the new linked case so fast the hot wax seal burned the spy's fingers. Anacrites had allowed the Seventh to continue with routine enquiries. Either they lacked the taint of association with Petronius and me, or he just thought they were too stupid to get in his way.

'As they are,' said Petro.

'You're tired.'

'I'm right.'

'Of course. So what do you think? Fusculus says the new official view is that the Triumphalis death indicates random killings on any road near Rome. It's supposed to tell us the Modestus death was just a traveller's unlucky accident.'

'Yes, apparently that is a luminous truth.'

'Modestus getting topped on his way into Rome has no relation to the Claudii but is pure coincidence?'

'Wrong road, wrong time.' Petro paused, as Maia came out with a dish of stuffed vine leaves, checking up that we were not enjoying ourselves too much without her.

'He needs his rest, Marcus.'

'We've nearly finished.'

'I know you; you haven't even started.'

'Buzz off and let us get on then.' Petro's tone was affectionate. My sister put up with it.

I chomped a vine leaf. Home made. Wheatgrain and pine nut filling in a slightly tart dressing. Mint. Good, but I stayed gloomy. 'Spill, sunshine.'

Petro took a snack between one thumb and finger, but merely waved it as he talked. 'Marcus, here is my personal list of anomalies. First, why did the Modestus killers cut off his hands? I still think for revenge: those hands had repeatedly written angry letters to complain about the Claudii. Someone must have heard about Cicero—murdered for railing against Mark Antony. Cicero's hands, which wrote his polemics, were removed and stuck on spikes either side of the head up on the rostrum where he had made his speeches.'

'One hand.'

'Pedant.'

'The allusion seems too literary.'

'No, it's not. Everyone knows what happened to Cicero. Even *I* know!' boasted Petro. He had been to school, but whereas my adult hobbies were drinking and reading, his were drinking and drinking some more. 'Besides, what do you think Nobilis and Probus do all day at their miserable shacks? They sit down with a learned scroll to improve their minds, don't they?'

'Show me proof! But I go with revenge against the petitioner's hands. Next anomaly?'

'I had had our doctor, Scythax, take a look at the remains before we got Modestus cremated. Scythax thought he was probably still alive when his hands were removed. Nobilis may know about the death of Cicero; he intended Modestus would appreciate his fate.'

'Meanwhile, the courier's boy never wrote poison pen letters.'

'No, he couldn't read or write.' Trust Petro to have asked the question. 'His body may have been stretched out like Modestus, but his slashed belly is different. Scythax tends to be cautious forensically, but he reckons the Modestus killer cut open the corpse after death. I mean, he probably came back and did it several days later.'

I cringed. 'What was that for?'

'Who knows why? Reinforcing his power, maybe.' Petro munched his snack now, thinking about perversion and frowning. 'Anyway, the courier was opened up the same day he died. We can be sure, because he set off in the afternoon and was found at first light next day. He was practically warm.'

'The murder sounds hurried—that's untypical of repeat killers.' I could tell from the way Petronius had paced his narrative, there must be at least one more discrepancy. 'What else?'

'Whoever killed Modestus, from the detritus left nearby, I suspect more than one man was there. And they stayed around the crime scene for several days. *After* the killing, I mean. Possibly someone came back to slash Modestus open—but I say, the bastards never went away.'

'Jupiter! This happens?'

'With perverts. Of course, people who hold other theories will argue that around the Via Appia tombs there are plenty of comers and goers, squatters and campers, so how can we tell?'

'And how can you?'

'As well as the post mortem filleting job, we found seats that had been moved out of the tomb; discarded amphorae; obvious food evidence. There was human shit and it was the right vintage.'

I winced. 'Your job is charming.'

'My job is to get it right and not let bastards bamboozle me.'

'If the Modestus killers had wanted to play with the courier's boy like that, all they had to do was take him away from the road out of sight. Instead they placed him right beside the road-edge ditch, where he was bound to be spotted immediately.'

'Funny, that!' observed Petro. 'The whole thing stinks—though a stupid spy might fall for it.'

He did need his rest and while he brooded, Petronius Longus fell asleep. I did not disturb him. I sat on there, letting him snore on the other daybed, while I continued thinking.

Maia looked out once. She brought me some warmed honey mulsum, silently curling my fingers around the beaker, then roughing up my curls. After these sisterly attentions, she left us to it.

31

It was time to look harder at Anacrites. Helena was right about how we could do that. Escorting my womenfolk to a soirée at his old-style Palatine mansion would not have been my choice, but his invitation had arrived and Rome is a city of civilised dining. Commerce and corruption of all kinds are furthered by social evenings of this type. I wanted to get close enough to him to work out why he wanted to be close to me.

At my members-only gym, Glaucus' at the back of the Temple of Castor and Pollux, I bathed and put myself in the safe hands of the sneery barber. First, I had Glaucus give me a fierce weapons practice, followed by a session with his most brutal masseur. When Glaucus asked if all this preparation meant I was off on another dangerous mission overseas, I told him where I was going that evening. His advice was to watch my footwork, watch what I was given to eat, but above all watch my back. He had met Anacrites. When the spy had applied to join the gym as a regular, Glaucus found he was so oversubscribed he could only put Anacrites on the very competitive waiting list . . . Anacrites was still there.

'Say no when he passes you the mushrooms,' Glaucus hinted. An old Roman allusion to poison. 'Better still, here's an idea. You got plenty of slaves off your old man when he died, didn't you? Take one along as your taster. Be sensible, Falco. You're paid up here until the end of the year—you don't want to waste part of your subscription.'

'I regard my slaves as family,' I protested with a righteous air.

'All the more reason to bump a few off!' replied Glaucus. Nobody would know he had a good-looking wife he doted on and an athlete son who was his pride and joy.

According to Helena it was more trying for a woman to get dressed when she wanted to look as if she had gone to no trouble than when she was trying to show vast respect to some possible patron in order to advance her husband (never applicable in my case) or to impress a man she was sizing up for passionate adultery (not applicable in Helena's, I hoped—though if that was her intention there was not much I could do about it; she was far too devious). I lay on the bed watching proceedings, naked and hoping the scent of the masseur's crocus oils would evaporate. His goo was useless for attracting women. Helena Justina had just wrinkled her nose in mild curiosity, as if I had come home with an arm missing and she was subconsciously wondering what was different about me. The hour which we could have filled with lovemaking went to trying on gowns, searching for girdles and picking through her jewel casket. When she was halfway through applying face paint, she rushed off to supervise Albia, who had decided that since her parents never took her anywhere, she would wear all the sparkle she possessed while there was an opportunity.

'We need to look as though we know it's not just borage tea and a pickled egg,' I heard Helena telling her. Two room doors had been left open, to facilitate the shrieks as the only good gown in the chest was found to have had honey spilled down it and the clasp on each chosen necklace broke under frantic fingers. 'But that we don't think enough of Anacrites to bring out our best.'

'And why is it we hate him?' Albia asked with her fastidious curiosity. She tended to act as if all things done in Rome were crazy beyond belief to anyone born in the provinces.

– 175 –

'No hatred. We treat him cautiously,' Helena reproved her. 'We find his jealousy of Falco a touch unhealthy.'

'Oh—as in, he tried to have Falco splayed on a rock for carrion birds in Nabataea?'

'Quite. Trying to arrange a long-distance execution was not acceptable etiquette.'

'So will the spy try short-distance Falco-killing this evening?' Albia sounded far too interested.

'No, darling. Anacrites is too shrewd to try anything with you and me there. I'd poke his eyes out, while you rushed for a lawyer.'

That was reassuring. I hauled myself upright and sorted out a tunic I was willing to wear.

'Oh Marcus! You're not going in that disaster. Wear your russet.'

'Too smart.'

I had always loathed the russet, which made me look like some praetor's pimpled equerry. Naturally, that was what my stylists made me wear.

At the Anacrites establishment, which he must have acquired with his Census earnings, the murderous watchdog had been sluiced with scented water and told to bark more quietly. That would be a bonus for the wealthy neighbours who were usually too scared to complain. The formidable gates had been oiled so they could be forced wide enough; Pa's old six-bearer litter sailed us through. We were cleared by the bestubbled porter and passed into the custody of liveried greeting slaves.

They were slick. So slick, Helena guessed Anacrites had hired professional party-planners. His house was busy with Lusitanians in matching snowy tunics. There were garlands in themed colours. A young lady facilitator in platform soles and a faux fur bustband picked out bijou little guest-gifts for us (I got dice, that would only land on three). At the spy's back door must be a train of carts bringing the accoutrements of outside caterers—bronze buckets of fancy seafood from specialist suppliers, slightly worn table linen, and their own griddles. For Anacrites, this evening clearly meant much more than a comfortable supper among friends.

I pinched Albia cheerfully. 'Assume the Trojan hog is on!'

The greeters whipped away our outer garments and shoes. A rumpus at the door announced further visitors. Since one of the voices was that of Camillus Aelianus—sounding a little weary perhaps—that boded ill. We had hardly reached the atrium and Albia already looked surly. Then I heard the hideous baritone of Minas of Karystos. He must have stiffened his resolve with cocktails before the party set out.

Helena and I shuffled past the atrium pool, towing Albia. Tiny lamps like fireflies, the kind designers think sophisticated, twittered around the pool, many already going out. While the newcomers were shovelled into their dining sandals, we found our way through the murk and came upon our host reclining on a reading-couch, like a man who was trying to calm his nerves.

He jumped up, wearing one of his slimfit tunics (great gods, the vain fool must have darts put in, to make him look trim). I was very put out that his was a brown shade rather close to mine. I'd half expected him to have a torc around his neck, but he had confined himself to matched gold cuffs on his upper arms. He exercised. He had enough muscle to show off, though his arms were oddly smooth, as if he had the hairs individually plucked.

'You invited my brother!' Helena barked at him. Anacrites had changed her from peacemaker to firebrand in one move. Even he looked startled.

'Dear Helena Justina—' Oh it was formal names tonight! 'Since Lucius Petronius and Maia Favonia unfortunately had other commitments, I invited *both* your brothers.' He made it sound as though he was doing her a favour, as if the noble Camilli were incapable of arranging a family party for themselves. What it really meant was that he only knew us. I was right: he had no friends. 'I hoped you would approve,' he whined.

Fortunately the band struck up.

He had three lyres and a light hand-drummer. They accompanied a short troupe of fairly good tumblers in almost new costumes, followed by a girl who sang brief Cretan shepherd songs after long explanations from a man in a shaggy goatskin cape. Ignoring this, we waved cheerily to Justinus and his wife Claudia, less cheerily to Aelianus, his new wife Hosidia and his tottering father-in-law. 'Cretan was the best I could get at short notice to compliment Greeks,' Anacrites whispered as he went to welcome the Camilli. As a host he seemed anxious, a new and surreal side to him.

We watched Anacrites wonder whether he could—or should—kiss Claudia and Hosidia, or if he should, or could, embrace Helena's brothers. (He had not hugged me. I'd like to see him try.) Minas, the bearded, exuberant law professor, threw himself upon Anacrites, whom he had never met, as if they had rowed the same oar in a galley for at least twenty years. Hosidia shrank against Aelianus, who nearly stepped back into the atrium pool. Claudia was too tall for the spy to kiss and she just shook hands with him briskly; the hem of her gown fell victim to the sting of the firefly lights but Hosidia considerately flapped out the sparks. Aulus and Quintus Camillus as one stayed at arm's length from Anacrites. I noticed they both wore heavy new chalk-white togas, ready for electioneering. They introduced their womenfolk, who then clustered with my two so they could all admire each other's outfits. Claudia, who had a warm heart, greeted Albia very fondly. Hosidia stood about looking supercilious. It was her natural expression, as far as I could tell.

'Would you like us to speak Greek?' Anacrites asked helpfully, in fluent administrative Greek.

'Naturally I speak Latin,' Hosidia answered—though she said it in Greek. That failed to solve anything; so we were headed for a bilingual evening—feasible, but distancing.

Two pale, flat-chested girls in long white uniforms arrived with snack trays. The snacks were small but tasty; there was no obvious sign that house-slaves had nibbled them. Young boys with their hair oiled into silly points brought the first drinks, in garish decorated cups that the caterers probably supplied. Minas, who needed no cheering up, cheered up loudly. The women guests then demanded that Anacrites give them a tour of his house. Looking worried, he let himself be swept off; he had the expression of a man who knew he had left a pile of dirty loincloths on his bedroom floor and failed to close the cupboard containing his winged phallus lamps.

This left Minas, the Camilli and me standing in a square, each holding a crayfish tail and asking one another what in Hades we were doing there.

Justinus reminded me that we knew from a previous visit Anacrites kept obscene statues in a secret room. Minas brightened, hoping for a private view. 'This should be a good night, Falco!' he boomed. I saw Aulus, who had a keen idea of Minas' liquid capacity, smile fixedly. 'I am so looking forward to it!' Minas confided to me, leaning close in a hideous aura of lunchtime wine and garlic. 'This man must have very great influence, I think? He knows important people? The Emperor, perhaps? Anacrites can do us favours?'

I nodded gravely. 'Tiberius Claudius Anacrites would be proud to know you believe that, Minas.'

32

We were called to dine.

The old dining room was indoors and a touch cosy. The hired hands had decorated its three crushed-together stone couches with coverlets in some shiny fabric the colour of pomegranate juice. They must have misjudged what kind of bachelor Anacrites was. A single rose, suspended from the centre of the ceiling, made the traditional statement that anything we said would be in confidence.

'Surely,' Albia piped up, all wide-eyed innocence, 'only an idiot would mention any secrets in a spy's house?'

'Now I remember your daughter!' cried Minas, clapping me around the shoulders so hard I nearly lost my footing (he had only just remembered *me*, I reckoned). 'This minx is too astute!'

'Oh these days intrigue is the only game in town, Minas.' Thanks to the bagginess of the russet tunic, a good wriggle helped me slide free of the Greek's grip. 'Anacrites loves people to come here and commit treason. He gets a thrill thinking they are his guests so he can't arrest them.'

Anacrites looked disorientated.

———

We were nine at dinner, naturally. To break convention would be too daring for our host. He must have given much thought to his placements, but when the rest of us arrived in the triclinium, Helena was shifting people around to avert awkward situations: making sure I could grill Anacrites; putting Albia and Aelianus apart; not imposing the bombastic Minas on anyone shy . . .

Minas thought he should take precedence, but this was Rome and he was foreign; he stood no chance. 'Both brothers Camilli are standing for the Senate—' Anacrites said, as he tried to guide them into his chosen places. They were talking about the races and failed to notice him.

'They'll be voted out,' snapped their sister.

'Oh thank you!' they chorused half-heartedly. She just grabbed each one and shoved him where she wanted him. For would-be empire-governors, the duo submitted like wimps. Albia was chortling at this, until she was frogmarched to the end of the inferior couch. 'Young girl's prerogative,' Helena soothed her. 'You get the easy exit to the lavatory and you can reach the food trays for seconds.'

Minas still took too much interest in which was the seat of honour. 'The one on the right-hand corner of the middle couch, I think . . . ?' Fired up by some tourist guide to Roman etiquette, he was aiming his big belly in that direction.

Helena shepherded me there. She pushed Minas to the other end. 'With the best views of the garden and statuary if we were out of doors—' Due to the deficiencies of Anacrites' house, we were facing a dowdy corridor. 'Marcus is the only person who has held a significant public post, Minas; he was Procurator of Juno's Sacred Geese.' If I was top man, and by virtue of supervising a flock of birds, that showed this dinner's low status.

Minas pouted. I grinned and to distract him I explained, 'It's a sad story, Minas. Government short-sightedness. I lost the job ignominiously, in a round of treasury cutbacks.' I always wondered if Anacrites had had something to do with it. 'Juno's Geese and the Augurs' Sacred Chickens were heartbroken to lose me. Their loyalty is touching, in fact. I go up on the Capitol regularly to see the clucks for old times' sake; I shall never lose my sense of responsibility.'

'You are fooling?' Minas was only half right.

'Forget convention. *I* think the best places are the centre of the couches—' Still struggling to seat everyone, Helena steered Anacrites between Minas and me. Aelianus had to go at the top of the left-hand couch, talking across the corner to Minas, with Hosidia behind him; Justinus was opposite Hosidia with Claudia above him, adjacent to me across the other top corner. Albia was below Justinus. He was a good lad and would talk to her; she would probably hope to upset Aelianus by being friendly with his brother. At the far end of the left-hand couch, Helena was stuck with Hosidia. Good manners would have placed Helena next to me, but she had demoted herself in order to put the spy in my range. At least I could wink down the room at her.

During the appetisers, our host led the conversation—as much as he could do, with Minas tipsily interrupting. We had seen him in action; as a symposium-crawler no one could touch him, even in Athens' exhausting party whirl.

The wine was better than good; Anacrites discussed it fluently. Perhaps he had taken himself to wine-buffery classes. At any rate, he served palatable mulsum with the appetisers, not too sweet, then a very fine Caecubian. One of the best wines in the Empire, that must have cost a packet. He also introduced us to an unfamiliar variety he had just acquired, from Pucinum; he was dying for us to ask where Pucinum was so he could show off, but nobody bothered. 'What do you think, Falco? The Empress Livia always drank Pucinum wines, ascribing her long life to their medicinal qualities.'

'Very nice—though the phrase "medicinal qualities" slightly puts me off!'

'Well, it kept her going to eighty-three, outliving her contemporaries—'

'I thought that was because she had poisoned them all . . .'

I asked for a separate water cup and drank the wine sparingly. Anacrites knew me well enough to have seen me do it before. I had a curious sense that tonight he wanted to relax for once—yet now he was torn, in case loosening up gave me some advantage.

While he continued to hold forth on vintages, I chatted to my other neighbour, Claudia Rufina. The three Camillus siblings were all lofty but Justinus had married a woman tall enough to look him in the eye; this Claudia now saw as necessary since he could be a rogue, an edgy character who needed constant watching. On a dining couch designed for our stumpy republican ancestors, she was having problems twisting herself to fit. But once she settled, Claudia gossiped with me on the current situation in the senator's house. 'Things are tense, Marcus.'

Minas had emptied the Camillus wine cellar in about five days. The amiable senator declined to restock, so Minas got huffy. Then Camillus senior hit on the idea that Aelianus and his bride should live next door; he owned the adjacent house, where his brother had once lived. It was decreed that Minas must stay with the couple. 'Julia Justa said, *So nice for him to see a lot of his daughter, before he goes back to Greece* . . . I don't think the professor intends going back, Marcus!'

'No; he is determined to be a big rissole in Rome.'

'I would have thought,' said Claudia, who was a kind-hearted girl, 'the newly-weds might be given some time to themselves—especially as they don't seem to have had much opportunity yet to get to know each other.' That was ironic. Claudia and Quintus would probably stick out their marriage (she had an excellent olive oil fortune which encouraged him mightily), but they were experts at communication failure.

'You presuppose, my dear, that either of them wants familiarity.'

'You cynic!'

'I've lived. Still, we must be hopeful . . . How are the lovebirds getting on?'

Claudia lowered her voice. '*They have separate bedrooms!*'

'How fashionable! Though not much fun.'

'They will never have children.' Claudia and Quintus had produced two small sons very quickly; she assumed everyone wanted the same.

At home we joked that Quintus could get his wife pregnant just by kicking his boots under the bed.

Babies were still a painful subject with Helena and me. To stop Claudia detailing the wonders of their newest son, I turned back to Anacrites. Forcing Aulus to endure a bout of Minas, I grabbed our host's attention. 'So! Tell us all about the big secret mission. Where did you go? How long did you stay? How many barbarians tried to garrotte you? Do tell me some at least tried. And what were you doing abroad in the first place, acting as the Emperor's messenger-boy?'

'You're just jealous,' Anacrites replied coyly.

'Cobnuts! Now, I don't mind you playfully pretending it's a state secret—just so long as you confess all.'

'It was nothing.' Everyone was now listening, so Anacrites had to answer. 'It seems that when his mistress Antonia Caenis was alive, Vespasian managed to discover for her that her ancestors came from Istria.' Minas looked puzzled yet again, so Anacrites explained that our affable old Emperor had lived much of his life with an influential freedwoman who filled a wife's place. 'Senators are forbidden to marry freedwomen. Apparently Caenis had not known her origins and I suppose it bothered her. Once Vespasian assumed power, he had access to the records. Someone finally looked up answers.'

'That's a romantic story,' Claudia said.

'It was true love.' Helena supplied the fact that Caenis had managed to visit her homeland for nostalgic reasons before she died. 'I met her; I liked her enormously. Did you know her, Anacrites?'

'I knew who she was, of course,' he said, in that careful way of his. From what I had seen, in a couple of meetings while she was alive, Antonia Caenis had more sense than to cosy up to the spy.

'I wondered if your backgrounds were similar?' Helena pressed. The spy, not deft with a spoon, concentrated on chasing a langoustine nibble around his foodbowl. I admired my sweetheart for many fine qualities, not least her ability to denude a silver comport of its most succulent seafood while seemingly engaged in chat. Helena served herself to three from the central table while he fumbled. If we had been seated together she might have passed one to me. 'So what were your duties in Istria, Anacrites?' Nobody else will have noticed, but Helena was aware of the way I was smiling down the room at her.

'Merely ceremonial. Falco would have been impatient with it . . .' I leaned on my elbow and glared at him sternly. Anacrites was just too good to show it made him uncomfortable. 'Vespasian endowed various public buildings, in honour of Caenis. An amphitheatre at Pola, for instance, needed restoration—'

'He *paid* for it?'

'He loved her, Marcus,' Helena called reprovingly. 'Go on, Anacrites.'

'I was sent to represent him at the inauguration. So, Falco, it was nothing sinister!'

I laughed off this weak attempt to make me appear paranoid. 'My dear fellow, any time you have the chance to cut civic ribbons in a two-bit foreign town, you do it. I am surprised you could be spared for such matters.'

He flushed slightly. 'Pola is a major city, *Colonia Pietas Iulia Pola Pollentia Herculanea.* I was owed leave. I was honoured to go. It suited me too,' he let slip.

'Oh?' I was on it at once.

'I have connections there.'

'Connections?' I patted his shoulder. 'Can we be learning personal secrets?'

Anacrites shifted. 'It is very beautiful along the coast.'

'Full of pirates, lurking in the rocky creeks, according to my Uncle Fulvius. He watched their movements for the fleet,' I told the spy, trying to make him think this undercover work had been for some mysterious higher agency. Fulvius was in Egypt now, or I would never have mentioned it. No rose suspended from a ceiling was protection enough; had Fulvius still been engaged as a 'military corn factor' (a ridiculous myth, because no corn factor is ever what he seems) he would not have thanked me for interesting Anacrites. 'So what was the real draw, Anacrites?'

'Oh . . . an opportunity to get my hands on some Pucinum wine!' The man was indefatigably slippery.

To his obvious relief the servers cleared the starter tables and brought in the main course. While this was organised, the tumblers tumbled off for a break and a professional singer swanned up to delight us. He must be all the rage; I recognised this caroller from Laeta's office. Immediately I wondered if he was Laeta's plant, observing Anacrites at play. The thought kept me happy until the new food-bowls were laid.

Time for business. (Anything to avoid listening to this singer.) 'So Anacrites, how are you getting on with the Modestus killing?'

'Don't ask, Falco!'

'I just did. Now listen, happy host, I am your guest of honour. While I stretch out on my elbow here in the best place, the consul's spot, my every whim is yours to fulfil—so come clean! What's the situation?'

'There has been another death.' The spy had a wide-eyed honest look that made me want to screw bits off my bread roll and stuff him like a trigon ball. 'It bears similarities to the Modestus killing . . .'

'But?'

'Either it's some sad mimic—plenty of people knew what happened to Modestus; the vigiles may have said too much in public—' Oh yes, blame them, you bastard! 'Or I think it is a ploy, Falco—falsely implying that the killer works from Rome. Of course, I am not fooled so easily. Modestus had been tailed on his journey; he was deliberately targeted. This was different.'

'Interesting!' I was shocked. Was Anacrites really so shrewd? I almost wondered if he had a nark in the vigiles' patrol house who had eavesdropped on Petronius and me.

Aware of my surprise, he applied fake humility. 'What do you say, Falco? I'd like to hear your professional evaluation.'

'Oh you seem on top of things.'

'Thanks. Did you know about the second killing? Have you discussed it with Petronius?' He really wanted to know whether we were still monitoring his case.

'Yes, we heard about it.'

'And what was his verdict?'

'We think a crazed copycat killer knifed the poor courier . . . So are you still looking for those Claudii?'

'Of course.' It was the right thing to say. He was smooth as a wet rat sliding down a drain. Still, I never expected Anacrites to be totally incompetent, let alone appear corrupt. He was too good to show what he was up to.

He turned away, readjusting a pomegranate silk cushion so he could converse again with Minas. 'We don't want to talk about a murder over dinner, Falco.'

You could tell he rarely entertained. He had no idea that far from being squeamish, guests would be eager to hear about gore.

When the main course arrived, he had overdone things. There was no need. His caterers were first class; we would have been flattered by anything they cooked. A couple of roasts, a simple platter with a fine fish, a vegetable mélange with one or two unusual ingredients, would have sufficed. But he had to over-impress. Although he had complimented Helena and me on the warm atmosphere of our Saturnalia gathering last December, Anacrites had failed to analyse it: good food, fresh ingredients not overcooked, a few carefully chosen herbs and spices, all served in a relaxed style with everybody mucking in.

Instead we had tired old Lucullan oysters—'I'm sorry, Falco; I know you were in Britain, but I could not get Rutupian!' After flamingo tongues and lobster in double sauces came the ridiculous climax. Albia squeaked and sat up on her couch in happy expectation: a major-domo clinked an amphora to call for attention, spare servers stood back expectantly, the tumblers' harpists (who must have finished their boozing break) rattled off dramatic arpeggios accompanying a drum roll. A pair of sweating waiters dragged in the Trojan hog. Though young, it was a big brute, presented on a trolley upright on its feet, wearing its hair and tusks. From the glaze on its cheeks and the delectable odours, it had slow-roasted most of the day. Fake grass, full of pastry rabbits, nestled around its trotters. A crown of gilded laurel topped it, wired on between the piggy's shining ears.

A master carver approached, perhaps the chef himself, wielding a vicious meat sabre. I wouldn't trust him on a dark night round the back of a seedy posca bar. His blade flashed in the lamplight. With one mighty sweep he cut open the boar's belly. Glistening innards tumbled out towards us, like raw guts. As Helena had said, they were sausages. While we still believed they were hot viscera, he tossed a quick-fire barrage into all our foodbowls. There were screams. Someone clapped briefly. Minas took a moment to grasp what was happening, then exploded with delight. 'Excellent, excellent!' He was so thrilled, he had to beckon a server to fill up his wine goblet. A hum of appreciative voices congratulated Anacrites, while Helena and I looked on patiently.

It was a shock—though not if you knew what was coming. The trouble with the tired old Trojan hog trick is it only works once. Was I jaded? I made an effort to look excited—well, mildly—though even Claudia forgot her natural generosity and muttered to me, 'Those Lucanian sausages look very undercooked! I don't think I'll eat them.'

The crackling was good, though full of bristles.

33

Some time while everyone was gnawing tough pork, then picking their teeth discreetly, I noticed that Albia had slipped away from the table. Her absence went unremarked by others. As the main course ended, people were behaving informally. One by one they went out for a natural break, on their return taking the opportunity to move around and talk to different guests. Justinus was now alongside his brother. Helena abandoned Hosidia and crossed the room for a chat with Claudia.

I was bored with Anacrites' well-clad back as he listened to Minas. Luckily the gloopy singer reappeared; he had picked up the Cretan shepherds' habit of explaining everything long-windedly—so often, of course, lamenting young sailors lured to their doom by sinister sea-nymphs or brides who had died on their wedding day. When he announced, 'The next song is a *very* sad one', I went to find a lavatory.

I explored in a desultory fashion, but I had been in the house before and seen all I wanted of the layout, décor and cold living arrangements. I found the kitchen, with the caterers engaged in washing bowls—most of them, anyway; I had passed a couple sidling about, probably pinching Anacrites' fancy curios.

The services were, as I expected, next to the kitchen—functional, but with the faint unscrubbed odour you expect in a male establishment. (I was well trained; in a strange house it is a man's duty to report to his wife what the facilities are like.) Emerging, I took a wrong turn somehow.

I ended up in servants' quarters, a series of undecorated small rooms that served routine purposes. There were sacks of onions, buckets and besoms. Even a spy has to endure the domestic—though I bet Anacrites put his onion-seller through an oral security test. That would explain why he had been sold mouldy, sprouting ones.

I spotted a figure ahead of me, slipping down a passageway. He did not hear me call out for directions, but he had left a door open and I heard voices. In one of the rooms, Anacrites' two legmen were sitting with a draughtsboard. I was surprised; I would expect him to keep work and home separate. Instead, the Melitans, as I called them, gave the impression this was a regular haunt. Their room had a sour smell that hinted of long-term use.

The duo were not playing, just talking. They could be arguing about whose turn it was to remove their food tray (there was a large jumble of used crockery and utensils piled ready to go back to the kitchen). They barely troubled to react to my appearance.

'Lost my way.'

Neither spoke. One waved an arm. I turned out of the room, pointed myself in the direction he indicated, and departed. After I walked off, their voices stopped abruptly, however.

They might not be Melitan, but they definitely were brothers. They had the same facial looks, the same dress code (dingy tunics; open-strapped shin boots), the same movements and accents (I had noticed they talked Latin). Most of all, the way they behaved together was the way Festus and I used to be: that blend of spats and tolerance only brothers have.

Back on familiar ground, curiosity drew me to a colonnaded peristyle, formally planted around a statue of three half-size nymphs. This was where the dining room really ought to be situated. I wondered if there was in fact a better triclinium than Anacrites had assigned to us.

I was looking for Albia. Sure enough, she was there on a low wall, looking in at the courtyard. She was just sitting, so I paused. Albia had gone out for a break from watching Aelianus being polite to his wife. It would be best if she could work through her heartache privately.

Someone else interrupted her reverie: Anacrites strolled through the colonnade opposite. Crossing a corner of the garden, he went straight over to Albia. He sat on the wall beside her, not so near as to make her nervous, though near enough to worry me.

'There you are!' he said easily, as though she had been missed, not perhaps by the company but by him. To reinforce his position as a careful host, he added, 'I am glad I saw you hiding here. Helena Justina told me all about your unhappiness.'

'Really!' He would have his work cut out with Albia. He played it well, saying nothing more until she asked in her blunt way, 'What are *you* doing away from your guests?'

Anacrites rubbed the tips of two fingers against his right temple. 'Sometimes commotion disturbs me.'

'Oh yes,' Albia, the unfeeling adolescent, answered. 'I heard you had your head smashed in.'

He managed to sound rueful. 'I don't remember much about it.'

'Does it affect your work?'

'Not often. The effects are random. Days may be good or bad. It's very frustrating.'

'So what happens?'

'I think I have partly lost my powers of concentration.' It must be three years since his head wound; he had had time to learn how to cope.

'That's awkward. You might lose your job. Do you have to conceal it from everyone?'

'Whoa!' In the teeth of Albia's relentless attack, Anacrites made it jocular: 'I'm the spy. I'm supposed to ask the heavy questions.'

'Ask one then!'

Anacrites leaned back his head against a pillar. He was savouring the peace and quiet, resting. 'Do you like my little garden?'

Oil lamps had been dotted around the rest of the house, though there were none out here, probably to avoid attracting insects. In the last light of evening, only outlines of climbers and topiary showed, though there were pleasant scents and a faint splash from some informal water feature. A boy grotesque, pouring from a vase, maybe. I did not see Anacrites as a two-doves-on-a-scallop-shell man.

'It's not bad.'

'I have it looked after by professional horticulturalists. They claim they need to visit every day to keep things trim. It costs a fortune.'

'Are you rich?'

'Of course not; I work for the government.'

'Spies don't do gardening?'

'No idea how to.'

'Falco can dig and prune.'

'Unlike your father, I never had a country background. Do you call Falco your father, by the way?'

'Of course.'

'I was not sure what kind of arrangement Falco and Helena had about you.' Anacrites was obviously hinting there was something irregular he could use against us.

'I have my citizen's certificate!' Albia slapped him down.

Anacrites jumped on it: 'Was that after appearing before an Arbitration Board?'

'Not necessary in a foreign province,' Albia sneered. 'The governor has full jurisdiction. Frontinus approved it. Didius Falco and Helena Justina adopted me.'

'So formal?' So necessary, with people like him out to get us.

'Well, there you are, Anacrites. You don't know everything about Falco!'

Though I grinned at the way she attacked him, I kept absolutely still. I was standing in shadow, by a great tangle of foliage supported on some kind of obelisk. Anacrites' eyes wandered one way and another. I reckoned he suspected I was somewhere watching and listening.

'You talk as if you think I am pursuing Falco! He and I are colleagues, Albia. We have worked together many times. In the year of the Census, we worked very hard in a perfectly good partnership; the Emperor congratulated us. I remember that as a happy experience. I feel very affectionate towards Marcus Didius.'

'Oh he loves you too!' Albia chopped the subject off. 'Tell me about Antonia Caenis and Istria. Why did she care so much about where she came from? Was she hoping to find her ancestors?'

'That I don't know. Perhaps she was. We all have a yearning to discover our background, don't we?' Anacrites' question was incongruous from him.

'I think what matters is the person we are now.'

'That sounds like Helena Justina talking.'

'She speaks good sense.'

'Oh yes; I too admire her immensely.'

'Are you jealous of Falco for having Helena?'

'Certainly not. It would be inappropriate.'

'Why are you not married?'

'Never seemed to find the time.'

'Don't you like women? Do you prefer men?'

'I like women. My work tends to mean keeping very much to myself.'

'Not many friends then? Or no friends at all? You were a slave too—like Caenis. Do you know about your own family?'

'I have some idea.'

'Really? Did you ever meet them?'

'My earliest memory is being among the palace scribes.'

'So you must have been taken away from your parents very young? Was that hard?'

'I never knew anything different. Where I found myself, we were all the same. I enjoyed my training. It seemed normal.'

'So—I always want to ask people this—don't you want to try to find your relatives? If anyone could do it, a spy should be able to.'

'I suppose you ask this question because *you* feel a driving need to find your own people?'

'Oh I shall never discover who I first belonged to. I accept that. I was orphaned in the British Rebellion. I'd like to think I am a mysterious British princess—that would be so romantic, wouldn't it? But I don't have red hair and the poor people I grew up with firmly believed I was a Roman trader's child. I suppose there were circumstances that suggested it, back when they found me. Because of the terrible events and confusion, that will be all I ever know. I am realistic. The uncertainties can never be cleared up, so some avenues in society are closed to me.'

'Is that why you are unhappy, Albia?'

'No, it's because men are deceitful pigs who use people for convenience then look after their own interests.'

'Camillus Aelianus?'

'Oh, not just him!'

'It is sad to hear a young girl speak so bitterly.'

'Now who is being romantic?'

'I suppose your anger is because Aelianus betrayed your hopes and married Hosidia . . . Hosidia what? Does she only have one name?'

'Her family know her as Meline, but "Hosidia Meline"—a Roman name then a Greek one—would sound like a freed slave. She is not one, of course. Some people despise professors, but it goes without saying, they wouldn't have got to be professors if they were poor. Minas must have a prosperous family if he went to Athens to learn law. Still "Meline" wouldn't do, not among senators. Vespasian may have got away with his mistress, but he is an unusual character. The Camilli have to look respectable.'

'I am very impressed, Albia. How did you dig all this out?'

'That's my secret. I've watched Falco. I could do his work. I could do yours.'

'I would be charmed to have you—but, unfortunately, we don't use women in the intelligence service.'

'Yes you do. I've heard of Perella, the dancer. There was a lot of talk about Perella in Britain. You gave her an assignment to eliminate a corrupt official.'

'Oh *really*?'

'Anacrites, don't bluff.'

'I know Perella, certainly. She is a superb dancer.'

'She cut a man's throat. To get rid of him and avert a public scandal. Everyone knew you sent her.'

'I heartily deny that rumour! What a slur on the integrity of our beloved Emperor and the high ethos of his staff. Don't spread this story, please, or I shall be forced to impose a gagging order . . . Anyway, you are much too sweet to want to do work like that.'

'I would not want to *do* it, but I would like to know *how*. Skills give you confidence and power.'

'I would say you have quite enough confidence, young lady. And you had better be kept away from power!'

'Spoilsport.'

'There you sit, looking neat, thoughtful and demure. That, I am sure, is how your adoptive parents are bringing you up. Falco and Helena would be shocked to hear the way you have talked to me.'

'Regretful, maybe—but not surprised.' She was only half right; I was startled by the way she took the spy on.

'Well, *I* am shocked, Albia.'

'You're easily shocked then. Why? You do filthy work. You are a spy and you co-operate with the Praetorian Guards. That means unfair arrests, torture, intimidation. Nothing I have said is so very outrageous, just honest. Life made me hard. Harder than the average Roman maiden of my new father's rank, or some pampered girl brought up in higher circles. I'm harder even than the daughters of poor craftsmen, who have to work in the family business, but who are free to chatter away their days until some dumb husband claims them. I come from the streets. I am sure you poked about and learned that about me.'

'Why ever would I investigate you, my dear?'

'It's what you do. To put pressure on Didius Falco.'

'That's a myth—and libel.'

'Better hire an informer then, to make your case in court . . . So you say you are above jealousy? Why then, Anacrites, do you do stupid things like stealing that case Falco and Petronius worked so hard on? They had their teeth into it, and are perfectly capable.'

Anacrites jumped up in a spurt of irascibility. 'Olympus! If the Modestus enquiry means so much to them, that ridiculous pair can have it back. There was nothing underhand; it just seems a suitable case for my own organisation! A normal redistribution of the work-load, once I was available to supervise.'

'So the terrible Claudii don't have some hold over you?'

'Who thinks that? Don't be ridiculous!' The spy was pacing about in the courtyard. Albia, my dogged, darling fosterling, stayed where she was. Briefly, Anacrites put both hands on either side of his fore-head, as if troubled again mentally. 'Falco asked me just now how the case was going. He was satisfied with my answer.'

'I doubt that.'

Anacrites stopped. 'Did Falco put you up to this?'

'Rubbish. He would be frothing at the mouth if he realised you were talking to me. What—out here in the dark, away from the com-pany, a young girl who has only just begun to go to adult parties and a man in a position of public authority, her host, maybe thirty years her senior?'

'Quite right!' Anacrites' voice was clipped. He held out an arm for-mally. 'I have enjoyed our talk, but I should return you to our fellow guests. Come!'

It was Albia's turn to stand up, swishing her skirts to put them back in order. She kept out of reach. 'I shall return myself, thank you. If we went back together, after so long away from the couches, my parents would be bound to think you had been making dreadful overtures.'

'Your father makes his own crazy decisions about me—though I would hate Helena Justina to suppose I harbour guilty thoughts.'

'You don't?'

'I do not.'

'You mean, because you respect Falco too much?'

'No, Albia,' replied Anacrites, returning to his insidious smooth-ness. 'Because I respect you.'

It was the perfect answer—if it was honest. Albia should be flattered, impressed and charmed. Producing that smooth reply just proved what I had always thought: Anacrites was deadly dangerous.

As he led her away, he looked back and his pale eyes swept the colonnades again. He was wavering, no longer certain whether I was hidden there. Knowing me, he just thought it must be likely.

Albia had kept him hopping. But much of what he said must have been aimed at me.

34

I let Anacrites and Albia go ahead. A tall, slim figure separated off from near another corner of the garden. A woman called in a low voice, 'Marcus! Is that you?'

'Helena!' We met along one of the colonnades. My hand found hers. 'So how long were *you* lurking there? Did you hear all of that?'

'Most of it.'

'I didn't put her up to it—so did you?'

I felt Helena bridle. 'I would never put her in such danger! I came to find her.'

'Did you really tell Anacrites about her yen for Aulus?'

'Of course not. Anacrites was lying, and I shall make sure she knows that. For one thing, whatever occurred between her and my brother—or whatever Albia thought at the time—she really has not talked about it. Besides, give me credit; I have more loyalty to her. Marcus, she's just a girl. He frightens me.'

'I was impressed by how she handled that.'

'It's not safe for her.'

'We'll have to see she never comes within his orbit.'

'Too late! He knows about her,' Helena told me morosely. 'He knows he can hurt you—us—through her. And I'm afraid she, too, will be hurt in the process.'

As we went around a really dark corner, I pulled her close to kiss her and take her mind off her fears. It failed to work on Helena, though it cheered me up.

Temporarily.

We ran into Aulus and Quintus, chortling in a corridor. They admitted they had nipped off so Quintus could show his brother the cabinet of obscene statues. 'How did you monkeys get in there?'

'We asked ourselves what you would do, Marcus—then we broke the lock.' Justinus spoke as if he had brought along a crowbar specially. 'The spy can blame his fancy caterers. They are crawling everywhere.' That fitted my fancy that Laeta was paying them to observe.

'And was the "art" collection revolting?' Helena asked. The lads assured her they were shocked. However, Justinus reckoned there were fewer pieces than when he stayed here last winter; Anacrites may have felt alarmed that other people knew about his filthy gallery so he had sold the most sinister pieces. A spy needs to avoid scandal. Besides, as I knew from Pa's business, he would have made a killing from any of the private pornography collectors.

We returned to the dining room, all in a jolly foursome, so Anacrites might think we had been together all the time. I had not yet decided whether to tell Albia about us eavesdropping. She was now staring at the tumblers' pratfalls, as if planning to run away to join them.

Claudia looked weary after being left alone to cope with Hosidia. I thought Hosidia brightened, as she watched Justinus sprawl back on his couch opposite her. Could his easy manners and good looks be attracting yet another young woman who really belonged to his stodgier brother? Claudia had once been betrothed to Aulus, but she dumped him—which her new sister-in-law had probably realised . . . But Hosidia would need some nerve to flirt with Quintus. If threatened, the once-shy Claudia Rufina fought for her rights with Hispanic bravura. In fact, being the senior bride in the Camillus family seemed to have fired up her confidence. Helena and I liked her; she was tougher than she looked.

Hey ho, I had convinced myself the Camillus family were about to enact a Greek tragedy . . .

Anacrites' evening was starting to deteriorate. Dessert was the least impressive course he provided. It consisted of browned fruit and lacklustre pastries. I reckoned Anacrites had got this far in the caterer's estimate then drew a line through any extras. He had a frugal streak. When I worked with him, it had always been me who went out for honeycakes to break the monotony.

While we toyed with grapes, Minas reappeared. He boomed that he had seen one of the chefs stealing a picture. Anacrites now seemed too deflated to deal with it. I jerked my head at the Camillus brothers. He was a host to avoid, but we were guests with manners. The lads needed no further telling. We three, tailed by the dispirited spy, marched to the kitchen to investigate.

We found the hired caterers packing up. Observed dully by Anacrites, Aulus, Quintus and I lined up the Lusitanian workers, pushed them about, searched them, insulted them, then went through their equipment. They had not been too greedy—just one or two small but good artworks that the spy might not have missed for weeks, a painted miniature pulled from a nail in a wall panel (that was what Minas had seen them taking), then a pitiful assortment of nick-nack bowls and cutlery. The two female servers were the worst offenders; they each had dainty reticules that doubled up as swag-bags.

One very suspicious item was a jewel, which Quintus found rolled up in a used napkin in the laundry hamper. 'This yours?' he asked Anacrites in some surprise. The spy shook his head initially; it was hardly his taste.

Suddenly he changed his mind. 'Oh—a girlfriend must have left it. Give it me, will you—'

'What girlfriend is this?' Aelianus joshed him.

'Oh you know . . .'

'Ooh! Anacrites has had a home masseuse!'

'Sent out for special services!' Justinus joined in.

'You dirty dog!' I said. 'I hope she's registered with the vigiles and you had her credentials checked. This could be a serious breach of security—'

Anacrites looked embarrassed. He was so close about his habits, assuming he had any, that being teased made him red-faced and uneasy. He was holding out his hand for the jewel but Quintus moved away, still inspecting it closely. Aulus stopped the spy, slapped him on the back, spun him around and clapped his cheeks as if he was a youth we had all taken to be 'made a man' by a sought-after courtesan in a luxury brothel. If that was the kind of woman he had summoned here, he would have paid through the nose for the house call.

We gave the caterers a stiff lecture. They were shameless, but we were drunk, so we kept at it with pedantic gusto. Minas loomed up and threatened to prosecute them, but it was not the kind of big law-work that would gain him notice; he wandered off again to search for more of the spy's fine wine.

Minas should have stayed: once he sent the caterers on their way, Anacrites brought out a small flagon of exquisite Faustus Falernian to thank us. We four sipped it together in the kitchen, though socially it was a stiff moment. This had never been a party that would extend to the small hours so I tossed back my tot, followed by the two Camilli. We were accompanied by mothers of young children, a girl, a newly married bride—all good excuses to disperse. Most of us felt weary too. The dinner had been hard going. Minas would have dallied, but when we returned to the triclinium, he was persuaded to tag along home with the Camilli.

We all thanked Anacrites who, frankly, looked done in. He made weak protestations that it was far too early for us to leave—then thanked us rather too fervently for coming. As he led us to our transport, which had already materialised at his entrance porch, he said he had had a wonderful evening. Compared with his normal lonely nights, it probably had been.

'I hope we have mended some fences, Falco.'

I kept my face neutral, watching Helena as she kissed Quintus

Camillus goodbye, undeniably her favourite of the brothers, as he was mine.

Aulus came up to me. Briefly he clasped hands. It was an unlikely formality, especially as I was being chilly with him over Albia. I met his eyes properly, for the first time since the news of his sudden marriage; amazingly, he winked. Something small and cold passed into my hand from his.

I curled my fingers on it. In the darkness of the lurching litter going home I opened my grip but could not tell what I had been given.

At our own house, oil lamps in our familiar hallway greeted our late return. I looked again. Upon my open hand lay the special cameo we had retrieved from among the soiled linen. The Camillus brothers must have done a swift lift-and-pass, neat as Forum pickpockets.

'Oh I like that!' exclaimed Helena.

It was oval, and looked like a pendant from a necklace; it had a granulated gold loop on top, though the chain was absent. The workmanship was fine, the design aristocratic, the cutting of two-tone agate quite remarkable. While a really expensive whore might afford such a thing, it was serious quality. That must have alerted Quintus when he handled it. He was not renowned as a connoisseur—or had not been before he married; Claudia came with her own overflowing necklace boxes, so why should he learn? Yet Quintus moved in society; he had seen plenty of custom gems, hanging from the crêpey necks and scrawny lobes of wealthy high-class women.

I understood exactly why Quintus and Aulus had palmed it. This bauble required investigation.

35

Anacrites was a sad case. Nobody else would turn up before breakfast to ask if last night's guests had enjoyed his dinner. That was his excuse anyway.

'I have mislaid that jewellery.' He had already trekked to the Capena Gate to enquire after the cameo. The two Camilli denied all knowledge, so he came to me. Anacrites still pretended this loss could make life awkward with the item's owner, though he did not want to give more details about which floozy that was supposed to be.

'What's her name, your bird of expensive plumage?'

'You don't need to know . . .'

He was in a dilemma, drawing attention to the piece, when he clearly wished we knew nothing about it.

I was determined to investigate that cameo's history. I lied, therefore, and said I did not have it. 'I'd forgotten all about it. Maybe those light-fingered caterers of yours saw somebody drop it and picked it up a second time . . .' No; he had been to ask them, he said. Jupiter! He must have been busy. 'Who were they anyway?' I asked. 'You'd have to lock up the family silver if you hired them, but that chef was wonderful.'

Briefly, Anacrites glowed under my praise. 'The organiser is called

Heracleides, sign of the Dogstar by the Caelimontan Gate. Laeta put me on to them.'

'*Laeta?*' I smiled gently. 'Taking a risk, weren't you?'

'I checked their credentials. They provide imperial banquets, Marcus.' Anacrites sounded stiff. 'Gladiators' last meals before a fight. Buffets for seedy theatre impresarios who are trying to seduce young actresses. All very much in the public eye. The proprietor has too much good name to risk losing it—Besides, the thefts were carried out by minions, mere opportunism. And I was protected. I had my own security—'

'I saw your house guests!'

'Who did you see?' Anacrites demanded.

'Your dilatory agents, playing board games in a back-corridor hole . . .' Some flicker disturbed his carefully cultivated, steady gaze. If I understood that half-hidden reaction, the Melitans were in for a nasty half hour when he next saw them. He could be vindictive. If they didn't know that already, they were about to find out. 'I meant, was a suggestion from Laeta safe for *you*, dear boy?' I gazed at him and shook my head slowly. 'Given his well-known wish to winkle you out of office?'

The spy's eyes widened.

'No, he wouldn't!' I cried. 'I'm being ridiculous. Laeta is a man of honour, he is above conspiracy. Forget I spoke.' Although Anacrites had imposed iron control on his face muscles, I could see he now realised Laeta might have wrong-footed him.

He changed tack quickly. Gazing around the salon where I had been forced to entertain him, he noted the profusion of new bronze statuettes, polished expanding brazier tripods, fancy lamps suspended from branched candelabra. 'Such lovely things, Falco! You're very prosperous, since your father died. I wonder—does it affect your future?'

'Will I give up informing?' I laughed gaily. 'No chance. You'll never be rid of me.'

Anacrites smirked. All last night's affability had dissolved with his hangover and he went on to the attack: 'I'd say your new wealth exceeds due proportion. When a man receives more from Fortune than he should, winged Nemesis will come along and right the balance.'

'Nemesis is a sweetie. She and I are old friends . . . Why don't you come out straight and say you think I don't deserve it?'

'Not for me to judge. You don't bother me, Falco. Compared with you, I'm fireproof.'

He had to have the last word. I could have allowed it because it meant so much to him—but we were in my house, so I patted back the ball. 'Your confidence sounds dangerously close to hubris! You just said it, Anacrites: presumption offends the gods.'

He left. I went off to breakfast with a lighter step.

Helena and I amused ourselves over the bread rolls discussing reasons why Anacrites could be so worked up about the jewel. After all, he had money nowadays. If some night-moth complained she had lost part of her necklace during their frolics, he could afford to buy her a new one to shut her up.

Some wrangles are meaningless and soon forgotten. Anacrites and I often exchanged insults; we meant them to bite and we meant every word, though it never stuck for long. But the clash we had that morning insidiously stayed with me. I continued to believe that cameo was significant—and I wanted to know why Anacrites had panicked.

36

The Heracleides company was run by one man who lived over a stable block. It was a large stable. Up in his elegant apartment he certainly did not tread on hay. His personalised loft had been floored with highly polished boards; a team of slaves must skate around with dusters on their feet each morning. Instead of mangers, there were sumptuous cushioned couches with dramatic flared legs like whole elephant tusks. He went in for ivory—always the snobbish side of flash. And the flared leg is much beloved by stagy folk (I was thinking like Pa.)

Heracleides ran his outfit from a line of stabled wagons that contained his staff's cooking and serving equipment. Where these staff lurked by day was not immediately obvious. Heracleides, I already knew, believed in distance supervision. He flattered clients with promises of individual attention, yet stayed away from their big night. According to him, his highly trained personnel had been with him for decades; they were safe to leave alone and his presence was unnecessary. At a venue, he would not so much as place a violet in a vase. I guessed his only interest was in counting the profits.

Younger than I expected, he was a pampered specimen—too much time at the baths, probably baths which offered stodgy saffron cakes and erotic massage. His tunic had a fringed hem; a narrow gold fillet bound his suntanned brow. You know the type: all high-stepping insincerity. Not safe to buy a rock oyster from, let alone a three-course dinner with entertainment and flowers.

Trying to impress me, he paraded his business ethic: love of fine detail, competitive rates and a long list of very famous customers. I wasn't fooled. I understood him straight away. He was a chancer.

I took a flared-leg chair, which needless to say had its back at the wrong angle for the average spine. One of the fancy legs was loose too.

I mentioned to Heracleides that sadly the staff he spoke of so highly had been involved in an incident last night. At once the operatives who had supposedly been with him for years became temporaries who must have come to him with false references, bad people whom he said he would never use again. I asked to see them. Hardly to my surprise, that was impossible. I stated calmly I would come back with the vigiles that evening and if the person I was looking for was not then present, Heracleides would be in trouble.

I spelled out the trouble: 'Got a function tonight, have you? Lucky you don't supervise in person or you'd be forced to cancel. Looks like you'll be stuck here answering five hundred questions about the status of your boy and girl helpers until the moon comes out. Any of them got form? Past arrests for pinching clients' pretty manicure boxes? Your women ever been on the vigiles' prostitute lists?' In the service industry that was inevitable. Waitresses were there to sleep with. 'And what about you, Heracleides—what's your citizen status? Did you answer your summons for the Census? Got any imported artwork you never paid port duty on? Where did all this charming ivory come from—would it be African?'

He tried to play tough. 'What do you want, Falco?'

'I want whichever of your staff picked up a fine cameo pendant at the spy's house. If they talk to me today, I can promise no comeback.'

'I wish I'd never taken that brief.'

'Think of this as structured learning. Now, show me your managerial expertise: kindly produce my witness.'

He liked the jargon. He disappeared to ask the group which of them was guilty. He wasn't long coming back. His minions must be curled up in the stable stalls downstairs.

'It's my chef. He's not available. I sent him on a meat-carving course. Sorry—you've had a wasted journey.'

'He slashed the Trojan hog with panache last night. He doesn't need extra training. You're lying. Let's make a little trip downstairs, shall we?'

We made the trip. I walked at my favourite pace, steady but purposeful. Heracleides stumbled more jerkily. That was because I was holding him up by the back of his tunic, so he had to walk on tiptoe. Draught mules watched thoughtfully as we appeared together in the stable.

'Call your chef.'

'He's not here, Falco.'

'Call him!'

'Nymphidias . . .'

'Too quiet.' I reinforced the request painfully. Heracleides yelled Nymphidias' name with much more urgency and the chef crawled out from behind a barrel. He was the man who stole the miniature painting yesterday, I knew. In view of his expertise with knives, I kept my distance.

I let go of the party-planner, shaking my fingers fastidiously. Heracleides fell headlong into some dirty straw, though of course I had not pushed him. I squared up to the chef. Not having his big carver with him, his bravado crumbled.

I extracted the facts fast. Yes, Nymphidias stole the cameo. He had found it in one of the small rooms down the corridor where I got lost earlier in the evening. In the room had been a narrow bed, a man's spare clothes, and a luggage pack. The jewel was in the pack, wrapped carefully in cloth. Everything else there had looked masculine.

I described the Melitans. The chef knew who I meant. They had both come into the kitchen at one point, asking for a meal. Nymphidias said it was a cheek—not in the party contract and they had demanded double portions too—but he prepared some food in a slack moment, which he personally took to their quarters as an excuse to look around. They were in the room where I saw them sitting, not the same as where he found the cameo.

It started to look as if all kinds of agents slept at the spy's house, on occasions. He must be running a kind of runners' dormitory.

'You see anyone else apart from the two who were hungry?'

'No.'

'Nobody who stayed in the single room, where you found the jewel?'

'No.'

I did not believe it. 'There was someone else—I saw him myself.'

'Party guests came to use the washroom. So did the musicians. That singer was hanging about like a spare part—we run into him at a lot of dos.'

'He's called Scorpus,' Heracleides put in, trying to seem helpful. 'Always takes an interest in how much money the hosts have, who their wives are sleeping with, and so on. Very persistent. It's all wrong; in our business you have to be discreet. These clients are high-status; they expect complete discretion.'

'So unprofessional,' I sympathised. 'He sings appallingly too. Whose nark is he? Who pays him?'

'You'll have to ask him.' Heracleides looked jealous, as though he thought Scorpus might receive more for information than he did.

'And who do *you* spy for?'

'No comment.'

'Oh him! I've met that shy boy "no comment" before! There are ways to make him less bashful—and they are not pleasant.'

I returned my attention to the chef. He said the spy's household staff had kept to themselves all evening, annoyed that outsiders had been hired. Apparently that was common. When Heracleides ran functions, he told his staff to make sure the house slaves did not spike drinks or spoil dishes. Anacrites dressed his slaves in green (how sickly; he would!); when they did wander about, they were easy to identify.

'So,' I enquired of Nymphidias, 'from its position and appearance, what did you think when you found this jewel?'

He sniffed. 'I thought whoever had it must have no right to it. It was hidden away too carefully. The rest of his stuff didn't look at all swank. The gem couldn't be his. So I might as well take it off him, mightn't I? Just the way,' he whined, with a new aggression in his tone, 'you've taken it off me.'

'The difference being,' I answered quietly, 'I shall hand it in to the vigiles, so they can find out who really owns it.'

Standing beside me, Heracleides laughed. 'Anacrites won't like that!'

He was right. But Anacrites would never know, until there was a good reason for Petronius and me to tell him.

Before I left, I took Heracleides out of hearing of his staff. 'One last question. Who is so keen to know what goes on in Anacrites' house?'

'I don't know what you mean, Falco.'

'Pig's pizzle. Anacrites is supposed to be the Chief Spy—but more observers sneaked in last night than deluded fathers and clever slaves in a Greek farce. What if I float the name Claudius Laeta past you?'

'Never heard of him.'

'You're tiring me out. Anacrites may be simple-minded, but I can spot infiltrators. Admit it; you do the same as Scorpus. You get paid to poke around houses, on likely nights . . . Indiscretions happen at parties. People drink too much, there is unfortunate groping, you overhear talk of an illegal betting syndicate, someone says Domitian Caesar needs a good spank, someone else knows about the Praetor's nasty habit—'

Heracleides looked wide-eyed. 'What habit?'

I had started a rumour. Well, it was probably true. 'Educated guess . . . We can make a deal. You tell me about Laeta, and I'll make sure you will hear no more about your staff's pilfering last night?'

'Can't help you, honestly. Oh leave it alone, Falco—we've got a good racket, and it's harmless. The hosts can all afford it. And we don't keep the stuff ourselves.'

'What racket's this?'

At once Heracleides regretted the slip. He soon drooped and confessed. 'We lift a few pretty things that look as if they may have sentimental value. We pass them to our principal. He goes along to the house a few days later. He tells them he has heard on his special grapevine about some property that belongs to them. He thinks he can get it all back, and will retrieve it as a special favour. Of course there is a premium to pay . . . You know.' I knew all right.

'So who is this?' It could not be Laeta. He had more class. Blackmail was his medium, not ransoming heirlooms.

'Someone I'm not prepared to mess with, Falco.' Well, the scam was almost irrelevant. I handled property-hostage hustles sometimes, but my present interest was in bigger things.

Heracleides seemed genuinely afraid. Joking initially, I finished up, 'That settles it. I shall have to assume that you work for Momus!'

Then the party-planner shuddered. 'Yes, but he scares me! For heaven's sake don't tell the filthy bastard that I told you, Falco.'

Momus, as well as Laeta?—Now this was really getting complicated.

37

I managed to screw from the party-planner directions for finding the torch singer. It took me an hour to locate his block, and iden-tify which attic he festered in. Scorpus was fast asleep on his bed. That's the beauty of witnesses who work late nights. You can gener-ally find them.

I sized him up before I woke him. He was chunky, though not athletic. He had a red face, a grey moustache, fairish hair receding badly. He looked like a tax lawyer. He probably played for them.

He slept in a disreputable loincloth; I threw a blanket over him. He woke up. He thought I wanted his money or his body, which he took in good part; then he saw that I was holding his lyre and he pan-icked. There was no need even to threaten him. It was such a good instrument it would have hurt even me if I had to smash it. He would talk. In great alarm he struggled to get up, but I pushed him back prone, using one foot. I did it gently. I didn't want this aesthetic type to collapse with anxiety.

'My name's Falco. Didius Falco. I expect you know that. And you're Scorpus, the disgusting highbrow singer of doleful dirges—'

'I play in the respected Dorian mode!'

'What I said. Minor keys and melancholia. If your listeners aren't sad when you start, by the time you stop, the poor idiots will be suicidal.'

'That's harsh.'

'Like life . . . Just lie there and co-operate. It won't hurt. Well, not as much as refusing, trust me . . . We can save time, because I know the score. Whenever there is a gathering at an expensive private house, with hired-in food and entertainment, half the specialist artistes are collecting and selling information. You certainly do it. I want to know your paymaster, and anything you saw of interest last night at the Chief Spy's house.'

He yawned insultingly. 'Is that all!'

'It's enough. Let's start with Claudius Laeta. Did he pay you to collect dirt on Anacrites—or have I got this the wrong way round: when you play for the great Laeta at the Palace is somebody else giving you kickbacks to observe him?'

'Both.'

'Ah Hades!' I twanged a lyre string vacantly, as if seeing how far I could make it stretch before it snapped. I can play a lyre. I use it for disguises. I know what happens when a string breaks and was really not keen to have whipping animal-gut flick at high speed into my eye. Scorpus could only see the threat to his precious instrument.

'Please don't do any damage!'

'Who's spying on Laeta? Momus? Anacrites?'

'Both—Everyone thinks I am working for them. Really I'm freelance.'

'Freelance, as in you'll take anybody's money? And you'll shit on anybody too?' I sneered. It made no impact. He was shameless. Well, I knew that from what he twangled for helpless listeners. 'You can do better than this, Scorpus.'

'What are you after?' He caved in. He had no interest in the fine practice of resistance. I was almost disappointed.

'I want to know what you saw.'

'Much the same as you did, I suppose,' he retorted defiantly.

'I was a guest. I couldn't look around freely, and anyway I've been in that house before. I know he has a pornographic art collection, so don't try to pass that off as news.'

'Has he?'

'He's sold a lot of it. Somebody must have warned him he's under observation.'

'I can't think who would warn that man of anything.'

'Then you have more taste than I supposed! What have you told Laeta?'

'I am bound to secrecy.'

'Let me unbind you.' I inspected the arms of his instrument, while prising apart the elegant yokes, forcing them against their cross-strut . . .

'Oh leave off, Falco! I had nothing to tell Laeta, except a list of who attended. The Greek with the big beard was dire, I have to say.'

'That Greek is a master of jurisprudence. He could sue you in three different courts for insulting him. He might even win.'

'He'd have to be sober!' The singer fought back with spirit. I had to stop this; I was starting to like him.

'I know that the caterers were stealing, for a ransom scam. You must have seen them at it, at other parties. I know who's paying them as well. Momus. You don't want to tangle with that bastard.'

'His money's good, if you're desperate.'

'So you work for Momus too?'

'Not if I can help it. Sometimes the landlord here is very demanding . . .'

I looked around. The place was bare and unappealing. Not as squalid as rooms I myself had parked in, but unsuitable for a court musician. He wouldn't want Laeta to spot fleabites. 'Whatever the rent, he's overcharging! You can afford better.'

'Who cares? I'm never here.'

'Have some self-respect, man!' I was turning into his wise old nurse. 'What do you spend your fees on?'

'Saving for a once-in-a-lifetime cruise to Greece.' That figured.

'Did it last year—not all it's cracked up to be. Still, book it and go now. You could die of self-neglect and your efforts would all be wasted. So—who were the tumblers and the band working for?'

'No one special.'

'What? We're talking about Cretan shepherds in hairy coats!'

'Cretan my rear end! The tumblers arrived last week from Bruttium and all the rest came straight over the Tiber from Nero's Circus.'

'You amaze me! And they have no money-making sidelines?'

'I didn't say that. I believe,' said Scorpus, with disgust, 'the strummers have been known to sell stories about indiscretions for the dirty scandal page in the *Daily Gazette*.'

I winced. 'That's low!'

'I agree—though I believe there is cash to be made.'

'Fortunately the Camilli—to whom I am related, by the way, so watch it—are models of tedious morality. As for Anacrites, snitching on him would be madness: you could end up holding your next musical evening with Praetorian Guards, answering an arrest warrant signed by Titus Caesar, before they drag you on a very short walk to your death.'

I plucked his lyre, reflecting that the musicians he sneered at as strummers had played seven-string lyres too—their instruments probably costing much less than this fine pearl-inlaid walnut specimen. The singer gave me a sideways scrutiny. 'So what were *you* doing there, Falco?'

'Oh all I got was indigestion and a sore head.'

Thinking this had made us friends, Scorpus tried again to get up. I shoved him back angrily. 'Oh get this over with! What do you want, Falco?'

'Who did you see? There were two agents lurking in a back room—was somebody else with them?'

He had had enough time between playing his sets for a thorough reconnoitre. He knew about the Melitans. But Scorpus claimed, convincingly it seemed, that he saw no one else; he did not know who occupied that other room, where the pilfering chef found the cameo.

I gave up and went home for lunch.

The singer had lied to me. I did not know it at the time, but when I found out afterwards, I felt no real surprise.

38

After lunch my secretary needed me to attend to business; in superior homes it might be the other way around, but not with Katutis. He told me what I had to tell him to do. I complied. Still, I was lucky to have my hour with him. Now I was known to have a secretary, other people continually borrowed him. Katutis was supposed to take down my case-notes and start collating my memoirs, but he spent whole afternoons writing out soup recipes, curses and laundry lists.

Next, Helena wanted to discuss household matters, which meant more meek compliance. My daughters then had an urgent need to show me drawings and ask for new shoes like those their friend three doors down had been given by their spoiling parents. Even the dog stood at the front door with her leash in her mouth.

Only Albia tried to avoid anything to do with me, but I took her out anyway. That would teach her to tell Anacrites she could do an informer's job.

I was taking the cameo to Petronius. By the time we reached Maia's apartment, it was so near to evening we only just caught him before he left for duty.

'Hold on. I want to show you this, off vigiles premises.'

He got the message.

With Albia watching, we inspected the jewel. It was carved from sardonyx, the redder form of onyx. 'It's like an agate, Albia—layered hard stone.'

'More education!'

'Listen and learn, girl.'

Petronius held the gemstone in his mighty paw while he tried to work out what was going on in the picture. It was a two-layered cut, in low relief. The onyx banding was white and red-brown, beautifully executed. The lower half of the design showed a gloomy bunch of captured barbarians. On an upper frieze, gathered around twirly horns of plenty, minor deities were applying triumphal crowns to the noble brows of bare-chested noble personages. An eagle, probably representing Jove, was trying to muscle in. 'Claudian imperial family,' Petronius guessed. 'They always have that clean-cut, very close-shaven look. They were all untrustworthy midgets really.'

Albia giggled.

'He's exaggerating, Albia. Lucius Petronius, being a great hulk himself, likes to make out anyone dainty is deformed. However, this is so special it may even have belonged to Augustus or someone in that family, either commissioned by them or given as a gift by a syco-phant.'

Petro's eyebrows shot up. 'It's that good?'

'Trust me; I'm an antique dealer. Without provenance it's hard to be sure, but I would say this could be the work of Dioscurides. If not his own piece, it certainly came from his workshop.'

'Dio who?'

'Augustus' favourite cameo-cutter. Well, look at the workmanship! Whoever carved this was brilliant.'

Petronius leaned towards Albia and growled, 'Have you noticed how Falco keeps sounding like a bent auctioneer these days?'

'Yes, at home we all feel we are living with a fake-wine-jug seller.'

'Rag away!' I grinned. 'Whoever owned this—I don't mean some mystery lodger at the spy's house—knew its worth. The purchaser, who may have been a woman because it has been a necklace pendant, had the money and the knowledge to buy real quality.'

'Someone in mind?' asked Petro.

'I hope we can tie it to Modestus' wife, Livia Primilla. From the nephew's vagueness when I asked about any distinguishing jewellery she wore, I don't think he would recognise it, but he said she wore good stuff.'

Petronius perked up. 'If it was her, and if she was wearing this when she disappeared, there is a chance we can identify it.'

He told us that the Fifth Cohort had picked up a runaway slave living rough near the Porta Metrovia, who was called Syrus. They were bringing him over to the Fourth that night, for quizzing about whether he was the Syrus given to the butcher by Sextus Silanus— the one who had waved Primilla off when she went to see the Claudii.

'Couldn't the Fifth have asked him for themselves?'

'They could have tried,' said Petro. 'But the slave's scared to talk and everyone knows Sergius is the best in the business.'

Sergius was the Fourth Cohort's torturer.

At this point I would have left Albia at Maia's house; sensing a brush-off, she insisted on coming to the station house with us.

Sergius was waiting for Petronius to arrive before he started. He had stashed Syrus in a small cell, like someone marinating a choice cut of meat for a few hours before grilling.

'You could just ask the man,' Albia suggested. It could have been Helena talking.

'Not half the fun,' said Sergius. 'Besides, the slave's evidence will only count if he screams it out while I'm thrashing him. The theory is, pain will make him honest.'

'Does it work in practice, Sergius?'

'Once in a while.'

'How can you tell whether what he says is true or not?'

'You can't. But then you can't tell when you're questioning a free citizen either. Most of them lie. That applies whether they have something real to hide—or are just being buggers on principle.'

I thought Albia might have been upset by the whip man's attitude, but young girls are tough. She listened quietly, filing away the details in that strange little head of hers. 'If this is the right slave, what will happen to him?'

'He will be whipped hard, for causing us trouble, then returned to whoever owns him.'

'No choice?'

'Certainly not. He is their property.'

'A non-person?'

'That's the definition.'

Albia accepted this as one more fact that showed Romans were cruel—assuming that idea was what caused her enquiry. Sometimes she was unreadable.

Albia turned her pale little face to me. 'Do you think coming from a rough, hard background, being treated badly in their slave generation, explains why those Claudii turned out as they are?'

'Maybe. But some groups, some families are feckless by nature. People carry their character defects from birth, whatever their origin. You find freedmen who are loyal, kind-hearted, hard-working and decent to live with. Then you find noblemen who are vicious, deceitful and intolerable to be around.'

Albia smiled. 'Helena would say, "I blame their mothers!" '

Petronius clapped her on the shoulder. 'There may be some truth in that.'

'So how does this theory explain Anacrites the spy?'

Petro and I both laughed. I said it: 'He is just a poor sad boy who never had a mother!'

Albia gave me a long look. She did not say, since she could see I had just remembered it, that until Helena picked her off the streets in Londinium, she herself had struggled with neither parent.

Petronius, a father of girls, recognised her mood. 'Falco is right. Most people do seem to be born with a character inbuilt. So you, Flavia Albia, are destined to be decent, sweet and true.'

'Don't patronise me!' Of course, being Lucius Petronius, he had charmed her.

We left it there. Sergius, with his long whip, was impatient to begin.

He got as far as ascertaining that the terrified fellow the Fifth had brought us was indeed the slave Livia Primilla owned. When she went to see the Claudii, she had given him instructions to wait three days then if she failed to come home, to go to tell her nephew. Syrus, who looked as if he had come from the interior deserts of Africa, was able to describe the scene: Primilla mounted on a donkey, wearing a round-brimmed travel hat. The slave was poor on garments but thought her outfit was in shades of dark red, with a long fringed stole that was also red or damson coloured. Petronius showed him the sardonyx cameo; he failed to recognise it.

One new piece of information emerged. Petronius demanded: how could her staff, despite their duty of care to their mistress, have let Primilla go off alone to see the Claudii—especially after Modestus had already gone missing? Syrus said Primilla had intended to meet up with someone: the overseer who looked after the property and who had first found the broken fences, a man called Macer. This was a development. This man had not previously figured in the disappearances. He must be one of the family slaves who had run away.

At that point, we were thwarted. Loud hammering at the mighty gates of the station house announced unwelcome visitors. The gates were kicked open. In burst a small group of large armoured men. Plumes danced in their glittering helmets. Violence curdled the air.

Three tiers of military cohorts kept law and order in the city; neither law nor order had much to do with the feud between them all. The Praetorian Guards despised the Urban Cohorts and they both hated the vigiles. But the Praetorians protected the Emperor and were commanded by Titus Caesar now; whenever those thrusting bullyboys strode from their camp and appeared in public, there could be no contest.

They burst into the exercise yard like dam water after a leak. There was no stopping them. Petronius did not try. Somehow Anacrites had learned we had the slavey; he had sent the Guards to snatch Syrus. They made it plain, it would be foolish to request a warrant.

'Take the ungrateful bastard; I don't want him. Our budget's too tight for feeding runaways.' Well, Syrus was a slave. Nobody was going to make an issue of it. 'I heard the Fifth had found him,' Petronius told the Guards' leader helpfully. 'My plan was to check the facts and send him up to the Palace with a note. You're doing me a favour. He's all yours.'

'Oh he is!' snarled the Guards' leader. 'Word of warning—don't meddle!'

'Are you speaking for Anacrites?'

'None of your business who I'm speaking for—back off, soldier!'

I could not believe the spy had been so crude—and it went against the careful pretence of comradeship he had been laying on thick at his dinner party. But that was him, since his head wound. He was highly unpredictable. Capricious mood changes damaged his judgement. The one thing a spy needs is self-preservation—and that demands self-knowledge.

Syrus was hauled from the interrogation cell by the Emperor's élite thugs while we stood around like puddings. Terror overtook him so his legs gave way; the Guards virtually carried him. His eyes rolled white and he shat himself. It had nothing to do with Sergius, who despite our teasing of Albia had barely touched him. Petronius was not preparing a witness statement; he had wanted answers, answers he could trust. Instead, as the Praetorians dragged the slave away, the poor creature knew his fate. He would be dead in a ditch within the hour. Anacrites, we were starting to suspect, either knew the answers already or he did not care.

Petronius cursed. He knew nobody would ever see that slave again. At least we still had the cameo. Petro retrieved it from a murky bucket of water where he had quickly dropped it when the Guards crashed in.

As for them giving us orders to back off, it was blatant intimidation. Nothing new for the Praetorians; not so new for the spy—but foolish. So stupid, in fact, that Petronius and I wondered if Anacrites had lost his grip.

39

You two great men have lost yourselves!' Albia was a frank wench; it was liable to get her into trouble. 'Why don't you ask the big question: if the cameo really belonged to Primilla, and if it was taken by a killer—*how did Anacrites get it?*'

I pointed out coldly that I had spent all morning among the dregs of artistic society trying to find out. 'Anyone else, Petronius and I would go along to his house, pin him to a wall with a meat skewer and demand an explanation. But the spy can't be handled like that. He claims it belongs to some woman he had had at the house.'

Petronius snorted. 'She must be desperate.'

'So many are, sadly,' Albia commented. 'That is how you men get away with things.'

'Helena is teaching her a lot!' said Petro.

'Sarcasm especially. It's always possible the spy does have a girl-friend.'

Albia biffed this aside. 'The jewel was found by the hog-chef, tucked away in luggage that we think belongs to the Melitan brothers. If they are Melitan. Or even brothers. Who said so? Nobody. This is just a fantasy Falco dreamed up last Saturnalia, when he had had too much wine with his hot water. I remember the pair of them watching our house, and the only thing we could tell was that they were idiots.'

'You ought to be at school, young lady,' Petronius instructed her. 'Not hanging around a vigiles house, causing upset.'

'I'm making sensible suggestions. And, by the way, I am home-tutored by Helena.'

'Oh take her home, Falco.'

'I can't. You and I have to talk about this cameo—'

'Send her then. Albia, be off with you!' Petro lowered his voice to me. 'I could assign a man to escort her—'

'I don't need a bodyguard!' snapped Albia. 'I'll go by myself.'

She went.

Petronius Longus stared at me. 'You let her walk in the streets alone?'

'Nothing else is practical. You allow Petronilla out unchaperoned, don't you?'

'Petronilla is a child. Much safer. Your girl is marriageable age.' He meant beddable.

We left it.

'She's right,' I grumbled. 'We need to explore how the cameo came to the Melitans.'

'Surely you mean the idiotic agents of unknown origin?'

'Bastard! I'm sure they look like brothers. Listen—if there is an innocent explanation for them having it, that saves us trying to link this to the Pontine killings. Maybe Anacrites really does screw women. Asking him for more details will be a waste of effort—but we could find his unknown-origin agents and ask them questions. He won't like it, but by the time he finds out, it's done. Can't you put troops out to look for them?'

Petronius groaned. 'I'd love to. I haven't got the manpower, Falco. If Anacrites keeps them close to him at home or in his office, those are no-go areas. I can't send troops into the Palace and I am not getting a formal reprimand for watching that swine's private house—

especially not on a case I was told to drop,' Petro concluded reasonably.

'Last night, he suggested they were his bodyguards.'

'Then the whole idea is definitely off.'

'You didn't tell me it was on.'

'I'm thinking about it.'

In the end, Petro taxing his brain proved unnecessary. One of my nephews turned up at the station house, bringing a message. Katutis had written it out. His writing was so neat, I always had difficulty deciphering the letters.

'What exactly is the point of your secretary, Falco?'

'Oh he goes his own way. That keeps him happy.'

Petro got his clerk to decipher. Albia had spotted one of the hangdog Melitans. Anacrites was watching my house again.

'The bastard! He's made this too easy for us—'

Petronius grabbed my arm. 'Now hang on, Marcus; we need to plan this properly—'

I nodded. Next minute he and I were scuffling in a doorway, laughing like ten-year-olds, as we each tried to be first through as we dashed out to run down the Aventine by the nearest steps to the Embankment. We knew that in taking on the Melitan we would be taking on Anacrites. Nothing of what happened next had been adequately considered. But with hindsight, it is fair to say Petronius and I would still have done it.

40

We separated and approached from two directions.

It was still light. The day's heat had diminished slightly, but blue sky still soared over the marbled bank, the Tiber, and the low hills opposite. The frenetic hum of city life had lost a little of its persistence as businesses slowed down and individuals thought about going to the baths. Those bath houses that had already opened would have just allowed admittance to their outer porticoes. Stokers were busy raising a smoke, ready for the formal entry to the changing rooms when the bell rang. There was plenty of banging and shouting, which carried further across the water as the last boat relays brought goods up to the Emporium from Ostia, making the weary stevedores curse as they longed to down tools and bunk off to wine shops.

Surveillance could not be easy. My house had no side or back approaches. The front looked straight out across the Tiber over the Transtiberina slums, towards the old Naumachia where Augustus had staged mock-sea-battles. Nobody here kept topiary in terra-cotta pots, suitable to hide behind, because if we did night-time drunks just rolled them over the road and pushed them in the river. Occasionally carts were parked, but as the Embankment was a main thoroughfare and a commercial artery, the street aediles had them moved to avoid congestion. All an observer could do was hang around in the road chewing a bread roll, hoping I would not appear in person and spot him. Last time the two so-called Melitans were watching us, the whole family used to wave at them as we came and went. Even the dog once ran up to wag her tail and say hello.

Albia was right. He was there. One of them, on his own. I wondered where his brother was. Maybe the two agents were taking turns—or if Anacrites was thoroughly obsessed with us, the other might be outside Petro and Maia's apartment. We would have to find out. My sister would become hysterical if she thought the spy was having her watched.

What we did next was totally unplanned. Petronius and I had been in this kind of dark situation once before, in Britain. An officer who betrayed our legion had to be dealt with. Justice was done. Maybe it gave us a taste for hard revenge. I for one had hoped we'd never find ourselves in such a situation again, but when we ended up here on the Embankment with the spy's agent, neither Petro nor I thought twice.

The man saw me coming, as I walked directly up to him. He was considering resistance when Petro tapped him on the shoulder from behind. We were already too close for him to run or fight. So we had him. We simply took him into custody.

At the time we presumed he thought Anacrites would rescue him. Perhaps he did think that. Perhaps we did. He may have expected we would merely argue about the surveillance, at worst throw a few punches, then order him to stop harassing me. That may even have been what we initially intended.

We searched him. It was no surprise to find that he was carrying: four knives of different sizes plus a short piece of rope that was only suitable for strangulation. We kept him standing in the road while we stripped him of this armoury, not bothering to be polite, though since it was a public place, we were not particularly brutal. He grunted a bit. Petro and I were feeling our way towards a decision.

Once we made him safe, we took him into my house. He had not expected that. Neither had we, to be honest; it seemed to follow on naturally from the search process. In this way we took him off the street and out of sight very rapidly—and we saved Petronius the potential awkwardness of imprisoning one of the spy's men at the station house. As soon as we stepped inside and the front door closed, everything became intensely serious.

We put him in a downstairs room. It was one of the damp ones I reserved for summer storage. In August he would not develop asthma or foot rot. The walls and door were thick. I pointed out that nobody would hear him call for help. Then we gagged him anyway. By this time, the black implications were growing. For him, there could now be no happy ending. For us, too, there was no going back.

We worked quietly. He endured it with resignation. This would not be a job for the vigiles punishment officer, Sergius and his metal-tanged whip; we would give it our personal treatment. The agent was an unimpressive specimen, but it was soon clear he would be professional. We bound his arms behind his back, tied his ankles together, then picked him up like a long parcel and roped him carefully to the top of a heavy bench, face up. We turned the bench on its end so he hung upside down, then left him to think about his situation while we went for refreshments and warned all my household that the room was out of bounds. Albia would probably have rushed straight in there, but she was out on one of her long solo walks.

Helena was apprehensive, though we tried to avoid her concern. She could tell Petro and I were beginning to feel raw. We had no regrets about our capture, but we had put ourselves in a grim deep hole. Helena drew herself up and said, 'I live here with very young children. I want to know what you are intending to do to this man.'

'Ask him questions.' Ask him questions in a particular way, a way that would produce answers—eventually.

'And if he refuses to answer?'

'We'll improvise.'

'How long should it take?'

'Perhaps a few days, love.'

'Days! You are going to hurt him, aren't you?'

'No. There's no point.'

'Am I to provide food and drink for him?'

'That won't be necessary.'

'I wish you meant he won't be here that long.'

'No. We don't mean that.'

'You cannot starve him.' We could. With this kind of man, we would have to. And that was just the start.

'Well, maybe a bowl of delectable soup, with an aromatic scent,' suggested Petronius with a smile. 'After two or three days . . .' To stand in the room and tantalise.

'What about toilet facilities?' Helena demanded angrily.

'Good thinking! A bucket and a large sponge would be wonderful, please.' We would clean up as we went. Petro and I had fathered babies; we could look after a prisoner hygienically. A regime of squalor has been known to work, but Helena was right; this was our house.

Our first conversations with him were civilised.

'Anacrites sent you—agreed? How long have you known him?'

'Couldn't say.'

'I can check the payroll. I have contacts.'

'Couple of years.'

'Who is the other fellow I've been seeing with you? A brother of yours, I'm thinking.'

'Could be.'

'Where is he?'

'Gone to see his wife.'

'Where's that?'

'Where he lives.'

'Don't be funny with us. You two look like twins.'

'And you two look like donkey-fuckers.'

'I'll overlook that, but don't push us. Do you have a name?'

'Can't tell you.'

'Are you from Melita?'

'Where?'

'Small island.' Ma had a Melitan lodger once. Thinking about it, at close quarters, this man was not olive-skinned, hairy or stumpy enough. He was hard to place—not from the East, but not from as far north as Gaul or Britain either.

'Don't insult me. I'm from Latium,' he claimed.

'You don't look like it.'

'How would you know?' A generation back, on Mother's side, I was from Latium myself. His accent was right: Latin, though countrified. This was almost the first occasion I had heard him speak. Three-quarters of Rome sounded just the same.

'What part of Latium?'

'Can't tell you.'

'Could be anywhere from Tibur to Tarracina. Lanuvium? Praeneste? Antium? Come on, what's the harm? Be specific.'

Silence.

'At least he never says, *Find out yourself!*' Petronius weighed in. 'He's being wise. That only leads to a big kicking.'

'Not our style.'

'No; we're soft little cupids.'

'So far.' I think we knew we were on the cusp of surprising ourselves.

'He doesn't like you, Falco. Perhaps he has a point. Let me talk to him. I expect he wants to deal with a professional.'

'Just don't thump him. You'll defile my house.'

'Who needs to touch him? He's going to be sensible. Aren't you, sunshine? Tell us your name now.'

'Find out yourself.'

Oh dear. Well, Petronius Longus had warned him.

We left him soon afterwards. It was dinnertime. For us.

4 1

We continued. One at a time, then in tandem. Long pauses. Short pauses. For the agent, existence became concentrated on events in this small room. When Petronius and I left the door open briefly, so he heard a child's cry or a rattle of pots in the distance, it must have seemed otherworldly.

'What's your name?'

'Can't tell you.'

'Won't, you mean. Why did Anacrites order you to watch my house?'

'Only he knows.'

'We may have to ask him, then. So much easier all round, if we can stop him knowing you were so easily spotted and caught . . . No, I'm wrong. He must realise by now. How soon do you think he missed you? Can't have taken long. Where is he, I wonder? What's he going to do about you? You would think Praetorian Guards would rip in here to grab you back for him. Has he given up on you? Perhaps he's away—could he have gone to the Pontine Marshes, working the Modestus case? Looking for the Claudii—have you heard about them?'

'Can't tell you.'

Petronius Longus suddenly spun the cameo in the air. 'Did you have this?'

'Never seen it before.'

'You or your brother?'

'Better ask him.'

'Now I'm depressed, Falco—imagine having to talk to two of them!'

'Suits me. One each. You could take yours to the station house, give him a real thrashing, use your implements. I could keep one here to play with.'

'Yours would talk first. You wear people out with your wonderful kindness. Villains cave in, weeping. They want the brutality they are used to. They understand that. You being their lovely benefactor just confuses people, Falco.'

'No, I think people respect humanity. After all, we could pull out his fingernails and crush his balls. Instead, what does he get? Moderate language and a pleasant manner. Look at this one—he admires restraint, don't you?—Oh don't hit him again; he's going to tell us everything without that . . . I still think he and the other one are twins. Twins can communicate through thought, you know. I bet his brother's sweating. What's your name again?'

'Can't tell you.'

'What's your brother's name?'

'Can't tell you.'

'Where did this cameo come from?'

Long silence.

42

Once, I thought he had been weeping while we left him alone. On my return, his eyes were dull, as if in the long interval of solitude, he had been remembering old pain. But his resistance stiffened. Someone had spent years conditioning this man. We could not touch him. He would endure all, without weakening and collapsing. He would ride it out, even curbing signs of hostility, until we gave up.

We were tiring of the game. He had stopped refusing to tell us things. He stopped talking to us at all.

'I'm going to throw a bucket of cold water at him.'

'No don't do that. This is my house, Petro. I don't want water everywhere. You go and have a bite. There's some really good goat's cheese, just came from the market this morning, strong and salty. And I've put out a flask of Alban wine; believe me, you really need to try it. Leave me with our friend here.'

Petronius left the room.

'Now, here we are, cosy and private. How about you tell me who you are and what you do for Anacrites?'

No answer.

I threw a bucket of cold water at him.

43

A development.
Helena Justina had been brooding ever since we first brought the man into the house. Now she braced herself, waited until everyone else was preoccupied, then came down to see what was happening.

We had the bench standing properly at that time. He was looking up at the ceiling, or he would have been, had he not appeared to be asleep. Petronius and I were standing back, arms folded, thinking up our next move. At that quiet moment, Helena must have been surprised by the ordinary atmosphere. She may have felt relieved by the lack of violence. Then she realised it was more sinister than it appeared.

Petronius and I greeted her affably. Outwardly normal, we could have been two men in a workshop who had been preoccupied with a big carpentry project; she could be the woman of the house just making sure two simple lags were not drinking nettle beer brewed in a billycan or reading pornographic scrolls. Our sleeves were rolled up high. Our attitude was businesslike; though drained by days of concentrated, unsuccessful effort, we were feeling weary.

The man on the bench seemed aware that Helena had entered the room. His eyelids flickered, though his eyes stayed closed. She stood there: more gaunt facially since she lost the baby, tall, positive though wary, dressed in drifting summer white, wafting a light silver-blue stole, as cool as refreshing sorbet chilled in a rich man's snow-cellar. He might smell her citrus perfume. He must hear the quiver of her bangles and her clear voice.

Observant and intelligent, she absorbed the scene. I watched her looking for signs of what we had been doing—while dreading what she might learn. There was nothing to see. Everything looked clean and neat. She focused on the man. She saw his exhaustion, how hunger, thirst, isolation and fear were bringing him close to hallucination, despite his ferocious will to resist. He had to fight now, to stop his mind wandering.

Helena realised how our task had dispirited Petronius and me too, how our power over the helpless man would soon defile us. Most men would have been corrupted from the moment the prisoner was taken and tied up, his helplessness freeing them from moral restraint. Even we had to struggle to avoid being most men.

'This is too brutal. I want you to stop.' The words were firm, but Helena's voice shook.

'We can't, love. It's about long-term sanction of bad neighbours' bullying. It's about murder, and official cover-ups of murder. He seems to be involved. If his activities have an innocent explanation, he only has to tell us.'

'You are being bullies too.'

'Necessarily.'

'He is close to collapse.'

'He has endured worse, we can tell.'

'Then you won't break him,' Helena said.

We ourselves were starting to dread that. We had learned that he had been ready for the ordeal. He had put himself into a state of passivity. His background must be bad. His past experience hardly showed physically; there were no old marks or scars. We could not deduce what his previous life consisted of, though we could tell he knew humiliation and deprivation. When we made threats, he knew that situation too. He was in many ways quite ordinary, a face in any crowd. He was like us, and yet unlike us.

Helena had come with a prepared speech. Petro and I stood at rest and heard her out.

'I have only agreed to what you have been doing because Anacrites is so dangerous. I am horrified by what you have done to this man. You have toyed with him, teased him, tortured him. You have obliterated his personality. This is inhumane. It goes on for days, he never knows what will happen in the end—Marcus, Lucius, can you explain to me what difference there is between your mistreatment of this man, and the way that the killers of Julius Modestus abducted and abused him?'

'We have not used knives on him,' said Petro bleakly. The urge to keep up pressure on the agent got the better of him: 'Well—not yet.' He gestured to the hideous collection we had taken from our abductee. 'Those are his. Assume he carried them to use.'

It was an instinctive response, not the real answer. I knew Helena, loved her, respected her enough to find a better reply: 'There is a difference. We have a legitimate purpose—the general good. Unlike the killers, we don't relish this. And unlike their victims, this man can easily stop what is happening. All he has to do is answer us.'

Helena still stood there rebelliously.

'He has a choice,' Petronius reinforced me.

'He looks half dead, Lucius.'

'That makes him half alive. He is better off than a corpse—by a long way.'

Helena shook her head. 'I don't approve. I don't want him to die here in my house. Besides, you are running a huge risk. Surely Anacrites could burst in to rescue him any minute?'

The man on the bench had opened his eyes; he was now watching us. Had mention of Anacrites revived him? Or did Helena's spirited speech awaken hopes he had not known he harboured?

Helena saw the alteration. She moved closer, inspecting him. His light-skinned, now heavily stubbled face had a faint scatter of liver spots or freckles. His nose was upturned; his eyes were pale, a washed-out hazel colour. He could be, as he had told us, from Italy, though he looked different from true dark-eyed Mediterraneans.

In a much lower voice, Helena spoke to him directly. 'Anacrites will not be coming for you, will he? For some reason he has abandoned you.'

The man closed his eyes again. He shook his head very slightly, in resignation.

Helena breathed in. 'Listen, then. All they really want to know is where that cameo jewel originated.'

At last he spoke. He said something to her, speaking almost inaudibly.

She moved away again and looked at us. 'He says it was found in undergrowth, out on the marshes.' Helena walked to the door. 'Now you two, I want him out of here, please.'

She refrained from saying, *That was easy, wasn't it?*

We refrained from pointing out he could be lying; he probably was.

When she had gone, Petronius asked him, in a quiet, regretful tone of voice, 'I don't suppose if we took you to the marshes, you would point out the spot where you say this cameo was found? Or tell us more about the context?'

The man on the bench smiled for once, as if he let himself enjoy our understanding; he shook his head sadly. He lay quite still. He seemed to believe that the end was coming. It looked as if he had decided there was no hope now, never had been any.

He spoke to us, the first time in two days. He croaked, 'Are you going to kill me?'

'No.'

We had our standards.

44

The next time I emerged from the room, I was shocked to find the hallway full of luggage. Sheepish slaves carried on moving chests out through the front doors, clearly aware that I had not been told what was going on. I bit my lip and did not ask them.

I found Helena. She was sitting motionless in the salon, as if waiting for me to interrogate her as roughly as we were dealing with the agent. Instead, I merely gazed at her sadly.

'I cannot stay here, Marcus. I cannot have my children in this house.' Her voice was low. Her anger was only just under control.

The usual thoughts passed through my head—that she was being unreasonable (though I knew she had tolerated what was going on longer than I could have expected) and that this was some overreaction in the grief she was still feeling after the baby's death; I had the sense not to say that.

I seated myself opposite, wearily. I held my head in my hands. 'Tell me the worst.'

'I have sent the girls away and now that I have spoken to you, I will be joining them.'

'Where? How long for?'

'What do you care?'

Flaring up like that against me was so rare, it shocked me. A terrible moment passed between us as I held back the urge to retaliate with equal anger. Perhaps fortunately, I was too tired. Then perhaps because I was so exhausted, Helena was able to see me as vulnerable and to relent slightly.

'I care,' I said. After a moment I forced out the question: 'Are you leaving me?'

Her chin went up. 'Are you still the same man?'

The truth was, I no longer knew. 'I hope so.'

Helena let me suffer, but briefly. Staring at the floor, she said, 'We will go to your father's villa on the Janiculan.'

She started to rise. I went across to her; taking her hands in mine I forced her to look at me. 'When I have finished, I will come and fetch you all.'

Helena tugged her hands free.

'Helena, I love you.'

'I loved you too, Marcus.'

Then I laughed at her gently. 'You still do, sweetheart.'

'Cobnuts!' she snapped, as she swept from the room. But the put-down she had used was a habitual one of mine, so I knew that I had not lost her.

I had to bring this to a finish.

Petronius and I had told the man we would not kill him. We could never give him back, however. Capturing one of the spy's agents was irreversible. So what happened to him next would involve more terror, cruel treatment and—soon, probably, though not soon enough for him—his death, even if it was not at our hands.

Petro and I had talked about a solution. We abandoned our efforts to extract information and made final arrangements. I had thought of a way to do this, so there would be no comeback.

I left the house, the first time I had been out for days. I went to see Momus. For an eye-watering sum, Momus fixed it up for me. I did not say who we wanted to put away so discreetly, or why; with his sharp grasp of a filthy situation, Momus knew better than to request details. When he wrote out a docket he just asked, 'Are you telling me his real name—or shall I give him a new one?'

We still did not know who he was. He was so hard, he consistently refused to tell us. 'Anonymity would be ideal.'

'I'll make him a Marcus!' Momus jeered, always one for a joke in bad taste.

I was startled how easy it was to make somebody disappear. Anacrites' man would be taken away from my house that night. The overseer who worked for the Urban Prefect was now expecting an extra body; when we delivered the Melitan, he would be infiltrated among a batch of convicts who were going for hard labour in the mines. This punishment was intended to be a death sentence, an alternative to crucifixion or mauling by the arena beasts. Protest would be pointless. Convicted criminals always claimed to be the victims of mistakes. Nobody would listen. No one in Rome would ever see him again. Chained with an iron neck-collar in a slave gang in a remote part of some overseas province, stripped and starved, he would be worked until it killed him.

We told him. I had once worked as a slave in a lead mine, so I knew all the horrors.

We gave him a last chance. And he still said nothing.

45

Soon after I returned home alone after removing the agent, Anacrites came to the house.

I had bathed and eaten. I had devoted time to making sure all trace of recent events had been removed. I was in my study, reading a scroll of affable Horace to cleanse my sullied brain. It was late. I was missing my family.

A slave announced the spy was downstairs. Would I see him? This was how things worked now; I would probably get used to it. Helena must have stiffened the staff, teaching them not to let visitors get past them. It gave a prosperous householder a few moments to prepare himself—much better than the days when any intruder walked right into my shabby apartment, saw exactly what I had been doing (and with whom), then forced me to listen to his story whether I cared or not.

I paused to wonder at the spy's timing—did he *know* we had shed our prisoner? Then I went in my house slippers to greet him.

He had no Praetorians. The other 'Melitan' was not with him either. He had brought a couple of low-grade men, though when I invited him up he left them below in the entrance hall. Taking no chances, I put slaves to watch them. I had known him when he only had available a legman with enormous feet and a dwarf; later he hired a professional informer, though he was killed on duty. A woman worked with him sometimes. This pair today were a grade up from basic, ex-soldiers I guessed, though pitiful; in a peaceful province they would have been relegated to rampart turf-cutting or in war they would have been expendable, mere spear fodder.

'I called in to wish you good fortune, Falco, on the Feast of the Rustic Vinalia,' Anacrites bluffed. I rarely honoured feast days, whether mystic or agricultural; nor did he, in my experience. I had sat with him in our Census office, yearning in vain for him to leave early to go sardine-munching at the Fishermen's Games in the Transtiberina or to pay his respects to Invincible Hercules.

'Thanks; how civil.' I refrained from bringing out a rock-crystal flagon of *rotgut nouveau.*

Anacrites favoured guarded sobriety while he was working—so different from Petronius and me, abandoning care at every opportunity and living on the edge. He made no attempt to cadge a festival drink. Significantly, as was also his tendency, he straightway lost his nerve. Despite having probably spent hours perfecting an excuse, he came right out with it: 'I have mislaid an agent.'

'Careless. What's it to me?'

'He was last seen outside your house. You won't object if I take a look around here, will you, Falco?'

'This is hardly an amicable gesture—and after we all had such a rollicking time at your hog-roast too! Still, help yourself. I dare say there is no point objecting. If you find him squatting on my property, I'll want compensation for his upkeep.'

This terse banter was interrupted by new arrivals. For an instant I thought the spy had brought the Guards after all. Someone banged the front door knocker in a military manner, though then a key scratched in the lock angrily: Albia. She had been roaming on her own again. I knew Helena had been unable to find her when the others left for the Janiculan; I was supposed to send the girl on. She looked disgruntled and, curiously, was accompanied by Lentullus.

'Thanks, jailor, you can go now!' she ordered him crossly. She stalked across the vestibule. From choice I would have ordered Lentullus to wait, so he could explain out of the spy's hearing. Albia turned back from the stairs and made furious signals for him to clear off.

Lentullus stood to attention and announced, 'Camillus Justinus asked me to return your young lady, Falco. He saw her outside our house, staring—it's a habit she's prone to recently.'

'Oh Albia!' I dreaded having to play the heavy-handed father.

'Looking is not a crime,' she snarled.

'You have been harassing a senator,' I disagreed, all too conscious of Anacrites listening in. 'If I know you, girl, you do your best to make your glare upsetting. Lentullus, please apologise to the senator. Thank Justinus for his kindly intervention, and assure them all this will not be repeated.'

'It's just that the Greek lady was getting spooked,' said Lentullus. 'The tribune said we'd better whip your girlie back home today and have a word with you about it.' He beamed at Albia, showing his admiration. 'She's a bit of a one, isn't she?'

'One and a half,' I grumbled. 'Anacrites, would you just excuse me for a moment while I sort out a reward for Lentullus—'

Anacrites waved me away, since he was then able to approach Albia. I heard the bastard offer that if she ever needed a refuge from family troubles, she knew where his house was . . . This evening had become a disaster.

Behind the spy's back I quickly passed to Lentullus the cameo jewel, pressing it against his palm the way Aulus had given it to me. Being Lentullus, he needed a really big wink to help him get the point. 'Remember the time we hid the tribune in that old apartment of mine? Can you find it again—above the Eagle Laundry in that little street? Could you possibly take a detour up there on your way back home?' I muttered where there was a hiding-place in my old doss, and Lentullus promised to conceal the jewel.

Albia had broken away from Anacrites and barged up, thinking I was talking about her. She sensed me making arrangements with Lentullus. 'I'll take Nux for a walk—if I'm allowed out?'

'You've just been out—but you are not a prisoner. Just stop stalking

Camillus Aelianus—and keep away from other men as well.' I meant the spy. Lentullus was too much of a clown to count.

I returned to Anacrites and his planned search of my house. 'Who are you looking for?' Better to ask, rather than admit I knew. 'Does your lost lamb have a name?'

'State secret,' Anacrites mumbled, pretending to make a joke of it.

'Oh, one of your precious bodyguards, would that be?' This was like trying to squeeze a dry sponge, one that had been desiccated in the sun on a harbour wall for three weeks. He nodded reluctantly, so I added, 'Aren't there two? Where's the other one? Doesn't he know what his brother's been up to?'

Anacrites shot me a suspicious glance. 'How do you know they are brothers?'

'They look like brothers—and in some passing conversation, they told me, you idiot. I don't waste my time trying to find out sordid details about your useless staff.'

Anacrites then set about peering into all our upstairs rooms, while I ambled along with him to ensure he saw nothing too private. I encouraged him to look under beds, if I knew there were chamber pots; I wished we had put snappy rat traps just inside cupboards. A toy donkey fell down a step and nearly made the spy take a tumble, but the beds were neatly made, shutters closed, lamps trimmed and filled. We had staff; order had seeped into my domestic life like a leaking drain. None of the slaves were discovered rifling papers or money chests, none were screwing one another in the guest rooms or playing with themselves alone in linen cupboards. Something about Anacrites made them all scuttle for cover even though I, their reassuring master, was escorting him, with my half-read scroll of Horace still tucked under my elbow and an expression of pained tolerance at his damned intrusion.

We glanced in every room, then went out on to the roof terrace. 'If he's up here, I'll throw him off.' By now I was curt. 'This has gone far enough. What's going on?'

'I told you—my agent has gone missing; I have to find him. He has family, for one thing; if something's happened, they will want to know.'

'Married?' I felt a strange need to know. I had shared three crucial days in that man's life. His worthwhile existence reached its end in my home. Petronius and I were his last civilised contacts. Remembering Helena's furious comparison, I wondered if psychopathic killers developed this warped sense of relationship with their victims.

'Yes, there is a wife—or so I believe.'

'Parents living?'

'No.'

'And he has a brother who looks like a twin.'

'They are not identical.'

'Oh you know something about them then, Anacrites?'

'I take care of my men. Give me credit for being professional.'

'An impeccable employer! He's probably fallen victim to a street mugger, or been knocked down by a wagon and hauled off to a healing sanctuary. Try the Temple of Aesculapius. Maybe he ran away because he couldn't stand his working environment—or couldn't stand his superior.'

'He wouldn't run away from me,' Anacrites said, with an odd expression.

We returned downstairs. On reaching the lower hall, Anacrites decided to search the ground-floor rooms. 'We don't use them,' I said. 'Too damp.'

He insisted. He looked ready for a fight with me, but I did not quibble.

When he looked in the room where we had kept our captive, Anacrites sniffed slightly. No trace of his missing man remained, though like a bloodhound, the spy seemed to harbour doubts. If I had believed in supernatural powers, I would have thought he was picking up the aura of a soul in torment. The room stood empty, apart from a well-scrubbed bench against one wall. The floor and walls looked spotless. The air was clean, pervaded only by a faint smell of beeswax where the boards had been given a buffing very recently.

'I used this as a holding cell,' I told Anacrites gently. 'For my late father's slaves—' Mentioning my bereavement made the bastard look humble. I wanted to kick him. 'While I was assessing which were for the slave market. And if, in your role as an interfering state auditor, you intend to ask—yes, I paid the four per cent tax on every one I sold.'

'I would not dream of implying otherwise, Marcus.'

Every time Anacrites called me Marcus it just reminded me how impossible it would be ever to call him 'Tiberius'.

He left eventually. I wondered if the unpredictable swine would come back for another attempt. Anacrites often did a job, then half an hour later thought of three things he had missed.

His 'search' was just a surface skim. He could be inept—yet he could also be more thorough when the mood took him. Tonight he just gave my house a casual walk-through. I even wondered if he had left his visit until now because he'd known all along where the agent was, and actually wanted to lose him from his payroll. After all, he knew I always spotted surveillance and would take against it. He had just claimed to be a concerned superior. When the Melitan went missing, it should not have taken him three days to act.

Luckily, at heart Anacrites was so obsessed with outsmarting me that once we engaged in mental tussle, he noticed little else. He seemed unaware that, while I walked him around, my heart was beating fast. When Albia left with Lentullus and called Nux for a walk, the madcap mongrel had raced downstairs eagerly. Our dog was carrying her latest toy. It was a short piece of rope; she liked to fight people for it, gripping on like fury, shaking it from side to side and growling with excitement. Nux would have offered to play the tugging game with Anacrites, had he shown the slightest interest. Instead, wagging her tail crazily, she scampered away after Albia.

As far as I could tell, the spy failed to spot that my dog's prized new toy had once been his agent's strangling rope.

46

Anacrites did not dare search Maia's apartment in person, though he sent his two ex-soldiers. They were very polite, especially when they found that only Marius (aged thirteen) and Ancus (ten) were in. They must have been warned to expect a termagant and possibly a large angry vigiles officer, so finding a scholarly boy and his very shy little brother caught them wrong-footed. My elder nephew wanted to be a rhetoric teacher; so, Marius practised legal disputation on them (the rights of a Roman householder) while they quickly peered about, found nothing, and fled.

Petronius heard about it later. He would have been furious, but by then something big had blown up. Something so big, that since no harm had been done at the apartment, he left the issue alone. He had noted it, though. He was adding it to the long list of outrages for which Anacrites would one day pay.

I was setting off to Helena at the villa when I received an intriguing invitation. I was to meet Petronius at a bar called the Leopard, one we never frequented. He suggested I bring my Camillus assistants. A cryptic note on his message warned us *Play by Isca rules.* Only I knew what that meant: it referred to a secret court-martial we once took part in. So, this was a meeting of high importance, to be kept from the authorities. Nothing that was said today at the Leopard would ever be acknowledged afterwards. No one could break faith. And for me, there was a subtle indication that somebody of status— Anacrites?—was about to be formally shafted.

Aelianus and Justinus were agog and turned up willingly at my house. We had a brief moment of tension when Albia stalked down to the hall while we were assembling. I overheard Aelianus plead with her, 'Won't you at least speak to me?'

To which Albia coldly answered, 'No!' She stormed out of the house, giving me a filthy look for my contact with Aulus. At least I knew this time she was not rushing to the Capena Gate to stalk him.

'You're an idiot!' said Quintus to his brother—who did not deny it.

When we arrived at the bar, Petronius was already there. He had a man with him. It was a large place. They were in a room at the back, which they had managed to keep to themselves. Money probably changed hands for that.

Brief introductions ensued. 'This is Silvius. He'll tell you himself what he does—insofar as he can say.'

The draughtboard and counters had been allocated to our room, a cover for us being there; we seemed like an illegal gambling consortium. While drinks were ordered, I sized up Silvius. He was lean, scornful, capable. Maybe early fifties. A semi-shaved grey head. One finger missing. Been around the houses—on good terms with the householders, maybe even better terms with their wives. I would not like him staying in *my* house. That did not mean I could not work with him—far from it.

'What are you thinking, Falco?' Petro asked, with a mild smile that meant he knew.

'Silvius is one of us.'

'Honoured,' said Silvius. He had an easy-going baritone voice that had ordered up plenty of flagons in its time. He had spent long nights in smoky bars, talking. Either he was a lyric poet, a speculative saucepan-seller—or he traded information.

The drinks came. Sides arrived simultaneously in pottery dishes. There would be no need for the waiter to trouble us again.

I saw Silvius eyeing the two young Camilli. Petro must have given him the rundown on us all. They had left their pristine togas in the clothes press and were turned out professionally: neutral tunics, serviceable belts, worn-in boots, no flash metal buckles or tags on their laces. Neither went in for jewellery, though Aulus had a rather wide new gold wedding ring; Quintus was not wearing his, but I thought he had had it on when he escorted his wife to the spy's party. You could just about take these two down an alley in the Subura without causing a rush of pickpockets, though they still had to learn how to pass along the streets completely unnoticed. At least they looked nowadays as though they might see trouble coming. As they thickened up in their middle-to-late twenties, each looked as if he might be handy when that trouble reached him. Their hair was too long and their chins too clean-shaven, but if we were soon to have action, I knew they would enjoy making themselves more scruffy.

'They will do; they are fit,' I said in an undertone. Silvius heard it without comment. Both Camilli noticed the exchange. Neither flared up. They had learned to accept how you edged towards acceptance in new professional relationships. When work was dangerous, each man had to make his own judgements about people he would be dealing with. Aulus leaned back on the bench and subjected Silvius in turn to scrutiny.

We raised a quiet toast, then set our beakers down again as Petronius prepared to speak.

'Is this about our Modestus case?' Having been to the marshes with us, Quintus was over-keen and jumped in. I laid a finger to my lips. Good-natured, Quintus shrugged an apology.

Petro began slowly. 'Marcus Rubella, my tribune, introduced Silvius to me, but officially, Rubella never met Silvius—and nor have I. *Officially* we surrendered the case into the safe hands of the honest Praetorians, together with their intellectual comrade, Anacrites the spy.

There's a poor interface with his organisation. We all let Anacrites play by himself.'

Aulus asked, keeping his voice level, 'Who are "we all"? The vigiles, the Praetorians, and whoever Silvius' people are?'

Petro gave a satirical growl. 'Here is how co-operation works, boys.' He branched into a lecture I had heard him give before: 'The Praetorian Guard provide the Emperor's security—hence the link with the intelligence outfit. Titus Caesar commands them, to keep them under control—though who will control Titus? They spend a lot of time nowadays arresting people whose faces Titus does not like. Upset Anacrites, and that could be us. The Urban Prefect is Rome's city manager. Duties include investigating major crime—note that. Then come the vigiles. Duties: sniffing out fires, apprehending street thieves, rounding up runaway slaves. When we catch minor criminals, we give them on-the-spot chastisement—otherwise we parcel them up for the Urban Prefect, who charges them formally. So another point to note, Aelianus: we have good lines of communication with the Urbans. Very good.'

I leaned on one elbow and pointed one forefinger at Silvius. Silvius nodded. He belonged to the Urban Cohorts.

The Camilli watched this interchange. Justinus asked pointedly, 'The Guards and the Urbans live in the same camp. Are they not natural allies?'

'You might think so,' admitted Silvius. 'Though not for long. Not once your keen eyes observed how the Praetorians behave like gods, looking down on the Urbans as their poor relations—while also thinking that the vigiles are puny ex-slaves, commanded by has-been officers.' Petronius spat out an olive stone. 'Pity the pathetic Urban who has bought the myth that it is easy to pass from one section to the other, merely on talent and merit,' Silvius continued in complaint. I wondered if that was what he had tried to do, and failed. 'No vigiles officer, I suspect, would even waste his time thinking it could happen.' Ah. Tell that to Marcus Rubella, whose dream was to rise on snowy wings to wear the Praetorian uniform.

'So you work in Rome,' Aulus pressed Silvius.

'Personally, no.'

We all raised our eyebrows—except for Petronius who calmly supped his drink and waited for Silvius to explain.

'The Praetorians,' said Silvius, with sly satisfaction, 'have to remain with the Emperor. The Urban Cohorts are free to roam. Our remit covers major crime—not only in the city, but anywhere within a hundred miles. Because, you see, any horrible criminal activity in that area might affect the sacred capital.'

'Now it makes sense,' said Aelianus. Even in the shaky hands of Minas of Karystos he had absorbed enough legal training to care about jurisdictions. 'For instance, the Modestus case would fall to you?'

'Yes, but Anacrites wants it.'

'So?'

'There is a magistrate at Antium—'

Justinus laughed. 'The invisible man!'

It was Silvius' turn to raise an eyebrow.

'When Modestus and Primilla disappeared, a posse from Antium was sent to investigate. Before Anacrites waded in and stopped our activity, Falco, Petronius and I tried to liaise with the magistrate but he declined to meet us.'

'You assumed Antium dropped all interest?' suggested Silvius. 'No, there is more to the man than that, boys. When he found nothing in the soggy marshes, it's true he went home and seemed to keep his head down. You may suppose he just spends his life enjoying the sea breezes at Antium, but this togate beach bum has a sense of duty—for civic rectitude, he could be one of our clean-living, right-thinking, porridge-slurping ancestors. Nor does bureaucracy scare him. Amazingly, he went on digging. He looked through records. Then one fine day, he was entertaining the Urban Prefect—our beloved commander, who, it has to be admitted, had gone out to Antium using official expenses in order to scout for a cut-price villa, to keep his bitching wife quiet. Over the men's sophisticated luncheon, words were exchanged of a diligent nature. Feel free to marvel.'

Aulus leaned in, scooping seafood from a dish. 'What have they found?' He had no truck with fancy narratives. Minas probably thought Aulus was not a natural lawyer, but his plain gruffness satisfied me.

'The magistrate has been following up reports of missing people, people who had disappeared while travelling mainly, so unlikely to have caused a local outcry. A list was prepared. Footmen were sent out into the countryside, some carrying long probes. And they *found*,' said Silvius, enjoying the chill he laid on us, 'two double sets of bodies.'

Aulus dumped a chewed prawn head in an empty saucer. 'So far.'

Silvius looked at me with only a trace of sarcasm. 'He catches on!'

'Thanks. I saved him from ruination: army and the diplomatic—he was a slow slug until I took on his training . . .' While Aulus seethed mildly, I pressed Silvius, 'You work outside Rome—so when the Antium big bug talked to the Urban commander, you were assigned to the case?'

'That's right. "Liaison officer". Keeping the locals on track—while letting them believe they have control.'

'Did you see the bodies yourself?'

He moved a little on his bench, disturbed by memories. 'Yes—one lot while still *in situ*. They were old bones. Nothing to identify. One pair much more recent than the other. Shallow graves, one trench to each body, each two of a pair lying close to each other—no more than ten feet separate—but the two pairs were half a mile apart. To find more, there will be a lot of ground to cover. The locals are still looking. And we've kept it secret.'

'People will soon know.'

'Sadly they will, Falco. So we need movement. I was sent to Rome to chivvy it up—only to learn the Modestus case has been passed over to the spy. I'm disgusted. This is no job for Anacrites. We Urbans won't cave in to him and the Praetorians. So our Prefect talked to the Vigiles Prefect. I've now been sent to communicate with you boys—very, very quietly. It's imperative the Praetorians don't know until they have to—and, until we can make arrests, nor must the Claudii.'

We all breathed in, or whistled through our teeth.

Petronius pushed aside his beaker. 'I'd like to hear more about the circumstances of these other deaths. How, when, where, who?'

'The graves are a few miles out of Antium. The oldest, just skeletons, may date back decades. The others are maybe five years old. How can anyone tell? A gravedigger from a necropolis was brought in to confer, but he couldn't say anything more specific. Because of their condition, impossible to say what had been done to them, though there could be cut marks on bones. We can't attach names—no clues to identity, though using the missing list, we may make guesses.'

'How were they laid out in the graves?' I asked.

'Arms at full stretch—like Modestus and that courier.'

'Any hands removed?' That was Petro.

'No. One corpse had an arm missing, but the grave had been disturbed, probably by animals. One had a foot off—maybe he kicked out and was given special punishment.'

'Any clothing or other items?'

'Nothing useful. Rags mostly. No money or valuables. It all looked careful, by the way. Marcus Rubella told me the courier's burial seemed rushed?'

'We're keeping an open mind on the courier,' I told Silvius. 'Even Anacrites thinks it could be a distraction, according to what he told me . . . Maybe it's him all along, trying to divert attention from the Pontine connection, to protect the Claudii.'

'Why would he want to look after those bastards?'

'Who knows? Have you met him? Do you know what he's like?'

Silvius spat contemptuously.

After a small pause Petro kept niggling. 'Did your four bodies give up any hints about the killer? Was there more than one, for instance? Did they stay on the scene afterwards, to commit further defilement?'

Silvius was pecking at snacks now, undeterred by the subject under discussion. 'The sites were too old. I wouldn't even say for sure that the deaths occurred where we found the graves. Two were in a lonely spot. It's a deep ravine, a place with a real sense of evil. We hated being there.'

'A ravine?'

'Water channel scoured out by a river at flood time. Dry in summer.'

Petro pushed back from the table, arms braced. 'So—this is the question: what makes you decide your very old corpses, discovered close to Antium, are linked to the Claudius family who live—insofar as we can call what they do living—away across the marshes.'

Silvius paused. He liked to milk a situation. We all waited.

'Petronius Longus, this is what I need your help for. There is a witness.'

'*What?*'

'Somewhere in Rome, we hope. Ten years ago, a young man fell into a street bar near Antium. He was hysterical and claimed he had been led off the road and nearly murdered by two villains. One man who seemed friendly and helpful had lured him, then suddenly jumped him and took him to an accomplice, an extremely sinister presence. He was obviously planning to commit terrible acts. The intended victim somehow escaped their clutches.'

Silvius himself shuddered, while the rest of us moved in our seats and variously reacted.

'Nobody took much notice at the time. If there was any kind of enquiry, it dwindled away fast. All the locals now think it was a couple of Claudii—Nobilis and one of his brothers. They were never interviewed, nor put in front of the victim for identification. They must reckon they got away with it. But we know the young man came from Rome—which of course wouldn't have helped him get attention in Latium. He is believed to have returned home after his ordeal. So, highly recommended Watch Captain with the interesting friends—' Silvius raised his beaker to the Camilli and me. 'You are requested to help me find him.'

47

All they knew was that the young man with the narrow escape was called Volusius. He was thought to be a teacher. Silvius had no details of his address in Rome. Petro had already tried the teachers' guild. A pompous official, possibly detecting that Lucius Petronius despised formal education, said he would ask his members but it would probably take time.

Petronius had cursed him for a piece of offal—but he managed to reserve this view until he was alone. Perhaps the guild master would come good. Wrong. It took him no time to 'consult his members'—in other words, he had not bothered. He said he had no member of that name on his current list and nobody had ever heard of Volusius. He declared the lad must have been an impostor. Petronius asked why would anyone ever lower themselves to claim fraudulently that they thrashed schoolchildren for a living? The guild master offered to demonstrate his big stick technique. Petro left, not hastily but without lingering.

The vigiles cohorts keep lists of certain undesirable professions (mine, for instance), though teachers are excluded. *Impersonating* a teacher, as the master had suggested, ought to be illegal but there were no lists for that either: probably because the pay was so low, fraud was in fact so unlikely.

Rubella still refused to allow Petronius to leave Rome. So by the time our meeting broke up, I had volunteered for another trip to Antium, to reinterview people at the bar where the escaped Volusius had turned up screaming for help ten years ago. If the bar was still there, which Petronius doubted, someone surely would remember a hysterical youth falling on the counter while screaming he had been abducted and scared witless. Even in the country, that must be more unusual than calves being run over by hay wagons.

The bar was there. It had been sold to a new owner who knew nothing about the incident. His clientele had changed. They knew nothing either.

Or so the bastards told me.

I pointed out quietly that if they left these killers on the loose, one of them could be a body in a shallow grave one day.

'Never!' a wall-eyed sheep-stealer assured me. 'All of us know better than to accept an invitation from Claudius Pius to go for a little walk down a marsh track to see his brother's spear collection.'

'Who mentioned Claudius Pius?' I asked in a level tone.

He rethought rapidly. 'You did!' he snapped. 'Didn't he?'

They all agreed that I had done so, despite it being obvious I had not. So against expectations I had discovered who lured away the victims—though this feeble conversation would not count as proof.

'Anyone seen Pius around here recently?'

Of course not.

'So tell me about "seeing the spear collection". How do you know that was the lure?'

'It's what the teacher said.'

'I thought you knew nothing about the teacher?'

'Oh no, but that's what people around here all reckon.'

'Anything else people around here know? Which brother's spears were on offer, for instance?'

'Oh Nobilis, bound to be. Probus has some, but nothing by comparison.'

'Any recent sightings of Nobilis?'

No. They said anyone who saw Claudius Nobilis would quickly look the other way.

'So what exactly are you scared of?'

They looked at me as though I was demented if I had to ask.

I was ready to give up. This bar might seem a safe haven to a young man escaping two murderers, but as a watering hole it was deadly. If this was the best place to buy a drink where I lived, I would emigrate to Chersonesis Taurica, die in exile like Ovid at the back of beyond, yet still think I had the best of it.

Preparing to leave, I glanced around the dismal place, then had one last try: 'I just can't work out what a teacher from Rome would have been doing on this road in the first place. None of them earn enough for a summer villa on the coast. I don't suppose "people around here" know why he came, do they?'

'He was coming to Antium to be interviewed for a holiday job.'

'Is that right!'

To my amazement, it turned out to be well known in those parts just which wealthy villa owner had summoned him. Incredibly, the rich man still had the same villa.

I never met the prospective employer, but it was unnecessary. He was the type who, faced with a potential hire who had come to grief, insisted that full details of the man's experience must be written down; in case Volusius tried to sue for compensation, presumably. A transcript still existed. I was shown it. They would not let me take it off the premises, but a scribe sat down and copied out the ten-year-old statement for me.

Volusius described meeting the man everyone now thought was Claudius Pius, who made friends and lured him off the road to meet his brother. Despite having no interest in weapons, the naïve young teacher found himself agreeing to accompany Pius. They went further than he expected, down extremely remote tracks, and he was already worried when they encountered the promised brother. This man was sinister. They met him in a clearing, as though he had been waiting. It made Volusius realise he had been deliberately stalked. He knew he had been brought here for evil reasons.

Volusius had made a terrible mistake. Although he felt he was about to be murdered, he managed not to show he understood his danger. Perhaps because there were two of them and they thought they could easily control him, the brothers were careless. Volusius broke away and managed to run off. Shaking with fear, he hid in a thicket for hours, overhearing a discussion about fetching a dog to track him down. As soon as he thought the men were out of earshot, he made a break for it, and ran until he reached the road and found the bar. The barkeeper at the time took him to safety at the villa where he had originally been heading.

The villa owner had clout. A search was conducted, though nobody was found. No one then made a link with the Claudii. Volusius gave a description of the two men, but it was too vague. If he had heard names, he could not remember them. He went into shock, too jittery to be of use as a witness. Some people even doubted his story. There was not a scratch on him. Nobody had seen him with the strangers. His fear might not be caused by trauma, but a pre-existing mental problem that made him imagine things. Enquiries petered out.

'And did he get the job?' I asked the slave I was talking to.

'Out of the question. He was a gibbering wreck. A man in that state could not be allowed to give lessons to respectable boys. He never even met them.'

'What happened to him?'

'He went back to Rome.'

'Was he fit to travel? After such an ordeal, didn't he panic at the prospect?'

'We kept him here a few days. He was allowed to write a letter and his mother came for him.'

'Got her address by any chance?'

'Afraid not, Falco.'

'We've lost him then . . .'

'Why do you need to find him? It's all here.'

'And it's invaluable, thank you. But we now believe the two men existed all right and there is an idea who they are. Volusius, as the only known survivor, might be able to identify them.'

'I bet he'd still panic, even after all these years.'

'Maybe. We have to hope seeing them in custody will reassure him . . . Tell me, what was the point of offering him a job here? Don't boys in a wealthy family have their own private tutor? Were they so dumb, they needed extra cramming in the summer holidays?'

'Excuse me! Quite the opposite. My master's sons had an all-round education in which they both excelled. This was to give them special lessons, because they were so gifted and mentally demanding.' It was to keep them occupied, I guessed, to stop them groping the maids and setting the house on fire. 'Volusius had a sideline—expertise in algebra.'

Now we were getting somewhere. The vigiles do not keep track of the miserable, half-starved souls who teach urchins the alphabet under street corner awnings, not unless there is a *very* large number of reports of sexual abuse; or, better still, complaints about noise. But in Rome, playing about with numbers carries dark undertones of magic. Like prostitutes, Christians and informers, therefore, mathematicians are classified by the vigiles as social undesirables. Their details are kept on lists.

48

I had one more task before I left Antium. I went to the workshop which had once belonged to the famous cameo-cutter, Dioscurides. He was long gone but an atelier still existed, where high-class craftsmen made every kind of cameo, not just from gems and from coral brought up from the Bay of Neapolis, but wondrous pieces carved from two-tone layered glass. I bought a small vase for Helena, an exquisite design in white and dark blue which I could either save for her birthday in October or hand over now to win her round if she was still being distant with me.

Remembering that I owned an auction house, I even made enquiries about bulk purchase—but the snooty salesmen sneered at that; they wanted only to deal direct with customers and take all the profits. Pa would have wangled some deal, I knew. I wasn't my father; I refused to become his ghost.

Exclusivity did help, however. When I asked about the jewel found at Anacrites' house, I was told they would have records of who made it, who bought it and when. I described it. They professed admiration for my eloquent detail. They sent me out for lunch. When I returned, a small piece of parchment was handed over, which they insisted was in confidence. The cameo had been made a long time ago for an emperor who died before it was finished; it had remained at the work-shop, awaiting the right buyer, until very recently.

Sadly, the eventual purchaser was not Modestus or his wife Livia Primilla, but a man in Rome called Arrius Persicus, who must have oodles of bullion, from the price he paid. It was not written down, though proudly whispered to me. The gem left the workshop only a few weeks ago. That too ruled out Modestus and Primilla. It also left no obvious link to Anacrites. Unless Persicus had disappeared myste-riously in the past month, the agent's claim to Petro and me that the cameo was found 'in undergrowth on the marshes' became suspect.

It was possible Persicus had been done in on his way back to Rome with his expensive new bijou. Petronius would have to check if he had been reported missing.

'Is he a collector of precious objects, or do you know who he bought it for?'

'Confidential, Falco.'

'Girlfriend, you mean?'

'We rather thought so.'

'I'm sure you get a smell for it . . . Is he married?'

'Presumably. He bought a second piece that day—very much cheaper.'

How sad life could be.

I returned to Rome, passing straight through and making my way to the Janiculan. Communicating with my own sweet wife Helena Jus-tina was now an urgent issue.

I dumped my luggage in the porch. Times had changed: I knew people would take it in for me. I could hear my little ones romping in the gardens, with Nux barking. Instinct drew me down a path away from them. I found Helena seated on a bench that had been set up close to where we held my father's funeral. A new memorial stood there, with an inscription to Pa and a sad last line naming our lost baby son. *Also Marcus Didius Justinianus, beloved of his parents: may the earth lie lightly upon him.* I had not been able to ask Helena anything about this; I had to arrange it myself. I had not even seen it since the mason set it up.

Helena's attitude suggested that she came here regularly. She was not weeping, though I thought I detected tears on her cheeks. If she was managing to mourn, that was an improvement on her previous tight, tense refusal to acknowledge what had happened.

After I met her gaze, I sat beside her in silence, then we looked at the memorial together. After a time, Helena of her own accord placed her hand on mine.

It was some weeks to Helena's birthday, but when we returned to the house I gave her the blue glass vase anyway. She was worth it. I told her that; she told me I was a hound, but she still loved me. 'I would have been just as pleased at your return without a gift.' A man in my line of work has to be cynical, but I believed her.

'Just so long as you don't see it as a bribe.' This would be our only mention of Petro and me keeping that man at our house.

'Even you can't afford the size of bribe you would have needed.'

'Oh I know. At least, unlike the wife of Arrius Persicus, you know I haven't bought a bigger present for some secret mistress.'

'No, darling. Spending even this much money must have been enough of a shock.'

'I'll get used to doing it. For you.'

'Well,' said Helena graciously. 'You had better go and tell Petronius Longus what you found out.'

'You're giving me a pass out of barracks!—Not tonight, though, honeycake. I'm staying in with you.'

'Don't overdo it, Falco—or I will think you have something to hide.' Helena Justina was almost her old self again.

I really felt too travel-weary to seek out Petro but sent a message to him with news of Volusius being a mathematician and Arrius Persicus buying the cameo. He would follow up these leads. I suggested we meet up for breakfast at Flora's next day. I burrowed back into domesticity—patted the children, tickled the dog, played mental tug of war with Albia about nothing much, bathed, dined, slept.

'Anyway,' Albia had demanded, 'what did you do with that scraggy bit of rope you took away from Nux? We spent hours searching for it while you were away.'

'I burned it. You don't need to know why—nor does the dog.'

'That was a waste. She loved her tugging rope.'

Nux was a scamp but I liked to think even she had standards. She might not have loved the rope if she knew what it was. Besides, with Anacrites repeatedly dropping in on us like an annoying uncle, the dog's toy had to be sacrificed.

While I was in Antium, he had even come up to the villa, Helena said. She told him I had gone to Praeneste for a client. She claimed it was a very attractive widow for whom I carried out unspeakable personal services; Anacrites had commiserated with her in apparent shock and sorrow.

'He said, *This is a new side to Falco.* So I snapped, *You are not a very good spy if you think that!* Don't relax,' Helena warned me. 'The man is not stupid. He didn't believe a word of it. Marcus, he will be wondering where you really did go.'

Next morning Helena arranged to bring the family back to our house. I had the impression she had been pretty well ready to do it even if I had not arrived to fetch them. I left the villa earlier. Even up here, I checked carefully that I was not followed. The spy was a man down now, though; perhaps he would stop haunting me.

Flora's Caupona was a decrepit drinks place in my family's part of the Aventine, run by my sister Junia. Luckily she had not yet arrived, since her mornings were occupied with the needs of her son, who was profoundly deaf. Junia had proved an inventive, devoted mother who spent hours coaxing him into basic communication. She had already had plenty of practice with her supremely dull husband, so perhaps her patience with little Marcus was not all that surprising.

In her absence the waiter Apollonius produced what the workers who formed the caupona's early passing trade had to endure as stamina food: stale bread and weak posca, the vinegary drink that is given to slaves and soldiers. Nobody who hoped for a sociable outdoor breakfast would ever come here. The tuck had one advantage, though; it was better, and safer, than what Flora's served for lunch.

Apollonius had once taught geometry at an infant school; he taught Maia and me. It would have been a neat coincidence if he had known the victim Volusius—a coincidence to find only in a Greek adventure yarn. In real life it never happens. 'Can't say I've heard of him, Falco.'

While I waited for Petro to show, I wondered glumly if the stricken young teacher half dead of fright at Antium could also have left his job and become a wine waiter. If so, in this city with hundreds of thousands of street bars, we would never find him.

I could tell by the jaunty way Petro approached that he had made progress. During the night shift, he said, the new facts I brought from Antium turned into excellent leads.

We told Apollonius to go into the back room and stay there, reading a long scroll of Socrates.

'What if customers come?'

'We'll serve them for you.'

'You can't do that!'

'My sister owns the joint.' Wrong. *I* owned the joint now; Junia just managed it for me. A terrifying thought.

'You mean you'll send my customers packing!'

'Relax. We'll call you.'

One or two latecomers did try to buy stuff. We told them we were hygiene inspectors and had to close the bar down. Then indeed we sent them packing.

49

Even after his shift, Petronius was buoyant. 'Let's start with the gem-buyer. Marcus, my boy, you've done well.'

'Persicus?'

'Persicus! He meant nothing to me, but Fusculus recognised the name.'

'Fusculus is a lad.'

'He's a sparkler. Too good, I'm afraid. Rubella will probably transfer him to another cohort for "career development".'

'How does he know about Persicus? We were not aware of him before, surely?'

'We could have been. He never showed on a statement, but while the Seventh Cohort were formally telling Rubella and me about that murdered courier, a couple of troops waited outside; talking to Fusculus, they gave up extra details. Their written reports are as skimpy as a whore's nightgown. I suspect their clerk can't even write—one of their centurions' halfwit cousins, who got the job as a favour . . .' He calmed down when I grinned. 'But their enquiry chief asked the right questions. The carter was forced to supply details of the courier's package, in case it was relevant—or the Seventh even found it.'

'Have they?'

'Don't make me weep! The carter said the parcel was a load of cushion stuffing, sent by a client to his country estate.'

'The client was Arrius Persicus?'

'Correct. This is the good bit. He's alive and well and has never mentioned losing any fabulous cameo.'

I guffawed. 'In case his wife finds out he has a girlfriend! Shouldn't cushion stuffing go the other way? Wool, feathers, straw—they all come from the country *into* Rome.'

'Exactly.' Petro tried to winkle crumbs of the stale bread we were gnawing from between his teeth. The crumbs clung on resolutely. Junia must have Apollonius spread it with cow-heel glue as some new gourmet fashion. 'The crucial parcel didn't sound significant initially—which was a clever ploy. The Seventh thought they could forget about it. So let's think: why dispatch a load of cheap stuffing via an expensive courier?'

'Obvious: something costly was concealed inside.'

'You bet.'

We sat quiet for a beat, thinking.

'Anyway—don't let's get too excited too fast. Fusculus has gone to ask the carter about it on the sly. We still have to pretend we're not intervening in Anacrites' case. If the cameo *was* in the courier's parcel, then it's a lead—but you and I need a long, hard think about the implications . . .'

'I'll start thinking too much now, unless you distract me. So, what about the teacher with the numerical sideline?'

Petronius perked up. 'Found him. Easy. The mathematicians list is one of the shortest: thank you, Jove. Volusius may have died eight years ago. At any rate, he vanished from our records—which is hard to achieve, once we have a rascal in our blotted scroll.'

I groaned. 'Dead end?'

'Not quite.' Petronius gave up on Flora's breakfast and threw what was left of his bread to a pigeon in the street. It flew off, affronted. He sniffed the acetic posca then dashed that into the gutter too. 'He lived with his mother, off the Clivus Suburanus, close to the Porticus of Livia. I'm whacked and old dames don't have enough verve to keep my eyes open. I'm going home to bed but you, being a layabout with time on your hands, may fancy a chat with her.'

I said I was always available to do work the noble Lucius found too much for him. And while he could only chat up pretty things of twenty, I was more versatile and could charm even older women.

Petronius let me get away with that, because he was bursting with one further fact. 'While I had the old documents spread around the room, my eye fell on something.' Calm by nature, he seemed excitable now: 'I found one of the Claudii!'

'Speak, oracle!'

'I'm sure it's him. Two years ago, a Claudius Virtus, newly arrived in Rome from Latium, appeared as a person of interest.'

'What had he done? Joined a dodgy religion?'

'Depends how you categorise cults, Marcus. We have him down as taking an interest in astrology.'

'Stargazing?'

'People-forecasting—wickedness. I hate that stuff. Life's dire without finding out in advance what will be dumped on you by Fate.'

'According to Anacrites, when he turned on me recently, when Fate gives you anything worth having, if you dare to enjoy your good fortune, remorseless Nemesis will fly up to snatch it away.'

'Is he sniping at your legacy?'

'You guessed. Is Virtus still living in the same place?'

'Who knows? We don't always update our records unless some name bobs up in a new offence.'

I said that in addition to Volusius' mother I would visit Virtus, but Petronius would not reveal the address. He would meet me for lunch after a few hours' rest, then we could go together. I promised to round up one of the Camilli, or both, to accompany us. Lunch could be at my house; Flora's had lost our custom.

'We should go armed. These bastards collect spears. The Urbans carry swords and knives—why don't we ask Silvius for back-up?'

Petronius Longus was a vigiles man and he would never change.

Despite the supposed joint operation with Silvius, he assumed a vague expression. 'Let's you and I just take a quiet recce first.' He was as keen on inter-cohort co-operation as a fifteen-year-old boy thinking about purity.

'Fine. We'll tiptoe up like cat burglars . . . I could knock on the door for a horoscope—but I don't want Virtus to look into my future and see when he and his stinking brother Nobilis will be arrested.'

'Don't worry.' Lucius Petronius had no faith in clairvoyance. 'He won't even be able to foresee what he's getting for lunch.'

'Right. What's your star sign, by the way? You're under the Virgin, aren't you?'

'Believe that, Marcus, if it gives pleasure to your childish mind.'

50

I sent a runner to tell Aulus and Quintus to come over for lunch. Meanwhile, I went alone to find the teacher's last known address.

It was a dismal mission. I found the apartment, in a tangle of narrow lanes on the way to the Esquiline Gate; indoors, as she generally must be, was the ancient, widowed mother. I guessed she had lost her husband young. Perhaps there had been a legacy; the rental where she lived—where she had brought up her only son Volusius—was cramped but just about tolerable. She was the proud kind, to whom poverty must be perpetually shameful. She had scrimped to get her boy an education, investing all her own hopes in his obvious potential. Although he became a teacher, because of his experience at Antium only disappointment followed. She was now half-blind, but taking in tunics to mend, to keep from starving.

Volusius was dead. His mother said he had never recovered from his fright that day at Latium. It affected him so badly he could no longer teach. He lost his job at the local school, then failed to find other work. He moped around as a loser, became mentally disturbed and committed suicide—threw himself in the river just after the second anniversary of being abducted.

'Did he talk about what had happened?'

'He could never bear to.'

'You went there to fetch him home afterwards. Was he in a bad state?'

'Terrible. He knew we had to pass the place where he had met those men. He froze at the memory. He was shaking so much when we tried to set off home, the people at the villa had to give him a sleeping draught and send us in a cart. Once I got him home, he woke up in familiar surroundings and just broke down crying. He kept saying to me he was sorry—as if what happened was somehow his fault.'

'I was hoping, if I could find him, he could describe the men who took him.'

The mother shook her head. *'Scum!'*

Such vehemence in the mouth of a civilised woman was ugly. The lasting effect on her was an extra consequence of the killings. This mother had not only lost her only son, too young, but all her own hopes. What happened to Volusius was on her mind daily. Now she lived alone, dwindling arthritically into fear and despair. There was no one left to take care of her. She was going to need looking after soon, and I could see she knew it.

When I said that now we thought we knew who the abductors were, she just waved me away. It was too late to save her son, so it was too late for her.

Angrily, I renewed my vow that this time we would find justice, for both Volusius and his mother.

51

Peace in the home. What a wonderful thought. If only I had it.

The Camilli had already arrived—anything to get away from Minas of Karystos and their wives. Nux was chasing around the house, barking loudly. Slaves were pursuing her, unaware that this only aggravated the dog's excitement. Albia would normally have waded in to sort this out, but she was shouting at Helena over me having invited Aulus. Julia and Favonia had picked up the idea of complaining and were wailing their heads off. As soon as I turned up, slaves began crying too; I could not see what that was about. Perhaps they were the ones I intended selling. I had not told them yet, but a list existed. They could have bribed Katutis to reveal it. Katutis was keeping out of sight, which clinched it.

Lunch. Very pleasant. Rather tense, but that is what lunch at home exists for.

No Albia. Helena had sent her on an errand to my mother. Ma would be taking me to task about the girl soon.

No dog. Worn out, Nux had fallen asleep in her basket.

No children. I had ordered them out of the room when Favonia threw a foodbowl on the floor and Julia giggled.

No slaves. I was not yet ready to treat a crowd of feckless strangers as extended family, with more domestic privileges than I allowed to my own relatives. I would house them, feed them, express gratitude and affection on a moderate scale—but no more. Nema, previously Pa's bodyslave, commented that he was very surprised by my attitude.

'We could have met at a bar,' Quintus suggested.

'Are you saying,' demanded his sister in a voice like an ocean breaker as it stripped barnacles off rocks, 'my house is badly run?'

'No, Helena.'

A meeting convened. Katutis appeared with a bunch of note-tablets and a hopeful expression; he was upset when I told him not to take minutes. 'Why else, Marcus Didius, would a man hold a meeting, but to have its conclusions recorded?'

'This is confidential.'

'Then good recording practice is to write "Confidential" at the head of the scroll.'

'So the next time Anacrites raids my house, he sees that and backs away bleating, *Oh I am not allowed to look at this!* In fact that's a certain way to make him grab it.'

Katutis slunk off, muttering like a malevolent priest.

The big, comforting presence of Petronius Longus soothed those of us who remained. Helena, whose meal had been interrupted by the various ructions, was still chewing flatbread. Dabbing chickpea paste ferociously on to her bread, she had the look of a woman who knew she would soon have heartburn. 'Oh don't wait for me to finish!' she scolded Petronius, in a tremolo of agitated bracelets.

Petro cracked on smartly. 'There is news. It's good—though it will pose questions. Since Fusculus proved the link to Arrius Persicus, I let him call on the carter, and thump him until he squeaked—'

'Can you not do anything without unnecessary violence?' Not a good idea to remind Helena about our treatment of the agent.

Petronius had the grace to look guilty. 'The carter now admits his spendthrift, two-timing client was indeed posting off a secret love token—and not for the first time. It was a routine arrangement. She's a lucky little pullet. This is why the carter panicked when his courier vanished—he thought the newly-wed had gone bad now he had a wife to support, so he pinched the gem. Later the carter kept quiet about that, in a misguided attempt to protect his customer.'

'Did the carter know what the hidden gift was?' Helena asked.

'A cameo on a chain. Persicus had bragged to him about it.'

'The chain is news,' I said. 'It's not been found. Who has got their sticky hands on that, I wonder? . . . Need we interview Persicus?'

'Not at this stage. If we want a deposition for the Prefect later, Fusculus can go along and scare him shitless then.'

'Back to basics then. The cameo comes from Antium, Persicus is sending it to his mistress. The gem is in some unconvincing wadding, in a parcel, in a pannier. The young bridegroom sets off on the donkey, no doubt whistling a jaunty measure and thinking about enthusiastic sex. Then what happened at the necropolis?' I ticked off possibilities: 'Better consider it: *did* the courier steal the gem?'

'No,' said Quintus. 'He wouldn't commit suicide and stuff himself in a shallow grave.'

'So was he robbed by somebody who knew what he was carrying? Did the carter himself set it up, even?'

'If so, he was foolish to report his courier missing.' Quintus again. 'And why would he kill his man?'

'As for someone else knowing,' Petronius said, 'Fusculus heard they were always very discreet when they had valuables to transport.'

'Models of good practice?'

'Fusculus said the carter swears the lad was tried and trusted. Could be relied on to avoid attracting notice.'

Aulus, who had been subdued since Albia had hysterics, recovered enough to add his thoughts: 'So, did the young man just classically happen to be in the wrong place at the wrong moment? Was his murder random—though then his attackers found our exquisite cameo in his donkey pannier and thought it was their lucky day?'

'That seems right,' I agreed. 'Being chosen by a cruising killer was an accident.'

'Someone who looked harmless, stopped him,' said Petro. '*Excuse me, what's the way to Clusium?—My pocket lodestone's broken . . .* I don't suppose this time the lurer said, *Do you want to look at my brother's lovely spear collection?*—but we'll never know.'

Helena had calmed down. She tidied bowls into piles. 'Now stop tiptoeing around the big question.' We men sat quiet, our backs a little straighter, our faces grave. 'How did someone in Anacrites' house get their hands on the cameo?'

Petronius drained his water cup. 'As far as the Seventh Cohort know, the donkey and its pannier disappeared. Suppose later, while Anacrites and his men were investigating, they found the donkey wandering?'

'Not right,' I said. 'He let the Seventh carry on with routine enquiries. Unlike you and the Fourth, he has no beef with the Seventh. Anyway if, for once, he actually found evidence, he would have boasted about it.'

Helena scoffed too: 'Even if his men had legitimately discovered the parcel, why did the cameo end up hidden in their luggage?'

'Are his agents screwing Anacrites—pinching evidence to sell?' Normally deadpan, Aulus looked cheery at the thought.

'Has been known,' Petro confirmed dourly. I knew the problem was endemic among the vigiles. House fires gave particular scope for pilfering from victims. 'But Anacrites knew about the gem, didn't he, Falco?'

'No, in fact.' I cast my mind back to the scene when the Camilli and I were pulling up the caterers for theft, with Anacrites watching us. 'When he saw the cameo, he first denied knowledge. He took a moment to realise what it must be. Am I right, lads?'

Both Camilli nodded. Aulus said, 'He looked annoyed—but he chose to protect the agents. Thinking fast, he came up with that limp story about a woman.'

'He became very jumpy,' added Quintus.

'Yes—jumpy enough for you to think the cameo was significant, and to palm it!'

'Ooh, naughty!' said Petro, grinning.

Helena frowned. 'Why would Anacrites protect his men if they are corrupt? Wouldn't he be livid that they stole evidence and jeopardised his chances of cracking the case?'

Petronius thumped a clenched fist several times on the table. The beat was measured, the meaning grim. 'You can have the wandering donkey theory—though I think it's bullocks' bollocks. Try this: during the courier's murder, one of his killers took the cameo. It was a trophy. It was secreted away to gloat over, the way killers' trophies are.'

I agreed: 'And it never left the killer. He took it home and hid the thing in his room. When Anacrites saw what the caterers had found, it took him a moment, but he knew what it meant. Why? Because he already knew he had a killer in his house. Work the rest out, lads—'

The Camilli made the connection immediately. Justinus said, 'The so-called Melitans are the two Claudii who work in Rome. They are Pius and Virtus.'

Helena sat back as it all made sense. 'Anacrites himself is protecting the Claudii—and not just since Modestus died. He has actively been their patron for much longer.'

I nodded. 'I'm slow. As soon as he let slip that his agents were twins, it should have rung bells. Too much coincidence.'

'It's good. It was another bit of very simple concealment,' said Aulus. 'Once you know, however, the subterfuge leaps out. I don't know how he thought he could get away with it for much longer.'

'Arrogance. He believes he is untouchable.' Petro claimed the big finish: 'Two of the murdering Claudii actually go out to kill *from the spy's house.* Anacrites himself has given the twins a base in Rome, providing them with a locale. He knows—but he still let them get away with it. So what is his game, Falco?'

Baffled by the spy's stupidity, I shook my head. 'He is crazy. I suppose he may be struggling to contain them. On an off-day, *he* may even stupidly have told them to provide a corpse north of the Tiber to distract attention from the Modestus killing on the other side of Rome.'

Helena had been thinking fast. 'Anacrites cannot have known originally what these men were. He must have taken them on to work for him—which we think was a couple of years ago—' That was what Pius or Virtus, whichever we had held captive, had told Petro and me, though I did not remind her of the circumstances. 'He found out later. Then he may have been attracted by a hint of danger attached to them. You know how he is; he would never admit that he made a mistake in hiring them.'

I agreed. 'When he learned the truth, he would simply convince himself he had chosen ideal staff. He would think having a colourful background made them just right for his work's "special nature".'

Justinus barked with laughter. 'So, being perverted murderers equates with "special intelligence skills", does it?'

Aelianus had once been a recruitment target; he knew the spy's sales patter: 'Anacrites maintains that spying is a little over the edge of legality. That's exciting. He sees himself as cunning and dangerous. He gloats that he can get way with using assassins "for the good of the state"—well, think about Perella.'

I thought it a good diagnosis: 'He would tell himself he could control them. But when he came back from Istria and discovered the Modestus murder had drawn attention to the Claudii, faced with them getting out of hand, he tried to take personal control.'

'Marcus, I'm afraid your involvement must have made it all worse for him,' Helena told me ruefully.

'Too right. Not only must he bury the problem before the Claudii are exposed, he has to distract me.'

Justinus blew his cheeks out. 'And there's no chance for us to expose his position, you know. He will only accuse us of interfering in some covert operation, endangering the Empire.'

'We are stuffed,' said Aelianus. He was young. He gave up easily.

I was older. I knew how the world worked. I was starting to think he had the right idea.

Petronius let out a grim laugh. 'Well, one of the twins is dealt with. Either Pius or Virtus has been removed from society—without us even realising who he was.'

I myself would not have mentioned that again. Helena glowered. The Camilli sensed awkwardness and did not ask what Petro meant.

Of course it explained why Pius or Virtus would never admit his name to us—and why Anacrites also glossed over his men's identity. It also explained why the agent—child of a cold, controlling father and a remote, neglectful mother, growing up with sadistic brothers— had managed to resist our interrogation.

And it explained the knives he carried. I tried not to look at Helena Justina as we both grasped that I had brought a perverted killer right into our house. I felt queasy remembering we had kept him here, in the same building as my wife and children.

Petronius may have picked up what Helena and I were thinking. He lowered his voice. 'So, Marcus Didius, my old tentmate, who volunteers to confront Anacrites?'

'Not us—not yet,' I answered.

Ever cautious, Petro nodded too.

52

Claudius Virtus lived in the Transtiberina. Petronius had found the address in the vigiles' lists. This was the Fourteenth District, a hike across the Tiber, an area I had always distrusted. It had a long history as a haunt of immigrants and outsiders, which gave it a reputation as a refuge for low-grade hustlers. Officially part of Rome for several generations, it retained a tang of the alien. Its dank air was imbued with murky hints of cumin and rue; alive with harsh, foreign voices, its dark, narrow lanes were populated with people in exotic cloaks who kept strange birds in cages up above on their windowsills. Carts here regularly tried to ignore the curfew. The vigiles, whose station house was just off the Via Aurelia, rarely made their presence felt, even to tackle the soft option of traffic nuisance. This area was attached to Rome, yet kept from full participation by more than the yellow-grey loop of the Tiber. The Transtib would always stay separate.

As I walked with Petro, Aulus and Quintus, I was still remembering that night at the spy's house. 'I saw someone else. Just a glimpse. I think he had been with the two agents. Could it have been Nobilis? Nobody we've questioned seems to have spotted him, though the chef did say Pius and Virtus asked for double portions with their meal—that could have been a cover for their brother. I certainly saw enough used dishes for three.'

'Description?'

'No good. He was too far away, and in a gloomy corridor. It was after dark by then, and Anacrites is mean with lamps.'

'So who do you think it was, Falco?'

'I don't know—but don't let's forget him. According to the caterer's chef, the third man was the one with the cameo.'

Virtus rented a room above a row of crumbling shops. It was in the same building as the bar we chose when we arrived, immediately above us. If he had been there, he could have jumped through a window and landed right on Quintus. But there was a fifty-fifty chance he had gone away, and would not be coming back.

The barman, who knew him, said Virtus had not lived there full-time for six months. He kept the place on, and had been coming back to check his stuff once a week. Not just lately, however.

'Sounds as though he's living in with a girlfriend? Keeping up with his rent because he thinks she's going to throw him out. Or he may want to dump her?'

'Not as far as I know. He's married, I believe.' That did not rule out Petro's girlfriend theory. 'Working in Rome to earn some cash, but he goes home.'

'Where would "home" be?'

'No idea, sorry.' We knew: the Pontine Marshes. The wife's name was Plotia. I had even met her. Petronius had searched the rustic shack where Virtus left her. Not much cash seemed to find its way back there.

'Where else might he go?'

'He mentioned a brother.'

'Pius?'

The barman shook his head. 'Means nothing, sorry.' He was very apologetic. According to Petro, as we went upstairs, the man in the apron should have been apologising for his lousy drink.

Petronius shouldered in the door. He didn't care if the occupant learned we were after him. The landlord could claim compensation; from the state of his building, he wouldn't come around to notice the damage.

It was a one-room apartment, its interior kept with the squalid housekeeping we recognised as the Claudius trademark. Flies lived here as subtenants; they soared about with the lethargic flight of insects that had gorged on unpleasant decay, close nearby. The smell in the room was familiar: an unclean, earthy odour I recalled from the spy's house, in those mean corridor rooms where the Claudii were lodged.

There was no space for four healthy adults. I volunteered to search, with Justinus. Petronius reluctantly agreed to wait downstairs in the bar with Aelianus.

'It's a simple room-search, Lucius. Let me handle it. Back off; you're worse than Anacrites!'

'I don't want you to cock it up.'

'Thanks, friend. Any time Quintus and I can shaft you in return, assume we'll be available.'

The 'stuff' Virtus came back to check was minimal. Apart from the landlord's basic furniture—sagging bed, lopsided stool, a skinny old sack on the floor for a rug—we found only a filthy foodbowl, empty wineskins, and a used loincloth which Aulus lifted up on the handle of a bald broom from the corridor then dropped in distaste.

We found no trophies from killings. However, hidden behind the inevitable loose wall panel, there were more knives. These were bigger and nastier than the ones we took off the agent.

After Quintus and I went downstairs again, Petronius insisted on going up to double-check.

'Jove, he's finicky!'

'Doesn't want to make a mistake with the Urban Cohorts watching.'

'Doesn't trust you, Falco!'

I asked more questions of the barman. This time he changed his story; he now remembered he had met the tenant's brother. His wife had appeared, curious about us. He was short and sparely built; she was shorter and enormous. She had met the brother too. The fond couple engaged in a hot marital argument; the barman maintained the brother was a scruff and a shambles, which the wife doggedly disputed. 'Kept himself nice. Good threads. Combed his hair.' They went on disputing, until it almost sounded as if they had seen two different brothers. Given the numbers of Claudii, this was possible.

'Fancied him?' asked Aulus, cracking the grimace he used for charm.

'Not likely—he had funny eyes.'

It was the wife who knew the real reason Virtus came back so regularly. 'He's one of Alis' regulars. He comes every Thursday.'

'Is Alis the local prostitute?'

'Not her! Fortune-teller. Just around the corner. She does a bit of witchcraft when people want to pay for it. Thursday is her night for seances. Virtus always went.'

As Petronius could not tear himself away from the room upstairs, I left the Camilli to wait for him. I strolled past a veg stall, a pot shop and a sponge bar, tripped around a corner by a fountain that was so dry its stone had cracked in the sun, and parked myself in a peeling doorway in order to inspect the fortune-teller's. The place I had been told Alis lived in was anonymous. These women work by word of mouth, usually hoarse whispers passed on in the environs of un-scrupulous temples. Anyone who has enough sixth sense to find a horoscope-hatcher, doesn't need her services.

After waiting a while, I went across and knocked. A frizzy baggage came to the door and admitted me. She was middle-aged and top heavy, wearing peculiar layers of clothes, over which were dried-flower wreaths with funny feathers sticking out of them. I expected a dead mouse to drop out any minute. The prevailing colour of her wardrobe was vermilion. It was amazing how many scarves and belts and under-tunics she had managed to acquire in that far-from-fashionable shade.

She moved with a shuffle and was slow getting around. Only her eyes had that sly, kindly glint you find in folk whose livelihood depends on befriending people with no personality, banking on the possibility that the vulnerable might part with their life savings and have no relatives to ask questions.

'My name's Falco.'

'What do you want, Falco?'

'You can tell it's not a love potion or a curse, then?'

'I can tell what you are, sonny! You won't fool me into drawing up a lifeline for the Emperor. I practise my ancient arts fully within the law, son. I pay my dues to the vigiles to leave me alone. And I don't do poisons. Who sent you?'

I sighed gently. 'No fooling you, grandma! I work for the government; I want information.'

'What will you pay?'

'The going rate.'

'What's that?'

I looked in my purse and showed her a few coins. She sniffed. I doubled it. She asked for treble; we settled on two and half.

She toddled into a corner to brew herself some nettle tea before we started. I gazed around, impressed that one elderly woman could have collected so many doilies and corn dollies, so many horrible old curtains, so many amulets with evil eyes or hieroglyphs or stars. The air was thick with dust, every surface was crammed with eccentric objects, the high window was veiled. I bet every superstitious old woman from a two-mile radius came here for her special Thursdays. I bet half of them left her something in their wills.

Nothing that smacked obviously of witchcraft was out on view. The desiccated claws and vials of toad's blood must be behind the musty swathes of curtain.

Eventually she settled down with her tea bowl and I learned Claudius Virtus was a regular at the seances. 'He was interested in the Dark Side. Always full of questions—I don't know where he got his theories. From his own strange brain, if you ask me.'

'Are you going to tell me what you do at your meetings?'

'We try to contact the spirits of the dead. I have the gift to call them up from the Underworld.'

'Really? And did Virtus ask about anyone in particular?'

'Usually he watched the rest. He tried to talk to his mother once.'

'Did she answer?'

'No.'

'Why would that be?'

Abruptly, Alis turned confiding: 'I got the creeps, Falco. I don't know why. I just felt I didn't want to be in the middle of that conversation.'

'You have some control then?' I asked with a smile.

The seer sipped her nettle tea, with the manners of a lady.

She told me Virtus had never missed a meeting until a few weeks ago. His mother—Casta—had died a couple of years before, he told Alis; he claimed to be close to her and said all the family adored the woman.

'My information is she was vicious,' I said. 'She had twenty children and was reputed to treat them all very coldly.'

'That's your answer,' replied Alis comfortably. 'It explains Virtus. He tells himself she was wonderful; he wants to believe it, doesn't he? In his poor mind, his ma is a darling who loved him. He misses her now, because he wants her to have been someone he should miss. If you were to say to him what you just said to me about his mother, he'd deny it furiously—and probably attack you.' I believed that.

Alis had winkled out of him that his father died before his mother, and that he had other relatives, some in Rome. 'More than one?'

'I gained that impression. He spoke of "the boys".'

'There are sisters too.'

Alis shrugged. She knew about the twin, believed he lived not far away, but had never set eyes on him. Plotia, the wife, had never been mentioned. When I commented that I was not surprised, Alis pulled a face and nodded as if she knew what I meant. Of course I despised this woman and her arcane dealings—yet in her frumpy, frowsty way, she was a good judge of character; she had to be.

'Did you think him capable of great violence?'

'Aren't all men?'

Virtus had ceased coming to the meetings, without warning. I took this as evidence that he was the agent we had sent to a hard death in the mines.

Alis put down her tea bowl. She sat motionless, as if listening. 'I don't feel we have lost him, Falco. He is still among those who wander the earth in body.'

I said I was sure she knew more about that than me, then I made my farewells as politely as a sceptic could.

This conversation had made me feel closer to Virtus now than in all the time Petronius and I had spent with him.

53

We men had a short case conference as we walked back towards the river. We would have preferred to stay at the bar, but that meant the helpful barman and his inquisitive wife would have listened. Anyway, Petro hated their drink.

We agreed it was futile for *us* to tackle Anacrites. However, the time had come to explore whether any higher authorities would take an interest. Camillus senior was on friendly terms with the Emperor; the senator might speak on the subject next time he was chatting with Vespasian. It would be tricky: so tricky, I shied off it until we gathered better evidence though I instructed Aulus and Quintus to tell their father what we believed. We had convinced ourselves, but that was not the same as proof.

Titus might be open to an approach, though his reputation varied from kind-hearted and affable to debauched and brutal. As commander of the Praetorians, he was Anacrites' commander too; that could rebound on us. If we failed to persuade him the spy was compromised, we could unleash a violent backlash from Anacrites—all for nothing. Even if Titus believed us, it could look as if *he* had misjudged his man. Nobody wanted Titus Caesar as an enemy. His dinner parties were more fun than the spy's—but he exercised the power of life or death over people who upset him.

I said I would have another word with Laeta and Momus. All the others thought that an excellent idea. They went to a bar near the Theatre of Marcellus that Petro reckoned was really well worth visiting, while they waved me off to the Palace.

I saw Laeta first, my preference. He did not turn me away. His method was to greet you with interest, listen gravely—then if your story was unwelcome politically, he let you down without a qualm. Unsurprisingly, he let me down.

'It's too thin. On what you've got, Falco, I don't see this going anywhere. Anacrites will simply say he made a mistake when he employed those men, and thank you for pointing it out to him.'

'Then he'll get me for it.'

'Of course. What do you expect with his background?'

'What does that mean?' I raised an eyebrow. 'As far as I know, his background is the same as yours. An imperial slave who made good—in his case, for unfathomable reasons.'

'He is bright,' Laeta said tersely.

'I've known pavement sweepers who could think and talk and grade dog turds to a system as they collected them—but such men don't end up in senior positions.'

'Anacrites was always known for his intellect—though he was more physical than most secretaries, which suits his calling. He had pliability; he could bend with the political breeze—which, when he and I were coming up the staff list, was a must!'

'He adapted himself to the quirks of emperors, whether mad, half-mad, drunkard or plain incompetent?'

'Still at it. Titus thinks well of him.'

'But you don't. You have a singer spying on him at home,' I threw in.

Laeta brushed it aside. 'The same man who observes me for Anacrites! Suspicion is a game we all play. Nevertheless, Marcus Didius, if you find genuine proof of corruption, I am sure I can persuade the old man to act on it.'

'Well, thanks! Tell me what you meant about the spy's background,' I persisted.

Laeta gave me a fond shake of the head—but then what he said was enlightening: 'Many of us feel he never fitted in. You compared him with me—but my grandmother was a favourite of the Empress Livia; I have respected brothers and cousins in the secretariats. Anacrites came up the ladder by himself, always a loner. It gave him an edge, honed his ambition—but he never shakes off his isolation.'

'Not isolated enough for me; he crushes up against me and my family.'

Laeta laughed softly. 'I wonder why?' He went no further, naturally. 'So, Falco, dare I ask: are you and your cronies still investigating the Pontine Marsh murders?'

I gave him a straight look. 'How can we, when our last instructions were to drop the case? Instructions, Claudius Laeta, which you gave us!'

He laughed again. I smiled with him as a courtesy. But as soon as I left, I stopped smiling.

Momus, I was certain, never had a slave grandmama who was cosy with the old Empress. He must have crawled out of an egg in a streak of hot slime somewhere. Any horrible siblings were basking in rich men's zoos or their heads were on walls as hunters' trophies.

Momus reacted eagerly to news of the spy's implication in sordid crimes, until I hankered for Laeta's measured thoughtfulness instead. Momus even promised to help—though he freely agreed it was hard to see what he could do.

'Momus, I still don't think the Claudii showed up and got jobs with the spy by accident. Are you ever going to tell me what you know about them?'

'Falco, if I knew how they control him, I'd be controlling him myself.'

'Do you admit you've put in people to watch him?'

'Of course I haven't,' he lied.

I left, reflecting ruefully that Momus had always been useless.

There was one more possibility.

Anacrites sometimes used a freelance on very special assignments, a woman. Helena and I had run into her a few times, and although I had a professional respect for her, we viewed her warily. She killed for Anacrites, killed to order. She took a pride in a beautiful performance, whether it was death or dancing. Dance was her cover. Just like her assassinations, it was clean, prepared in every detail, immaculate and took your breath away. Her talent gave her access to people Anacrites wished to remove; distracted by her brilliance, they were at her mercy. As often as not, no connection was made between her dancing and the discovery of a shocking corpse. Her name was Perella. She used a thin-bladed knife to slit her victims' throats. Knowing her method, I never let her stand behind me.

The first time I met Perella, before I knew her significance, it was at her home. Though a few years had passed, I managed to find the place again: a small apartment near the Esquiline, inexpensive but endurable. She let me in, barely surprised to see me. I was given a bowl of nuts and a beaker of barley water, urged to take the good chair and the footstool. It was like visiting a great-aunt, one who looked demure but who would reminisce about times when she juggled three lovers all at once—and who was rumoured to still do it, passing them on to the baker's wife, when she felt tired.

What made me remember Perella was my encounter with the mystic Alis. Perella, too, was of mature age and build; in fact more years of age than it was kind to mention. The skilled diva remained supple. She had power too; not so long before, I saw her kick a man in the privates so hard she wrote off all chance of him producing children.

'Didius Falco! Whenever I see you, I feel apprehensive.'

'Nice courtesy, Perella. And I take you very seriously too. Still working?'

'Retired—generally.' That figured. Her hair, never stylish, had once passed for blonde; she was letting the grey work its way out through the lopsided chignon. The skin on her neck had coarsened. But her self-containment did not alter. 'Yourself?'

'I had the chance—came into money. I decided work was in my blood.'

'What are you working on?' Perella was eating pistachios as if all that mattered was splitting their shells. She tossed off the question like casual conversation—but I never forgot she was an agent. A good one.

I let time pass before I answered. Perella put the nuts down. We gazed at one another. I said quietly, 'As usual, my role is complex. I cannot trust my principle—insofar as I have any, given that the case I was investigating for a dead man's nephew was then grabbed by Anacrites.'

Perella folded her hands on her full waistline, as if she was just about to ask me where I got my stylish wrist purse. 'My whimsical employer!'

'Still?'

'Oh yes. You mean the marsh bugs, I suppose? He sent me there, if you're interested.' I must have looked surprised. 'I can swat flies, Falco.'

'And which fly,' I asked with emphasis, 'was he wanting you to swat?'

'A vicious coward called Nobilis.' Although Perella worked for Anacrites, he never quite managed to buy her loyalty. She was more likely to connive with me, a fellow professional. 'Nobilis must have heard I was coming, so he fled abroad.'

I could not blame him. 'So that's why he vanished! How did he know you were coming for him?'

'I wonder!' scoffed Perella. She implied Anacrites let it slip.

'Do you know where he went?'

'Pucinum.' Where had I heard that name recently? 'Fled into hiding with his grandma,' Perella said, sneeringly. 'That's where they come from, those animals. I could have gone over there and dealt with him easily.'

'Did Anacrites run out of cash for your fare?'

'Much more intriguing! Anacrites was going that way himself.'

'Aha! So Pucinum is in Istria!' I whistled through my bottom teeth, to give myself thinking time. 'I've remembered—he bought wine there on the trip . . . Has Anacrites done the business? Has he finished Nobilis himself?'

Perella gave me an odd look. 'Well, just like you, I'm off the case. But, just like you, I never let go. He didn't. Nobilis is back, according to my sources. Seen in Rome. Anacrites must have reprieved him.'

'Or he just bungled it.'

'Not so,' said Perella softly. 'Claudius Nobilis came home on the same ship as the spy. The pair of them together, tight as ticks.'

'Anacrites brought him back? But not in leg irons—I haven't seen a trial announced!'

'Surprise! You'd think,' Perella told me in disgust, 'if he wanted Nobilis dead, as he told me, he could have found the chance to put a boot in the small of his back and shove the bastard overboard. Anacrites is handy enough—and I hear you know all about that!'

'What?'

'A little bird twittered "Lepcis Magna"?'

'That birdie must fly absolutely everywhere! I'll wring his neck for tweeting.' Anacrites had fought as a gladiator at Lepcis. It was illegal for any but slaves. Citizens who fought in the arena became nonpersons. News of it would make Anacrites a social outcast; he would lose his job, his ranking, his reputation, everything. I smiled gently. 'You *are* well informed. It's true; he spilled blood on the sand. But that information is mine to exploit, Perella. I was there.'

'I won't step in—even though I want his job.'

'*You want his job?*'

'Why not?' Indeed! The Praetorians would never accept her, yet Perella was just as shrewd, experienced and ruthless as the current incumbent. More intelligent, in my opinion. She had the talent. Only the ancient traditions of keeping women beside the hearth interfered with her qualifications. No tombstone yet had ever said: She kept the house and worked in wool—*and slit a few throats for security reasons* . . . 'You could destroy Anacrites, Falco—and presumably he knows it. Can you ever feel safe?'

'I have protection: other witnesses. If he touches me, they'll tell. So he's the one who lives in fear. I'm saving the information for the sweetest possible moment.'

The dancer took up her barley water peacefully. She still sounded like a well-disposed aunt, giving me career advice: 'Don't wait too long, my dear.'

54

I found my team, not as tipsy as I feared, merely unreliable. I said it was good to associate with happy men. Petronius had to work, or at least take a nap at the station house. The Camilli, being persons of leisure, rolled along with me. They had reached the clingy phase, where I was their best friend. Trailing them like seaweed stuck on an oar, I went up the Aventine to Ma's house, intending to collect Albia.

She had left, for home my mother said. 'Anacrites was here—he drops in, to see I am all right,' she confided in Aelianus and Justinus hoarsely. 'He knows my own don't give me a second thought. When I am found stone dead in my chair one morning, it will be Anacrites who raises the alarm.'

I cursed this libel and sat down on a bench. The Camilli did likewise, fitting in fast, as people did at Mother's house. They were clearly thinking: what a dear little old lady. She sat there, tiny and terrible, letting them believe it. Her beady black eyes rested wisely upon them. 'I hope my good-for-nothing son hasn't taken you drinking.'

'They were drinking; I was somewhere else, working,' I protested. 'Now I shall have to take them to the baths, have them home to dine, and sober them up for their trusting wives.'

'I don't expect trust comes into it!' reckoned Ma. The senators' sons looked shifty. Belated doubts about the dear little old lady filtered through their blearied brains.

Ma then described a cringe-making scene at her house earlier between Anacrites and Albia. 'He said "I always admire Junilla Tacita; you should come to her when you are troubled, dearie".' He cannot have called Albia 'dearie'; it was the word Ma used, to avoid truly accepting this outsider as a granddaughter. Albia saw Ma's reservations; she only came up here when Helena sent her. 'We all had a nice chat, then when your Albia was ready to go, he *so* kindly offered to see her home. Beautiful manners,' Ma insisted to the Camilli.

Aulus said in a solemn, lawyer's voice, 'You can tell a man's character by the way he treats young women.' He thought he was being satirical: big mistake, Aulus.

'You are the one who broke her poor little heart, are you?' asked Ma, with her crucifying sneer. 'Well, you would know all about character!'

I judged it time to leave.

Albia was safe at home. Anacrites had left her on the doorstep, merely sending in greetings to Helena; he probably knew this would only increase her anxiety—and my wrath. Albia failed to see what the fuss was about.

She dined with us, despite Aulus being present. Nothing kept Albia from her food. So she overheard us relating our progress. Helena summed up: 'Virtus has been dealt with; let us not remember how. He said Pius had gone home to the Pontine Marshes. Perella believes Nobilis is back in Rome, though you have no leads, unless it was him Marcus saw at the spy's house. Now we know the "Melitans" are his brothers that does seem likely. You won't get in there a second time to look. Relations with Anacrites are deteriorating, and he will hardly invite us all to dinner again—'

With yelps of pain, her brothers and I pleaded to be excused if he did.

'I could go to his house!' piped up Albia. 'He is perfectly nice to *me*! He says *I* can go at any time.'

'Keep away from him,' snapped Helena. 'Have respect for yourself, Albia.'

'Don't listen when he makes out you're special!' I said crushingly, 'Saying he's never met anybody like you is a very old line, sweetheart. When a man—any man—who has a collection of obscene art invites a young girl to visit, there is only one reason. It's nothing to do with culture.'

'Is this from experience, Falco?' Albia asked, disingenuously. 'How did you meet Helena Justina?' murmured our little troublemaker.

'I worked for her father. He hired me. I met her. She hired me as well. I never invited her to my horrible hutch.' Helena turned up there of her own accord. That was how I knew enough about strong-minded girls to be afraid for Albia.

'Was it when you lived at Fountain Court? I've seen it! I went with Lentullus, hiding that cameo. Is that how you know how the art invitation works, Falco? Did you lure girls up to your garret, pretending your father was an auctioneer so you had curios to show them—then when they had climbed all those stairs and found out there was nothing, it was too late and they were too weary to argue?'

'Certainly not,' Helena interrupted calmly. 'Marcus was such an innocent in those days, I had to show him what girls were for.'

Albia broke up in giggles. It was good to see her smile.

I topped up everybody's water cup while I tried to reassert the myth of a respectable past.

We agreed it was time to go after Claudius Pius. Assuming his brother had told Petro and me the truth, then Pius was visiting his wife, that fragile soul Byrta. It meant another trip into the marshes, though at least that would let me go over to Antium and liaise with Silvius, of the Urban Cohorts. Petronius had checked with Rubella, who still refused to release him from Rome, even to work with Silvius. So Justinus, with his experience on our first trip, won the ballot to come with me.

Next day at dawn, I was all packed and about to mount a mule outside my house, when Helena ran out after me. She told me anxiously that Albia was not in her room. Our conversation the day before had had unwelcome results. The girl had left a note—at least she was that sensible—to say she was going to Anacrites' house *'to have a look around'*. If she went last evening, he had kept her overnight.

'Don't worry,' Helena reassured me, though her voice was tense. 'You get off—I'll fetch her back somehow.' I wanted to stay, but I had five slaves chomping at the bit behind me and had made arrangements with Justinus to depart at first light. 'Leave it to me, Marcus. Don't fret. Take care, my love.'

'Always. You too. Sweetheart, I love you.'

'I love you too. Come home soon.'

As I rode through Rome in the thin air of a very early morning, on my way to collect Justinus at the Capena Gate, I thought about those words. How many people have said them as a talisman, but never saw their precious love again? I wondered if Livia Primilla, the elderly wife of Julius Modestus, had spoken the words when her husband rode to challenge the Claudii. If I failed to return from this journey, Helena Justina would come after me too. I should have told her not to do it, not without an army. But that would have meant planting the suggestion that her brother and I might be in serious danger.

At the Capena Gate, Aelianus emerged to wave us off. He was mildly jealous, though as an assistant he always enjoyed being left in charge. I mentioned what had happened to Albia. 'Aulus, it's not your affair. Obviously this is awkward for you, but could you check with Helena that everything is all right? Will you tell her I had a thought as I came through the Forum: if she goes to see the spy, take my mother.'

'Will he listen to your mother?'

'Mediation! Helena will know—in a crisis with an enemy, it's a fine Roman tradition to send in an elderly woman, with a long black veil and a very stern lecture.'

Justinus suggested leaving behind Lentullus, who could bring us news later.

So Justinus and I, taking a handful of slaves as back-up, rode off once more to Latium. Thirty miles later, as near we could get discreetly, we camped overnight, not showing ourselves at any inns where landlords might give advance warning of our presence. We planned the traditional dawn raid.

At first light, with the promise of an unpleasantly hot late August day, we reached the end of the track. Here, we knew, three of the Claudius brothers lived when it suited them, in poverty and filth, with two skinny, subdued wives and innumerable wild children. We had already passed the shack where their brother Probus mouldered; we saw no sign of him, nor his ferocious dog, Fangs.

The woodlands were sultry. Fetid steam rose from depleted pools as the marshes dried out through the summer. It must have rained recently; there was a dank, unpleasant smell everywhere. Clouds of flies rose up from tangles of half-decayed undergrowth, skirling in our faces in predatory black curtains as we disturbed them. The insects were worse than we remembered, the going more difficult, the isolation drearier.

We rode up as quietly as possible. We all dismounted. With drawn swords, Justinus and I went straight to the hovel where Pius and his wife lived, while our slaves checked around the back. We banged the door, but there was no answer. The hutment which belonged to Nobilis looked as deserted as before. While we continued knocking, a man appeared in the doorway of the third hut. A woman's voice sounded behind him.

'What's that noise?' he shouted. It was the other 'Melitan'. I recognised him, and he recognised me—though he cannot have known quite how familiar he seemed. Anacrites had said the twins were not identical; maybe this one was half a digit taller, a few pounds heavier, but there was little in it.

'Claudius Pius?' If so, he was on the wrong doorstep, growling over his shoulder at the wrong woman. Mind you, it did not surprise me that one of the Claudii should be screwing his brother's wife.

He rounded aggressively. 'No. I am Virtus.'

I believed him. We had muddled them up. I should have known. Anyone who has ever seen a theatrical farce would expect the wrong one to pop out of a doorway. That's what you get with twins.

55

He could be lying. Impersonating each other to fool people is a lifelong game for twins. When I was at school, the Masti were famous for it; their loving mother helped by always dressing them in identical tunics, with their hair curled in the same ridiculous quiff. They spent their days tormenting our teacher, then later were reputed to swap girlfriends. Causing confusion would have gone on for ever, if Lucius Mastus had not been run over by a stonemason's wagon. His brother Gaius was never the same afterwards. All the joy went out of him.

Virtus had the same build, skin, freckles, light eyes and upturned nose as the man Petro and I had captured. I felt uncomfortable with it, though I did not believe the telepathy of twins could have told him what his brother went through. I suppose I had a bad conscience.

After grumbling noises from indoors, Byrta sidled into view next to him. In the act of re-draping her clothes, she hitched a scarf around her neck. Maybe it was to hide love bites, if she called their relationship love. It was some rich red colour, decent material. I supposed Virtus must have brought it for her from Rome as a present.

She vouched for him being Virtus not Pius. I said he had to come with us. He reluctantly complied. His wife did not rush to pack him a travelling bag. We searched his home before we left, but found nothing, not even weapons. If he really was Virtus, he had left his armoury in the Transtiberina apartment, so it was now secured at the Fourth Cohort's station house. The woman stayed behind with their children.

We asked about his brother Probus. Virtus said men had come and arrested him—Silvius and the Urban Cohorts, presumably. 'Why didn't they get you at the same time?'

'I heard them coming.'

We took him with us to Antium, where we joined up with Silvius. Silvius confirmed he had Probus in custody. Probus seemed to be breaking ranks and denouncing Nobilis, though it was too early to say if he would distance himself enough to give us evidence. When Silvius wanted to question Virtus, I had had enough with the other twin, so I gave him the prisoner without quibbling. Justinus and I sat in. I insisted on that.

In two days of hard questioning, Virtus said little useful. His line now was that he had never had anything to do with any of his brothers' cruel practices—and, as he knew well, we had nothing to tie him to the murders.

'None of us ever knew what Nobilis was up to.' That tired cliché. 'These things you are saying about him and Pius are terrible. Thank the gods our father will never know about it.'

'Aristocles was no moralist! Look at the disgusting rabble he and Casta produced. Strong family bonds, have you?' asked Silvius, insinuating.

'Oh I see your game! I repudiate my brother. I reject Nobilis. If he and Pius did those things, I dissociate them from our family. They shame us. They are blackening the family name.'

'*What family name?* Don't make me spew.'

Virtus just stared at Silvius. He was not a clod. None of them were. That was how those of them who committed the crimes had covered up their tracks for so many decades.

'We'll get the truth,' sneered Silvius. 'Probus is here in custody, you know that. Your Probus seems a fellow with a conscience. Probus has begun telling us a lot of helpful things—all about his perverted brothers.'

'Probus is just as bad as them,' scoffed Virtus.

When Silvius needed a break, I was given a go. 'Tell me about your connection with Anacrites, Virtus.'

'Nothing to say.'

'When did you find out about him?'

'Around two years back. We went up to Rome and asked him for work. He thought he could use us, so it was fixed up. I know when it was, because our mother had just died.'

'Casta? Was her death something to do with you going to see Anacrites?'

'Yes and no. When we lost her, we felt cast adrift.'

'Oh you poor little orphans!'

'Have a heart, Falco!' Justinus broke in, grinning. Silvius let out a short laugh too. He had bad teeth, not many left.

I had remembered something someone told us about Casta. Unexpectedly, I strode up, grabbed the prisoner by his hair, then turned his head to demonstrate he had part of an ear missing. 'Did your mother do that to you?' I yelled.

'I deserved it,' said Virtus, immediately and without blinking.

We had to stop then, because news came in about the discovery of more bodies.

Justinus and I went with Silvius to inspect the site. On the way, Silvius owned up that the Urbans had been using Claudius Probus for the past few days to help them identify places where his brother Nobilis might have buried corpses. 'We believe Probus is himself implicated in the abductions, though not as the principal.'

'How did you make him talk?'

'We had to provide immunity. The way it works, Probus suggests places that Nobilis liked—secret lairs he had, on his own or with Pius.'

'Pius was the one who lured the victims; he brought them to Nobilis?'

'Seems so. These spots are difficult to access, so Probus takes us and points out where to look.'

'He knows too much about it to be innocent.'

'He admits that. He says he was young, and coerced by his brothers. He claims he became too horrified and stopped joining in.'

I hated him being given immunity. Sometimes you have to compromise, but if Probus was directly involved in the deaths, immunity was wrong. Silvius just shrugged. 'When you see the terrain, you will understand. There is no other way we could ever find the bodies. My seniors conferred. It's worth it, to clear up the old disappearances.'

Silvius was quite right about the dreadful terrain. The first place we went was a forest, a few miles out of Antium. A thick canopy of slim-trunked scented pines, intermingled with stunted cork oaks, filled this thickly wooded area. At ground level, dense brushwood impeded movement. Nobilis must have used a narrow track. A slightly wider access had been bashed down by the Urbans. Following a guide, we struggled along it to a dell. We went in silence. When we reached the activity, the shocked hush continued, broken only by rustles and chopping spades as work went on slowly at the sordid scene.

Bodies had been excavated and placed on flattened underbrush. There were eight or nine, of different ages; their poor condition prevented an exact tally. Most were now collected in proper array, but the bones of one or two could only be hopelessly jumbled on a sack. The troops had lifted most remains from their resting places and laid them in a row—except one. One body lay apart and they had not touched it. One was new.

The men stood back. Silvius, Justinus and I went to look. While the workers waited, watching us, we surveyed the remains, pretending to be experts.

Most of the recovered bodies had been found in the ritual position, face down and with outstretched arms—the mark of the Modestus killers. There were no more severed hands. Petronius must have been right that this was the letter-writer's particular punishment for making appeals to the Emperor.

We had all seen dead men. Dead women too. We had seen flesh battered and bones treated disrespectfully. Even Justinus, the youngest here, must already know the swift sag of the stomach that comes in the presence of unnatural death. That smell. The mocking way skulls grin. The shock at the way human skeletons can hang together even when entirely stripped of meat and organs. The worse shock, when long-dead bones suddenly fall apart.

What lay here was in one sense no longer human; yet these bodies were still part of the wider tribe we belonged to. Most had died years ago. Many would never be identified. But they called on us as family. They imposed responsibilities. I cannot have been the only one who silently promised them justice.

The newest corpse was a woman.

'How long?'

'Two days, at most.'

Her killer must have been fleeing from the forest almost as the first troops approached. Perhaps the noise of them stomping down thickets had disturbed him. Perhaps he even glimpsed them through the trees.

She lay on her own, not with the others. Those who found her had felt she was different—still close enough to living to count as a person, not simply anonymous 'remains'. Indeed, it would have been possible to recognise her face—had her killer not battered her badly. She had suffered; large areas of her skin were discoloured by bruising. Someone suggested much of the beating was inflicted after death; we preferred to think so. Either her trunk was swollen because of what had happened internally during the violence, or she had been pregnant. Unlike the other bodies, which were deposited face down in scraped graves, this one had been left unburied and looking at the sky. She had not been ripped open. He had not finished with her corpse.

Around her neck still lay a gold chain that must have been the means by which Nobilis managed to get close to her again. The expensive granulation looked like the hanging loop on the Dioscurides cameo. I could see the fastening. I forced myself to bend down over the body, unhook it, and remove the chain. It had dug into the flesh, but I pulled on it as gently as I could.

'I know who this is.'

I recognised her dress. I remembered that sad rag from when she was brought to see Helena and me in the inn at Satricum. It was Demetria, daft daughter of the morose baker Vexus, obedient lover of the foolish grain seller Costus—and one-time wife of Claudius Nobilis, the pernicious freedman who so relentlessly refused to release her from his possession, that he finally came after her and slaughtered her.

56

Word of the grisly discoveries in the forest had inevitably spread. The bodies were carried out on hurdles; we left a small group of men still searching. When we came back to the road, a crowd had gathered. A few, who must have lost friends or relatives in the past, rushed forwards as the cortège emerged from the woods, and had to be held back by troops. Also there, though keeping to themselves in a tight knot, was a group of women I was told were from the Claudius family: three sisters, plus the sisters-in-law, Plotia and Byrta.

They neither spoke to us, nor we to them. They stared, blank-faced, as we removed the dead. It seemed to me they would never speak, never assist with any knowledge they had of the crimes, never even defend themselves. Others kept away from them; who could believe these women were truly innocent of the crimes their men perpetrated? How could they really have known nothing? They would be ostracised. They and their children were further casualties. A grim cycle would repeat itself. The children would grow up angry and isolated. Already none of them knew anything except neglect and violence. Which descendants of Aristocles and Casta could ever escape the stigma of this bleak family? To start a new life would be too hard; to learn new behaviour impossible.

I knew Plotia and Byrta had been friendly with Demetria, but her corpse was well covered; we kept her identity secret until we informed her family. Silvius and I did that. First, we sought out her father, Vexus. From what he told us, we were partly prepared when we visited the cottage where Demetria had lived with Costus. Costus had been taken in by his mother two days ago. Our news would not surprise him; he must count his lover already dead. Two days ago he had come home from his work to find Demetria gone. Their home had been trashed. Every pitiful stick of furniture they owned was wrecked. Vegetables and grain were scattered in the road outside. Pottery, skillets, brooms, rush lights, and a few personal possessions, were all stamped on, thwacked to pieces, shattered and smashed, the quiet means of domestic life pointlessly desecrated. And on the street door, we found a crude symbol: fixed with a long nail through its head was a doll.

A shiver ran through me. I recognised this savage witchcraft.

I knew now who came and destroyed my darling sister's treasured home on the Aventine two years ago. Anacrites must have sent some of the Claudius brothers to frighten Maia and her children; his messengers included the depraved Nobilis.

57

Despite the long summer days, it was nearly dark when we turned in at our inn that night. Silvius had still not finished; he had gone to report to the magistrate.

The finds in the wood were only the start. Painstaking work would now begin on the few scraps of material from the graves which might provide clues, with attempts to work out physical details of the human remains—height, body-weight, sex—if it were possible. Only that way might at least some of the bones be identified, to close missing-person cases and give release to distraught survivors.

From one comparatively recent body, which had boots a local cobbler recognised, we knew the troops had uncovered Macer; he was the overseer who worked for Modestus and Primilla—the man who was beaten up when he remonstrated with the Claudii about the broken boundary fence and who accompanied Primilla when she went to challenge them about her missing husband. We knew we had not found Livia Primilla. I can say now that nothing of her ever was discovered. Her nephew would only ever be able to guess what must have happened.

I was ready for bed, though my head was thrumming with today's experiences. I would not sleep. I sat up with Justinus, neither drinking nor talking. We were staying near the beach; most places at Antium fringed the coast so not only rich men's villas but even ordinary homes and business premises had good views. Stars and a slim moon rose over the motionless Tyrrhenian Sea. The beauty of the scene was both calming and subtly disturbing. My young brother-in-law and I, experienced in dark adventures together, remained silent. Our terrible experiences today removed any need to communicate.

Suddenly we heard familiar voices. One was Lentullus. The piping tones of that nincompoop split the night with cries of mundane bewilderment as he tried to find us. Justinus smiled at me ruefully in the feeble outdoor lamplight; he half rose and called out. My secretary Katutis burst on the scene with Lentullus. They joined us, excitedly. Food and drink had to be supplied. There was a minor commotion, soon reduced as the hungry travellers ate.

While Justinus organised, I demanded, 'Has Albia been found?'

'Oh she's all right!' Lentullus assured me, ripping into bread ravenously.

Katutis had burrowed under his long tunic to produce a letter from Helena. 'She wrote it herself!' He was annoyed at this breach of etiquette. I felt off-kilter because letters between Helena and me were rare. We were infrequently apart for long.

I took the sealed document aside, taking a lamp so I could read in privacy.

Helena wrote to tell me a lively story.

For a couple of days back in Rome, much activity had revolved around my foster-daughter. Helena now knew Albia had betaken herself to the spy's house, convinced she could discover for us whether he was harbouring Claudius Nobilis. It began well. At first Anacrites kept up the pretence that he and Albia had some kind of special relationship. Once she wheedled her way in, she used the age-old excuse of needing a lavatory; then she hastily explored the corridor of utility rooms where I had seen Pius and Virtus playing draughts. She found the room with a third bed. Baggage was still there. Unfortunately, so was the occupant. Albia came face to face with Nobilis. She knew it must be him from the sinister way he turned on her; Albia was terrified.

Luckily for her, Anacrites appeared. She wondered if he had actually been watching her progress. He sent Albia back to the main part of the house. Being her, she disobeyed and dawdled. She heard Anacrites quarrel with the man. He shouted that now Nobilis had been seen by Albia, he had to leave; the only safe course was to go home to Antium. Anacrites said he would deal with the girl.

Albia did not wait to see what that meant. She ordered a little slave boy to tell his master she would seek sanctuary in the House of the Vestal Virgins—the one place in Rome, she said, that not even the Chief Spy could invade. Then, although the spy's house was always heavily secured, our streetwise Albia found a way out.

Now she had to decide where to hide for safety. Coming home that night was out of the question; Anacrites would follow her. Helena did not tell me in the letter where Albia was, although she said she knew. Her mother, friend of a retired Vestal, had obtained curious inside information. The spy had turned up at the Vestals' House in the Forum, mob-handed with Praetorian Guards. The idiot tried to enter this sacred place that was barred to men. He outraged the Vestals, those revered women whose sanctum had been inviolable since the foundation of Rome six centuries ago (and just when, chortled Helena, they had settled down for the night with hot mulsum and dunking biscuits). When they caustically denied any knowledge of Albia, Anacrites refused to believe them. It was horrible to contemplate how severely the Vestals slapped him down in return. Only he would have taken on a group of vicious professional virgins who had six hundred years of training in how to reduce men to shreds. He retreated ignominiously.

All this had taken place before Helena and I realised Albia was missing. Next day—very soon after I left for Latium—Anacrites turned up at our house, alone, pretending to be concerned about her. Of course she was not there either. Helena showed him the door.

He tried my mother's house. This was another bad mistake and as a result he had now lost her previously unshakable goodwill. Ma was dozing in her chair—anyone of sense would have tiptoed out again. He woke her. He was so het up, Ma could see he intended Albia no good. Despite her devotion to this worm whose life she had saved, Ma rallied; she might have been lukewarm about having Albia in the family, but in a crisis Ma always defended her grandchildren. Furious, she ordered Anacrites to leave, threatening to upend an onion casserole over his sleek head. Even he had to see their cosy relationship had ended.

Anacrites next convinced himself Albia must have run to Helena's father, to ask the senator to intercede with the Emperor. This was the spy's worst mistake. She was not there—never had been—but my winsome father-in-law became incensed when Anacrites forced a house search on him. Camillus Verus called for his litter and immediately had himself carried off to complain to Vespasian.

Not content with jumping into this vat of steaming dung, Anacrites stormed next door to the house where Aelianus now lived with his wife and the professor. Minas of Karystos was ecstatic at the outrage. Wielding a wineflask in one hand and a bread roll in the other, he rushed from a late breakfast to pronounce loudly on the rights of a citizen to live without interference. Unbeknown to us previously, he was a populist democrat, fiery on the subject. Even with omelette in his curly beard, he was good. He bounced outside into the street, seeing his big chance to advertise his hireable expertise to all the well-heeled inhabitants of that fine patrician quarter. Before a rapidly expanding crowd, Minas had already quoted Solon, Pericles, Thrasybulus the defeater of the Thirty Tyrants, Aristotle of course, and several extremely obscure Greek jurists, when aediles turned up to investigate the street disturbance. The aediles did nothing; they were so impressed by his luminary erudition and the interesting points he was making, they brought him half a barrel to stand on.

Anacrites did not find Albia. Officially, her whereabouts remained unknown.

As I read on in weary amazement, Lentullus crept up to me with his usual confiding manner. He burped shyly. 'Falco, I know where your girlie may have gone—'

I raised a finger. 'Stop! Don't say it! Don't even think about it, Lentullus, in case Anacrites can read your brain.' In fact not even the devious spy could untangle that ball of wool, but Lentullus sat down obediently by me on the bench, full of joy that we were sharing this Big Secret.

While he carefully kept quiet, I read the rest of Helena's letter. That was personal. You don't need to know.

Afterwards, I folded up the document and tucked it inside my tunic. We all sat a while longer, listening to the whispers of the dark ocean, each contemplating death and life, love and loathing, the long years of tragedy that had brought us here, and the hope that at last we were ending it.

A faint breeze had got up and morning was not far away, when we said our goodnights and for a few short hours all sought our beds.

58

A lot of things had happened in the past few days. I told Silvius what we could now deduce about Nobilis and his movements. Anacrites had ordered him to leave Rome; Nobilis must have obeyed, much at the same time as Justinus and I left. We could easily have encountered him on the road down here.

His killing of Demetria confirmed his arrival. He must have been doing that while we were in the marshes arresting Virtus. We knew Nobilis must have carried out the attack on his ex-wife alone, because both Pius and Probus had been in custody. With troops swarming everywhere, he was probably pinned down in the Antium area. We set up a search.

If he went into the Pontine Marshes, we had no hope. The wild bogs stretched for nearly thirty miles between Antium and Tarracina, and between ten and fifteen miles across. This great rectangle of terrain was impossible to monitor. Nobilis knew the marsh intimately, had roamed there since childhood, had lived there all his adult life. He could elude us for ever.

Catching Nobilis quickly was now imperative. We had to hope that activity during the forest search had prevented him slipping away. The troop movements could have trapped him close to Antium itself, or forced him west. We searched the town—no luck. A polite house-to-house was set up among the handsome coastal villas. Of course we encountered resistance from their wealthy owners, who would rather put up with a depraved killer in their midst than let the military check their property. Each huge spread possessed innumerable outbuildings, any of which could be a hiding-place. Justinus and I spent half a day attempting to mediate with the rich and secluded; Silvius had reckoned us respectable (a senator's son and a man with his own auction house) so he assigned us the role of winning over the landed classes. For the most part, they saw it differently, though only one set the dogs on us.

We held a midday conference. Silvius had convinced himself that once Nobilis knew we had found the forest bodies, he would not just hunker down but would try to leave the area. Available roads were either north along the coast, taking the Via Severiana towards Ardea, Lavinium, and ultimately Ostia, or else the main road that skirted the northern edge of the marshes. That would take him over to the Via Appia, on the way to Rome. In Rome, could he still call on Anacrites for protection? Even if not, Nobilis could easily vanish into the city alleys as so many criminals had done. Ostia, if that was his choice, would give him access to ships bound for anywhere.

We pulled everyone off the property searches. It turned out to be the right choice. While we were still sitting around our lunch packs, co-ordinating our next moves, Lentullus edged up to Justinus and me. He asked if we wanted to know something funny about an ox cart that had just passed. The driver had seemed like any of the locals who pottered around. 'He looked all right—for a farmer, if that's what he is,' said Lentullus. Lentullus had come from a farm originally. 'And guess what—he had an ox that was just like Nero!'

'*Spot!*' Quintus and I roared at him, as we scrambled to our feet.

We all mounted up; we had a mix of mules and donkeys. Checking our weapons, we piled in pursuit. If this was just some inept ox rustler, we would look stupid, but we knew where Nero had been stolen so none of us believed that.

The countryside was gently rolling; when he turned off down a dirt track, we were close enough behind to see him leave the highway. A bullock cart can put on a fast turn of speed, a fully grown ox less so—and Nero had always been a plodder. Nonetheless, it was two miles before we caught up. It was Petro's ox all right, but by then abandoned. No mistaking that dun-coloured hunk of beef, with his mournful low and his permanent stream of dribble. He was even hitched to our own cart, the one we had had to leave in the marshes after the ox was taken. There was no time to make jokes about salvage rights, but Petronius and his po-faced brother would be delighted.

Nobilis had left the cart and taken off on foot. I made Lentullus stay with the ox. His bad leg would have hampered him, and those two simple souls could look after one another while the rest of us, the hard men, tracked our killer. We stayed on mule-back as long as possible, but soon, like him, we had to leg it. He vanished down a deep ravine and there was no choice but to follow him in.

'I know this place,' said Silvius. 'It's where we first found bodies!'

Italy is a strange country geographically, so long and narrow, with its great spine, the ever-present Apennines. They were there in the distance, low-looking grey ridges far away but visible beyond the undulating foreground plain. Even in summer, towering clouds rise over those hills. You can see them as you approach Rome. After storms and in winter, rain pours off the Apennines. Trapped water causes the Pontine Marshes. Here close to Antium, groundwater lay very close to the surface but instead of forming marshes, rivers carved phenomenal channels through the alluvium, down which they sucked the surplus to the sea. For century after century it happened, creating strange caves, deep seasonal gullies, and incredible ravines. You would not know they were there. From above, the countryside seemed featureless. The presence of these gullies made farming harder, so only a short way past Antium was a near wilderness. In this dire place, Claudius Nobilis had struck down one of the deep ravines. There was nothing else to do: trusting our souls to the gods—those of us who believed in gods—we went in after him. A few who did not believe in a deity until then may have offered a swift apology for doubting and beseeched divine protection after all.

Why does it always happen to me? In the course of my work, I had been at the bottom of some ghastly holes. This was another appalling experience. Nobilis had scrambled into a fissure in the earth that became fifty feet deep in places, though never much more than six feet across. The sides rose perpendicularly. Soon we felt quite cut off from the world; we feared we would never manage to return. No place I had ever been in contained such a sense of menace. It felt like one of the approaches to Hades.

He kept going. Hours seemed to pass as we struggled slowly after him. The ravine's formation reminded me of straight-sided rock-cut corridors I had seen in Nabataea, places so narrow a claustrophobic man would have to turn back afraid. In high summer, it was dry. One of our men, who had local knowledge, told us that when the rains came, such a ravine would contain raging water to waist height. In summer its soggy bottom fed the sturdy roots of unyielding under-growth. The going was almost impossible. Bright green frogs croaked everywhere; flies tormented us. Sweat poured off us as we strove forwards. As we trampled on, scratched and torn by ferocious scrub plants, we became rapidly exhausted.

The place nearly defeated us. We were not the first to come here. Generations of criminals must have used this hateful crevice. They used it to hide themselves, their loot, their weaponry. They left behind sordid litter. Bodies must have been dumped here too. They would never be found. The undergrowth would conceal them, the floods would carry them away.

Ahead of us, the killer also struggled. He knew the ravine of old, yet found no easier way through it than we did. If paths had ever existed, harsh foliage had reclaimed them. Its prickly growth was impenetrable. The atmosphere, the heat, the smell, drained us. Being in a group, we just about kept up our spirits, and were closing the gap between us and our quarry. Nobilis was alone. He was on his own for ever now, and he knew it.

In the end he could go no further. With no way out, he turned on us. We never saw him coming but suddenly we heard him, as with a long, wild yell, he crashed out of hiding. With barely time to react, we bunched closer, bringing our swords up defensively. For an instant it did seem his intention was to break out past us. The ravine was too narrow, the tangled thicket too dense. His animal howl of defeat, despair and rage continued. We braced ourselves.

Nobilis flung himself straight at us. So this man, who had killed so many people with his own crude weapons, used us and our raised swords to kill himself.

59

Once we dragged out our blades and the corpse fell to the ground, we stood in shock. Silvius recovered first and rolled him over. We gathered round, to inspect the remains. We had to see, once, the man we knew to be the killer.

He looked younger than Probus and the twins. There were likenesses. We could see he belonged to the Claudii. He was bigger, more unkempt, over-heavy. Dead as he was, he lay staring at the sky in a way that made us shiver. Camillus Justinus, a man of refinement, stooped down quickly to pull the eyes shut with one thumb and forefinger.

Just before he did so, Quintus looked up at me. 'That barman's wife in the Transtiberina may have seen Nobilis. She said he had peculiar eyes.' He spoke with the same throwaway manner Helena would use in company, tossing me something to think about, for discussion later. I said nothing, but I looked—then I drew the same conclusions.

We left the body there. We were exhausted. Dragging it back up the ravine would have finished us. If his siblings wanted to collect Nobilis for burial, let them.

———

'Myself, I like to go to law,' said Silvius, back in Antium. 'A quick show trial, and a bloody execution. Deterrent to others. Suicide-by-cohort never works the same.'

Since the Urban was in a vengeful mood, he then let on that Claudius Probus was to remain in custody.

'What happened to his get-out clause?'

'Ah, Falco, I just remembered! I am not empowered to offer it. Immunity from prosecution is reserved to the Emperor—and he, I gather, never intervenes in criminal cases . . . So it's thanks for the help, Probus—but tough luck!'

The surviving twin, Virtus, was also in trouble, potentially. Despite his insistence that he kept aloof from his brothers' activities, Justinus had remembered something: 'When we picked him up at their shack in the marshes, I noticed his wife, Byrta, was wearing a good quality scarf in a dark red material. Silvius, if you can ever find any of the runaway slaves who belonged to Modestus and Primilla, you must show them that scarf. Primilla was wearing something like it when she left home.'

Piece by piece, we were linking the Claudii to their victims. We also had the unusual chain that Nobilis must have given to Demetria; I was confident that belonged with the cameo taken from the Rome courier on the Via Triumphalis. Petro would send the cameo for comparison; Silvius would take it to the Dioscurides workshop for absolute confirmation.

We asked both Probus and Virtus about their connection with Anacrites. Both blanked us. In my view, now Nobilis was dead, they were afraid they would bear the full burden as public scapegoats, but they believed the spy would extricate them. I thought they were wrong. 'No; he will distance himself now. I know him. He will sacrifice the Claudii to save his own career.'

'I thought they could put pressure on him?' said Silvius.

'We still don't know what—though Justinus and I have a theory we intend to check. I suggest you process Probus and Virtus here in Antium. Do it fast, Silvius. But if you can, please give me a couple of days, before you send word to Rome about Nobilis.'

'What's the plan, Falco? I can see you have one.'

'Let me keep it to myself. Silvius, you don't want to know.'

Silvius and the Urbans stayed in Latium to process the survivors' trial. I and mine set off for home. Lentullus was bringing Nero and the ox-cart for Petronius, which meant the usual maddening slow progress. It took us a day to reach Bovillae. Next morning, Justinus and I left Lentullus to drive in without us, while we rode on ahead up the Via Appia.

We passed through the necropolis where the corpse of Modestus had been found. After that came the Appian Gate, then a long straight run through garden suburbs until we hit the dark shade of two leaky aqueducts at the Capena Gate. I excused myself, and left Quintus to pass on greetings to his parents and his wife. We arranged that he and his brother would come to my house the next day, for a catch-up meeting.

I moved on, reached the southern end of the Circus Maximus, where I veered left. Since I had a mule to do the hard work, I pressed him up the hill. He carried me uncomplainingly to the crest of the Aventine, with its snooty ancient temples on the high crags, around which beetled the vibrant plebs of this place where I was born.

After life on the coast, I felt assailed by the busy racket. More shops and workshops were crammed together on this one hill out of seven than traded in the whole of Antium. The crowds were loud—singing, shouting, whistling and catcalling. The pace was fast. The tone was coarse. I drew in a deep breath, grinning with joy to be home again. In that breath I tasted a strange brew of garlic, sawdust, fresh fish, raw meat, marble dust, new rope, old jars and, from the dark doorways of ill-kept apartment blocks, the reek of uncollected sewage in flabbergasting quantities. My mule was jostled, insulted, barked at and cursed. Two hens flew up in our faces as we wove a passage through garland girls and water carriers, ducked out of the way as a burglar dropped down off a fire porch with his clanking swag, turned off a narrow road into one that was barely passable. At the end of *that* lay the disguised entrance of the sour alleyway called Fountain Court.

A pang of nostalgia hit me like last night's undigested Chicken Frontinian. The street was not much wider than the ravine where Nobilis killed himself. The sunny side was shady and the shady side was glum. A deplorable smell rose and wavered around like a bad genie outside the funeral parlour, while a fierce fight about a bill was spilling on to the pavement by the barber's. To call it a pavement was ridiculous. The customer who was threatening to kill Appius, the barber, was sliding on molten mud. To call it mud as it oozed in through gaps in his sandal straps was optimistic. I rode by without making eye contact, though my sympathy was with the barber. Anyone so stupid as to patronise a tonsure-teaser who had the sad combover Appius gave himself should expect to get fleeced. Even a *quadrans* was too much to pay.

I dismounted stiffly at the Eagle Laundry and tied up the mule among the wet flapping sheets in what passed for a colonnade. Lenia, the laundress, emerged nosily: a familiar figure, all frenzied red hair and drinker's cough, tottering on high cork heels, unsteady after her afternoon bevvy. She winked heavily. She knew why I was here. I gave her a wave that passed for debonair, and as she snorted easy insults, I set off up the worn stone stairs. My rule was, three flights then take a breather; two more then pause a second time; take the last flight at a run before you collapsed among the woodlice and worse things that littered your path.

The doorpost of my old apartment still had the painted tile that advertised my name for clients. An old nail, carefully bent about ten years ago, was still hidden in a pot on the landing; as a spare latch-lifter it still worked. I put the nail back, pushed open the door very gently in case someone jumped me; I went in, feeling an odd patter of the heart.

It looked empty. There were two rooms. In the first stood a small wooden table, partly eaten away as if it were fossilised; two stools of different heights, one missing a leg; a cooking-bench; a shelf that once held pots and bowls but was now bare of fripperies. In the second room was just a narrow bed, made up neatly.

I called out that it was me. I heard pigeons flutter on the roof.

There was a folding door from the main room to a tiny balcony. I jerked the door with a special hitch that was needed to move it. Then I stepped out through the opening into the old, incongruously glamorous view over Rome, now bathed in warm afternoon sunlight. For a moment I soaked up that familiar scene, out over the northern Aventine to the Vaticanus Hill beyond the river.

Albia was basking on the small stone bench. Coming from Britain, she adored the sun. The building was so badly maintained by its landlord Smaractus that one day the whole balcony would fall off, taking the bench and anyone who was sitting on it. For the moment it held. It had held for the six or seven years that I lived here, in view of which it was easiest to continue to have blind faith than to try and make the unbearable Smaractus carry out repairs. The kind of builders he used would only weaken it fatally.

My fosterling wore an old blue dress, tight plaits, a simple bead necklace. She sat with her fingers linked, pretending to be happy, calm, and unafraid. There was no chance she was afraid of me. I was her father, just a joke. But she must know her situation. Someone else had terrified her.

'I thought I would find you here.' She made no answer. 'You had better stay until I have a chance to straighten things out with Anacrites. Are you all right, Albia? Do you have food money?'

'Lenia gave me a loan.'

'I hope you fixed a good rate of interest!'

'Helena came. She settled up.'

'Well, I'll send you an allowance until it's safe to come home.'

'I won't be coming,' Albia informed me suddenly and earnestly. 'I have something to say, Marcus Didius. I love you all, but it cannot be my home.'

I wanted to argue but I was too tired. Anyway, I understood. I experienced deep sadness for her. 'So we failed you, sweetheart.'

'No.' Albia spoke gently. 'Let's not have a family argument, like other tiresome people.'

'Why not? Arguments are what families are for. You have a family now, you know that. You're stuck, I'm afraid. Try not to be estranged from us, the way I was from my father.'

'Do you regret that?'

I grinned abruptly, even laughed out loud. 'Never for one moment—nor did he, the old menace! . . . Have you told Helena this big idea of yours? Striking out on your own?'

'She was upset.'

'She would be!'

Albia turned to me, her face pale, her blue-grey eyes dark with panic despite her attempted bravado. 'You gave me a chance; I am grateful. I want to stay in Rome. But I am going to make myself a life, a life that is suitable and sustainable. Don't tell me I cannot try.'

Huffing gently, I squashed in on the bench beside her. Albia moved up, grumbling on principle. 'So let's hear about it?'

Uncertain of my reaction, she confided, 'I cannot have the life you hoped to give me. Adoption only half works. I stay provincial—if not a barbarian. Someone who hates us might find out where I came from. In this city, spiteful rumours could damage you and Helena.'

'Anacrites?'

'He intends to do it.' Albia spoke quietly; all self-confidence had drained out of her.

I wondered how he had so badly crushed her spirit. 'And what about you? Did he try something on?'

'No.' Albia was inscrutable. She had made up her mind not to tell me. If Anacrites had seduced or raped her, she would spare me incandescent anger; she would protect Helena, too, from the pain of knowing. But even the fact that Anacrites had lured her into danger gave me motives to pursue him.

'You sure?' Pointless question.

'He was not the same. He had changed—or at least had stopped hiding what he is really like. You were right about him: he looked lecherous. I decided straight away I must escape. Then I found Claudius Nobilis.'

'Did *he* lay hands on you?'

'No. He meant to. But Anacrites barged in and said "leave her to me".' Albia shuddered, looking older than her years. 'Repulsive man!'

'Don't you think we are all the same?' I teased, alluding to her opinion of Camillus Aelianus.

To my surprise, Albia smiled sweetly and replied, 'Not quite all of you!'

'So, Flavia Albia, you are leaving home. What are you planning?'

'To live here. Do what you did.'

'Right.'

'No argument?'

'No point. So you want to be an informer? Well, that could work.' I put my head back against the rough surface of the wall, remembering the experience. Part of me was envious, though I hid it. 'Start small. Work for women. Don't accept any job that comes along—gain a name for being picky, then folks will feel flattered if you take them on. It's a hard life, depressing and dangerous. The rewards are few, you can never relax, and even when you achieve success, your miserable cheating clients will not thank you.'

'I can do this,' Albia insisted. 'I have the proper attitude—the right bitterness. And I have sympathy for desperate people. I have been orphaned, abandoned, starved, neglected, beaten, even in the clutches of a violent pimp. There will be no surprises,' she concluded.

'I see you have convinced yourself! Nothing scares you—even when it should.' The romantic in me wanted to have faith in her. 'You are too young. You have too much to learn,' I warned, as the father in me took over.

'I have been pushed into it before I'm ready, so it's not ideal,' replied Albia coolly. She had spent several days here, thinking up answers to thwart me. Then, because Helena Justina's teaching had made an impression, she added demurely, 'But I shall have you to teach me, Father.'

My throat went raw. 'First time you ever called me that!'

'Don't get overexcited,' Flavia Albia answered matter-of-factly. 'You have to earn it, if you want it permanent.'

'That's my girl!' I exclaimed proudly.

I stood up, easing my stiff back. I needed to see Glaucus at the gym, get back in shape. Before I left the apartment, I made a few adjustments to the old potted rose trees, pinching off dead wood from spindly branches. 'Professional question, Albia: when you encountered Nobilis—did you notice his eyes?'

She jumped up eagerly. 'Yes! I wanted to tell you—'

'Save it. Come down to the house tomorrow. It will be a good exercise in moving around Rome unrecognised.'

'What for?'

'Family conference. We need to talk about Anacrites.'

60

I awoke late. I was alone, Helena's side of the bed long cooled. I could hear the house thrumming with movement and casual noises, everyone going about their business without me, as they must have done while I was absent, as they would do if I stayed dozing. I was the master, but expendable. However, a wet snuffle under the door from Nux waiting patiently outside told me the dog was aware of my homecoming last night.

I let her in, endured a quick greeting (she was a polite dog), then allowed her to jump on the bed, which was her real purpose. The whiskery fright was not allowed on beds or couches; that made no difference. Nux curled up and went to sleep. I washed my face, put a comb through my curls, dived into a favourite tunic. I was ill-shaven, hungry, stiff from travel and subdued. I had no casework I was aware of and would have to look for clients. In most respects I could have been back in the life I once led in Fountain Court. Once again, I felt mournful and bereft of my youth.

Downstairs, slaves saluted me with only mild disdain. A good breakfast and my alert assistants were waiting. My wife came in and kissed me. My children appeared in the doorway, made sure it was me, then ran off back to their games. A buffet slave refilled the bread basket with warm rolls as soon as I took a serving, poured hot water on to honey for me, cut smoked ham slices. The napkin laid upon my lap was fine linen. I drank from a smooth Samian beaker. When I came to rinse my hands again, scented water in a silver bowl was immediately offered to me.

I had forgotten I was rich. Helena saw my reaction; I noticed her amusement. 'Jupiter!'

'You'll get used to it,' she said, smiling.

My new status brought responsibilities. Clients were lined up, awaiting favours shamelessly.

I dealt briskly with Marina, wanting money of course, then ignored a message from my sister Junia about the caupona needing a refurbishment. Helena said there were queries at the auction house, not urgent; I could attend to them when I visited the Saepta. Next came another, much more serious, family problem. The usher (I now required one, it seemed) ushered in Thalia.

She was visibly pregnant, puffing slightly. It had not persuaded her to wear less revealing clothes. The two Camilli, waiting for me to be free for our planned meeting, exchanged startled glances. Arrayed in a few wafts of gauze and long strings of semiprecious beads, Thalia patted the bump that was supposed to be Pa's offspring. 'Not long now, Marcus!'

'How are you feeling?'

'Terrible! The python knows; he's off colour, poor Jason.'

'Still dancing?'

'Still dancing! Are you hoping exertion will bring on a miscarriage?'

'That would be irresponsible.'

'Gods! Money has made you so sanctimonious!—Now listen, I need to talk to you.'

'Well, make it quick. I'm about to begin a business meeting.'

'Stuff that,' replied Thalia. 'A little child's life is at stake here. We've been let down, Falco, this poor baby and me. I've had words with that scheming shark, Septimus Parvo—your devious father's utterly useless lawyer.'

'He seemed competent.' Thalia's annoyance was cheering me up now.

'You would say that. He tells me he has looked into things further and the will's rotten. It won't hold up. My poor little one has been cheated—and he is not even born yet!'

'I don't know what you mean, Thalia.'

'According to Parvo,' she enunciated with high distaste, 'if a legacy is given to a posthumous infant, the child must be born of a legal marriage.' Thalia was a tall woman of majestic stature; as she rounded on me fiercely, I felt some alarm. 'Geminus said Parvo would sort everything out for me. I know what's gone on here. This is a fiddle. You bastard, Falco—you must have put him up to it!'

Not for the first time since my father died, my first thought was to lay wheat cakes on a divinity's altar and exclaim, *Thank you, for my good fortune!*

Aulus leaned forward, his face serious. 'Parvo is quite right, if you don't mind me saying so.'

'My brother Aelianus,' Helena told Thalia helpfully. 'He has had legal training.'

'I don't trust him then!' Thalia scoffed. Aulus took it well.

'There can be no doubt, I'm afraid, Thalia.' What an excellent fellow Aulus had turned out to be. 'Didius Favonius remained married to his wife of many years, the mother of his legal children.' Helena may have discussed all this with Aulus. He was a better scholar than we expected, but only with advance warning. He must have looked up the law specifically. 'Everyone at Geminus' funeral saw Junilla Tacita taking her place as the widow. She was acknowledged as such by all those friends, family and business colleagues who knew her deceased husband. Moreover,' Aulus continued relentlessly, 'to become an heir, the child must be referred to in the will itself. I do not believe a codicil will count.'

'All that is as may be!' Thalia could be worryingly firm. 'I am here to make arrangements. Things have to be set up properly.'

I gulped nervously.

'Here is the deal, Marcus Didius. When this child is born, it has to be looked after. Don't expect me to do it. I can't take a baby on tour with the circus! My animals would be dangerously jealous, it's not hygienic, and I don't have the capacity.'

'That's very sad,' Helena interrupted. 'Children give so much pleasure and can be a comfort, Thalia.'

'He'll get in the way!' Thalia replied, as riotously honest as when she discussed her sex life. Then she dropped me in the midden. 'You will have to bring him up, Falco.'

'What?'

'I thought about it. This is what Geminus wanted. You know it is. He told you in that codicil: you were to see my baby as your own sister or your brother. You can't argue with a *fideicommissum*.' She was calm. She was composed. Before I could bluster excuses, Thalia added the death blow: 'The best thing will be, Marcus darling, if as soon as he is born, you take him off me and adopt him.'

I closed my eyes while it sank in. I had expected troubles to come with money. I knew some of them would be complex, many crushing. Cynical though I was, nothing of this magnitude had crossed my mind. There was no escape, however. Pa had landed me absolutely.

I said I had to consult Helena. 'That's right,' Thalia agreed composedly. 'Then the dear little thing can grow up with you two, and be part of your beautiful family.'

Those quick brown eyes of Helena's told me she foresaw everything, just as I did.

So I acquired a 'brother', who was almost certainly not my brother but whom I had to adopt and endure as my son. I would have shared the money with him fairly willingly, but now I had to give him a decent chance in life as well—quite another proposition. This could only go wrong. Helena and I anticipated from the start that little Marcus

Didius Alexander Postumus (as his mother would name him, poor noddle) could never be grateful. We would offer him a home, education, moral guidance and affection. Pointless. A soulless waste of effort. He would be difficult to raise and impossible to console for the arbitrary fate that had been dumped on him. He was bound to seethe with jealousy and resentment. And I would not even blame him.

Thank you again, Geminus.

61

There had been slaves pootling around us, but we dismissed them. Katutis did not even try to argue; he was learning.

We sat in the salon. Helena had moved things around while I was in Latium. We reclined on day-couches with bronze fittings. Cushions in soft shades of blue and aqua lay under our elbows. The walls, newly painted last year, were respectable tones of honey and off-white, plain panels delineated by fine tendrils and elegant candelabrum motifs, intermittently relieved with discreet miniature paintings of birds, done in faint brushstrokes. These were civilised, though unpretentious surroundings. With her own sure taste, Helena had scaled down from when my father lived here, using less grandeur than when he had the place bursting with antiques. The salon made a quiet setting for the sombre discussion we were about to hold.

Others soon joined us: first Albia, then Petronius and Maia. I had considered including Ma, but my habit of keeping secrets from her was too great. Helena rose to close the double doors for privacy. Before she resumed her seat, she stood for a moment: tall, wearing white with coloured bands and informal jewellery, just a matron at home, as ever on the edge of domestic harassment, always alert in case she was called away to scorched meat in the kitchen or bruises in the nursery . . . It would not happen today. Arrangements were in place. Here she was, the woman I loved, taking on the wider role of a Roman wife and mother: steering her family towards great decisions and the righting of intolerable wrongs.

I smiled at her faintly. She understood what I was thinking. I had made a good choice.

Helena said, 'This will be a family conference—in every sense, because we are all members of a family, and families are what we have to talk about. Nothing that is to be said in this room today may be mentioned outside it to anyone.'

'*Sub rosa*,' said Aulus.

'Isca rules,' nodded Petro.

'*Our* rules,' my ever-caustic sister Maia corrected him.

A formal family conference is the symbol of emergency in Roman society. It happens rarely, because it only happens after outside measures have been tried and have failed. A fallback when public systems have collapsed, it is used for both utterly private reasons and for arranging a challenge to political tyranny. This is the last meeting before assassinations, executions, exile or disgrace. This is where wives are summoned to account for adultery by stern old-fashioned husbands, then humiliating punishments levied with unpleasant aunts' encouragement. It is where necessary usurpation of rulers is plotted. Where suicide or honour killing is carried out, after rape or other violation.

Our family council was where seven of us, my closest and dearest, assembled to unpick the full connection between the Claudii and Anacrites. Then we would decide what to do about it.

First, Quintus reported events in Latium. I watched him, tall, still boyish in appearance though increasingly firm in manner. He had his father's straight rather spiky hair, his mother's bearing and good looks. He was more slightly built than his brother, though Aulus had lost weight since his marriage: stress, presumably.

Quintus was concise, his tone almost pleasant. He could have been assessing routine logistics for a fort commander in a frontier province, as he concluded: 'We never had a chance to interrogate Claudius Nobilis. Everything else about him has to be conjectural—except one thing: his eyes. After he died, Marcus and I noticed they were odd. Nobilis had pale eyes, eyes that were neither one colour nor another. Part grey, part brown. Extremely unusual.'

I heard Maia catch her breath as she made the link. Albia was twisting her hands in her lap.

'Neither of the twins, nor Probus, had that aberration,' Quintus continued, after a quick glance at Maia. 'Marcus and I checked the survivors. But we all know one other person whose eyes look two-coloured with some tricks of the light: Anacrites.'

Helena took up the story, taking the narrative from her brother as smoothly as the sacred torch is passed in a Panathenian relay race. 'This explains many things. Let us go back to two slaves on an imperial estate in the days of the early Empire: Aristocles and Casta. Of course they could not marry while they were in slavery, but let's assume they met, matched and even perhaps began to have children then. They were freed, some say to get rid of them because they were so difficult. They had many offspring. Some died. Some of the girls broke away, at least partly, and married. The eldest was Justus, who died not that long ago, perhaps of a bad conscience. Nobilis was among the youngest, pushed out more, perhaps; having to jostle more for attention, maybe even for clothes, space and food.'

My turn. 'One of the boys was called Felix. His brother Probus sneered: *Felix, the happy and fortunate—and a clever little sod too; well we lost him early, naturally* . . . How did they "lose" him? We know now. When he was three years old his intelligence was officially noticed and he was removed from the family. In Rome, he was arbitrarily assigned a new name. It happens to slaves. So the man we know as Tiberius Claudius Anacrites began life as Claudius Felix. He may not always have remembered where he came from—but he certainly knows now.'

At that point, it was Maia, Maia who might have been expected to be harshest, who put in a word for him. 'Imagine how it might have been for a child so young to be forcibly removed from the people he thought were his own.' Shaking her head, she went on in a low voice, 'Aristocles and Casta may have been distant, even violent, as parents, but I dare say they screamed and shouted when they had to give him up. From what we know, they were possessive; he was theirs, their property.'

'Casta may have tried to hang on to him physically,' Helena agreed. 'I know I would. Imagine the scenes—with the child hysterically weeping, torn from his mother's grasp by brutal overseers. Next, with Casta's screams ringing in his little ears, he was taken many miles away, nobody telling him why or where he was going. Perhaps he felt it was a punishment for some unknown naughtiness. Plenty of punishment went on among the Claudii—he knew that concept. Dumped at the Palace, he wakes up in a cold dormitory. Other children there were strangers. They may all have been older, may have bullied him.'

'He says his subsequent childhood seemed normal to him,' I said. 'But was it really? He learned to survive—but trauma and fear moulded him.'

Petronius had been listening with distaste. Now he stretched his long legs and frame, looking too bulky for the couch. 'I'm more intrigued by where he is today. In adulthood, do you think he was aware who his family were?'

'I doubt it,' I said.

Petro grinned. 'We could ask him.'

'You could. I wouldn't. He would only lie. In fact, as long as he can, he has to. He cannot hold a high imperial post as a known relative of murderous criminals.'

'So we're getting to the heart of this, Falco. What happened to reunite them?'

'Two years ago, or thereabouts,' Helena reminded us, 'the mother, Casta, died.'

We were all silent for a while, wondering what that had been like, for the large sprawling family that Casta had ruled with her mixture of cruelty and indifference. Aristocles had gone before her. Casta's death destroyed their equilibrium, Virtus told me.

Aulus leaned forwards. 'I bet there was a mighty big funeral. The full wailing, hypocritical orations. All sorts of sentimental grief. And presumably it was around then that somebody thought of contacting their long-lost brother Felix.'

'Anacrites went to the funeral,' stated Maia. She was looking down at her feet. Maia was sitting sideways, adjacent to Petronius. Her feet were small, pressed together tidily, wearing stylish shoes in ox-blood leather. Maia looked at them as if she was wondering where the decorative footgear came from.

'It begs the question,' mused Helena, 'how did his siblings find him?'

Again Maia unexpectedly had answers. 'He told me once. He had a letter from his mother when she realised she was dying. After all, where he was taken as a child would not have been a secret. Casta must have followed his progress, either from affection or the possessiveness we mentioned. Anacrites answered her summons but when he got there it was too late. I never knew the funeral was in Latium; he kept quiet about his people living in the Pontine Marshes. It was just after I met him he told me, as a conversation gambit.'

'Was he upset?' asked Albia.

'He seemed so.'

'He could have been acting.'

'There was no reason for that.'

'That's him, though. Defying logic.'

'His feelings need not concern us,' I said. 'The funeral was his downfall. Once they knew who he was, his brothers latched on like para-